Blame It On The Tea

A Pride and Prejudice Twist

Blame It On The Tea

A Pride and Prejudice Twist

Sara O'Brien

Blame It On The Tea

ISBN: 978-0-557-28980-6

Book and cover design by Sara O'Brien
sobrien1971@yahoo.com

For my friends at The Meryton Literary Society, and especially my exceedingly patient beta Maryanne (MAB) who had to put up with me through thick and thin, and of course my ever patient and supportive mother without whose support I could have never done this. Thank you with all my heart!

Prologue

Elizabeth awoke in her room at Hunsford Parsonage with her mind still in a haze. The tea that Mrs. Hanson had given her the evening before was still causing her mind to be muddled. Somewhere in the recesses of her mind, she thought that she could recall a visitor… *Mr. Darcy! Yes, I think I recall him being here, but for the life of me I do not recall what was said! Oh, I hope I did not embarrass myself, or say or do anything rash!*

She sat up in the bed and felt a great amount of soreness in her bottom and legs, and tried to get out of bed to work the discomfort away to no avail. With her first few steps she felt an unusual tenderness in the place between her legs as she walked to the water basin to wash her face. Within a few minutes the young maid, Margaret, came to see her mistress' guest, and Elizabeth felt a need to have more than a cool basin to clean up with, and requested a bath be brought up for her.

Within twenty minutes the water was ready and she requested to be left alone to tend to herself. Removing her nightshift, Elizabeth felt some wetness and noticed blood on her thighs. *Odd… my courses were almost two weeks ago. They should not be due for another two weeks!* She thought no more about it and commenced to sit in the tub in order to clean herself up. The warm water helped to relieve some of her discomfort, though not entirely.

As she lay back against the edge of the tub and closed her eyes as she tried to recall the events of last evening. *What happened last night when Mr. Darcy visited, and how did I end up in my bed with my nightshift on? Perhaps Margaret or Mrs. Hanson helped to get me to bed after that gentleman left?* Trying to clear her mind of the fog that still enveloped her, Elizabeth had almost fallen asleep when Margaret came to check upon her, and help her to dress.

"Margaret… Do you recall how I managed to get into bed last night?"

The maid gave her a strange look as she answered, "No ma'am. I though' you ad got yerself ready las' nigh."

"Why do I not recall it though?"

"Do'no, though I think tha you ad even went ta bed a' fore the gemen left, 'cause e let 'imself out. I 'couldn even say ow long e stayed, 'e was so quiet when 'e left!"

For a moment, Elizabeth pondered the information, but was still unable to piece the information together to make enough sense out of it. *He must have considered me abominably rude then to have gone to bed even before he left the parsonage!* She thought to herself with humor before she felt some guilt over her behavior... so unlike herself.

"I do not suppose that you have any idea how long he might have been here... or... or if there were any loud... discussions?"

The maid studied her for a moment before she answered, "Nooo ma'am, I 'ain't 'eard a any arguing at tall, an usually we do hear 'bout stuff like that!" She assured her, then as an afterthought she added, "Though I migh say tha ya seemed to 'ave been a bit restless, 'cause you seemed ta be thrashin' 'bout in bed a bit an moanin', but after a bit ya seemed ta settle a bit. I checked on ya 'bout an hour er so after I heard ya in th room, and you were sound asleep."

"I see." Elizabeth was still trying to place the events of last night together as Margaret was putting the finishing touches of her hair, when Charlotte came in to check up on her.

"How are you feeling this morning, Lizzy? I heard you slept rather ill at first last night."

"I think I am feeling a little better but I do not think that I shall be taking anymore of Mrs. Hanson's medicinal teas anytime soon. My mind is still in a fog, and I woke up rather sore this morning."

"Oh, well then I suppose you will not be taking your usual morning walk today then?"

"I... I do not know. Perhaps I may just postpone it until later. I may simply rest after breakfast, and then take a walk later this afternoon."

"That sounds like a good idea. You look a bit peaked yet, and your father would not forgive me if you took ill while visiting me here."

"Oh Charlotte, I shall be fine. I am only a bit tired after yesterday, and I think I can credit the tea from last night for my current condition."

"Very well then Lizzy, but promise me that you shall take it easy until you leave us. If I send you back home in worse shape than you came, Mr. Bennet will likely not allow you to visit me again."

"I promise to take care, after all... I shudder to think of missing out on more of Lady Catherine's condescension."

The two friends laughed at Elizabeth's reference to Mr. Collins noble patroness, and as soon as she was ready they went downstairs to join the clergyman in breaking their fast. As promised, Elizabeth did rest for the remainder of the morning, and after lunch she felt improved enough to walk in the groves near the parsonage.

Rounding a corner in the groves, Elizabeth had almost literally run into Colonel Fitzwilliam.

"Oh, I am sorry for my clumsiness, Miss Elizabeth. Are you all right?"

"Yes colonel, I am fine, just a little embarrassed to have been caught woolgathering." She blushed as she greeted him properly. "I hope that you have survived my carelessness though?"

"Think nothing of it, ma'am. I am quite sure that you have many a good reason to be *woolgathering* now..." the colonel added jovially. "What with planning a wedding and all..."

Elizabeth looked at him thoroughly confused as she asked, "W-what wedding would that be sir?"

The colonel looked at her oddly for a moment, and then broke out in a wide smile, "Oh, I am sorry Miss Elizabeth..." he laughed as he pulled out a letter addressed to her, "My cousin took the liberty of informing me of your engagement this morning... just before he left for Meryton." He quickly added, "I hope that you do not mind that he made me privy to your betrothal? Darcy only wished for me to deliver that letter to you, and of course I thought it rather singular of my *proper* cousin to do such a thing. He proceeded to explain your circumstances, and I was more than happy to oblige him. Oh... and I promise not to tell a soul. You can both count on my discretion." He finished with a wink and a smile at her.

As her companion spoke, Elizabeth felt a cold sweat wash over her, and by the time he had finished with this piece of information, she felt very faint. *Oh dear Lord! What have I done? What happened last night at the parsonage to make Mr. Darcy think that we are engaged? Unless...? No... that cannot be! I would surely have remembered something as important as that! But then there was the tea Mrs. Hanson gave me and I cannot recall how I even managed to get into bed by myself.* When she said nothing more to him, the colonel again looked at her and his expression was one of alarm.

"Miss Elizabeth... are you quite well...?"

His voice seemed to be coming from far off, and she heard nothing more as darkness enveloped her. The next thing that Elizabeth remembered was waking up in her bed at the parsonage, with a very concerned looking Charlotte Collins, Maria Lucas, Colonel Fitzwilliam, and some elderly looking gentleman hovering over her.

Charlotte was sponging her forehead with a cool cloth, and she heard her say, "I think she is coming to, Mr. Robbins."

The elder man glanced up to her face as he held her arm by the wrist with his fingers. He spoke to her directly, "Good afternoon Miss Bennet. How do you feel?"

She looked to each one of the rooms occupants starting with her friend, and ending with the man she assumed was Mr. Robbins, "I-I… do not really know, sir. I do not know what came over me-or how I came to be here."

"What do you remember before you fainted, Miss Bennet? Did you feel… unusual at all…?"

"N-no." She paused for a moment until she remembered her headache yesterday, but before she could speak a word about it, both the colonel and Charlotte spoke up simultaneously.

"She had complained of a headache yesterday…" they gave each other a kindly smile, before looking back at her.

Charlotte spoke up again, "She took some drought last night as well and seemed rather out of sorts this morning, but I must confess I thought her much better after lunch, else I would not have allowed her to walk out." She sounded almost guilty.

"I see, so this was not necessarily something that just came on all of a sudden?" the elder gentleman asked Elizabeth in response.

"Well, I… felt well enough after lunch to go out walking and by then my headache was gone, and I feel fine now, sir. Perhaps it was just the heat and that I walked too much with the warmer weather?"

"Perhaps, Miss Bennet, but I think that you should rest for a couple of days, and no more long walks in the warm weather. Oh…" Mr. Robins looked at Charlotte, "Pray… what was it that your housekeeper gave Miss Bennet last night?"

"Uh… I am not exactly sure, but I shall go and get her and you can see for yourself what it was." Charlotte offered.

"Please." The physician requested.

Charlotte left the room quickly, leaving Elizabeth to ponder what had happened from last night on. She could not fathom being engaged to Mr. Darcy at all, yet the colonel insists that he told him that they were. *Why would such a proud, arrogant, and wealthy gentleman want to marry me? He has only looked at me to see faults! No… no, this must be a mistake! There has to be some logical explanation!* As soon as Elizabeth finished that thought, Charlotte arrived with Mrs. Hanson.

"Mr. Robbins, this is our housekeeper, Mrs. Hanson. She gave Lizzy some of this last night for her headache." She offered the bottle containing the minty smelling herb. The physician sniffed the drought, and looked at the housekeeper.

"Mrs. Hansen… was this some form of mint from the garden?"

"Y-yes, sir. I use it occasionally for such beastly headaches, but I must say nothin' like this 'as ever happened before."

"No doubt, but I think what you have here is a very potent amnesiac herb. If it is what I think it is, then it is no wonder Miss Bennet seemed out of sorts. A simple drop or two of opium would have been better, but what is done is done. For now, Miss Bennet I would prescribe some rest…" he looked towards Charlotte and the housekeeper then and said, "and *absolutely no more* of this at all."

"Yes sir." Both the housekeeper and Charlotte agreed.

"Well then, I propose that we all leave and let the patient rest."

They filed out of the room, but before the colonel left he approached Elizabeth with no little anxiety, "Miss Elizabeth… I am sorry if what I disclosed to you distressed you in any way. I assure you of my discretion, and I will not tell another soul until Darcy gets back from Longbourn. He would throttle me if anything happened to you while he was gone."

Elizabeth's eyes widened but she was unable to say anything. Her mind was still trying to grasp the fact that Mr. Darcy had somehow come to the conclusion that they were engaged after last night, yet she could remember none of their visit. She laid in bed trying to sort things out in her mind, but the more she thought about it the worse her head felt. *What am I to do? Perhaps papa will turn him away and tell him 'no', but what if he does not? What will he tell papa?* She continued to worry until the new drought that Mr. Robbins prescribed stated to take effect.

When Elizabeth finally awoke again it was dark outside and the parsonage was quiet. She managed to pull herself up to a sitting position and looked around the room trying to figure out what time it was. When her eyes cleared she could just make out that it was eleven o'clock. Focusing more on her surroundings, she saw a small tray of food with some water and froze when she saw the letter underneath the serving tray. *The letter from Mr. Darcy!* Elizabeth stared at it for a moment before she reached over to retrieve it. Being naturally very curious she quickly broke the seal to read what he had written to her.

Saturday 8 April 1809,

Rosings Park

My dearest Elizabeth,

Please forgive me for leaving so hastily both last night and this morning. I wanted to speak with your father as soon as may be, and return to you as quickly as possible. After our heartfelt encounter last night it was torture to pull myself away from you, however I did not wish to risk such a scandal that it would certainly have caused were we to be discovered. I am sure you can understand that. When I left you at the parsonage my soul desperately ached for you, and I consol myself with the thought that we shall hopefully soon be together forever as husband and wife.

On another note, and after reading the above, I wish to convey my most sincere apologies for my ungentlemanly behavior as well. My only excuse can be my enthusiastic and undying love for you overrode my senses, and thus I acted so abominably. I also wish to let you know that I respect you just as much if not more than I had before- if that is possible. You are so beautiful, and how you responded to me last night made my heart soar, you have no idea. I always knew that you had such a passionate disposition, but to be the recipient of such is beyond compare the very best thing in the whole world.

That is the other reason for my leaving so early today. I fear that passion so much that I am not certain that I can control myself when it comes to you. This brings me to a most important point; I think it best under the circumstances if we marry sooner rather than later. The thought of the consequences to our actions begs me to ask you for your consent to a hasty wedding sooner rather than later. I worry that to wait may put you in some jeopardy, and I love and care for you too much for that to happen.

I shall close with my assertions of my utter devotion to you, for now and forever.

Your devoted husband-to-be,

Fitzwilliam Darcy

Elizabeth read through the letter several times to try and make sense of it all, and more importantly try to remember what happened last night. She continued to be befuddled as to his references to '*last night*'. *What did I do... and more importantly, what did we do? He seems to indicate a huge impropriety, but for the life of me I do not remember anything!*

As Elizabeth read through the letter again, she was struck by the tender regard, and deep seeded feelings that he conveyed to her, and it struck her that this was a totally different side of the man she knew as Mr. Darcy. There were no words of hauteur, or arrogance, and he said that he loved her.

Astounding! I cannot believe that a man such as he could feel such a way towards me! I thought that when he looked at me, he only did so for censure, but... was I wrong? And what about Mr. Wickham? How could this man act in such an abominable way to his father's favorite, and yet act so... so kind and loving towards a woman who can hardly oblige him?

The enigma that was Fitzwilliam Darcy continued to baffle Elizabeth until she finally found herself too exhausted to think anymore. Though her conscious thoughts of the mysterious, handsome man had faded, her dreams about the same individual were more vivid, and...realistic. She tossed and turned all night until dawn.

~*~*~*~

As Fitzwilliam Darcy tried to sleep Saturday night, the only thing he could think about was his beautiful Elizabeth lying in her bed with her dark hair spread out on her pillow. It was difficult to find slumber when he kept imagining her in his arms. He had always thought that she had a passionate nature, but tonight surpassed all of his expectations, and he did not want to give up his euphoria to the night yet. His dreams had never been so lovely, nor had he felt this way with any other woman, and soon she would be his wife.

It was that last thought that finally induced him into a restless slumber as the evening unfolded again in his mind... and dreams. Early tomorrow morning, he would ride out to Meryton by way of London in order to send a note to the Archbishop of Canterbury to apply for a special license. From town he would ride on to Longbourn and meet with Mr. Bennet as soon as possible. He knew that that gentleman would likely not be made too happy by his precipitous application for his favorite daughter's hand, but it could not be helped. Her well being was foremost in his mind.

His conscience bade him to feel some remorse for causing this need for hasty nuptials. If it had not been for his behavior they would have plenty of time for planning a decent wedding befitting the future Mrs. Fitzwilliam Darcy, but now that was not to be. Their actions may have resulted in some far reaching consequences, and he did not want her to shoulder those repercussions herself-much less unmarried.

He resolved to ride out at first light, not only to take advantage of the daylight but also to avoid his aunt, Lady Catherine. She was usually one of the first people up in the household, and he most certainly did not wish to encounter her before he rode out to apply for another's hand in marriage. *There is no way that I wish to explain to her where I am going, and I know that I cannot prevaricate very well... and I refuse to have Elizabeth exposed to my aunt's vitriol due to her disappointed hopes!*

He thought about leaving Rosings and taking his beloved with him, but he knew that it would likely only make Mr. Bennet even more displeased with him. *He will be angry enough if I have to explain why we must marry in this manner. I shall have to get word to her somehow, though to let her know where I have gone. I do not want her to think I have seduced her with empty promises and then left her after second thoughts. Richard! I shall ask him to deliver a note to Elizabeth when he goes out walking!* Darcy grimaced, thinking about sending his cousin off to meet up with his beloved fiancée. He had seen and heard how much Richard appreciated her beautiful eyes, and lovely womanly figure and her witty personality to the point of making him want to do his cousin serious injury.

She is mine now though and there is nothing that Richard or anyone else can do to change that! I shall have to tell him of our engagement, and swear him to secrecy. It would not do for him to go blabbing about my personal business to Anne or Lady Catherine. They would only make things more difficult for Elizabeth, and I will not stand for their rude, arrogant behavior towards her! No, I shall write her a note, and make one out to the archbishop and dispatch them as soon as may be, and hurry on to Longbourn. The sooner I get these things done, the sooner I can get back to her, and we can begin our life together.

Oh... I have to send a note to Georgiana as well! She must come down from Pemberley for our wedding, and maybe Richard can keep her at Matlock House with the earl and countess for a little while we become more acquainted. I am sure that she and Elizabeth will get along very well. Maybe they will even become as close as Elizabeth is with Miss Bennet are. But... what shall I do about Bingley? I do not wish to lose his friendship, yet I think it would be too soon for him to be in the company of Jane Bennet without being in danger. Perhaps we shall just have a quiet ceremony with only close family, and announce it as soon as we are married. Under the circumstances that seems more practical anyway.

Darcy finally exhausted himself thinking about all of the details necessary in getting married hastily and fell asleep. By morning he was re-energized as he went about dressing for his early morning ride without the assistance of his valet. Before he left to go to the breakfast parlor, he had to deliver the note for Elizabeth to Richard.

As he knocked on the door he steeled himself for the onslaught of questions his nosy cousin was bound to pepper him with.

There was a faint and aggravated, "What?", heard beyond the door, and Darcy entered stealthily.

Richard had barely opened his eyes and was trying to go back to sleep when he saw Darcy.

"Do not tell me you want my company for a ride this early in the morning Darcy. This is even early for you... or are you trying to avoid the she dragon?"

"Humph, no Richard I only came in to let you know that I must away to town today on some urgent business, but I will be back hopefully by tomorrow. I only came to ask a favor of you."

By now Richard was sitting up in his bed sleepily, but waking more each moment in concern.

"What do you need? Is it something to do with Georgiana...?"

"No! Lord no, she is fine..." Darcy shuttered at the thought of anything else happening to his sister after last summer, and thought of Wickham not only trying to make inroads with her, but then Elizabeth later on in the fall. He quickly made a mental note to tell Mr. Bennet to be careful where that rogue was concerned as well least he try something with Elizabeth's sisters.

"Well then... what is it?! What do you need me to do?" Richard asked impatiently.

"Oh..." Darcy snapped out of his private thoughts, "I need for you to deliver this note to Miss Bennet today... as soon as you can. Will you do that for me?"

Richard stared disbelievingly at him for a moment before slowly answering, "All right... but may I ask why my usually stoic, reserved, and *proper* cousin is writing a note to the very lovely Miss Elizabeth? I mean... you have to admit that it smacks of impropriety, Darcy. What will she think?"

"Do not get yourself worked up Richard. When I left here last night, I went to the parsonage..." Richard raised his eyebrow to signal his interest in the subject, and Darcy continued, "And I asked *Miss Bennet* to marry me."

Richard jumped out of bed and clapped Darcy on the back, "That is marvelous news, Darcy! You are a lucky man, I hope you know... and you have great taste. Why... if I were in your position, I would have jumped at the first chance I had to propose to her."

Darcy frowned at his cousin's choice of words, still feeling insecure about his easy relaxed manners with Elizabeth, but consoling himself with thoughts of last night.

"Well it is a good thing for me then, that you are not!" He said a little roughly, then his voice softened a little, "And I cannot agree with you more as to my luck. Elizabeth is everything that I would ever want in my wife and companion of my life, and I am a most fortunate man."

"I should say so, but what shall the she devil and Anne say when they find out that you are engaged, and it is not to Anne?"

"They will not be finding out, Richard, because you will not say a word until the deed is done, then they can do nothing about it! Besides... you and the rest of our family have known for as long as Lady Catherine has been proclaiming it, that I am not, nor have I ever been, engaged to Anne. That is just our aunt's delusional thinking, and please do not mention where I am going to her either. I will deliver my request for a special license when I go through town, and then head on to Elizabeth's family's estate, Longbourn to formally request her hand from Mr. Bennet. I do not wish to be away from her for more than a day if I can help it."

"Ah... well then, consider it done, cousin. You can count on me to keep things under control in your steed. I shall make sure that your fiancée is in good hands while you are away. Oh... and make sure that you do not injure yourself while you are away... The ladies in town would be so disappointed should I have to take Miss Elizabeth as my bride instead of you."

He gave Darcy a cheeky grin, to which Darcy's jaw tightened as he glared back at his cousin. "Do not even joke about that Richard!" He left Richard in his room laughing at his sudden serious demeanor. *By G-d I shall be very careful on my journey! It would not do to have Elizabeth put at risk for the censure of all society, or worse... having to marry my cousin for protection!* The thought was enough to make him shutter.

Before he broke his fast, he called for the footman to have his horse readied, and sat at the vacant table in the breakfast parlor where the ever efficient staff already had some repast set out. *Good, I am starved after my exercise last night!* He ate with gusto quenching his ravenous appetite, and surprised some of the kitchen staff who had only seen him eat in moderate portions before this morning. As soon as he was done he set out for the stables, and was quickly on his way to town.

He briefly thought of stopping by the parsonage before he left Hunsford, but reconsidered thinking that Elizabeth may still be abed and very tired after last night. There was also the added risk of raising Mr. Collins, and under no circumstances did he want to raise his suspicions. *He would be the first to run to Lady Catherine and tell her about my early morning visit to Elizabeth! I will be back quickly enough... maybe even tonight, and ... no I could not see her after I get back! I will likely not be fit to be seen after all of this riding, and I would not even have enough energy to properly greet her.*

Darcy continued to think through what he wanted to say to Mr. Bennet, and how he was going to convey the need for a hasty wedding. He knew that he did not wish to confess to his beloved's father that he had taken liberties with Elizabeth. *No... that would only make him angry, and what if he says 'no' just because of that? I shall not mention it unless absolutely necessary, but I will not lie to him either. He deserves the truth, and while I am at it, I should let him know that George Wickham is not a man to be trusted either.* The last thing Darcy wanted to think about was *that* waste of a man.

It had been nearly eight months since the Ramsgate fiasco and Georgiana was nowhere near her normal self yet. *I am sure that when Elizabeth and I are married they will grow as close as she and Jane are, and hopefully it will help to have a woman closer to Georgiana's age to relate to. Lord knows I have no idea how else to get through to her. I should have killed that blackguard when I had the chance, then he would not be able to impose himself on anyone else again!*

Darcy found it difficult even now to erase the image of George Wickham standing next to Elizabeth in the street at Meryton. The moment he saw them together he wanted to dismount off his horse and throttle him, but restrained himself for the sake of Elizabeth's sensibilities. As soon as they announced their engagement, Darcy vowed to ensure that Wickham was not allowed anywhere near Elizabeth ever again. Knowing George, he would likely try to use his engaging manners to manipulate her into helping him... or worse. Darcy's mood blackened as he thought about his past with his childhood friend, and he traveled onward to town trying to exorcize those ghosts from years past.

I shall have a new beginning with her though, and let the past go. We will make happy memories and forget about all of our pain. Darcy arrived in town around lunchtime and managed to eat quickly and change into a new outfit at his home before he headed to Longbourn. By noon he was on the road to Meryton and his destiny, but not before he made his upper staff aware of the need to ready the mistress' rooms, which created quite a bit of speculation amongst the privileged few servants.

By the time he arrived at Longbourn it was almost four o'clock in the afternoon, and he had cleaned up at Netherfield, making sure that he looked presentable, before calling upon Mr. Bennet. As he rode up the drive he could make out three faces staring through the window at him. *No doubt Mrs. Bennet and the two youngest girls! I am thankful that Elizabeth will soon be away from here and living with me at Pemberley. We could not be far enough away from her family for my tastes... well... maybe Mr. and Miss Bennet are all right, but the others!*

He involuntarily shook his head at the thought of her other relations, thankful that he was able to pry Bingley away from Netherfield before he made a huge mistake of marrying without affection or any special regard. He handed his card to the housekeeper and requested a private audience with Mr. Bennet.

Within a few minutes, the same woman was showing him to the library and announced him.

"Mr. Darcy to see you, Mr. Bennet, sir."

The elder gentleman rose from his desk near the hearth and welcomed him, "Mr. Darcy... It is a surprise to see you, of *all* people here. Pray... is Mr. Bingley come back to Netherfield?" He looked past Darcy towards the door as if expecting another visitor as well, and Darcy donned his usual stoic and impenetrable mask.

"Ah... no, sir. I have come alone, and as far as I know Mr. Bingley is still in town." *Not that I could easily decipher what he is doing based on his writing skills.*

A surprised looked passed over Mr. Bennet's face "Well then... what can I do for you, Mr. Darcy? Oh... can I interest you in anything to drink?" He held up a canter of brandy.

Darcy advanced into the room, "No... thank you. I have actually come to make a personal request, sir."

"Of me?"

"Yes, sir. I have come from Hunsford... Rosings Park actually... and wanted to talk to you about your daughter..."

Mr. Bennet turned to him in alarm, "Is there something wrong with my Lizzy? Is she well?"

"Ah, yes, she was well when I last saw her..." *Even better judging from her reaction to me, but I will damned to admit it to you!* "Mr. Bennet, what I want to ask of you is your permission to marry your daughter, Elizabeth."

The old man's face paled as he looked at Darcy, and he sat down heavily on his chair behind his desk.

"W-what did you say?"

Darcy was beginning to wonder if Elizabeth's father was actually somewhat deaf. *It would not be hard to imagine wishing to be in this household*, he thought to himself, but recalled the conversation at hand.

"Sir," he began a little louder, "I am asking your consent to marry your daughter, Elizabeth."

"No need to shout, sir, I heard you the first time. I simply cannot fathom how it is you have come here to make such a request... and for my Lizzy, of all my girls!"

"Mr. Bennet... I assure you that I know of what I am speaking, and it is your daughter, Elizabeth that I wish to wed. I have only come here to gain your consent... and, ask for us to be able to wed within the month."

Again the older man looked at him with such an expression of fright, "But... but how... why...? What has happened to bring this sudden engagement about? The last time I spoke to her, she acted as though she thought..." His words died upon his lips, as the two men stared at each other.

"Sir, I assure you that your daughter and I have formed an attachment, and she has agreed to be my wife. In fact, we had only spoken of it last night..."

"Is that so?" He asked skeptically.

"It is, and we... or rather I wish to marry within a fortnight if possible. It will soon be planting season, and I need to be back at my estate in Derbyshire beforehand, and... I had hoped to bring Elizabeth home with me then." *Well... it is not* technically *a lie; planting season is coming on soon. No need to let Mr. Bennet know we have need to marry sooner for another reason.*

Mr. Bennet sat in his chair staring at him, as if he thought he was mad.

"Mr. Darcy forgive me for my being so shocked. It is just that when my Lizzy left here, she had not indicated any preference for you... or any man for that matter. You can have no doubt as to how... surprising this news is to me considering."

"It is understandable, sir, and I assure you that it has come as a surprise to me as well, but I assure you that last night your daughter Elizabeth made me the happiest of men by accepting my hand in marriage, and now I have come to ask *you* for her hand as well as your blessing and consent."

The room was silent for a minute before the master of Longbourn spoke again, "Forgive my hesitancy in granting your request, but it is such a... a... surprise. You must understand my reluctance to grant this without first speaking to Lizzy... and in any case I think that a fortnight is simply... well..." he frowned, "out of the question."

Darcy felt himself breaking out into a cold sweat, not wishing to have to give any more of an explanation to Elizabeth's father for their seemingly impulsive need to wed, but in a split second he decided that it may be the lesser of the two evils.

"Um... Mr. Bennet... I... uh... would beg of you to reconsider- not that I have any objection to you speaking with your daughter, it is just that... it may not be in everyone's best interests to... wait very long." He finished softly.

Mr. Bennet sat straight up in his chair while staring incredulously at him.

"What is *that* supposed to mean, *Mister Darcy*?"

Darcy recognized an angry father when he saw one. He did not begrudge him that under the circumstance either. In fact it was probably akin to how he felt towards Wickham when he discovered the truth about his and Georgiana's plans to elope, but it did not make it any easier for him at the moment.

He looked contritely at Mr. Bennet and said as levelly as he could muster, "It means that it would not be in her best interests to wait for very long, sir."

"Am I to understand that there is a *reason* for such urgency then...*sir*?"

"Not urgent, exactly, but a good reason to expedite the process."

"What *happened* between you and my daughter, *exactly*, Mr. Darcy?"

By now the tension in the room was palpable, and Darcy by no means wanted to anger the man any further, but he knew that the time for reckoning was here.

"Some things that should not have, but they are done now and I wish to rectify the situation as soon as may be. It is for Elizabeth's protection more than anything else... though I would have proposed to her regardless."

The sudden sound of Mr. Bennet's hand hitting the desk top reverberated around the room, and actually startled Darcy, but he held his ground, and looked squarely at Elizabeth's father. By now the man looked as if he could fly across his desk and throttle him, but his glare spoke volumes.

"I will ask you this once, sir, and by G-d you had better answer me truthfully, did you force yourself upon my daughter?"

"No! I did not force her to do anything, if that is what you are asking, sir." Darcy answered defensively.

"I cannot believe that my daughter, *Lizzy*, would behave in such a way, or... allow any such liberties! The only explanation would be for her to have been out of her senses to act in such a way!"

"Mr. Bennet, I assure you that I did not coerce or drug Elizabeth. I love and respect her too much to dishonor her like that!" He said defensively.

"*Love and honor*? How can a man behave in such a way towards a maiden, and say that he loves and honors her?" He asked incredulously.

"Sir… it was neither intended nor planned. It happened when we let our emotions cloud our good judgment, but now that it has happened we must do our best to protect Elizabeth. I also wish to add that I am not in the habit of behaving in such a way, and you may ask anyone in town about my reputation. It is impeccable, but I can understand if you have your doubts right now."

He heard a snort coming from the elder gentleman, but proceeded on, "Elizabeth is the only woman I have ever wanted to wholly share myself with, and I wish that I could take it back and give her everything that she deserves, and I will try to make it up to her. I assure you that she will be treated very fairly with regards to her settlements as well… she will want for nothing. You must understand that this is not just for me but for her also."

Mr. Bennet sat back again in his chair and suddenly looked very old. Darcy understood, and prayed that he would consent if not for him then at least for his most beloved daughter's sake.

"Well… it seems that I have *no choice* but to consent to my daughter's marrying you, though my blessing has yet to be seen. I still wish to talk with Lizzy before a date is set, and I can only hope and pray that you understand what a treasure you have found yourself Mr. Darcy, because if you do not then you will live to regret it!"

"I do know what a treasure she is, sir, that is why I chose her. As far as the date is concerned… I will leave it for you and your daughter determine."

"*How very gracious of you.*" Mr. Bennet replied sarcastically.

The two gentlemen sat across from Mr. Bennet's desk looking at each other thoughtfully for another couple of minutes, before getting down to the business of the marriage contracts, and settlements, ending with a promise to have their attorneys review their agreements and make further suggestions to the final documents. They had agreed that they would meet in town by the end of next week to review said documents, and so long as everything was in order they would be signed. Mr. Bennet also requested that Darcy deliver a letter from him to Elizabeth upon his return to Rosings Park, which Darcy promised to deliver.

He knew that his last request to Mr. Bennet may be justly denied, but he asked anyway, "I know this may sound selfish under the circumstances, but would it be possible for me to bring Miss Elizabeth along with her traveling companion back to town in my carriage? I hate to think of her having to travel via post with strangers, and my coach is always well guarded… plus I will be traveling with a colonel in the regulars."

"Is that supposed to make me feel any better about it, Mr. Darcy?" Mr. Bennet asked dryly.

Darcy had the good grace to blush before he answered, "Not particularly, but I felt you should know whom I would be traveling with, and the man in question happens to be my cousin, so I can assure you that he *will not* be acting inappropriately towards your daughter… or anyone else's if I can help it."

Mr. Bennet gave a slight smile for the first time that afternoon, "I think then, that I may be able to trust you in a carriage with two other people, and perhaps another escort of my choosing. My brother Gardiner had already offered to send one of his men to escort Elizabeth and Maria Lucas to town…"

"Then he shall join us as well, if that is what you would prefer."

"It *is* what I would prefer."

"Very good then. I will leave you with my card from town and my other card from Pemberley should you need to get in touch with me for any reason, my staff know how to contact me."

"Until later then."

"I look forward to it, Mr. Bennet."

Darcy left Longbourn and mounted his steed headed back to town. It had entirely sliped his mind that they had not even touched upon the topic of George Wickham until Dracy was nearing town. It was nearing six o'clock and he knew that he would not make it to Rosings until tomorrow. He was already too tired from the heated discussions and haggling with Mr. Bennet to ride all night. Remembering the comment from Richard about pursuing Elizabeth 'should anything happen to him' also cooled his enthusiasm as well. *Lady Catherine will be furious with me for traveling on a Sunday, but I will not spend another moment away from Elizabeth if it can be helped.*

It was ten o'clock that evening when Darcy arrived exhausted, faint, and hungry at his house in town. As soon as the housekeeper, Mrs. Jones, saw him she gave him a large glass of water and ordered him up to his bath and a meal was sent to his rooms. The older woman had her husband, who was also the Darcy house butler, tend to the master personally. By eleven that evening Darcy had bathed, eaten and almost literally fallen into bed.

Chapter 1

The next day, Darcy woke up from a very pleasant dream to a loud knocking on his door. It was already eleven o'clock on Sunday morning, and it took him a full minute to realize that he was in his house in town and not with Elizabeth at Pemberley. Being awakened thusly did not sit well with him; consequently he answered the caller curtly. Being awakened thusly did not sit well with him; consequently he answered the caller curtly.

"Yes? What is it?"

The door opened slowly to admit his valet, Mr. Hobbs.

"I am sorry to disturb you Mr. Darcy, but Colonel Fitzwilliam is here calling upon you."

"Colonel Fitzwilliam? Here in town? Why is he here at Darcy House, and so early in the morning?"

Hobbs gave him an odd look before he answered, "Uh... Mr. Darcy, sir... it is after eleven o'clock, and the gentleman has only just arrived."

Darcy started at his man's information, and looked over to his clock on the mantle. True enough, it was now past eleven o'clock and not only had he missed church, but he was now far behind in his quest to get back to the Hunsford parsonage... and Elizabeth. He was brought out of those thoughts when he noticed his rather anxious valet.

"Uh... Hobbs, can you have some hot water brought up, and ready my things for travel within thirty minutes? Oh... and tell my cousin that I will be down as soon as I am done dressing."

"Yes, sir... right away, sir..." He bowed to his employer and turned to leave the bedchambers.

When the man did not move fast enough for his tastes he urged, "Quickly man! Quickly!"

Hobbs scurried towards the door as Darcy hopped out of his bed and made his way straight to his private sitting room to where his smallest safe was tucked behind a small portrait of Pemberley. When he opened the safe, he brought out a rather ornate jewelry box while holding it reverentially. Inside it held a few of the more valuable Darcy family gems- one being more important than all the rest.

Darcy pulled out the sapphire and diamond ring with which every Darcy heir had presented his bride for at least the last four generations, staring off distantly as he thought about what his father had said to him about the requirements he should look for in a bride... wealth, title, and many accomplishments that had no use- at least to him.

You were never particularly happy, father, and I shall not repeat your mistakes. You never loved my mother-I could tell that from a very early age. I was just your ornament to show off to visitors until it was time to be put away again! Well... me and my children will know what it is to be loved and cherished-and with such a mother as Elizabeth, we will know what it is to live and be happy.

Thinking of his fiancée made him smile. *Elizabeth... you do not know how very much you mean to me. You are the air to a drowning man, so beautiful, so lively, so... passionate.* The remembrance of Friday night made him flush. Before then, he could only assume by her demeanor that she would be a more adventurous and less inhibited lover, but never in his wildest dreams would he have ever thought her to be so... so... *seductively unencumbered*

When he had gone to the Parsonage that evening, the housekeeper led him to a small sitting room on the second level of the house where Elizabeth appeared to have been tending to some correspondence. She seemed genuinely surprised to see him which only endeared her to him more because of her modesty. His admiration quickly converted to alarm though, when she stood to greet him and stumbled, lunging forward, which brought him forth to rescue her from the floor and a potentially nasty injury.

As he held her in his arms, he asked, "Are you well, Miss Elizabeth? Should you not sit down?"

She stared into his eyes for a moment blinking rapidly, before replying, "Y-yes... Mr. Darcy I am well. I only suffer from a little headache. I shall be all right, I thank you."

Darcy was not entirely convinced that she was indeed well. When he attempted to help her stand, she seemed off balance. Not wanting her to fall, he assisted her over to the settee where he deposited himself next to her.

"I do not mean to nay say you Miss Elizabeth; however you do not look yourself at all. Are you certain you are feeling well? Is there something I can get you, a drink maybe…?"

"No! No… Thank you, but Mrs. Hanson has already given me a drink of her medicinal tea for my headache. I shall be well in a bit."

Darcy continued to stare at her in disbelief, until she finally looked back up and into his eyes. Her brow arched charmingly, as she continued to gaze at him. *If only you had an idea of what that does to me Elizabeth, you would not do that.*

"I am sorry about my not so graceful welcome to you Mr. Darcy. I think that whatever Mrs. Collins housekeeper has put into the tea has made me rather… dizzy when I stand at the moment." She arched her brow again, as if asking him his purpose for being there.

It took Darcy a moment to recover his initial shock of her state, before he replied to her unspoken query.

"Mr. and Mrs. Collins had said that you were not feeling well, and I had come to see if you were ill-"

"As I have said before, Mr. Darcy, I only suffer from a headache… nothing more…"

Elizabeth's eyes were starting to look a little glassy, and Darcy began to worry that she may not realize just how… unlike herself she looked. She continued to stare silently at him, making him feel self conscious.

"Is there something amiss, El… Miss Elizabeth?" He looked down at his attire to make sure that nothing was out of place, "You keep staring at me…"

"You have the darkest brown eyes, sir, did you know?"

Darcy felt his cheeks burning, so surprised was he by her commentary that he too was silent for a moment as he held her gaze. *Perhaps she does know what she does to me? Maybe that is why she is acting so… different than I have ever seen her before. But I must respond to her open flirting.*

"I do not know how dark my eyes are at the moment Miss Elizabeth, but I do know that yours are the finest I have ever set them on."

"Humph! I wonder what you are playing at, sir? I know for a fact that you only found me 'tolerable' at the Meryton Assembly when we were first thrown into each other's company…" She tried to rise from her seat, but when she made to stand she fell back-right into Darcy's lap.

Her sudden appearance in his lap nearly negated her last words. Darcy struggled to keep his varied emotions in check with her biting words as she spoke them, but her gyrating against his groin area as she tried to move off his lap did nothing to alleviate that. Unfortunately his mind had taken a turn towards his baser instincts due to her movements at that moment. The feel of her bottom writhing against him brought to mind many of his dreams where she had done the same thing only less attired.

Without forethought, he instinctively grabbed her by the waist to try and still her movements, which only caused her to glare at him from behind her.

"Miss Elizabeth, please… you are… I am.."

Before he could say more, he felt rather than saw her hand go to his now very aroused member. The sensation of her hands there made him moan involuntarily. Her hand stilled, and she looked at him with alarm.

"Oh… I am sorry, sir. Did I hurt you?"

If you only knew how well that felt, you would not even ask, my love. Out loud he said to her, "No… not exactly, Eli… Miss Elizabeth. It is just that when you were squirming…"

"I was not *squirming* Mr. Darcy! I was trying to get up off of you! Oh…!"

She leaned back against him hard as she tried to move again, and Darcy could feel her putting more weight upon his lap. Her body went as limp as a noodle. In that instant he knew that he should call for help, but under the circumstances he knew if he did then Elizabeth would be utterly compromised in the eyes of the household staff, and the thought of Mr. Collins talking about this to his aunt, Lady Catherine… *Insupportable! Although… she would have no other choice than to marry me if that were the case.*

"Elizabeth… uh… Miss Elizabeth… please wake up." He patted her hand and tried to fan her with a newspaper that sat next to him.

I need to get her to her bed so that she can rest! Obviously she was more ill than Mr. and Mrs. Collin led me to believe! Not surprising considering the people in question! Such low connections, yet… she is so lovely. As carefully as he could, Darcy arose from the settee with Elizabeth in his arms and walked to the door carefully opening it so as not to make a sound. He knew that should anyone see him at that moment they would know what was going through his mind. After peering out into the hallway, he glanced upstairs to where the bedrooms must surely be, and ascended the stairs with his precious cargo as quietly as possible.

When he got to the landing, he had a decision to make; *which room is Elizabeth's?* There were five doors leading in various different directions, and he had to decide where to look first. *Logical thinking would have Collins looking out towards the road so that he could see who was coming or going, so the door on the right can be ruled out, so the door next to his must be Mrs. Collins room. Now as to which room would be next... My guess is that Mrs. Collins would keep her closest friend as far away from her husband as possible.* His logic took him to the farthest door to the left, and sure enough, when he opened it, he saw what he knew to be her pelisse and bonnet laying across the chair by the library desk. Backing up against the door to shut it, he acclimated himself to his surroundings

As carefully as possible, he laid Elizabeth down on the bed, but before he could withdraw his arms from underneath her, her fine eyes shuttered open. They gradually opened more until they were wide with... he knew not what. Suddenly he feared what she might think of him bringing her to her room, but she did not say anything-only kept staring at him.

"You are so warm." She closed her eyes again as she leaned into his chest, trapping his arms between herself and the mattress.

He froze as he knelt beside her soft form, watching her facial expressions as her lips curled into a pout. He was a man after all with manly needs and he ached to claim those lips as his own. To feel the soft warmth of them as they caressed his own, and touch her tongue with his own, feeling the velvet of her mouth. Before he knew what he was about, he was in truth kissing her and after a moment she was kissing him back. He could taste the mint in her mouth from what he assumed to be her tea from earlier, and he wanted to taste more... of her.

Soon he felt her soft hands snake around his neck and migrate to his hair, and his hands were gradually released to be able to run his hands through her tresses. The soft silkiness intoxicated him, but soon enough he wanted more as his body started to demand it of him. He was utterly lost to her and he knew it as his body surrendered to her with all his heart.

Chapter 2

It did not take long for the Darcy townhouse to come alive as the master barked out orders to have his horse readied within the hour so that he could join Elizabeth back in Kent. He quickly made his way to the breakfast parlor and was unsurprised to see his cousin, Richard, already partaking of some food.

"What brings you to town, Richard? Do not tell me that Bonaparte has launched an offensive against us and you were quickly summoned to town." Though Darcy was in good humor, he could recognize that his companion was non-pulsed with his jovial attitude. Suddenly he felt remorseful of having said something so flippant about his cousin's occupation

"I was only speaking in jest Richard. Seriously... what *are* you doing here on today of all days?"

Richard looked at him closely before answering, "I came rather urgently for a couple of reasons-both to warn you and also to discuss what exactly happened at the parsonage the other night when you had left us at Rosings."

There was a certain edge to Richard's speech that gave Darcy a pause, and he flushed at the thought of what he had done, but he thought, *I will be damned to divulge everything that happened between Elizabeth and me that night*. He knew that he could trust the man with his and Georgiana's life... and now Elizabeth's, but he would not have his cousin think her wanton for their night of passion for anything. He carefully chose his words before responding to the unspoken challenge.

"I admit that we may have breached propriety with our meeting alone at the parsonage Richard, but I knew that we should be leaving Kent soon and I had few other options than to meet her there,"

"Was she expecting you then?" Richard's eyebrows furrowed.

"No! She had no idea of my feelings for her, but she did seem to return them,"

"Are you certain of that cousin, because when I meet her the next afternoon in the park and mentioned your '*understanding*' she looked at me as if I were the whole of the French troops moving in upon her. In fact... *that* is one of the reasons why I am here today."

Darcy looked at him in alarm, silently begging him to continue with his reasons for being there.

"I see you look surprised. I am not though because your dear '*fiancée*' fainted when I happened to mention the whole of the circumstances of her receiving a letter from you and how I came to be the one to deliver it to her."

He grew anxious at the news that Elizabeth's sudden illness and asked with great concern, "*What*? Is she... is she all right? What did you do? What happened to her? What did you say to her, Richard?"

"Calm yourself, Darcy. I caught her before she fell to the ground, of course, and then I immediately took her back to the parsonage. Mrs. Collins called for the local physician who came immediately, and he examined her and talked to Mrs. Collins about Miss Bennet's strange symptoms. What concerns me is what the good physician said ..."

He hesitated to relate the rest of the tale until Darcy grabbed him and shook him.

"What did the man say, Richard?"

Richard shoved him lightly causing him to loosen his grip.

"Apparently the Collin's housekeeper had given Miss Bennet some herb in her tea and that herb was apparently very potent-in fact so potent that it could render a person completely unaware of their... um... behavior. That is what has me so concerned, Darcy. I think that it is entirely possible that your Elizabeth is unaware of your proposal... or what else may have happened that night."

His face paled. He knew in his heart that he should feel guilty for what had transpired that evening, but he felt sure that Elizabeth was almost as willing a participant as he was, and her reactions to him were so... passionate. *She was acting quite... forward, and quite... not herself, but when she said such things... and did such things, how was I to act differently? A man who felt less might have.* Suddenly the horror of what he had done struck him full force. He had taken his dearest Elizabeth's virtue without much forethought believing that she felt just as much for him as he did for her.

She must truly hate me now for what I have done. How could she forgive me for having taken her without restraint...? His thoughts were interrupted by Richard's voice.

"She does not recall anything from last night, Darcy, and I do hope that you did not do anything that would have been witnessed, because I think that you need to have another discussion with your intended before any announcements are made." He shook his head and added, "At any rate the physician also sent me to town to fetch this botanist just to be sure that Miss Bennet will not have any further episodes of amnesia. I thought it only right to notify you of what has transpired since you left us."

Darcy nodded, "Of course we should bring the man to Hunsford. Richard... please see to it that the gentleman is taken to her directly."

"Of course, I have already sent word to him." Richard added with a sigh, "I am sure that she will be fine and when she is recovered you can make your addresses again. Lord knows any woman would count herself lucky to have such a rich catch as you."

Darcy looked at his cousin sharply, "I know that many women of town have thought that they might '*catch*' me, but Elizabeth is not just any woman and I shall thank you to remember that, Richard."

"I know that she is not." He murmured before he slowly left the parlor to make the necessary arrangements.

Darcy was wracked with guilt for his behavior, but what was most distressing is that Elizabeth may not even recall that they had engaged in very inappropriate and intimate activity that may have very far reaching consequences. His honor required for them to marry if for no other reason than for her protection. His next conundrum was figuring out how to relate their activities without her resenting or even hating him for it.

With his appetite now gone, he called for his horse. *The first thing I need to do is go to the parsonage and beg for a private audience with Elizabeth, but how the devil am I to try to explain all of it?*

As Sunday morning dawned, Elizabeth woke up sore again. This time it was most of the muscles in her body, and she cringed when she sat up and walked to her bathing room. Her head was still fogged up with the vivid recollections from her dreams-most which included Mr. Darcy. Though she knew she was a maiden, she could not explain the images she recalled seeing in her sleep. The view of his body completely unclothed closely resembled the prints of the sculpture Adonis in her father's books.

Why am I imagining such things? And of him! Then again, how could he possibly have gotten the idea that I would agree to marry him? I can hardly stand him, let alone sentence myself to a lifetime with him... at least voluntarily. Oh... but Colonel Fitzwilliam said that he went to see papa yesterday! Good Lord what will he have to say to me when I return home? He was likely very displeased- to say the least, when Mr. Darcy approached him for my hand.

How can I explain it to him when I do not even remember any of it? Elizabeth felt the hot sting of tears of frustration building up within her and quietly despaired of ever being able to recall the events of Friday night. *Not only have I lost a whole evening, but I also managed to get myself engaged to the world's most disagreeable, proud man!* It was in this mood that the maid, Margaret found her.

"Beggin yer pardon ma'am, but Mrs. Collins sent me in ta tend ta yer bath, but she begged me ta tell ya that neither she nor Mr. Collins expected you to join them at services today." The maid was looking at her awkwardly which only made Elizabeth feel even more self conscious.

"W-why would Mrs. Collins say such a thing, Margaret?" Elizabeth was trying to hide her reddened face from the maid.

The young woman hesitated with her reply before saying, "I think it's on a count o' Lady Catherine."

Elizabeth puzzled over what the maid was talking about. "What about Lady Catherine?"

"Oh Miss... from wot I heard, the old lady's been in a lather 'bout you an Mr. Darcy..."

"What about me and Mr. Darcy?"

"'Bout you an him be'an engaged! Why... it's been all over th' place!"

Elizabeth startled at this new bit of information, but the maid did not seem to notice as she began her chores. It was bad enough to know that Colonel Fitzwilliam had been told of her engagement to Mr. Darcy, but now... apparently several other people knew as well. *Had he made an announcement before he even left...? Or did he make the announcement when he came back from Longbourn? Oh the nerve of that man! I do not know if I can even be civil to him at this moment!* Almost as suddenly as she thought that, she remembered what Margaret had said.

For a brief moment she amused herself while thinking of Lady Catherine's reaction to gaining such relations, all while her own plans were being thwarted! *I can just imagine what she is saying about the match right now!* Elizabeth chuckled at the idea of the harridan venting her spleen to the parson, while Collins simpered beneath her. *Poor Charlotte...having to deal with them alone!*

How I wish that I had Jane with me right now. She could comfort me. Jane... poor Jane! What would she think of me marrying the man who separated her from her Mr. Bingley? If only Mr. Darcy had minded his own business and not interfered with theirs then they would likely have been wedded by now! Just wait until I see him! I will give him a thing or two to think about!

It was with these thoughts that Elizabeth soaked in her warm bath until she heard a soft knock by the front doorway. Strange, Margaret usually comes through the servants doors.

"Yes?" Elizabeth answered.

"Elizabeth? It is me... Charlotte. Can I come in for a minute?"

Elizabeth sat up in the tub and draped a towel over herself before she beckoned her friend to enter.

"It is all right, Charlotte. You can come in now."

The look on her friends face told her a few things and begged a few more questions. She grew impatient waiting for her friend to speak.

"Charlotte, out with it. I know that you have something on your mind, and by the looks of you, I may not want to hear it."

"You know me too well, dear Elizabeth. I would imagine by now, that you know that we are all aware of... of your... engagement to Mr. Darcy."

Elizabeth sighed, "Yes. I heard from Margaret that there was talk of it..."

"Why did you not say anything to me yesterday? I had thought he might be in love with you from what I have observed, and I guess I was correct. It is amazing-"

"Charlotte... you do not think that I have forgotten all of my principals? You should know better than that! I do not even recall what happened to lead Mr. Darcy to think that we are engaged. In fact... I do not even recall him asking me to marry him... not really."

"Well obviously something happened to make him think that the two of you are engaged. Why else would the colonel ride to town on a

Sunday, to seek out some help for you... unless... unless he were trying to find favor with you as well..."

"I seriously doubt that. He was congratulating me on our *engagement* yesterday, and besides that, not two weeks ago he was telling me that he must marry economically, and in case you have forgotten-I have done little to entice him there."

"Hmmm, good point, but still he did ride all the way to town by the suggestion of Mr. Robbins. That reminds me... the doctor thought it might be a good idea to bring a botanist to examine whatever it was that Mrs. Hanson put in your tea. You still seemed a bit out of it yesterday and even into last night. I will not even repeat what you said in your sleep."

"Why? What did I say?"

"It does not bear repeating. With all of your moaning and talking, Mr. Collins was certain that someone else was in your room with you, and insisted I go check up on you. Of course you were alone, but the noises you made... I was a bit... concerned."

"*Charlotte*-what did I say? I cannot remember."

"Lizzy... they were sounds not usually heard from gentlewomen, at least not in your situation. I quite thought you may be having a nightmare... or..."

"*Or what?*"

"Nothing... it was nothing. I am sure you were just having a bad dream. T'is another reason for me to request that you stay home for today. I think it may be in your best interests to rest some more, and maybe your fiancé will even be able to join you later."

"Humph! My fiancé! I hope that he forgets that I was ever here! *I do not want to marry that man!*"

"But, Lizzy... do not be a simpleton! The word has already gotten around to Rosings, and likely through all of Kent by now, *and* I understand that he has gone to Longbourn yesterday to ask Mr. Bennet for your hand in marriage! It is as good as settled. Besides why pine over Mr. Wickham now? He is to marry Miss King anyway, and if you marry then your family's future shall be secure."

Elizabeth shot Charlotte a sharp look. "For your information my *good friend*, I do not recall *ever* agreeing to marry him. I am not even *sure* that I did. Furthermore, I am quite reconciled to Mr. Wickham's engagement to Mary King. In fact I am happy for *him*, and as far as my family's security goes... it would have been secured a long time ago if it had not been for Mr. Darcy's *meddling* in Mr. Bingley's affairs!"

"Whatever are you talking about, Lizzy? How did Mr. Darcy meddle in Mr. Bingley's affairs, and what has that got to do with your family's security?"

"Do you not remember my sister, Jane... sweet innocent Jane, who was quite smitten with Mr. Bingley, and he who was as equally smitten with her?"

"Lizzy..." Charlotte began softly, "Jane was not exactly what you would call overt in showing her feelings, and I can see how Mr. Bingley-who hardly knew her well enough to know that, would not be able to tell what her true feelings were for him. Did I not tell you before that a woman ought to show more affection than she feels? You can hardly blame him, and if he was as weak as to listen to another to direct his heart. Obviously his feelings were not strong enough for her. If he were truly in love with Jane then he would have stood his ground, and found out the truth of her feelings. Not left at the briefest word from a friend never to return!"

"But this '*friend*' is a proud arrogant... unfeeling..."

"Do you hear yourself? Are you still angry at him over his unfortunate remark at the Assembly? Listen to me when I tell you that that man is obviously in love with you, else he would not be '*lowering*' himself to marry a woman with no title and little in the way of a dowry. He is ten times the consequence of any man of your previous acquaintance, and he pays you the highest compliment."

"But Charlotte, how can I marry a man that I do not love..." she picked up her pruney fingers and frowned.

"Elizabeth... sometimes we women must look at the practical side of things, and forget about our childish romantic notions. He is a man of great consequence and pays you an even greater compliment by offering you marriage. Now... I am not saying that you have to bow to his every whim, but as you can see," Charlotte held up her hands, "There are ways to manage your husband without having to be much in their company."

Charlotte finished by handing Elizabeth a towel, and said to her friend, "Think about what I have said, and then think about what it could possibly do for Jane. Who knows... you may even be able to reacquaint her with Mr. Bingley." She smiled to Elizabeth and left her to her cold bath.

~*~*~*~

Elizabeth did do a great deal more thinking about what Charlotte had said, but still found it difficult to reconcile herself to the prospect of a loveless marriage. She had always vowed that when she married, it would be for love, and now she faced the prospect of marriage to the last man on earth she would ever want to marry... barring William Collins, of course. She shuttered at the thought of being married to *that* man, and having to bear his attentions. *I wonder if Charlotte has any advice on avoiding her husband in those circumstances as well?*

She knew that should she actually go through with this marriage, she would eventually have to bear Mr. Darcy's attentions. *He will want an heir, I am certain of that! Most men of his standing want at least one male heir, and if the first is a girl... ugh! I cannot think about this!* Why *am I actually considering going through with this?*

Her agitation became such that she thought she should take a nap while the house was empty. Her headache had returned again, but there was no way she would to take anything else for that now. *Last time I took a drought, I ended up engaged. Next thing that would likely happen is me ending up married!* She closed her eyes and tried to remember what had led up to this whole disaster in the first place. Soon she had found sleep again.

Darcy kneeled next to her on the bed and she noticed his eyes were so lovely and dark as his set met hers. Elizabeth's eyes closed for a moment thinking his arms around her felt exquisite. This man was like a raging fire, so warm... so... so strong, she never wanted this feeling to end. Her fingers made their way to his silken curls, and down his chest. It seemed instantaneous that their clothing was removed... and Elizabeth thought to herself that his form was as beautiful as a man's form ever could be. His lips felt so soft on her skin, and when he touched her... her body responded to him traitorously as he continued to caress her curves to her most private of places. His skin was on hers, rubbing, caressing those areas.

Suddenly she felt a sharp pain ripping through her. Something large was rubbing her there to the point of pain. When she opened her eyes, she saw him above her, whispering into her ear. His voice was so soothing and she calmed down, even through the pain. Within minutes there was a warmness within her... unlike anything she had ever felt before. The pain was gone then, and the soreness lingered, but he was still there. His body was warm against hers as he held her tight. It felt so wonderful... so safe. She drifted back to sleep, and awakened to an empty bed and room. Where did he go? Or was it all a dream?

Elizabeth's eyes flew open as she shot up in the bed. She had never in her life seen a real man in all his glory, but to have recalled Mr. Darcy in such a state and so closely resembling the prints in her father's den were very upsetting. Her good breeding would have prevented her from doing anything so wholly inappropriate as to allow a man into her bedroom, let alone do such things as she saw in her dreams. To say she was agitated would have been an understatement. She continued to dwell on her remembrances of her dream and the significance of them, but was still unable to make any sense of them.

By Sunday afternoon, she had nearly succeeded in distracting herself from the thought of being married to Mr. Darcy, when the parsonage received a very agitated visitor. Mrs. Hanson's announcement of Lady Catherine DeBourgh was anything but necessary. The woman could be heard shouting orders from outside the parsonage, and Mr. Collins was seen from the upstairs window scurrying outside to pay his patroness homage while she barked at him. By the time the lady arrived in Charlotte's sitting room, she had already made it clear that she was furious, and it was laid clearly at Elizabeth's door.

When the woman stormed into the room, she made immediate demands of Elizabeth.

"I must *insist* that I have a word with you Miss Bennet... *in private!*"

Elizabeth was too stunned to object to the woman's demands and acquiesced in silence by a nod of her head. Almost immediately Mr. Collins offered the use of his study, but Lady Catherine refused his offer.

"No! We shall take a turn about the gardens... where it is more private!"

The horrified look on Charlottes face told Elizabeth that they were likely thinking the same things, and that this was anything but a social call. The two women headed outside to the garden. Lady Catherine did not even wait for Elizabeth to don her pelisse as she made her way towards the trellis. As soon as they were out of earshot of anyone, the old harridan rounded on her object.

"Miss Bennet, you can have no doubt as to why I have come here today."

Elizabeth thought she may have several ideas, but did not wish to give the woman and opening. Being the object of that woman's impertinent questions at her home was one thing, but coming to here hosts house to accost her was quite another. She decided to play on here near innocence.

"I assure you ma'am, that I do not know why you have honored us with your presence today."

"Miss Bennet! I have recently heard a most malicious rumor that you and my nephew, Darcy, are engaged and I have come here to have you contradict it!"

"If you thought it untrue, I wonder that you took the trouble to come here."

"Miss Bennet! I am not to be trifled with! I do not believe my nephew capable of making such a grievous error in judgment as to form an attachment with such a low and unconnected person such as yourself, but I have come here now to hear you contradict this information! Tell me at once... are you and my nephew, Darcy engaged?"

Elizabeth was furious at her treatment by this rude, obnoxious, and condescending woman, and as much as she wanted to deny that she and Mr. Darcy were engaged, the truth was she did not know for certain what the facts were or where she stood in that respect. She opened her mouth only to shut it once more, and repeated that action a couple more times, but just before she was about to reply, a loud baritone voice boomed out, "Yes aunt, I am engaged to marry Miss Elizabeth Bennet, though I do not know what concern it is of yours!"

The women turned abruptly to see the nephew in question as he approached them.

"Darcy! *What has gotten into you?* You are engaged to Anne! You two were formed for each other since you were in your cradles, and I will not stand aside and watch as you ruin your life to marry this... this... temptress! *What has she done to you?* Has she used her wiles to force you into offering for her... is that it?" The old woman demanded.

When Mr. Darcy had shown up, and verified that they were in fact engaged, Elizabeth's mind froze, although her stomach starting turning summersaults. A wave of nausea passed through her, and she could only make herself look on as Mr. Darcy and his aunt argued over the veracity of his assertions.

"Lady Catherine, that is quite enough! I will not have you assault my fiancée in such a way! As to Anne and I being engaged that is only your wishes, not mine. We are not, nor have we ever been engaged, and as to Miss Elizabeth ruining my life, I hardly doubt that. She is a gentleman's daughter and I am a gentleman, thus far we are equals. Elizabeth could only be a complement to my life, and I shall insist that my fiancée, and soon wife, be treated with the utmost respect!"

"You cannot be serious Darcy! She will make you the laughing stock of society. I must insist that you end this little charade before anyone of worth gets word of it!"

"I shall do no such thing, Lady Catherine, and I have told you at least twice now that I will not stand for you-or *anyone* else treating Elizabeth with such disrespect. We are to be married, and shall do so as soon as possible…"

This news came as a complete shock to Elizabeth, who was now standing behind the taller gentleman. Her mind went into another spin when she heard his pronouncement. *What? When was this decided? What has my father to say about this*? As she continued to wrap her mind around the certainty of his assertions, she felt herself swaying at this new development.

"Why such a hurry, Darcy? Or is there another reason for you to make such hasty plans? Come now… if she is with child, you could easily afford to send her away somewhere. Once her confinement was over, you could even keep her as your mistress… after you marry Anne, of course."

"Enough! I will not stand here and allow you to say such vicious and untrue things about my future wife! She is every bit as honorable as the other women of our society-*likely even more so*. Besides… I will not have the sort of relationship as my own parents… or you and Sir Louis had. I wish to be happy in my marriage, and I do not wish to settle for some empty headed sycophant who has no true thoughts in their head or any regard for me at all!"

"That is the way things are done in our society, nephew. It has been the way for many generations…"

"And at what cost? They were miserable, and did not know what was truly valuable. At least in marrying Elizabeth, I will have a real treasure. She may not be wealthy, but she has more accomplishments than that of any other woman I have ever known-even more than Anne."

"Darcy… if you marry this… this woman, I shall see to it that our society never recognizes her. She will be a nonentity!"

"No wife of mine shall ever be seen as such, and if people are foolish enough to feel as such then they are not worth our acknowledgement at all. Society in general has more sense."

"Is this your final word, then Darcy? Will you deny your mother's last wishes for this... harlot?"

Elizabeth was becoming more offended by Lady Catherine's words, but she could not force herself to say anything, for Mr. Darcy continued to defend her honor, and insisted that he thought he might be happy with marriage to her. *What is Mr. Darcy going on about? We could hardly oblige each other when we were in Meryton, and now he professes that he wants to marry me? Astounding!* She was so engrossed in her own thoughts that she almost missed part of the conversation between Mr. Darcy and Lady Catherine.

"You shall not sway me from taking anyone other than Miss Bennet as my wife. My mind is quite made up."

"I know how to deal then, Darcy! You will regret this for the rest of your life!" Lady Catherine stormed off from where she had come.

When Elizabeth saw a flash of blue, she realized that the whole episode had been witnessed by not only Charlotte through her sitting room window, but Mr. Collins, Colonel Fitzwilliam, Anne De Bourgh, and a handful of servants. Everyone seemed to be staring at them. The whole scenario was so overwhelming to Elizabeth's overburdened mind that her knees grew weak and she began to feel like a trapped animal. Her skin went cold as her vision narrowed. Everything went blurry but for the most beautiful brown eyes looking down upon her with such tenderness. Her mind kept repeating, *'This must be a dream! This must sampling be a very confusing, tangled dream!'*

Elizabeth did not know it, but the man belonging to those beautiful brown eyes had her in his arms, holding on to her for dear life. As Fitzwilliam Darcy carried his beloved Elizabeth back to the parsonage, no one missed the concerned look upon his face as he regarded his precious cargo. The door to the back of the building opened up to admit them, and they were quickly followed by Colonel Fitzwilliam, who offered to go and retrieve Mr. Higgins who was likely on his way to Rosings Park at that moment. Charlotte, Mrs. Hanson, and Margaret led him up to Elizabeth's room where he laid her gently upon her bed. Immediately the women went about to care for their charge as Darcy looked on. He refused to leave her side until she woke up again-much to Charlottes chagrin.

Chapter 3

When Elizabeth finally opened her eyes again, the soft brown ones that she remembered seeing last appeared before her again. She regained her bearings and realized that they were not alone. Her bed was surrounded by at least three other people. Charlotte, of course, was by her side, along with Mr. Darcy opposite the matron, and some other gentleman.

"Good evening to you, Miss Bennet. I believe you have had quite a tumultuous weekend... and all after having some very potent tea." The as of yet, unnamed man addressed her.

Charlotte was first to speak up, "Yes Mr. Higgins. She has fainted twice since yesterday."

"And after having this medicinal tea, for a... what was it? A headache?" The man tisk-tisked. "Such a price to pay, hmmm?"

"The question is Mr. Higgins, how much longer will this go on? She will be well, will she not?" Mr. Darcy asked with a hint of worry.

"Yes, sir. Your fiancée should be recovered from the effects of the tea by tomorrow, and if not I suggest that she be evaluated more thoroughly. From what I have seen though... I think you have nothing to worry about." The man finally turned to address her again, "Have you had any more recurrences of your headaches, Miss Bennet?"

"N-no, sir. I think that I have just gotten a little overwhelmed with... well... everything that has happened recently. I think that I shall be well..."

"But if something happens to you again, Elizabeth, it would be better to be in town where there are physicians who could better care for you. In fact... after this afternoon's episode with Lady Catherine, I have directed my staff to pack my things and take them to the inn here in Hunsford. I will not stay another night under my aunt's roof- not after she attacked you as she did, so I am already packed. According to Mrs. Collins, she could easily have you readied to leave by tomorrow mid-morning then we can arrive in town by mid-afternoon..."

"But my Aunt and Uncle Gardiner are not expecting me for another week, and I do not even know if the post can take me tomorrow..."

Mr. Darcy wore a half amused half frown on his face before he said, "Elizabeth... surely you do not think that I would allow my fiancée to travel alone in a post carriage? You will travel with me, and if you require an escort, then Mrs. Collins can either send Miss Lucas or if she does not wish to go so early, the maid Margaret may go with you-"

"Excuse me, Mr. Darcy, but I think that I can make some decisions for myself... in fact I think you take too much upon yourself. You have once again presumed too much."

By the look on Mr. Darcy's face, Elizabeth knew that she had wounded him, but at the moment her emotions were at war within her and she was finding it hard to feel remorseful. On one side was a man who defended her so gallantly to his own arrogant aunt, and declared his affections, and on the other side was a man who had separated his best friend from her dearest sister... and those feelings could not reconcile with what she had at first felt about the man. Her sense of independence was trying to assert itself at the moment though, and her ire concerning his presumption about their status was hard to contain.

It took the gentleman in question a moment to reply, "I am sorry if you feel that I am being overly cautious, Miss Bennet. My only intention was to see to your well being. I do not wish for anything else to happen to you, and in my haste to protect you, I fear that I spoke rather quickly, but..."

Charlotte broke into their conversation at that moment, "Lizzy... there are other things that you need to know as well. You must understand that Lady Catherine is likely to be more than a little displeased with... well... a lot of things after today, and Mr. Collins has already been talking about sending you away." She paused as she gave Elizabeth a sympathetic look. "I am sorry to have to tell you this now, but under the circumstances I think it may be for the best if you do go to town early."

"Miss Bennet... Elizabeth... I am sorry to seem so high handed, but Lady Catherine can make things even more miserable, and if you stay here you could only be made more uncomfortable-to say the very least. She is frightful at best at the moment, and that cannot be good for you right now."

No doubt Lady Catherine could make even the most stolid person react to her tirades, but I am able to defend myself, Elizabeth thought petulantly. As she looked around the room however, everyone seemed to be agreeing with her friend and Mr. Darcy.

"Miss Elizabeth," the voice of Colonel Fitzwilliam could now be heard. She had not noticed him up until now and she paid him more heed, "I have just come from Rosings Park, and can verify everything that has been said here thus far. Lady Catherine is absolutely livid, and... well... Mr. and Mrs. Collins may have their hands full for now."

Elizabeth considered his words. She had already experienced that lady, and could only imagine having to stay indefinitely and listening to her rants. It still grated on her nerves to have everyone else dictate to what she should and should not do. Common sense ruled in the end as she considered her options. *I could not stay here when Mr. Collins will only make things impossible to bear, and then risk having the old woman accost me again is not worth it to stay anyway. As to my travel arrangements though... I am not as certain.*

"Charlotte...? Is Maria ready to go back home, do you think? Or would she prefer to stay and come home later?"

"In light of what we have all witnessed, she thought it might be best for her to leave sooner rather than later. She certainly has no wish to endure Mr. Collins lamentations over our '*disgrace*'."

All of a sudden the feeling of shame came over Elizabeth. Not so much for what happened, but for the repercussions that followed. She did not even know what she was going to say to her father when they finally reunited. He will be so disappointed in me for... engaging myself to Mr. Darcy, but then he is not the man I thought he was. What shall papa say when he hears what happened this afternoon? Likely the absurdity will amuse him... and nothing else will be said other than to tease me! She also worried about what impression her early arrival would have on her Aunt and Uncle Gardiner. *They are not even expecting me for another week. What shall I tell them if I arrive at their doorstep with two strange men in such a carriage? Oh, what a mixed up mess this had become! And still I have no idea how it all happened!* That was the most frustrating thing to Elizabeth-she still had no recollection of how this had all come about.

Realizing that she had not replied to her friend she made her decision, she said, "I suppose that you are right about me staying on here any longer. It would not be pleasant for anyone. My greatest concern about this plan is that I am not expected at Gracechurch Street for another week…"

"I can have one of my footmen sent to your family's residence this evening with a message, then he can ride back in the morning, and you and Miss Lucas can travel with Colonel Fitzwilliam and me to town."

Elizabeth still felt unsure in this situation, and wished beyond everything that she could recall what happened on Friday night, but the only person who could fill in those questions was a man that confounded her more than any other of her acquaintance. She did not want to travel four hours in a coach to town with a man that up until very recently, she thought could not abide her presence in his -let alone wanted to spend the rest of his life with her.

"Mr. Darcy… would it be possible to have a private word with you before we make any further arrangements?"

She looked to everyone in the room but the man she had addressed, pleading silently with her eyes for some time to discuss their arrangements. Charlotte frowned for a moment, Mr. Higgins only raised his eyebrows, and Colonel Fitzwilliam smiled at his cousin conspiratorially. Charlotte seemed to know that she needed some time to talk to the man who would soon become the most important figure in her life.

Her friend finally agreed to her request, "All right, Elizabeth, we will give you and your fiancé a few moments to discuss things, but I must insist that the door be left ajar-for propriety's sake."

"Of course." The couple said in unison.

Once everyone else had cleared out of the room and Charlotte left the door slightly cracked as promised, Mr. Darcy reached for her hand and smiled at her.

"I was hoping that we may be given a few moments alone, although I did not imagine that it would be like this." He half smiled.

Elizabeth stared at him for a moment with mixed emotions, not knowing how she would make an opening with him. Then she started hesitantly.

"Mr. Darcy, you must understand that… this has all… come as quite a shock to me. I… I must confess that I do not know how this has come about."

"Elizabeth," She was still rather uncomfortable with his presumed familiarity with her, but let it pass as he did not seem to notice her discomfort, "I have always admired your modesty, and I think that it was one of the first things that attracted me to you. Well… that and many other things."

"Sir, I do not know what to say or think. I must confess that I barely recall your visit this past Friday even, let alone your proposal or my acceptance…" He looked stricken at her confession, but quickly schooled his face to reflect his haughty appearance as she continued, "especially after our acquaintance in Hertfordshire. In fact I still acute remember hearing you say, 'she is tolerable I suppose, but not handsome enough to tempt me'," His face paled at her speech, "I had no idea that you thought of me other than to see some defect or other, and even here you did not seem to be very impressed with my presence."

"Elizabeth, I do not know what to think of your *confession*, but it has given me grief ever since I have made that most unfortunate remark at the Meryton Assembly, and I regretted it ever since I said it. As to my behavior towards you while I stayed at Netherfield Park, I must confess that I struggled against my attraction to you and acted in a way as to prevent you from developing any expectations. When I saw you again… here visiting Hunsford, I knew my struggle was a hopeless cause. I sought you out while you were out in the park walking, and tried to make conversation with you as best I could, but I am not good at reading people… that much is true. As to our being engaged, I might have thought less of you had you not been surprised at my addresses, but the feelings that I have expressed earlier were honest, and true."

"I appreciate the sentiment, yet sir; you have not answered the material question. How is it that we have come to such an arrangement?"

Elizabeth saw his face flush, before he looked to the floor and took a few deep breaths before looking straight at her to answer, "That is a more complex answer Miss Elizabeth, especially in light of the fact that you do not recall most of the evening in question. I do not know how to answer other than to say that you had responded to me… most… delightfully." Again he diverted his eyes away from her.

"Mr. Darcy… you do not expect me to accept that as an answer, do you?"

"Miss Elizabeth... Elizabeth, please call me Fitzwilliam, and no, I do not expect you to accept that as an answer, but it is all that I can say at the moment, other than rest assured that it is in your best interests and sensibilities at the moment not to delve too deeply into my reasoning. Suffice to say that we are doing the right thing by marrying."

Elizabeth could feel her ire rising again at his dismissive attitude. *The nerve of this man! Thinking he knows what is best for me, and what is he all about in saying that* 'we are doing the right thing by marrying'? *Did he compromise me in some way, and we were observed? Well it is not as if it matters now anyway! After what happened this afternoon, we shall have to marry-else me and my family will be disgraced. Jane would have no chance at all to reunite with Mr. Bingley and I do not even want to think about poor Mr. Wickham!* The idea that she had been left no other choice but to go through this sham of a marriage frustrated her more than she wished to acknowledge, and she felt tears burning in her eyes and then they started to fall down her delicate cheeks.

Mr. Darcy reacted to her tearful state with hasty concern, "My love... please do not cry. All will be well. I promise you that we shall marry as soon as possible, and this will all be forgotten."

"How can it be forgotten when it was not even *remembered*?" Elizabeth sobbed.

Darcy approached her and sat upon the bed to embrace her while still holding her hand. "Shhhh, shhh, my love, it is just as well that you do not recall it-for then we can make new memories together."

"But... what *did* happen? Obviously something significant must have happened to force us to marry in such haste, and I assume that you have already been to see my father...?" Mr. Darcy nodded his head in confirmation and Elizabeth asked, "He must have given his blessing if you are saying that we are marrying soon."

"Ummmm, yes he had given his consent, in fact he wrote a letter for me to give to you." He reached into his coat and retrieved a letter addressed to her from Mr. Bennet. "He asked that I give this to you when I saw you."

Elizabeth took the letter and read the address then turned it over in her hands, as she said, "Thank you." To Darcy.

He was hesitant as he asked, "Will you consider my request to marry soon, Elizabeth? I have already received the special license from the archbishop, so we may marry at any time ..."

"Please, sir... give me some time to acclimate myself to the idea of our getting married. It has come as a surprise, and now you wish to make such haste, yet I need time."

Mr. Darcy frowned again, but grudgingly agreed not to force the issue. "Of course, of course I will give you some time to acclimate yourself to the idea, but I still hope that we can marry within the next fortnight..."

"Again, sir, I ask you to give me a little more time... to become accustomed to this. You would not allow your sister to marry in such haste, now would you

Those words seemed to suffice, for Mr. Darcy immediately went silent and even seemed a bit remorseful over his insistence. After a brief pause he answered her.

"No... no of course I would not wish for her to feel pressured to make such a decision..."

"Then please... do this for me."

"But you will still consent marry soon?"

Well it is not as though I have any choice in the matter, now is it? She thought, but said reluctantly, "Y-yes. Now... would it be possible for me to have a few moments alone to read my letter?" She indicated the dispatch that she was still holding.

He nodded his head, "Of course. Oh-what shall we do about removing to town tomorrow?"

"I think that it would be in everyone's best interests if we leave tomorrow as soon as you and your staff are ready. If I may have my writing desk with my supplies I will pen a note to my Aunt and Uncle Gardiner, and you can have it sent to them as soon as I am done."

Mr. Darcy readily agreed to her requests, and ensured that she had everything that she needed to write to her family then left her to read her letter, but not before kissing her upon her lips. The gesture took her completely by surprise, but it was not necessarily a bad one. His lips were so soft, and tender, and when they met hers it caused her to feel a sort of electrifying elation. She could scarcely understand her body's betrayal of her. Though he had committed a breach in propriety she was not of a mind to call him out for it at the moment. When the door closed behind him, she took the letter from her father and reluctantly broke the seal to read it.

Longbourn

8 April 1809

Dearest Lizzy,

I cannot tell you how surprised I was that Mr. Darcy came to pay me a call today. I would have thought that the king himself was more likely to show up at our doorstep than that man, but imagine what a shock it was to learn that he had come not as a social call, but to ask for my second daughter's hand in matrimony. This daughter, whom I might add, had thought him rather disagreeable, and haughty-or so she protested vehemently before she left for Hunsford.

It was brought to my attention that there may be some urgency in this matter, though I do not know exactly what happened, and I would just as soon not know all of the details as nothing can be done to change it. It pains me to think that you shall be marched up the aisle. I cannot believe that you would voluntarily have behaved in such a way, and I am concerned that perhaps something must have happened to force your hand with the man.

Lizzy if this be the case, then please reconsider your choices. I would not have you forced into an unequal marriage-especially one that would endanger your well being. If you wish, you may return home and we shall deal with the consequences should there be any. I have not made any announcements here pending confirmation of your acceptance, and I have requested that Mr. Darcy do likewise.

Let me say again that I would ask you to thoughtfully reconsider. Though the man may be rich, and you would have more fine clothes and fine carriages than Jane would have if she were to have married Mr. Bingley, I would not have you miserable for the rest of your life. I will await word from you to know how to react.

Your concerned father,

Thomas Bennet

Elizabeth's emotions reasserted themselves, and now she wished more than anything to know exactly what happened the other night when Mr. Darcy came to the parsonage. Apparently something must have to cause such urgency, but it did not help that she had no idea now, how to approach her father. She had, after all, officially agreed to marry Mr. Darcy, but her father did say that he would support her in whatever decision she made. With a moment's consideration, she felt that they should wait the appropriate amount of time before their wedding in order to assure her father that they were not doing so blindly.

Papa will feel a little better if Mr. Darcy and I give him and each other some time to become accustomed to the idea of our marrying. Maybe we should not make any announcements about our betrothal, but tell everyone that we are courting? Though it will not likely be long before the events of today are known, we can have some time to give the appearance of propriety. That will give them less to talk about than a hastily arranged wedding, and maybe I could even convince him to reunite Mr. Bingley with Jane? Yes... I think that would be a splendid idea!

It took her a little more time to think about what she would say to her Gardiner family, but finally she felt that the best approach would be the most direct one.

Hunsford Parsonage,

Sunday 9th April, 1809

Dearest Aunt and Uncle Gardiner,

You will likely be amazed at what I have to relay to you, but I am engaged to Mr. Fitzwilliam Darcy of Pemberley in Derbyshire, but we are not making any announcements until we have some more time to get to know each other better. I know how it must sound, but I tell you this earnestly. Recent events have caused us to make these arrangements, and I do not have enough paper to write to you about what has occurred. Suffice to say that due to my engagement to Mr. Darcy, things have been strained with my cousin's patroness, Lady Catherine De Bourgh.

Lady Catherine happens to be Mr. Darcy's aunt and is less than pleased with this new development. She had apparently planned on her daughter, Anne and Mr. Darcy marrying ever since they were in their cradles, and has made things rather difficult here. Due to the strain between our relations, Mr. Darcy along with his cousin, Colonel Fitzwilliam, have offered to bring me and Maria Lucas to town tomorrow. I do hope that this will not be a great imposition, and I also request that my engagement not be generally know as of yet. Though my father has given his consent, he has made no general announcement, and I would wish to inform Jane myself.

    Mr. Darcy's messenger will be returning to Hunsford in the morning, therefore if you have any message to send back with him, he may bring it back to me. I will add God bless you all, and I shall look forward to seeing you tomorrow should you find your way to having me upon such short notice.

Your loving niece,

Elizabeth Bennet

    When Elizabeth finished sealing her letter, she rang for the maid, and requested that Mr. Darcy be sent in. When *that* gentleman approached, he seemed a little more reluctant to her, and she sensed his remorse for everything that had occurred. With a slight smile, she handed him her letter to be sent to town along with the directions. She finally made her requests regarding their *courtship*, feeling that he was likely to accede to them under the circumstances.

    "Mr. Darcy… I understand that you have expressed to my father some need for urgency for our nuptials, but he did not say why, and I still wish to know what exactly happened the other night."

    "Miss Elizabeth, please understand that I feel great remorse over everything that happened then, and wish that I could take some of my actions back-especially now that Mrs. Collins has informed me what the situation was. It is difficult to say what occurred though without violating your sensibilities, and I promise that I shall confess what happened to you, but please give me some time to figure out how to explain it."

    Although Elizabeth was less than pleased with his response, and she was tempted to issue a challenge, something of his looks made her reconsider. She reluctantly agreed to allow him that, but made her other requests, feeling that they would be just compensation for her wait for an explanation from him.

    "Very well then, but I do have two other requests. *First*, I wish for you to let Mr. Bingley know that my sister, Jane, is in town and not only that, but that she has been there these past three months. I am not saying that he must be dragged over to visit her or anything, but he should know that she only went in hopes to maintain some acquaintance, and that his sisters were less than forthcoming in their reasons for leaving Netherfield Park. Miss Bingley had in fact said that he was planning on marrying your sister, Georgiana."

"*What?*" He did look truly surprised at her pronouncement, which gave her some hope for her dear sister's chances of a happier outcome.

"Oh… were you not aware that Miss Bingley wrote to say that one of the reasons for their all leaving Netherfield was so that he might be allowed to spend more time with Miss Darcy, and that they anticipated that your families would be united."

"That is absolutely false!" He stopped himself, suddenly realizing that he should direct his anger elsewhere. "My sister, Georgiana, is only fifteen-and though she will soon be sixteen, she has not even been presented yet. Besides, she does not see Bingley as anything other than a brother."

His words gave Elizabeth some comfort, although she wanted to ensure that he would agree to inform his friend of Jane's presence, and not prevent them from becoming reacquainted should both parties desire to do so.

"Then am I assuming that you will inform the gentleman of my sister's present address, and *not* prevent your friend from forming an attachment should they *both* desire it?"

Though he looked at her strangely, he nodded his head. "Agreed."

"And one last thing… we shall not make an announcement made generally known… at least not for a little while…"

"But, Elizabeth… surely you do not believe that after what happened here today… and in front of so many people, that word will not get around? Though I am not a betting man, I would wager that by tomorrow even, word of our betrothal will have come to town. Soon enough it will be in the papers…"

"Then we shall take our chances, and know how to deal if the time comes. Even if we do make the announcement, I would like some time to… to at least be courted properly. I do not think that that is too much to ask for, is it?"

"No… certainly not-but we should not wait too long…"

"Would you care to explain that to me then, Mr. Darcy?" She challenged somewhat angrily.

He said no more about her last question, and only shook his head. "I will agree to your requests Elizabeth, but promise me that should you start to feel any worse or different even, that you will let me know as soon as possible?"

She did not know what he was talking about, and assumed that he meant the effect of the tea, but she did agree to his wishes, "Agreed."

"I shall take comfort then in knowing that we shall be wedded in the future and for now... I will let you rest as I see to our travel arrangements for tomorrow and..." he held up her letter, "I will send a messenger to deliver this immediately. Is there anything else that you require before I bid you a good night?"

"No... I thank you, sir."

He nodded his head to her again before he left her for the evening, and she lay back in her bed, praying that she was not making the biggest mistake of her entire life. *Papa, I hope that you understand, and I do not disappoint you, but somehow I sense that he is not what we had all thought he was.* She thought of her fiancé, but still could not reconcile the man she knew in Hertfordshire to the man who presented himself at the parsonage. As she drifted off to sleep again, her dreams from last night returned, only this time she could actually recall some of the sensations and even scents that went with the images. As she tossed and turned, the rest of the parsonage were subjected to her moaning in her sleep yet again.

~*~*~*~

The Hunsford party was assembled the next morning at the parsonage, and Elizabeth and Maria Lucas's valises were secured on Darcy's carriage. Darcy sat next to his cousin, Colonel Fitzwilliam, as Elizabeth sat opposite him and next to Maria. They had a few stilted conversations between them, but most of her attention was drawn to the colonel who always seemed to have such an easy unassuming manner.

"Miss Elizabeth, Darcy tells me that you are going to make him wait to make you his bride, and yet you are brave enough to allow him to go back to town."

"That is correct, but I do not know that I am brave for *allowing* him to do anything. In fact was it not you along with him who requested that we all remove from Kent?" Her voice was light and teasing, with just a hint of annoyance in it.

"Touché," the colonel replied, "But it is amazing that any woman would not just snatch him up, and march him down the aisle. Darcy here, is quite the catch in town, did you know?"

She was amused as she saw the man in question scowl at his cousin, who only laughed at his cousin's expression.

"Oh? And is that due to his handsome good looks?"

Colonel Fitzwilliam guffawed and replied, "Possibly... but then he does have other inducements as well."

She looked again to the man sitting across from her, and noticed him looking out the carriage window with a bright blush upon his cheeks trying hard to avoid her gaze.

"I am sure that you know *all* of Mr. Darcy's good qualities much better than I, Colonel Fitzwilliam, and I do hope to discover them in time."

Elizabeth spoke more to that man than the colonel, however, and Mr. Darcy turned to address her, "I intend to demonstrate them all to you, Miss Bennet... without any reservations at all." He said huskily.

Colonel Fitzwilliam smiled and said, "Yes, I have no doubt that you will, Darcy... as soon as she sees your house on Grovesnor Street-not to mention *Pemberley!*"

The colonel continued to talk, but Elizabeth paid little attention to what he was saying. Her notice was drawn to the silent man sitting next to him -whose eyes were dark and intense as he stared at her, and Elizabeth could feel heat well up within herself as she was drawn to the passionate expression in those eyes. She blushed furiously and looked out the window next to her, not venturing to look in his direction except when she felt little chance of discovery. There were a few times that she thought she could detect a slight smile come over his face as she looked in his direction though, and she thought it made him look even more handsome.

She continued to dwell upon that enigmatic man as she drifted off into a slumber as they traveled towards town, and did not awaken until they had arrived in front of the Gardiner's home on Gracechurch Street. She could see the faces of her relatives as they peered out of the windows, and Mrs. Gardiner had come out to greet them wearing a concerned look upon her face.

The gentlemen descended first, and Darcy helped Elizabeth and Maria Lucas out. Mrs. Gardiner studied the two gentlemen for a moment before she greeted Elizabeth.

"It is good to see you Elizabeth, and I must say that I am thankful that you had written to your uncle and me last night, otherwise the surprise of the article in this morning's paper would have been much more shocking."

Everyone stared at Mrs. Gardiner, not knowing to what she was referring to.

Chapter 4

Fitzwilliam Darcy had never been so furious with another human being in his life than he was at present with Lady Catherine. When he arrived at the Gardiner's residence and met Elizabeth's Aunt Gardiner, he was impressed by that lady's comportment... especially considering the circumstances. After they were shown into the parlor, Mrs. Gardiner showed them the offending article as she frowned deeply.

He read through the gossip section until his eyes rested on an alarming paragraph. After seeing what was written, it was not difficult to guess who was behind this heinous slander against himself and Elizabeth, and although she was not known to his acquaintances in town, it would not be long before everyone knew who she was.

Elizabeth had been reading over his shoulder, and he heard her gasp and then sob, "It is not true! It is simply not true!"

Darcy dropped the paper to reach for her hand while his cousin retrieved the paper to read:

' It has been disclosed that a gentleman, FD, from Derbyshire has recently broken off his longstanding, though unannounced engagement with a lady from Kent. According to sources, this has come about after his having made arrangements of a particular sort with an EB from an estate near Meryton in Hertfordshire. Though not much is known about that lady, our sources divulge that she has relatives in town that reside on Gracechurch Street, and she occasionally resides with them there.

Though there have been many ladies among society who have aspired to become the next Mrs. F.D., it seems that the gentleman...'

Richard huffed in disgust, and Darcy saw that he was shaking his head as he read the article.

"Unbelievable... I did not think that the harridan would do something so... tasteless!" Richard exclaimed.

"Obviously she is bent on revenge, but I have to admit that this is beyond what I thought her capable of!" Darcy responded and realized what Richard said. "Wait a minute, Richard... what do you mean by, you did not think that she would '*do something so tasteless*'?"

"Oh... uh... Well yesterday when I went back to Rosings to retrieve our things, our aunt was talking to someone-and before you ask, no I do not know who it was- and she was saying that she would ensure that everyone knew the truth about you and Miss Elizabeth. I just thought she was spouting off her rhetoric as before, but... I am inclined to agree with you. She is obviously bent on revenge, and this *is* most likely her handy work."

There were so many things going through Darcy's mind at present, and none of them were too pleasant. He desperately wanted to run Lady Catherine through for her maliciousness, and though he knew she could be difficult when she did not get her way, he never envisioned her running the risk of ruining Anne along with him-not to mention causing such a scandal in society with the family name. Though he was not pleased to have his name dragged into the gossip columns, he was even more furious about Elizabeth being hurt in the process. With her in mind, he wanted-nay, needed to have her consent to announce their engagement in order to lessen the effects of such slander.

He took a deep breath, turned to his beloved, and looked straight into Elizabeth's eyes, "Elizabeth... I had never imagined that my aunt would stoop so low, and I am heartily sorry about this, but... I think that we have no other choice now than to announce our engagement officially."

Elizabeth struggled to regain her composure as Mrs. Gardiner tried to sooth her. That lady gave him a sympathetic look and a wan smile, and then spoke in low tones to Elizabeth though he could not make out what she said to his fiancée he could see her calming influence. Elizabeth nodded her head and sat down before she responded to him. For a moment he thought she might just wish to break *their* engagement, but knew that Mr. Bennet would never allow that-especially in light of what he already knew.

"Mr. Darcy, I... I think you may be correct in what you said, but... I still must insist upon a longer engagement than what *you* have proposed. I think that should we wed now, it will only add to this... this... I do not even know what to call it. It is far beyond a lie, and it will undoubtedly affect not only me, but all of my sisters as well."

"Then do I at least have your leave to make an on. announcement in the more respectable papers- this afternoon even?" At once he felt self conscious and as if he may have put his foot in his mouth for insulting Mrs. Gardiner's choice of reading material, but upon seeing no reaction from her, he thought no offense was taken.

Elizabeth looked to Mrs. Gardiner as if to ask her consent and that lady nodded her head to her niece. Finally she answered him.

"Yes, I will give you leave to make the announcement, Mr. Darcy, but please... do not announce any definite date as of yet. I wish to confer with my family... especially my father and eldest sister, Jane, before anything is decided."

At her last words, Darcy was reminded that he had a few other tasks to perform as well and wanted to have a private word with Elizabeth before he left, if only to reassure her of his commitment to keeping his word to her. He looked at Mrs. Gardiner for a moment, wondering if she would allow such a liberty.

"Mrs. Gardiner... ma'am, would it be possible for me to have a private word with Miss Elizabeth?" At her hesitancy, he promised, "We shall leave the door open a bit to allow for propriety, but I would like to discuss some things that she and I had agreed to before coming to town."

"All right Mr. Darcy. You may use my husband's study, and one of the maids can stay out in the hall." She turned to Elizabeth and said, "Perhaps when Jane gets back from her walk in the park with Mr. Bingley and Jessa, you can discuss things with her as well?"

Elizabeth looked at her aunt with wide eyes, and shot him a look of surprise as well. One of her eyebrows rose rather enticingly, and she offered him her arm to escort him to the study. Once they were ensconced in the spacious room filled wall to wall with books, she spoke first.

"Mr. Darcy... I do not know what to say about everything that has happened thus far since... well ever since we have known each other. I have to say that I have gone through many a quandary over your complex moods and behaviors, and yet you still manage to astound me. I am sure that you know to what I refer at this moment, though I am by no means complaining... I wonder how you managed to reunite Mr. Bingley with my sister so quickly?"

"It is simple. When I sent the messenger to town last evening with your letter to Mr. And Mrs. Gardiner, I also sent a letter to Bingley as well. I let him know that Miss Bennet is in town and has been for some time, and I... hope you will forgive me the presumption, but I gave him this address."

She smiled at him with her bright beautiful eyes that would light up at any pleasure of hers, and for a moment he forgot about their current predicament. He knew that it may be even more difficult for him to get her to consent to a wedding date within the month after what Lady Catherine had done, but realizing that they had more pressing matters to discuss he pressed on.

"Elizabeth... may I call you by your given name?"

She smiled at him and said, "Yes."

"Good, and will you call me 'Fitzwilliam'?"

Again she said, "Yes." Rather shyly.

"Thank you." He replied softly, "I am sure that you want to put your best foot forward in light of this..." His voice started to rise, "Malicious... this... tripe, but... it may not do us any favors in the long run if we wait for very long. I understand wanting to have your family with you-especially your father and Miss Bennet. I would also like to arrange for my family-aside from Lady Catherine, of course, to be with us as well, but I do not think it would be prudent in the long term to wait. People may begin to view what she has said as truth, and I do not want your reputation hurt anymore than it already has been."

"But, Mr. Dar... sorry, Fitzwilliam... if people see us marry so soon after this is, then they may think that we truly did have a reason to do so, and by waiting we can give them proof that we are an honorable and respectable couple."

not, he thought to himself. *If you only knew the whole truth of it, Elizabeth, you would likely never wish to speak to me again, but how can I convince you that we need to do so without disclosing the whole of our intimacy?* He could not think of a way to tell her that they may already be in some danger, but could not fathom how to tell her without causing her to despise him. After debating for another moment he thought that they could leave *that* debate alone for now. *Damn Lady Catherine Anyway!*

"I think that we should keep an open mind about this, Elizabeth. After all, we do not know what may happen between now and when we will marry, and I would rather not set us up for more censure should we plan for a later date and need to move the date up for some... unforeseeable reason." He was almost pleading with her.

"What else could happen, sir? It is not as though my honor has not already been impugned, and I doubt that anything else could happen to make us marry in such haste. I would much rather behave as any respectable couple would, and we shall deal with those in society who wish to question us with the truth. Those who are sensible will not be foolish enough to believe everything that is said in the scandal sheets anyway.

Her words only demonstrated to him how very naive Elizabeth still was about the world in general and his society in particular, but it also caused him huge pangs of guilt over what he had already done with her and could not confess. She was still ignorant of what had happened Friday night, but that may just be their biggest threat yet. One of these issues he could easily guide her on, but another he had no clue how to manage.

"Elizabeth... you do not know the society that I have known my entire life. They are not all as sensible as you, and they seem to enjoy the pastime of gossip more than anything-regardless of the veracity of what is said. As to the rest of the world, one would hope that they could see the sense in things, but they only know what they hear, see, and read. Unfortunately my aunt has chosen to risk her own daughter's reputation by spreading these lies in order to ruin your reputation and force my hand, but know this... I will stay by your side, no matter what."

"You say this now, but what if it will affect your own sister's prospects?"

Darcy thought he may have found a way to press her hand and ventured, "It may have already done so, after all it is already out in circulation that I have kept you as my mistress, and it is not as if *that* will help her in the future." *At least not with any respectable families,* "Perhaps if we were to marry sooner the rumors will quiet down, and by the time she is presented next year, society will have moved on to another scandal or two, but... if we wait, it may only drag on, thus affecting her presentation."

"Mr. Dar- Fitzwilliam, I will not be forced into a hasty arrangement. I scarcely know you well enough as it is, and I want to ensure that we will be compatible, before..." She took a few deep breaths, and he could see her eyes tearing up, making him feel even guiltier over his behavior.

He approached her and wanted very much to embrace her yet he was unsure how he would be received. Finally he decided to try and comfort her, drawing her into the strong warmth within his embrace.

She sobbed again as he held her tightly, and lightly kissed the top of her head while running his hand up and down her shoulders.

"Elizabeth… I am sorry that this has turned out the way it has, but I meant what I said about showing you all of my good qualities… at least I hope that you will agree that they are my good ones once you have seen them."

She looked up into his eyes and said, "I think that I already have seen at least a few of them, but I also have so many questions, and I have heard so many things about you from… from Mr. Wickham…"

Darcy immediately tensed up at the mention of his old nemesis. He had hoped that he had seen the last of that blackguard last summer, and then he show up in Meryton. *Why did the cur have to come there of all places-and meet with Elizabeth of all people! Why does he continue to haunt me wherever I go? And no doubt he has spread his lies about me to gain her sympathy while using his charm and easy manner to fool her! No more, Wickham! You have hurt too many people that I love, and now she will learn the truth about you!*

"Elizabeth… I can only imagine what George Wickham has said about me, but I am almost certain that whatever it is-it is quite likely far from the truth."

She pulled away from him as she looked into his face. It seemed as though she was trying to garner some truth from his expressions, which must have conveyed enough for her to ask, "Tell me, sir, if you will, what your side of the story is… please?"

At first, Darcy was hesitant, but then began to reluctantly divulge his history with George. As he talked about how his father had always treated the steward's son even better than himself, to the point of neglect, he had to stop for a moment. He was reliving the pain of what he thought of as rejection from his own father who was blind to the treachery of the very wicked Wickham.

Darcy had to stop himself as he started to describe George drawing a young chambermaid to a room in the attic, locking the door with the key, and violating her. He was sure that Elizabeth could hear his despair at not being able to stop him until it was too late, and by the time the lock was jimmied, George had already assaulted the girl. Within weeks she was sent away from Pemberley due to her disgrace for coming with child, even though Darcy tried to relay the truth to his father. George managed to convince the old Mr. Darcy that the girl had *seduced him*. It was almost certain that that was not an isolated incident either from the talk of the household staff.

When it came to telling of George attempting to elope last summer with Georgiana, Darcy could hardly contain his furry. By the time he had finished with his story, Elizabeth sat on the divan next to him with her mouth agape and eyes wide open with eyes that now expressed such sympathy towards him, and he thought he could see some unshed tears in those warm orbs. *Are those tears for me?* He wondered.

They sat there in the study at the Gardiner's house for another few moments before a not so subtle "Ahem," was heard coming from the archway. A middle aged gentleman stood at the entrance to the room looking at the couple with an expression that expected some answers. Darcy wondered how much he had heard of his narrative on Wickham and Georgiana. The other parts of his story he worried less over, but he did not want anyone that did not need to know to hear about her near disgrace. They both stood to greet the newcomer and Elizabeth introduced her uncle to him.

"Uncle Gardiner... we did not see you..."

"Obviously." He replied.

Darcy studied the man for a moment, before Elizabeth made their introductions. He noted a man that appeared fashionable and refined, and he also had an intelligent expression-something he would not have expected of Mrs. Bennet's relations... well blood relations anyway.

"Uncle Gardiner, may I present Mr. Fitzwilliam Darcy? Mr. Darcy this is my uncle, Mr. Edward Gardiner."

"Pleased to meet you, sir." Darcy addressed the gentleman.

"Likewise, Mr. Darcy." He stood in silence for a moment before he requested a private audience with him. "I was wondering if I could have a few moments of your time, sir, to discuss some issues brought up in the paper this morning if I may?"

"Certainly." Darcy knew which items to which he referred and only hoped that he could satisfy Elizabeth's uncle that he was not some rake and bounder.

"Uncle Gardiner... I should like to stay as well. This does involve me as well..."

"Lizzy," Mr. Gardiner addressed her rather sternly, "I need to discuss this situation with Mr. Darcy-*alone*. There are a few things that should not be brought up in the presence of ladies..."

"But, sir..." she protested.

Mr. Gardiner held up his hand to forestall her, "Elizabeth, I assure you that I will leave your gentleman in one piece. It is only information that I seek, but I am afraid that some of the subjects are not suitable for your ears, so I shall request that you await us outside until we are finished."

She looked between the two of them with pleading eyes, but Mr. Gardiner would not be moved, and so she was forced to leave them to converse alone. Darcy already felt bereft of her, but focused his attention to his host who studied him for a minute before he began.

"You probably already know what I wish to discuss with you, Mr. Darcy."

"Ah… yes, sir… I am afraid that I do, and I hope that I can ease your mind by saying in my own defense that I have *never* been engaged to anyone, let alone broken an agreement such as that."

"That is a relief. The other issue that was alleged, I know to be false. Our Lizzy would never do anything so outrageous or dishonorable, so I can imagine that the rest is also a falsehood. That alone tells me that whoever put this out must harbor some significant resentment towards you… I am sorry but I cannot imagine Lizzy having *any* enemies, and so I am guessing that this was more directed to harm you."

"No offense taken, and you are at least partially correct about whom I believe put this out. They are resentful for my not choosing their daughter for my wife, but I have never given them any reason to believe that I would either. Unfortunately that person has a pique with Miss Elizabeth in that she is my intended, and that is their reasoning beyond anything else, to ruin Eliz-Miss Elizabeth's reputation. I assure you though; that has no bearing upon my steadfast intentions towards your niece."

Mr. Gardiner offered him some port which he gratefully accepted.

"That is a relief as well… but then I would not have expected anything else from the man Elizabeth has chosen for the companion of her future life."

Darcy flinched at Mr. Gardiner's choice of words. He knew that Elizabeth would not just settle for a spouse who could offer her the security of a social position or even wealth. She wanted more from her companion than physical comforts, and she deserved his respect for holding on to her principals without giving into the pressures of the outside world. At that moment he vowed that he would do everything within his power to deserve her. *That* would be his life's mission.

"Thank you, sir. I hope to eventually deserve her." Darcy said softly.

"Here, here." The other gentleman held up his glass and took a drink. "I do not suppose you have set any date yet for your impending nuptials?"

"Ah… no, in fact we were discussing that before you came in. We both want our families with us, but as to a grand affair… I am not too sure that that would be very wise."

"I agree. With such rumors flying about, it is probably not a very good idea and frankly I do not think that Lizzy will mind that either… although, I am sure my sister may try to change your minds on that."

"I will let Elizabeth decide what she wishes to do. It is the least I can do for her."

Mr. Gardiner smiled at him sympathetically, "Do not be so hard upon yourself. It is not as though you spread this lie in the paper, sir. I imagine that this person must be some associate of yours that had some hopes that you would take their daughter off of their hands?"

"Something like that… It was most likely my…" he took a deep breath wondering what Elizabeth's uncle would think when he heard that the person responsible for besmirching her good name was none other than his own aunt. "Aunt… Lady Catherine De Bourgh."

The frown upon that gentleman's face foretold his displeasure. "Excuse me?" He asked as if to ensure that he was not hearing things. "Your aunt? Why on earth would she do such a thing? She very nearly ruined her own daughter's good name as well dragging her into this."

"Yes, sir, but that is apparently the length she is willing to go to try and separate Elizabeth from me. As I had told her though…" Darcy went on to relay what his conversation entailed from Sunday with Lady Catherine to the amusement of Mr. Gardiner. He also disclosed that he was announcing his engagement to Elizabeth that evening . He would send notices to the major papers, and hopefully the gossip would die down. He cared very little what others thought of his supposed engagement to Anne. Most all of his good friends were already aware of his aunt's proclamations from a long time ago, and they had more sense to believe what they read in the papers anyway.

By the time Darcy and Mr. Gardiner finished their discussion, it was getting late and Mrs. Gardiner invited he and Richard to dinner along with Bingley who had arrived while the gentlemen were still in the study. Joining the rest of the party, he greeted the newcomers and was introduced to the eldest of the Gardiner children. Jenna who was all of ten years of age, but behaved more mature, reminded him very much of how he imagined Elizabeth as a young girl. For her part, the young lady could even converse well with adults, and while he was attending her he had not seen the frown his friend directed towards him.

When his attention was drawn towards that quarter of the room he saw Bingley staring at him with a less than pleased expression. Darcy felt the guilt at that moment for having separated Bingley from his one true love. He could not imagine being separated from Elizabeth, and knew that he would be devastated if he thought she felt absolutely nothing for him. *Well, Bingley my good man, I do not blame you in the least for being so angry with me. I only hope that you will forgive me by the time you marry your Miss Bennet, else it shall make for some very uncomfortable family gatherings.*

The whole family plus guests gathered around the table and were seated informally, as they were able to choose their dinner companions, and Darcy had no other preference other than to be next to Elizabeth. The Gardiner family was a stark contrast to the Bennet family in that no one talked out of turn, and manners were observed at all times. He thought that perhaps at least the two eldest must have spent some time with these relatives, judging by their seeming closeness and affection.

By some chance he was also seated across from Bingley, and wanted to make some inroads into healing the breach between them thus decided to try to engage him in conversation that required more than a 'yes' or a 'no'.

"Bingley... What have you decided to do about the summer travel plans to the north?" *There, he will have to answer me, and this will give me some indication as to whether he will still want to join me and Georgiana... and hopefully Elizabeth at Pemberley.*

Bingley looked at him rather surprised at having addressed him with such a question, and showing how good and amiable a man he was, he answered, "I... ah..." He looked at Jane Bennet briefly then back to him, "had not really decided, yet. I know that if we do not go to Pemberely Caroline and Louisa will be very decidedly disappointed, but I may go back to Netherfield to reopen it... and stay there for a little while to… to reacquaint myself with the neighborhood." He smiled shyly to his lady.

Darcy noticed that his remarks were also observed by Elizabeth, as she wore an approving smile as she looked on. When she looked up from her sister and his friend, he saw a genuine soft-and he dare hope, loving gaze from Elizabeth. Throughout dinner he would occasionally glance to her, and sometimes he would catch her doing the same towards him. His heart was as light as a feather, as he thought she may be coming closer to gaining some affection for him. He knew that he would do anything to see her look at him with such unbridled adoration, as Jane Bennet bestowed upon Bingley.

By the end of dinner Charles Bingley seemed as if he had never even been upset with him, but Darcy thought that perhaps his companion during the meal had something to do with that. Even Elizabeth appeared to be in a better mood as they removed from the dining room to the large parlor eschewing the separation of sexes. The children were sent upstairs after the meal at the direction of their parents, and surprisingly they gave few protests, even though they now had their two favorite cousins staying with them.

While they set out a card table for Bingley, Jane, Richard, and even Miss Lucas came to join them after she had settled from her walk with Miss Bennet earlier, to play lottery tickets. Darcy took a few moments to talk with Mrs. Gardiner who had asked about a familiar shop in Lambton. He was surprised that she knew the place so well, and even more surprised to learn that she grew up not five miles from his home at Pemberley.

"I remember there was a horse chestnut tree over by the smithy… is it still there?"

"Yes… You know the town well, Mrs. Gardiner."

"I should. After all I spent the first fourteen years growing up there. It is such a beautiful place; I still miss it even after all of these years."

"You would think that I kept her locked up here in town, but I have promised to take her up north this summer when we go to the lakes. Who knows… if we have enough time we may be able to go to the Peaks on our way up there." Mr. Gardiner paused for a minute as he looked at Elizabeth, and said, "I suppose now that you and Elizabeth will be getting married she will not be able to go with us."

This garnered Darcy's attention immediately. "You were going up north this summer?"

"Yes… in fact we had even discussed going through Derbyshire, but it all depends upon how much time I can take away from my businesses."

"If you would like, I would be delighted to have you as my guests…which will hopefully be *our* guests at Pemberely." He looked at Elizabeth and saw her smile at him with such pleasure, it gave him goose bumps.

Mr. and Mrs. Gardiner looked at each other and smiled. They seemed to be communicating their pleasure to each other, and Mr. Gardiner spoke for them, "You likely know that issuing such a generous invitation-in front of my wife, no less will demand that I accept your kind offer. I think that I would likely be forced to sleep out in the stables should I refuse." The couple laughed at his lighthearted answer.

"I look forwards to you joining us then." He raised his eyebrow to Elizabeth, who only smiled at him coyly.

The entire party seemed to have forgotten about the news earlier that had everyone out of sorts that morning as they entertained themselves with cards, conversation, and camaraderie, until the butler announced some new arrivals to their party.

"Mr. and Mrs. Bennet, and Miss Mary, Miss Catherine, and Miss Lydia Bennet to see you, sir, madam."

The sound of Mrs. Bennet's high, agitated, and shrill voice was enough to make Darcy want to recoil. When that lady walked into the room, she immediately addressed Elizabeth.

"Oh, there is that disobedient, ungrateful, unruly child! What you are doing to my poor nerves!" She yelled at Elizabeth without regard to anyone else in the room, to his and her horror.

Chapter 5

Darcy heard Mrs. Bennet's shrill voice admonishing Elizabeth about something he had yet to comprehend as soon as the woman came into the Gardiner's sitting room. He immediately felt the need to protect Elizabeth and stood up to move between her and her mother. When *that* lady was no longer in view of his beloved, but now stared at him, she startled then frowned *up to* his face.

"Mr. Darcy..." she addressed him angrily as she tried to maneuver around him, "I do not know what has been going between you and Elizabeth, but I am here to tell you that I do not approve! Not one bit! And as to *you*, young lady..." she tried again to peer around him to speak to her daughter, "you were brought up better than to go running about the countryside in such a wild manner, but noooo, your father would not curtail your behavior, and now *look* at what we *all* shall have to suffer for it!"

She produced a newspaper similar to what Mrs. Gardiner had earlier, and tossed it behind Darcy at Elizabeth. He had never experienced a lady-other than Lady Catherine-behave in such a way, and it made him angry.

"*Mrs. Bennet,*" He spoke in a commanding tone to the matron, "I can assure you that my intentions towards Miss Elizabeth are quite honorable, and no one shall have to suffer for whatever lies others have purported about us." He saw a few sets of eyes directed at him as he said the last, and some were more surprised than others.

Elizabeth's mother looked as if she was the last to grasp what he had said and what it meant, but when the look of understanding finally registered; her *happier* effusions were as obscene as her more hostile ones.

"Oh...? Oh, Mr. Darcy... you a-and my Lizzy...! Oh, how wonderful! How magnificent, and you as good as a lord! Who would have ever thought it possible that you would ever want to have such an unruly girl as her?"

Darcy felt every bit of the offense for his betrothed, and saw Elizabeth cringe as her mother continued to make her loud effusions over his declaration. Now more than ever, he desperately wished to be married to her if not for his undying love and devotion, then for his desire to protect her from her mother's unseemly behavior. He made eye contact with his fiancée, hoping that she could read the sympathy within him. The corners of her mouth turned up, and he sensed her understanding.

With all of Mrs. Bennet's blathering and speeches, he had nearly forgotten that Mr. Bennet had also arrived with the rest of his family, and was standing next to Mr. Gardiner who had been exchanging private words with him. Within moments, Elizabeth's father stepped up to direct his wife attention away from Elizabeth, but not before shooting him a stern look of consternation.

"Now see there Fanny, our offspring had done nothing untoward and managed to garner the notice of this once..." Mr. Bennet raised his eyebrow as he looked at Darcy, "reticent young man... and I am sure that he will see to it that things are set to rights. Is that not the situation, Mr. Darcy?"

Darcy knew that his soon-to-be father-in-law was all but demanding that he declare himself in front of the whole room, and he was at the point where he was more than happy to confirm that he intended to make Elizabeth his wife.

"Yes sir, you are correct."

"Well then, I suppose it would not be out of the question to request a word alone with you tonight, if you would be so obliging?" Again the older man raised his eyebrow that he could swear looked just like Elizabeth's in the same pose.

"Uh, I would be more than happy to join you, Mr. Bennet."

Mr. Bennet spoke to his brother-in-law, "Edward, would you be kind enough to allow us the use of your study for a few moments, please?"

"Of course, Thomas... make yourself at home." The gentleman answered.

Elizabeth started to speak in protest at not being included in the discussion, "Papa... if you are going to discuss something of such importance that involves me, then I insist on being included in the conversation..."

Her father held up a hand and gave her what Darcy could only describe as a stern glare that would not brook any opposition, and said to her, "Lizzy... what I need to discuss should be done between gentlemen, but I assure you that once we are done, I will include you in the conversation. Now... if you will excuse us?"

Elizabeth watched them leave and their eyes met briefly. She seemed concerned, but for which reason, Darcy could only guess.

Mr. Bennet led him to the study, and closed the door firmly behind them. At first, he felt as if he were going to be reprimanded for addressing Mrs. Bennet as he did, or allowing such slander to be put out about Elizabeth and himself, but her father headed to the sideboard and offered him some port, which he gratefully accepted , before they both sat down opposite each other near the hearth.

Mr. Bennet took a drink before he addressed him again, "Mr. Darcy I am sure you are wondering how it is that we have come to town so quickly after this..." he frowned and shook his head, "tripe, has been put out?"

"Yes, I had wondered at it briefly, but obviously someone must have come from town and brought it to your attention..."

"Precisely, and unfortunately it may very well have made the rounds in Meryton by now. The source of our distress came from none other than our neighbor John Lucas, who apparently had some business here, but once he saw this gossip in the paper, he brought it straight home to Lady Lucas's attention, who promptly brought it to Mrs. Bennet's attention. I am sure you can imagine how much of an uproar *that* created. Surprisingly she did not go into hysterics, as one might imagine, but insisted that we come straight to town to avoid the scandal that would surely erupt, and she..." he looked at him with a hint of amusement, "demanded that I *make* you marry my Lizzy."

Darcy felt great relief at that moment, fearing that Elizabeth's father would want to take him to task for everything that had happened with regards to the article in the paper. Though he knew he was not guilty of allowing such information to be put out about him or Elizabeth, he still had other feeling of culpability related to their need to marry sooner than later. *I may as well discuss our plans for marrying, and perhaps enlist Mr. Bennet in persuading her to agree to an earlier date, he thought to himself.*

"Mr. Bennet, I feel that under the circumstances, we should discuss a wedding date sooner rather than later. I would not want to create problems for you or your family and I am more than willing to make things right between Elizabeth and myself. I just feel that in light of everything... well it makes good sense in order to avoid any further scandal."

"Mr. Darcy... I think that we are getting ahead of ourselves. I still would wish to talk with my daughter about what her feelings are between the match, and while I can see that she has obviously warmed to you since last fall, I would not have her rushed to the alter over some malicious gossip, or some minor liberties taken in privacy."

Darcy was concerned now, that the gentleman did not fully understand the necessity of a wedding sooner and pressed on.

"Sir, I think it only fair to say that... well... I am ashamed to say that the liberties that were taken were more than minor and though they were not observed..."

Mr. Bennet looked at him sharply as his face paled, "May I ask... What is that supposed to mean?"

Darcy looked away from the gentleman and walked towards the window looking out to the street. Mr. Bennet took a deep breath before beginning again, "Did you... did you, sir... *take her*?"

Darcy was now wholly ashamed of his actions, but knew that now was the time to confess everything-at least to Mr. Bennet. He looked away from Elizabeth's father and nodded his head slowly.

"Yes." He said quietly.

Mr. Bennet drew in a sharp breath, and let it out quickly. His nose was flaring, as he said, "I had thought-nay-hoped that when you had come to me on Saturday that this was not what you were referring to!" He let out an expletive before saying, "I would have thought better of you, sir, but now..."

"Mr. Bennet... sir, please understand that I take complete responsibility for what happened. My only excuse can be the force of my feelings for your daughter, though I do know that what I did was reprehensible. I have to say that she was, apparently, not herself either. She had been given some drought that... unfortunately make one behave differently than they normally would..."

"I do not suppose you are going to try to convince me that you had also partaken of the same drought?" He asked sarcastically.

"No sir, I did not, but as I have said it makes one behave differently, and... apparently Elizabeth does not recall what happened."

"That is at least a relief to me, but that still does not explain *your own* behavior."

The man seemed to have aged in minutes and Darcy felt even more remorseful for having done such a thing, for he was taught differently, but when around her, his senses caused him to act differently though that was no good reason to throw all of his good breeding out the window.

"Sir... I know I have no right to ask this now, but.... Under the circumstances do you not agree that we *must* marry sooner?"

"There is no question that you *must* marry, though I do not know how I can tell her that she must do this... I must." He looked at Darcy again and admonished, "She was an *innocent* when she left me! I wonder how you managed to..." He sighed heavily. "Elizabeth had no idea about the relations between men and women, although she knew enough of the farm animals, and she has enough curiosity to try and find out things, but..." He shook his head again, "it makes little difference now though, does it?"

"Mr. Bennet... I wish that I could take back what happened, but I cannot. As I have said, she was not... herself when it happened-in fact... she... she does not even *know* what happened. The only thing that I can do now is to make certain that should she... have consequences from this that she is not exposed to censure and ridicule. I understand that this may be of little comfort to you, but I do appreciate your daughter's wit and intelligence. In fact... I love her dearly. I had struggled against it for so long, but... I could not overcome it, and I knew that I could never even consider marrying another besides her."

The gentleman studied him for a minute wearing a deep frown, before he said, "How is it that she *'does not even know what happened'*, sir? What did you do to her?"

Darcy was taken aback by the insinuations of Mr. Bennet's words, but knew that he had to defend his honor while explaining modestly what had occurred that evening.

"Mr. Bennet... I had gone to see Elizabeth at the parsonage on Friday last in order to ask for her hand in marriage. When I arrived and was taken to the parlor she was... She had taken a draught for her headache, but I had no idea of that at the time. She seemed her usual self if a little unsteady on her feet, which was a little odd, but then she began to... sway. She fainted and I would have called for help but for our position on the settee-she had been... sitting upon my lap. I felt it best under the circumstances to put her to bed and my intention was to lay her down and that was all. I swear to you upon my honor I was going to call for her maid, but then she awoke and…"

"And you took advantage of her!"

"No… well, perhaps it may be seen as that, but that was not my intention. It just…" He could not lay this upon Elizabeth's shoulders. It was his fault that this happened, but he did not want Mr. Bennet to think that he was just marrying Elizabeth out of duty.

"Sir… I have loved your daughter for so long, and could scarcely get her out of my mind since I had last seen her in Hertfordshire. When she seemed to welcome my attentions that night, it was impossible for me to reign myself in. I take full responsibility for what happened, but I must say that I am not just doing this out of my sense of duty. I truly love and care for her and I want to protect her. I would also like to say in her defense… according to two physicians, whatever herb it was that Elizabeth was given seems to cause amnesia when ingested. That is why she is not aware of… of what happened. Had I known this at the time, I would never have… allowed things to go on as they did. "

The look of sadness, anger, and disappointment flashed across the man's face as he took it all in. HE looked like a defeated man. "Very well then, there is nothing to be done about it now. Though I am greatly angered by your behavior, I will not allow her to suffer because of that, and she seems to have come to term with it. Still… I have no idea how to tell my Lizzy that she must marry, nor why it has to be so urgent, and… she has to know. I do not want to be the one to tell her, Darcy. That I will leave for *you* to explain. She will likely be angry with you as well, so chose your words carefully or else you may suffer for a very long time."

"I will." Darcy replied softly.

"Please send her in. I wish to have a private word with her before we discuss this any further."

Darcy did as he was bid, and went to the parlor where the rest of the company was congregated at present. When he entered the room everyone's eyes were upon him, as they followed his path to Elizabeth.

He leaned down to whisper to her, "Go to your father. He is waiting for you."

She looked at him for a moment and he gave her what he hoped was a reassuring smile. When she got up and walked to the door, Darcy noticed that everyone was watching them, including Richard and Bingley. As his cousin and friend gave him questioning glances he shrugged his shoulders, and tried to feign an ease he did not feel.

Mrs. Bennet, who had been talking between Mrs. Gardiner and the younger Miss Bennets, could be heard to say, "When Lady Lucas showed me the article, I was sure we were all ruined. I thought of all of my girls, it would be most like Elizabeth to go and do something so foolish, but then again... should he decide to marry her, she may not be that foolish after all."

That woman finished by glancing towards him. At that moment Darcy wanted to take Elizabeth as far away from her mother as possible and marry her as soon as may be. *She dares to call Elizabeth foolish, yet she is the most ridiculous mother I have yet to come across! Elizabeth has got to be the most intelligent, witty, and passionate woman of my acquaintance. And you, Mrs. Bennet never could appreciate her as she should be!*

He sat there for a couple of minutes listening to his soon-to-be mother-in-law, glaring at her and contemplating doing her some physical injury until his thoughts of how that might be accomplished were interrupted by Bingley.

"I have to say, Darcy that this has been quite a revealing day. Not for all of my fortune would I have ever bet that *you* would be surrounded by such intrigue." He said in low tones so as not to be overheard.

"Then that makes two of us Bingley. I confess that I am surprised that you are even talking to me under the circumstances though."

"Yes well... I was very surprised and hurt that one of my closest friends would be involved in separating me from my angel, but then... you did write to me to let me know she was here in town so I suppose that I may just be able to forgive you after all."

"Thank you, even though I do not deserve it."

"Oh, come now, Darce-you know I could never stay angry at you, and I know that you only thought you were protecting me-even though it was a bit misguided." He gave him a half smile, "And now that I have Miss Bennet's assurances that she has forgiven me for my neglect of her, I wish to discover what part my *sisters* played in this duplicity."

"May we discuss this at a later time, Bingley? I am in no mood right now to confess all of my wrong doings in one evening."

"My, you are rather sure of yourself. To think that you would be able to confess *all* of your wrong doings in just one evening... one would think you were a saint!" He teased.

"Hardly! My errors of late seem to be mountainous."

"Oh, I would not be too hard on myself, Darcy. These things have a way of sorting themselves out, although... this bit about you and Miss Elizabeth is rather... alarming. Not that I believe any of it, but it certainly puts her in a bad light."

"I know, and I intend to make things right with her, in fact... we are engaged to be married."

"*Married?*" Bingley asked incredulously.

"Yes, married and do not act so surprised."

"But... how can that be? I mean... it is good of you to offer, but I did not even think you two could abide each other while we were at Netherfield, although... I did wonder at the ball. She was the only woman you asked to dance, and that is a rarity for you. I had thought you were doing so for my benefit even."

"No, Bingley. I have admired her almost since I had laid eyes on her."

"But how can that be? You two were always drawing swords with each other. If you were using real weapons one of you would have surely been dead by now, and I am not so sure it would have been her."

Darcy chuckled at his friend's reference to their verbal sparring, and could even acknowledge the truth of her quick wit. They were always very well matched when it came to witty repartee-her more so in larger gatherings, but they were equal in many more ways than one. That thought was sobering. All along he had been thinking that he would be raising her up in circumstances-that almost all of the benefits would be to her with their marriage, but now he saw that she was as much of an asset to him as he would be to her.

As he was lost in thought, Richard came over to join their little group. "This morning I would never have guessed that this day would have turned out like it has-even considering what I already knew." He looked at Darcy, "It seems as though your intended's family was not made aware of your engagement before now."

"No Richard, Mr. Bennet wanted to talk to Elizabeth before an announcement was made."

"Ah, I see. So are we to assume that that is what he is doing right now?"

"I would imagine it is."

Bingley said nothing, but seemed to be paying close attention to what was being said between the two cousins. He was about to say something when Elizabeth entered the room with Mr. Bennet.

The patron requested everyone's attention, and when he had it he said, "I doubt that I need to say this judging by all of the anticipatory looks I see, but never the less I shall make this official. I have given my consent for Mr. Darcy and Elizabeth to marry."

A few giggles, and a shriek could be heard coming from the corner of the room where Mrs. Bennet sat. Mrs. Gardiner looked to Darcy who was joined by Elizabeth, and smiled at him sympathetically. He nodded his head to her, and looked towards Mr. Bennet who had approached Mr. Gardiner after he made the announcement. Briefly, Darcy wondered what had been decided upon for a date, when Mrs. Bennet approached them, along with Elizabeth's sisters and Miss Lucas to offer congratulations-or so he thought-until Mrs. Bennet began to talk of arrangements for the wedding.

"Oh, I knew how it would be! Lizzy, you sly thing you! You will have such fine things, so many carriages, and what pin money… Oh, and we must not forget your wedding clothes. I would have been so much more prepared for Jane and Mr. Bingley's announcement, but we will just have to get to work planning this. Now… I know you have not likely had any time to discuss a date, but what do you think about June? That would give me enough time to get all of the fabrics in for your trousseau, and have enough flowers to decorate the church at Meryton... come to think of it; perhaps we should even consider July… we shall have to talk to the rector as well to set the church…"

Darcy became more horrified at each passing word that spewed from her mouth, and saw Elizabeth's color heighten even more. He wondered how much longer he could tolerate the incessant proclamations, until he really was afraid of doing her mother some harm.

Finally Mr. Bennet joined them along with Mr. Gardiner, and said to his wife, "Fanny, give us a chance to discuss this, and as for waiting until July-I am afraid that that is out of the question. With such a scandal brewing, we must act quickly to stem the tide of rumors, therefore we shall have to think of a date much sooner…"

"*Sooner? Are you out of your mind*? How am I to plan something befitting a wedding such as this demands any sooner than July? No, no, no, it cannot be done sooner than then Mr. Bennet."

"Yet it must, and if you do not feel that you are up to the challenge, then I suppose that I shall just have to request the assistance of Margaret and Jane. I am sure that Elizabeth will understand the need for a more simple fare… Is that not right, Lizzy?"

"I do."

She was more quiet than usual, and Darcy began to pay her more attention. Her color was still heightened, and he worried over her health and peace of mind. *Surely Mr. Bennet would not have divulged what happened the other night? He said that he would rather I tell her.* He studied her again, and occasionally saw that she looked at him out of the corner of her eye, but she hardly looked at him directly after she came back from her discussion with her father.

More than anything, he wanted to have a few moments alone with Elizabeth, or at least to have some privacy to talk to her about what she had discussed with her father.

Mr. Bennet must have noticed his absent state of mind, and advised, "I think that we should allow them a few moments of privacy in order to talk, Fanny. Do you suppose that we can impose upon you a little longer for the use of your study, Edward?" He asked their host.

"Yes, of course, Thomas. I will have one of the maids stay out in the hall and leave the door cracked."

"Very well then… Off with you two." He ushered them both to the door, and quietly advised Darcy, "She was not too pleased with me when I insisted that you two marry soon, but I have not told her why, or at least the real reason. I should warn you though, she is a very curious creature and you will not be able to keep things from her for very long."

"I shall endeavor to remember that, sir."

"You do that." He replied seriously.

When he and Elizabeth were finally alone in the study, she was still not looking at him, and he worried that she was angry with him over this whole ordeal.

"Elizabeth… I cannot tell you how sorry I am about everything that has happened. I *had* hoped to at least give you some time to become accustomed to me before we wed, but I am afraid that under the circumstances it is not possible."

She looked up at him sharply, "Yes... I know, but that is not what distresses me." She gave him an embarrassed looked, and he encouraged her to continue with a slow nod of his head. "It is just that I know you must not think very highly of my mother... especially after the Netherfield Ball and..." She was wringing her hands, and he could tell that she was nervous about discussing her family with him. He instinctively reached out to take her hand to comfort her, and she smiled at him. "I know how mortifying it is to hear her talk as she does, and I can only imagine what it must be like to hear her say the things she does. It is painful for me to see her expose herself-and us in turn-in such public places."

"Elizabeth, please do not make yourself uneasy. I cannot hold what your mother or any of your relatives says against you-especially after what my aunt has likely arranged to have printed in the papers about us. In fact, I think that I would much rather listen to your mother's effusions than my aunt's condescending speeches any day."

She seemed to relax after that, and he said seriously, "Have you and your father discussed how soon we will marry, or do you have some sort of an idea when this can be accomplished?"

"Papa says that this may very well spread throughout the country if we do not act quickly. I had argued that we had really only started to know each other well a short time ago, but that I knew you to be an honorable man, but... still I do not think that this warrants us marrying in such haste. Would not an announcement in the papers suffice to stem such gossip?"

Though Darcy felt such guilt and remorse at having taken such advantage of her, he could not bring himself to tell her the real reason they must marry so quickly, and he thought quickly to the reports in the paper.

"Perhaps, but recall that the article that has caused all of this, has also accused me of jilting another woman, *and* it was reportedly because I have taken you as my mistress. I hardly think that an announcement will stop the gossip unless it is followed swiftly by a wedding. That way everyone will know that we are not just trying to put them off from the truth." *And my aunt will have no time to put out anymore lies about us.*

She seemed to be contemplating what he was saying, but asked, "Will it prevent my sisters from suffering from ridicule and shame though, if we were to marry quickly?"

"Truthfully I cannot predict what some people will do or say, but overall I think that it might help that we lent the legitimacy of our union to the respectability of yourself and your family. I know that there will always be some-especially in my circle that look for ways to besmirch someone's respectability to make themselves feel better. I usually pay them no mind however.

Nodding her head slowly, she said, "Then I suppose that I will agree to a wedding soon. I was hoping to be able to marry from Longbourn though..."

"If that is what you wish, then we shall do so. My only request is that we use as many resources as possible to accomplish it quickly, and if you would like... you may use my sister, Georgiana's modiste to make your dresses."

"But, we cannot afford such luxuries...", Elizabeth protested.

"I will cover whatever it costs...", he insisted.

"We cannot allow you to do that. "

"Why ever not? You will be my wife soon enough, and then it will be my responsibility anyway.

"What if word gets around that you were paying for my trousseau? Our respectability will come into question..."

"Elizabeth, Mrs. Marshal will not say a word to anyone about her payment arrangements. She has worked for the Darcy family ever since my mother was alive. She is like a very trusted servant-like family almost. *Please* allow me to do this for you. It is the least I can do after what has happened."

She looked as though she were considering his offer, and then finally agreed, "All right, I will allow her to make *my* dresses, but *only* mine. I know that my mother will protest, but I do not want your sister's modiste to dread the day she ever heard my name."

Darcy was about to protest, but the look on Elizabeth's face said that she would not brook any arguments to the contrary, besides he already felt that he had gotten more than his fair share of concessions recently.

"Agreed. Then the next question is when do you wish to marry?"

"I do not know, but I assume that as soon as the arrangements are made, and at least the gowns for that day are finished we can marry." She paused momentarily as if remembering something. "Mr. Darcy, what about your sister? Will she be able to join us?"

Darcy had almost forgotten about Georgiana, and the fact that he had not even told her that he was attached to anyone. *What shall I tell her?* He thought to himself. *She needs to be informed, but what will she think about our hasty nuptials-especially after Wickham? I cannot bear to tell her how I have acted so abominably. Although should anything occur, she will already figure it out.*

"I will write to her immediately, and have her companion bring her from Bath... or better yet, I can send Richard to retrieve her. They can join us in Meryton, and I doubt that she will need any new gowns. She has already had some new ones made up before she left. As soon as she can come we will marry-if that meets with your approval?"

"Yes, I think it will work." She smiled at him for the first time in at least two hours.

"Then I suppose that we should inform Mr. and Mrs. Bennet of our plans? I imagine that everyone is anxious to know what we are going to do, and not just within this household."

He glanced at the clock and saw that it was almost ten o'clock. *Have we been here for five hours already? It seems like we only just arrived, and yet so much has happened.*

They left the study and joined the others to inform them of their plans to go forth with the wedding as soon as Georgiana could be sent for, and the dresses made for the ceremony. When Darcy heard Mrs. Bennet make her loud protests, he was glad to be able to use the excuse that it was time to leave. His only regret was having t leave Elizabeth behind to deal with her. *At least she has Mrs. Gardiner and Miss Bennet to help her. I seriously doubt that any of the other girls will be of much use. They seem to be as silly as their mother.*

He wished to have one last private moment with Elizabeth before they left the Gardiner's, but that was not to be. One of the Gardiner's servants came to inform Mr. Gardiner of a small crowd that was gathering in front of the house. They all looked at each other with a sense of dread.

"They say tha' they're lookin fer one of the Miss Bennets, sir. I think they're press er somthin li' tha'."

Mr. Gardiner asked the man, "You did not tell anyone anything about who is here did you, John?"

"No, sir, even though they'd offered me an' Joe a guinea each to spill fer some infermation."

"Good heavens, Darcy. I think we should have your carriage brought out back. People do not need any confirmation as to the whereabouts of your... fiancée." Richard said as he looked out at the crowd through the window.

Elizabeth eyes widened as she looked through the slit in the opening of the curtains. She said nothing as he joined her to see how many people were standing just outside of the residence, and he lost count at thirteen. Darcy could taste the bile rising in his throat, and knew that they had not heard the last from Lady Catherine.

Chapter 6

Elizabeth backed away from the window and turned to face Darcy. The horror she felt at that moment was mirrored in his expression. Now she was certain that Lady Catherine De Bourgh was behind this, and she was furious. *That insufferable woman! To think that she could bully people into bending to her wishes!* Darcy touched her arm to gain her attention, and she looked up into his face.

"I am so very sorry about all of this Elizabeth. I... well, I am sure you know who is likely behind it, and I feel terrible about my aunt dragging you into this."

"But she did not *drag* me into any of it. I was a central part of the reason why she did this."

"No!" He said a little harshly at first, but then said a little more calmly, "It makes little difference to my aunt who I marry if it is not to be Anne... and it would *never have been her. That alone* was the cause of this. Lady Catherine feels that she must always have her way, but do not worry. I will not allow her to ruin you or your family." The corners of his mouth turned up for a moment which made him look even more handsome to her.

"I appreciate that, but what of your own reputation?"

"Do not worry about me. I... I have an excellent standing in the upper circles, and... even more connections than Lady Catherine."

She chuckled, but then sobered, thinking about the crowd that had gathered outside. *Surely him being here so late will not look good? Perhaps we should discuss making this announcement earlier than usual... though if we announce it to the masses that have gathered, how appropriate would it be? Then again, they already think that I am the cause of a broken engagement, so what is one more impropriety?*

Impulsively she spoke up, "Do you suppose that we should announce our... arrangement...?" Elizabeth began.

"*Tonight?*" Darcy asked incredulously. "Are you sure? When...?"

"I... I think that for the peace of everyone here it might be best if we... if we marry sooner. It will not change anything if we wait and it may only make things worse for... everyone."

Darcy grasp her hands and looked her directly in the eyes, "But I thought that you wanted to wait... Elizabeth, I do not want you to feel pressured into marrying just to appease me. I want to make certain that you are all right with doing so. Is it truly what you want?"

She nodded her head as he replied, "Yes, I think that it would be a good idea to get the news of our official engagement circulating and set a date, but that is not the only reason. You have already proven yourself to be earnest about your intentions, and I do not know how to explain, but everything within me is telling me to do so."

"Very well then, perhaps we shall decide a definite date tomorrow." He smiled widely at her.

Elizabeth returned his smile and repeated, "Till tomorrow, then."

He motioned for his cousin to come join them. "Richard, I think that we should just face this head on. If we do not, then they will continue to print these lies. Let us enter the carriage in the front and deal with it there. Should they ask about any arrangements, then we may truthfully inform them that we are to be married, and that I have never been engaged to any other woman than this one."

"That sounds like a good plan, but do you really think that they will believe it now?" the colonel asked.

"It does not matter whether they believe it or not. Soon enough it will be proven true, and though I hope that this does not negatively affect Anne, I can do nothing about it. It was her own mother who did this to her in the first place. Perhaps she shall be fortunate not to be found out publicly, but I doubt that it will be the case. If I should be pushed any further, she will not be able to escape it either."

Elizabeth continued to worry over what would happen next with Lady Catherine and what else she was capable of. She had always thought that people of her society would not stoop so low as to expose their own children to ridicule-*at least purposefully*. While the gentlemen conferred with each other, her new fiancé continued to talk in earnest with her father, uncle, Mr. Bingley and Colonel Fitzwilliam. Occasionally she would see Darcy glance at her and the corners of his mouth would form a faint smile then change suddenly to his serious mien when he turned back to the gentlemen.

It did not take long for Jane to join her and breach the subject of what had been on everyone's mind that evening.

"Lizzy… will you tell me what happened in Hunsford between you and Mr. Darcy? Obviously you have formed some better opinions of him since you left town before."

Elizabeth smiled at her sister, not quite sure how to explain things. There were some parts of her discussions with Darcy that she could easily share, but then there were parts she thought better left unsaid.

"I am not even certain how this all came about, Jane. It seemed so sudden, but yet he assures me that he has felt such strong feelings for me for so long."

Jane was forever the eternal optimist and smiled at her sister again, "I knew that he must have admired you even in Hertfordshire. His eyes always seemed to be seeking you out, and even then I thought he might admire you."

"And as it turns out… you were correct all along, though… I never saw it… not until now anyway."

"But do you love him, Lizzy? Please do anything other than marry for… for love…"

"Jane… you must realize that if Mr. Darcy and I do not marry, then we shall all be ruined, and… I could never do that to you… besides… I think that I admire him, and… maybe even more than like him."

Jane laughed at her before becoming serious. "I had always hoped that we would marry for love… to men who love us as much as we do them, and I think he may even love you more than anyone… at least as a man ought to love a woman."

"Well Mr. Bingley seems to be quite smitten with you as well, but I have to confess that his inconstancy does worry me…"

"Oh, that… Yes, we had talked in the park when we went for a walk, and… Oh, Lizzy… he says that he loves me-that he has loved me this whole time since he left Hertfordshire, but he was so unsure of himself, and how I felt that he… well he was misguided into thinking that I did not feel for him as he did for me."

"No doubt that his sisters had much to do with that."

"But it was me who did not show him how much I cared for him, and for that I have suffered needlessly."

"Do not blame yourself, Jane! Had it not been for some," Here Elizabeth was still feeling some irritation towards Darcy even though she knew that it was not entirely his fault that his friend was so easily talked into staying in town, she shook her head and began again, "He would have come back to Netherfied and you would have been happier."

"But, Lizzy... I would not want him to marry me without knowing what I felt. We were both wrong. Me for not showing him how I felt, and him for not following his heart. So you see... we were both guilty, and now we have forgiven each other."

"Jane, have you and Mr. Bingley come to an agreement?" Elizabeth asked with a hint of teasing, and a raised eyebrow.

Her sister smiled at her, and blushed, but before she could say anything else, Darcy, Mr. Bingley, and the colonel had joined them.

"Elizabeth," Darcy addressed her, "We must be going now, but I will be back tomorrow after your father and I meet with my solicitor to arrange the marriage settlements. I will see you after we are done, and then we can discuss the wedding details afterwards. Richard..." He nodded his head to the colonel, "Is going to Bath to retrieve Georgiana, and as soon as they can get to Hertfordshire, they will join us."

Elizabeth thought she heard a hint of strain in his voice, but she was not certain. She felt a tinge of disappointment that he was leaving, but happy that he would be back tomorrow, and was already looking forward to their reunion.

"Will you see me out?" He asked her quietly.

"Yes... of course." She answered.

They silently walked to the foyer along with most of the party sans her three youngest sisters and Maria Lucas, who stayed in the parlor and continued to catch up on the gossip from home. Jane said some quiet words to Mr. Bingley who smiled at her and replied likewise before he bid them all a good night. He waited for the colonel and Darcy to walk out with him. *Hmmm.... He probably does not want to face such a crowd alone*, Elizabeth thought with amusement.

Darcy came to her side and whispered, "I shall miss you until we see each other tomorrow." He raised her hand to his lips and kissed her there tenderly as his eyes bore into her.

She felt her knees go weak, but still managed to hold her own weight. "I look forward to it." She looked at him through her eyelashes, and bit her lower lip, worrying that she was being a bit brazen in front of her relatives, and his cousin and friend.

No one seemed to be paying them much attention, until Colonel Fitzwilliam said to him, "Come Darcy, we ought to go now before Bingley here loses his nerve." That gentleman gave them a wry smile.

He looked at her once more before bidding the rest of the party goodnight. As they stepped out onto the front porch, she could hear the loud questioning from multiple people, and saw him as he slowly tried to weave through the people waiting outside becoming swallowed by them. He was jostled to and fro and she could just imagine him giving his impervious glare. There were a few shouts from the crowd asking what he thought about the article in the paper from this morning, and if he had any comments or rebuttals. He stopped suddenly, and turned so that she could just make him out.

Darcy was staring straight at her as he said, "As a matter of fact... *yes*-I do have a comment and a rebuttal to the reports from this morning. It is my great pleasure to announce to everyone that Miss Elizabeth Bennet has done me the honor of accepting my hand in marriage, and she is and will be the only woman that I have ever asked to be my wife."

He smiled softly to her, before slowly making his way towards his carriage with his friend and cousin. Suddenly there was some shouting, and shoving ensued. She could tell that he had made it to his conveyance, but the colonel and Mr. Bingley had been pushed back away from Darcy's coach before it lurched forward, and sped off down the street rather dangerously. She stood rooted to the floor of the front foyer, disbelieving what had just happened.

Colonel Fitzwilliam started shouting orders at people, and turned to Bingley to say something, before mounting the horse that was brought in front of the house along with the carriage. He quickly galloped after the coach that had just dashed off with her fiancé. She felt so helpless and horrified as some unnamed ruffians absconded with Mr. Darcy then in another moment she wanted to take off running after them, but she knew in an instant she would never catch them.

Everyone within and outside of the house was in shock, especially Mr. Bingley since he was one that had been shoved away from the carriage. He managed to make his way hurriedly up to the house, and Mr. Gardiner bade him to enter. Though she could hear the voices within *her* screaming, no noise came out and gradually, her mother's hysterics registered through her fright.

"*Oh, good heavens*! Oh, Lord... w-what has happened? What is to become of our *dear* Mr. Darcy? Who would *do* such a thing?" Mrs. Bennet ranted, as Jane and Mrs. Gardiner came to her side to try and calm her.

"Please Fanny! Enough of your nerves! Can you not see that it will do us no good at all... least of all Elizabeth! Now we will have to send for some help... immediately, and... I do believe that Colonel Fitzwilliam is in pursuit of the perpetrators, but I must have some calm!" Mr. Gardiner bellowed out.

Elizabeth's Aunt Gardiner had already summoned both John and Joe from the back and urged them to get some assistance from some of Colonel Fitzwilliam's own corps from Knightsbridge. Luckily he knew exactly where to direct them, and they were sent off to get more help in quick order. Mr. Bennet urged Mrs. Gardiner and Jane to take Mrs. Bennet up to one of the spare bedrooms, and stay with her until she was more calm, then he turned to the four young girls staring at them from the parlor entryway.

"You should all go upstairs as well. Something tells me that we may be in for some long days ahead. Mr. Bingley... would you care to join us in the study?"

The rest of the men and Elizabeth went to Mr. Gardiner's study quickly. Once they were shut in, they looked at Elizabeth with surprise, as though they had not seen her come with them until now.

"Lizzy..." Mr. Bennet began, "do you not think you should go upstairs now? It is getting late, and we have much to discuss."

"I will not go anywhere, papa, until I know that Mr. Darcy is well, and has been returned!" She protested.

"Elizabeth... there is nothing that you can do at the moment, and I am sure that you must be exhausted after such a long day. Rest assured that as soon as we know anything, we will let you know."

"How do you expect me to sleep after what happened?" She cried indignantly. "And how can you remain so calm after what you have just witnessed?"

"What other option is there? It will not help things if I were to go into hysterics as some others may do." He turned to Mr. Bingley and asked, "Do you think that the good colonel is in great danger?"

Mr. Bingley stood there looking at Mr. Bennet as though he had grown a second head.

"*It is possible sir*. Though he is always armed and well experienced with combat he may be injured. I think that if I could get a horse then I may be able yet to catch up to Colonel Fitzwilliam and Darcy..."

"I seriously doubt it, Mr. Bingley. Though we do have horses between us to ride, I am afraid that they would not be able to keep pace with animals such as yours and Mr. Darcy's, and we would not wish for you to risk your safety." Her uncle Gardiner informed him, as he handed him a generous glass of whiskey.

"Then I hope that my horse does not give out before he apprehends the two men who did this!" Bingley replied with agitation. "I also hope that they do not start shooting at him…" He started pacing back and forth while running him hands through his hair.

"Did those men have weapons, Mr. Bingley?" Edward Gardiner asked.

"Uh… I think that is a distinct possibility. They had shoved the colonel and I back as soon he had entered his carriage, and threatened to kill him if we tried to enter." He shook his head, "I felt so… helpless!"

Elizabeth felt the tears well up within her, and tried to fight them back. She did not want to cry in front of a whole room full of men-especially when she had just demanded that she be allowed to stay. Her mind was screaming, *they may hurt or kill him. How could I bear it if anything happened to him?* To her it was a startling revelation of her inner feelings towards Darcy.

Mr. Bennet seemed to realize that she was not bearing up so well as she silently shed some tears. He wrapped his arms around her and tried to reassure her, "Do not fret Lizzybear. We will find him, and then you two can marry and live happily ever after."

She smiled at his childhood reference to her, and hoped that he was correct.

"Perhaps Colonel Fitzwilliam has even managed to apprehend them by now, and they may be on their way back here. Mr. Bingley did say that he was very experienced in combat, after all."

She hoped rather than thought that that would be the case. Though the colonel was a single man and had a fast horse, Darcy's carriage had four matched and well built horses. *They may not be able to find him easily, but why would Lady Catherine have such a thing done and with a crowd and so many witnesses surrounding them…?*

"Miss Elizabeth…" Mr. Bingley addressed her.

She looked to him, and he said, "I am sure that you know by now that the colonel and Darcy are more than cousins-they are more like brothers in fact, and he will not allow anything to happen to Darcy. I am sure that everything will turn out fine."

"I hope that is so." She said in a subdued voice.

Elizabeth knew that there was not much that she could do at present, but sit and wait, and pray that he was brought back in one piece and unharmed.

Within three quarters of an hour after the Earl of Matlock had received word of his nephews kidnapping and the disappearance of his son, and managed to descend upon the Gardiner's residence along with at least two dozen cavalrymen and their superior officer. He did not seem too interested in introductions as he wore worried concern all over his face and wanted more than anything to get right down to business.

Apparently Colonel Richard Fitzwilliam was very well liked and respected within the army, and they all wanted to do what they could to bring back one of their best men. They began an investigation immediately, and by six thirty Tuesday morning, they had figured out the logistics of where they could be, sent out Bow Street runners to investigate, and received even more offers to help find the two missing gentlemen.

Elizabeth was beginning to feel overwhelmed with all of the soldiers within the house, and when Lydia, Kitty, and Maria Lucas saw that the whole downstairs of the Gardiner's home filled to overflowing with uniformed officers, she had her hands full trying to keep them out of the way of the investigation while the men tried to work. She, along with Mrs. Gardiner, Jane, and Mary, and occasionally Jenna tried to help by serving tea or coffee, and pastries to the men, Lydia was kept busy flirting with a few of the lower ranking younger officers. By three o'clock that afternoon Elizabeth was too exhausted to do anything but wring her hands.

Looking out towards the street, the crowds had been replaced by uniformed officers of His Majesties Army. They were interviewing nearly everyone in the neighborhood who might have seen or know anything, but thus far no one seemed to have much information. She continued to grow more frustrated until her father met her out in the parlor.

"Lizzy, I know you are worried, but they are doing everything possible to find Mr. Darcy and Colonel Fitzwilliam. You are not doing yourself any favors by staying up moping about and pacing and you have not slept hardly one wink since last evening. Maybe you should get some rest."

"Oh, papa... I cannot rest! Not right now, and I feel as though I have so much... pent up, frustrated energy. I think that if I can just get out and... and walk maybe it will help a little."

"Well if you feel you must, then perhaps you can take Mary along with you..."

"No... no, I feel like I need some time alone... just to think, and clear my head without listening to her pontificating about this whole situation. Besides, there is a whole neighborhood teeming with soldiers. It is not like anything will happen to me."

Her father looked at her skeptically, and then reluctantly agreed to allow her out, but not alone. "Very well, but you must at least take Nate with you... and do not stay out too long. I know for a fact that you have only had a total of thirty minutes sleep since last night."

"I am quite capable of looking after myself, and how could you know such a thing?"

"Because... I was up with you. I have little doubt that you, of all my girls are 'quite capable of looking after' yourself, yet I must insist on Nate joining you for my own peace of mind, if not for your own safety."

She smiled tiredly at her father realizing how much he worried over her future husband and kissed him on the cheek before going to the foyer to retrieve her pelisse and bonnet. Soon she was on her way to the park which was only about a block and a half from the Gardiner's home being trailed by the young stable hand and trying to keep her distance. She made her way through the outer edges of the park, and then ventured to go inside to watch the children with their mother's and nannies feeding the ducks in the pond with some breadcrumbs.

Elizabeth found herself lost in thought as she watched the children play, and she sat down on a bench to observe them, completely unaware that she herself was being observed by someone other than the servant. She thought about everything that had happened over the past few months, feeling rather foolish for overlooking her betrothed's good qualities, all while putting more stock into the word of his greatest enemy-up until then anyway. It was beyond her how she was blinded to a man with so many principals and morals, while she was taken in by such a scoundrel.

"George Wickham..." She said to herself.

"At your service madam." Came a reply just then.

Elizabeth startled at the sound of his voice. When she looked up she was blinded by the sun, but could make out his tall form with his blonde hair, and his uniform... there was no mistaking it was George Wickham standing right in front of her.

"You look rather surprised to see me, Miss Elizabeth." It was more a statement than anything.

"I am rather surprised to see you in town, Mr. Wickham. I had thought that you were still in Hertfordshire..."

"Oh, that... yes, well... after news of the kidnapping of one of my oldest friends from Derbyshire, and the disappearance of his rather popular cousin, Colonel Forster gave me leave to come join the search here in town."

He moved to sit down right next to her, and rather closer than strictly appropriate, and she moved closer to the edge of the bench to put some space between them. *I wonder that Nate says nothing to Mr. Wickham's closeness.* She looked around them for the servant, but did not see him anywhere. *Where has he gone?*

"Are you looking for someone Miss Elizabeth?" Mr. Wickham smirked.

She looked at him closely before answering, "My companion who seems to have lost himself." She paused again before answering his first comment. "I had thought after what you told me about your relationship with Mr. Darcy that you were more estranged than anything."

He laughed at her reference to his earlier story about his hardship at the hands of her fiancé, but he continued on, "Yes well... I can let bygones be bygones... for certain inducements..."

"And what, pray, would be your inducement to come and help him now, sir?"

"You forget, Miss Elizabeth... we are friends are we not? And I had heard that you, my friend, have become engaged to my *old friend*, Darcy."

By now he had scooted even closer to her and his eyes were raking across her body like a lion in a field full of gazelles. She shivered involuntarily, trying to put more distance between them, now alarmed that her escort may have abandoned her to the overly familiar man.

"*Mr. Wickham*! I must insist that you stay right where you are! Now I *do* appreciate any help that anyone is willing to give in the search for Mr. Darcy and Colonel Fitzwilliam, but I do not see what it is you are after! Please speak clearly; sir-else I shall leave!"

"Fair enough..." He said smoothly, "I may know somebody who may be able to help you find your Mr. Darcy-Oh...and we must not forget his sidekick, Colonel Fitzwilliam as well."

Elizabeth was by now incredulous at his means of address, but he had intimated that he could help her to find her fiancé, and she ventured, "Who? Who do you know that could help us?"

"Me." He said with a smug look.

"How is that possible? There has been a whole army looking for them since last night..."

"Ah... but that leads us to the whole crux of this though. You see the whole problem is that none of them have any idea where to look for them."

"And you do?" She asked incredulously.

"Yes." Again he answered smugly, with his smile growing.

"And how is that, sir? The only people who could know such a thing are the ones that kidnapped them..."

When Elizabeth realized what it was she said, she looked at him with wide eyes to see him bring a handkerchief reeking of strong odors over her face. She swung her arms at him as she tried to get off the bench and run for safety, but he was too strong for her. As the fumes filled her nostrils, she felt her limbs growing heavier until she blacked out.

Nate was nowhere to be seen.

When Elizabeth and the servant did not return to the Gardiner's residence by six o'clock that evening, the Gardiner's, Jane and Mr. Bennet became alarmed. It was not like her to go off for a walk of that length and not return by supper. What was worse... the most trustworthy Nate was missing as well. Their main concern was for her safety after what had happened to Darcy the night before.

Through all of Mrs. Bennet's protests, they went to the park to search for them, but when the missing party could not be found, they summoned some of the soldiers to assist in the search. When they found an unconscious and bleeding Nate in the shrubbery they feared the worst for Elizabeth.

Had the same person who took Darcy come back to steal Lizzy away after beating her escort in broad daylight... in front of a whole park filled with people, and surrounded by soldiers? Mr. Bennet wondered.

The physician that was summoned to examine Nate found him to be still unconscious. They would have to wait to find out what if anything he could recall. The physician could not give them any positive reassurances as to if that would even be possible given his current condition. Mr. Bennet grew frustrated about the lack of any intelligence about his most favored daughter and even a little worried about the young stable hand.

"Thomas... I have spoken to one of Colonel Hill's men, who said that they saw a man carry a woman-who seemed to have fainted from the park. He was accompanied by a soldier, but none of the men here know anything about the woman, the servant, or who the soldier was carrying the woman." Edward Gardiner said. "Whoever took Lizzy has got to be well organized and must have had help."

Upon hearing that his daughter may have fainted, and someone took her both filled him with hope and dread. In his mind he knew that it was not a benign incident, especially in light of young Nate's condition, but he refused to believe that he would never see his beloved daughter again. His other concern was; what if anything the servant could tell him about where they may have taken her? Immediately he went to confer with Colonel Hill about his missing daughter and the injured stable hand.

When he gathered some of the principals involved with their search, as well as the higher raking officers they were unexpectedly joined by Lord Andrew Fitzwilliam, who heard of the newest incident, and wanted to see what they had learned-if anything.

After they were all briefed of the new situation, the earl wondered, "When did this all happen, Mr. Bennet?" How did she manage to go missing? Where was her escort... or were they the ones involved?" He looked at Colonel Hill accusingly.

"Sir," The colonel addressed the earl, "I can assure you that *none* of my men would do such a thing!"

"Then how is it that a man wearing a uniform walks away with another man who happens to be carrying an unconscious woman... and no one thinks a thing about it?" He demanded.

"If you will recall-it was rather warm outside today, sir, and as far as anyone knew, she had succumbed to the heat, *that* is why no one thought anything about it. As to Miss Bennet's escort-they found him beaten and shoved in some shrubs! And before you ask... I have gotten a list together of all of the men who were here today, including those in the neighborhood who were going door to door to question everyone. I and my most trusted men are interviewing everyone, but so far... we have come up empty handed."

"How can you be so sure that it is not one of your 'most trusted men' who is behind this?" The earl demanded.

"*Sir*, I do not have any scallywags among my company, and I can assure you that I would not put anyone that I do not trust upon a case involving a good friend of mine-who just so happens to be your son, and a ranking officer in His Majesties Army! *Now*... if you will let me do my job, instead of stand around and bicker with you we might be able to get somewhere a little faster!"

Though Thomas was worried about his daughter's welfare and that of the unconscious Nate, he was momentarily amused by the battle unfolding on in front of him, and he understood their angry words were born out of frustration more than anything else. He did want to bring some facts out as he had seen them however, and he cleared his throat to gain their attention.

"Sirs... I know that this has been a very long day, and we would appreciate having our loved ones returned to us, but it will not happen soon if we continue to bicker and blame." Two of the men glared at him, but he continued, "As I see it right now... there is either a man out there who is using a stolen uniform or is legitimately wearing one, and he is party to my daughter having gone missing and beating-most severely-one of our trusted servants. Obviously he has at least one accomplice, and I suspect that they may have been the same men who have taken Mr. Darcy and Colonel Fitzwilliam. There is also the fact that they had taken the two men last night and then returned again for my daughter this afternoon-so they must not be far from town."

He turned to look straight at the earl as he said, "It has also occurred to me that just yesterday, someone made some allegations about a non-existent arrangement between Mr. Darcy and a young woman from Kent, but whomever made those allegations also tried to besmirch my daughter's reputation. Now that an *'official'* announcement has been made, I tend to suspect that perhaps whoever made these allegations might also be behind the disappearances of our loved ones."

He glared intently at the earl, as the man sat staring back at him. Though there was no announcement in the papers as to who the *'jilted'* woman was, and the earl likely had no idea that *he* had already been informed as to her identity, he wanted to earl to offer his intelligence to this.

Finally the other man spoke, "I *may* have *some* idea about who that person might have been, but... I seriously doubt that they are behind the abduction of my son and nephew, or your daughter. Non-the-less... I shall go first thing in the morning to talk to them, but do not get your hopes up, *sir.*"

"That is all we ask of you, *sir.*" Thomas replied.

They spent the rest of their evening plotting the half distances from London to nearby towns and figured a few that would take eight hours ride in a coach. A small town near Hunsford was one that was on their list, and by the next morning the Earl of Matlock boarded his coach bound for Rosings Park.

Chapter 7

The coach ride to the cottage near Hunsford was rough at times and filled with a deathly silence. George Wickham for one had no desire to converse with Denny's dense questions about why they needed to take Miss Elizabeth, and he had no intention of revealing his true design in kidnapping her either.

Though our last attempt at abduction was no great success, this one was most assuredly much more pleasant. Elizabeth is so much easier to manage, and so much more lovely than Darcy. He would be furious if he knew that I was holding his fiancée... even more so when he sees what I am going to do to her. He chuckled to himself. His thoughts were interrupted again by his companion's questions.

"I still do not understand how taking Miss Bennet will help us, George. The earl and Lady Catherine De Bourgh are not likely to pay us well for the likes of her, and her family is not wealthy by any means!"

"Shut up, Denny! Do you not understand that since you let Darcy and Fitzwilliam get away, we have to have some way of inducing them to come back? By taking her, it will ensure that they will return, and then we can deliver them to Rosings."

"I had nothing to do with them getting away! It was one of those other goons that you hired that was supposed to be watching them. I was busy writing to Colonel Forster, letting him know that we would be away a few more days due to our latest... dilemma."

"It makes no difference; you were the one that was *supposed* to be watching them! It is fortunate that I know how to think quickly though. With Darcy's fiancée in our custody, he will have to return, and by then she will be utterly ruined."

Denny bristled at Wickham's statement, "Now look here, George. I did not sign up to go abducting young maidens. My part of the deal was to help you bring Mr. Darcy to his relatives. As it is, if they catch us then we could be hung!"

"We *will not* be hung, Denny. Our patroness will make sure of that. Right now she cannot afford to be found out, and the Darcy and Fitzwilliam families cannot afford the scandal it would cause if the truth were known."

"Still... I do not understand why you must *tie up* the lovely Miss Bennet. She was already unconscious!"

"Why? Are you forgetting what happened earlier? Come now Denny, I have other plans for her and you can have a go at her as well... after I am finished with her."

Silence fell over the carriage again as they traveled to their destination. Both gentlemen lost in their own thoughts.

As the sun started setting in the horizon on Tuesday evening, Elizabeth's eyes were fluttering open. The first thing she saw was a relatively small vase filled with water, and she heard the voice she had last heard hours ago.

"It is so good of you to join the living, Miss Elizabeth... I was beginning to despair that perhaps I may have used too much vapor, and done you some serious harm, but... it appears that you are well after all."

She wanted to make a rebuttal, but could not as she realized that he had placed a gag on her. By now her mouth was so dry and parched, she was not certain that she could make a noise even if she wanted. The furry she felt for being taken, and then treated in such an infamous way must have been conveyed to him through her eyes judging from his next words.

"I can tell by the look in your lovely eyes that you are already mentally berating me for having tied you up, but I thought it necessary under the circumstances. We wanted to ensure that our bargaining piece did not escape as Fitzwilliam and Darcy had. Oh well... no matter, they could not have gotten far, and if your dear lover is as concerned about you as he professes then he will not go too far... at least I would be disappointed if he did..."

He started towards her leeringly, however he did not get too far when Mr. Denny came into the room.

"What? Are you starting without me, George? We were to draw straws for the privilege of enjoying her..." Mr. Denny said in protest, as though she were not even in the room.

Mr. Wickham let out an expletive before saying, "I had to do most of the work here, Denny! Besides, it was me who had the connections to the sponsor for this job anyway! You should feel fortunate that I may let you watch." He gave out a wicked laugh and continued while directing his attention on Elizabeth, "Oh... do not worry, Elizabeth. I shall wait until we have Darcy safe and soundly tied up to watch what I shall do with you. You really have no idea what a pleasure that will be, now do you? Who knows... you may just prefer me to him."

He laughed again, as he drew his hand upwards from her ankle to her knee. By this time Elizabeth's mind was racing wildly. Her body shuttered at his touch, and as much as she tried to shrink away from him, she could not move with her hands tied to the bedposts, and her feet were bound likewise. The voice in her head was screaming, and she felt the tears well up in her eyes at what he was insinuating.

Lord what has happened to Colonel Fitzwilliam and Darcy? What are they going to do to us if they find them? She did not want to think about his threats towards her, for she was fairly certain by now that he was not making any empty ones. *Please do not let them get hurt. Please let them get away, and get help. They can save themselves... I doubt that Mr. Wickham would let that stand in his way of... of...* She began to sob quietly, at the thought of what he had insinuated he was planning to do with her. Mr. *Darcy will not want me after this... I will be ruined by his worst enemy and he will want nothing more to do with me...*

"Now, now... no need for tears, dearest Elizabeth. We do not want anyone thinking we were mistreating you do we?"

He brought his hand up to touch her face and drew his fingers down her jaw to the neckline of her dress, as she was turning her face away from him. She could feel his eyes resting on the place where his fingers were, and wondered if he was going to do something to her right then. Elizabeth tried to shout at him through the gag, but it only sounded like a low moan.

"Patience, patience, woman. In due time... we would not want to begin without our main spectators do we?"

She felt the horror of what Darcy must have endured at the hands of this villain. Anger and outrage overcame grief and sorrow for what he had already suffered at this monster's hands. Elizabeth wondered what could possibly cause a man to do such things. Her mind continued to plot of some way to distract them from doing what they insinuated. The idea of being violated in such a way caused her to want to wretch, but she had nothing in her stomach to bring up.

Wickham's sudden address to his coconspirator interrupted her thoughts. "Denny, I do not suppose that you have arranged for our mounts to be brought here, have you?"

"No... I thought you were going to do that."

"Do I have to do *everything*? What did I bring you along for if you were not going to help with those minor details?"

"Ummm, I believe that you needed some assistance to apprehend a certain gentleman and then his lady. Lord knows you could not have done it yourself."

"Just shut your pie hole, and go see to our dinner." Wickham snarled, "I need to go to the main house to discuss our arrangements with... our benefactor. See to it that you have everything settled before I get back. We cannot afford any more sloppiness."

"I was not the one who left them unattended to go to the pub!" Mr. Denny answered him.

"For once, will you just shut up and do as you are told? They were tied up anyway, and I was not the one who did that! I have to go and see what the others have heard about this latest *incident*. As soon as I know anything, I will be back...." He pointed at her and directed Mr. Denny, "and do not take your eye off of her, whatever you do."

He slammed the door as he left, and she was alone with Mr. Denny who stared at her with an unreadable expression. He walked over to her, reached out towards her face and she flinched as he removed the gag.

"I do not think that you need this Miss Elizabeth. Even if you were to scream, there is no one to hear you."

He offered her a glass of water and helped her to sit up as much as her bindings would allow so that she could drink. She did not want him touching her, but she was grateful for the assistance until she recalled what he said to Wickham earlier.

"Why are you doing this, Mr. Denny? What is Wickham offering you, that you would be willing to risk your life for?"

"Ah... that is the *material* question, is it not, Miss Elizabeth? Simply put... it is for the money, although the inducement of being able to sample one Hertfordshire's beauties is another."

His eyes wandered down her form, and she moved as far away from him as the ropes would allow. He snickered a little before he explained further; "Yes... Wickham has promised me other... things as well, but... I cannot partake of them until your fiancé is brought back here. *She* wanted to make certain that Darcy could witness your ruination you see, and I must say there are many who are more than willing to contribute to that for such an inducement..."

"But... why? Who has put you up to this?"

He smiled enigmatically and shook his head, but did not answer. "You know good and well that I cannot divulge that information, and as to why?" He laughed again, "It must be a falsity that you have already been taken... *if* you do not know what it is that I refer to. Do you know that some back in Hertfordshire are saying that you have been Mr. Darcy's mistress since last fall?"

Her eyes widened, "No! That is not true! That is a lie!"

"Oh? Do you mean to say that it is a lie that you have been his mistress? Or that it has been since a time other than this past fall?"

Elizabeth felt like slapping him for his impudence, but she could barely move her bound hands so she turned her head away in disgust as tears burned her eyes. She did not wish to hear anymore from him, and after a few minutes sitting in silence he decided to get up from her side and see to their dinner as he had been directed, leaving her in the darkening room with just a hint of firelight from the grate. *Thank goodness for the solitude... I do not know how I shall bear up. Oh, please Darcy, I pray that you are safe, and no harm comes to you or the colonel.* Tears began to run down her cheeks again as she thought of the future.

Just a few days ago she would have been happy to have been rid of Mr. Darcy, but now she despaired that he would never want to set eyes upon her again after this whole ordeal. His safety was also of great concern to her. She did not want any harm to come to him, especially after she learned about his childhood growing up with George Wickham. The events of the day left her feeling exhausted not just physically but emotionally as well, and she was finally fell into a fitful sleep.

George Wickham walked towards Rosings Park in dread. He knew that his benefactor, Lady Catherine, would likely vent her spleen over Darcy and Colonel Fitzwilliam's escape. That was one of the material reason's he had not made it back before now. He dearly wanted to see Anne-it had been so long since he had her and waiting to take Eliza Bennet was getting to him, but he knew that her mother would be furious should she learn about their affair so he had kept his distance.

He and Anne De Bourgh had been involved off and on for almost six years. More so due to his instigation than hers and he did that because she occasionally gave him money, but when her mother began to press her harder to marry her cousin she had withdrawn from him. In truth, Anne *wanted* to marry Darcy, but realistically she knew that *he* would not have *her*, and she was almost relieved… *almost*.

She had waxed eloquent about how handsome her cousin was, and how if they married they could unite their two estates and become even more wealthy and powerful, until George wanted to do him serious harm. His inducement to help her obtain her goal now was her offer to keep him while being married to Darcy because she would have even more funds, and Darcy was not likely to want to keep her company as was George. Wickham rationalized that he could always have another woman or two so long as she did not find out, which gave him some comfort. She was his ticket out of the dismal life of working for a living and he would do anything to keep it. The added bonus of cuckolding his long time nemesis was another bonus to the arrangement as well.

The current situation with him helping to abduct Darcy was arranged by Anne-not that it took much convincing for him to agree to help. She had talked to her mother about using George as he always seemed to know how to access Darcy, and he would be more than willing to do so quietly for a pretty penny-or pound as the case was here. The only thing that they had not anticipated was Fitzwilliam being his usual valiant self and coming after them.

How was I to know that Fitzwilliam would still be there at the Gardiner's residence? Ha! He was probably flirting with the ladies and could not drag himself away! If he had not been there we would still have Darcy, and this whole thing would be resolved, but… it may work for me after all. That Eliza Bennet was ripe for the picking at Meryton, and now I will actually get to sample some of her fruit!

His reverie was broken by the change in the sound of the gravel as he approached Rosings back entrance. Lady Catherine was insistent that he not enter through any other door. She did not want anyone other than some of her close staff knowing of their acquaintance. When the butler showed him into her private sitting room, she immediately burst into a tirade about his mishap with Darcy and having gained the attention of Fitzwilliam as well.

"What were you thinking, dragging Richard along with Darcy? You know how they are always together! You should have been much more careful! Then having to return to town for that… that *woman!*"

"But, your ladyship, she was the key to keeping them in check, and they will not say or do anything that may put her in harm's way."

"Now we have that *harlot* to deal with, but you know how to handle her *do you not*, Mr. Wickham?"

"I know exactly how to handle her, ma'am, and as to your nephews… I shall see to it that they are not harmed. I had even planned to have the pair of them observe myself and Miss Bennet."

"See to it that you do, Mr. Wickham. See to it that you do. You will not get another farthing if you muck this up anymore." She said in her usual impervious voice. "Now, be gone and do not come back until Darcy is back and ready to marry Anne. I have no doubt that he will not wish to see that… chit after you and your associates have your way with her."

He thought he could see a slight upturn in the corners of her mouth when she said the last, but he could not be certain, and he was more than anxious to be away from her presence. Sauntering back down the hall, he went to the back door to Anne's dressing room. *If I am lucky, Betsy will be in the back and I can get a little relief before I head back to the cottage.*

When Darcy had been shoved back into his carriage forcefully, he immediately went into a defensive position. He still had his walking stick, but knew that even if he could wield it and do some damage, the carriage was still moving too fast for him to leap out safely. For a split second he wondered what happened to his two footmen and his driver, but thought that they, like him were also ambushed.

Though it was dark in the carriage, he could make out the forms of two men. One of them he had known almost all his life and the other he had met only the past fall in Meryton.

"What are do you think you are going to accomplish by abducting me, Wickham?" He growled.

"Ha! It is not a question of what I will accomplish, but what will others accomplish?" Wickham laughed.

"Do you mean to tell me that someone else put you up to this?" Darcy demanded.

"Truthfully it did not take too much to 'put me up to this', my *dear old friend*."

"*Who*? Oh, never mind '*who*'! I think I can imagine who would pay you to do such a thing, but what I wonder is why? What does Lady Catherine think she will accomplish? I will never marry Anne, not even if she threatens me with bodily harm!"

"Well as appealing as that thought is, Darcy, I cannot beat you as I would *love* to. I have been told that you must be in presentable condition for your nuptials tomorrow, and what a sight you would be if I did what I wished to do to you right now."

"Your pugilist skills were never as good as mine, Wickham. What makes you think that I would be the one worse for the wear should we engage in such a battle?"

To his challenge, he was met with laughter. "Darcy what makes you think that I need to engage in any battle with you to best you? All I need is an assistant and some good fumes." Suddenly Darcy smelled a strong odor and before he knew it, a handkerchief was smothered over his face as he fought against his attackers, but he was quickly falling into unconsciousness, and then all he saw was a black nothingness.

When he came to he heard some laughter in the back ground, and felt a sharp jab in his ribs.

"Darcy! Darcy, wake up!"

The voice was very familiar, and sounded like... *Fitzwilliam! What the devil is Richard doing jabbing me in the side like that?* He was gradually trying to wake up, but his eyelids still felt heavy.

"Richard, what do you want, can you not see that I was sleeping?" He asked still unaware of his surroundings and more than a little irritated that his cousin had interrupted a most pleasant dream.

"Really? And here I thought you were playing possum! Come now, you big horse! Get up... before they come back!" Richard whispered in a harsh voice.

Immediately Darcy's eyes flew open, to see that he was lying on a hard floor in a cold room bound up next to Richard who was thrashing about wildly. After a few more gyrations, he had managed to free his hands, and quickly untied his ankles then moved to Darcy's bindings. He was more than a little surprised that he had not noticed before that he was lying on a hard surface, but now his back was aching and he wanted to stretch for a moment before moving around.

It only took another few seconds to recall what had happened the last time he was awake, and he instantly became furious that Wickham had abducted him then tied him up. Before he could get too worked up, Richard reminded him that they may not have too much time before their captors returned.

"Hurry up and stretch or do what you need, Darce! We need to get out of here, and I think I see a window over there." Richard pointed to a window a few feet away from them. "We are on the second floor, but if there is a tree or some vines or a trellis we can climb down, and make it to the nearest town, then we can get some help."

"Wait a minute... how do you know that we are on the second floor, Richard?"

"Because I heard the sounds of footsteps on the stairs, which leads me to my next point... we need to get out of here *now*!"

To demonstrate his point, Richard dragged him near the window, and opened it as quietly as he could muster. When he gained his bearings, he saw that they were indeed on the second floor of a building, and he thought he saw a trellis about two feet away from the window.

"I am going to try to reach the trellis and make it down, and as soon as I reach the ground follow me, understand?" he was still whispering quickly.

"Yes. I would much prefer to make sure that it is safe before I risk breaking my neck."

Richard glared at him through the darkness, but he paid little notice. He wanted to return to town as quickly as possible to assure Elizabeth that he was all right. He watched as his cousin easily made his way down the vines, only once letting out an expletive when he cut his finger on a splinter. Once he saw that the trellis was at least stable enough for Richard he followed suit, and was safely on the ground.

They began walking towards the woods alongside the road making sure that they remained hidden from anyone that would pass them by. Darcy wanted to know what time it was and figured that it must be at least two in the morning by his estimation, judging how dark it was outside, but he could not be certain. He was worried about Elizabeth and her family having witnessed the whole scene of him being taken away forcefully, and wondered at Richard's presence as well.

"Richard... as I recall... were you not shoved away from the coach after I got in?"

"Yes."

"Then how is it that you managed to be tied up alongside me?"

"Well, as it happened, Bingley's horse was not yet tethered to the carriage and I managed to mount him and pursue your errant carriage until we got to the outskirts of town, when they had to stop to change horses... well they ended up changing carriages as well. I was about to apprehend them, but then found that instead of three men there was a fourth, and it was a little too late. He hit me over the head-hurt like hell too, but it was enough to bring me down, and they tied me up and dragged me along with you."

"Ah, I see... so you thought that you could apprehend three men by yourself?" Darcy was a little amused by his cousin's bravado.

"Yeah... I know it was kind of foolish after thinking about it." Richard admitted.

"Kind of?"

"All right it was pretty foolish, but in my own defense, it *was* for you, Darcy."

"I thank you, Richard. I do appreciate the gesture, but next time... maybe you could follow at a safe distance and see where they are going?"

"Next time? What makes you think that there will be a next time? Are you planning on being abducted again in the future?"

"Lord I hope not. I do not think that I would make a good captive." After pausing for a moment, he said in all seriousness, "I wonder how Elizabeth is faring right now? She must have been quite frightened."

"She shall be fine. I am sure that with Bingley, Mr. and Mrs. Gardiner, and Mr. and Miss Bennet, she shall be all right."

"I noticed you did not say anything about Mrs. Bennet..."

"I am neither blind nor stupid, Darcy. I saw how she was with both you and your intended. I cannot imagine what it would be like to have such a mother..."

"Yes... I know..." Darcy said softly.

"What? What is the matter Darcy? Are you having second thoughts due to Miss Elizabeth's mother?"

"No! No, not ever! I just... I cannot fathom her having grown up in such a home."

"Yes, it is rather remarkable, is it not that she and Miss Bennet grew up in the same house with Mr. and Mrs. Bennet and the three younger girls. They are a bit... exuberant, but..." Richard paused for a moment before he asked, "Say... Darcy... did you not say that you had managed to separate Bingley from a woman whose mother was so scheming, and that her family was... rather wild?"

"What is your point, Richard?"

"It was Miss Bennet, was it not?"

Darcy looked at him sharply, but said nothing.

"I can tell by your non-reply that it must have been. I... I do not know how to tell you this, Darcy, but... I may have mentioned to Miss Elizabeth something about that."

"There was no '*may*', Richard. She told me that you had mentioned it to her, and believe me she was none too pleased."

"Oh dear... I am sorry about that. Had I known..."

"You would have kept your big mouth shut?" Darcy queried.

"Yes, but then... how is it that if she knew then she agreed to marry you?"

Darcy felt pangs of guilt at how things really happened, but did not wish to confess all to his cousin this night, while they were escaping their captors. He knew that soon enough he would have to confess all to Elizabeth and until he did no one else had any more of a right to know.

"It is a long and complicated story, Richard and right now I am more concerned with reuniting with my fiancée than telling all to you."

Richard snorted but seemed to know enough not to ask any further questions, and let the subject rest. They walked for at least an hour coming into more and more familiar landmarks, as they realized that they had come into Rosings Park. Darcy was not surprised in the least that Lady Catherine would have something to do with kidnapping him, and guessed that it was in pursuit of her quest to see him marry Anne. He began to think of ways to confront her when Richard spoke up.

"Say, Darcy?"

"What is it now, Richard?" He was becoming more and more irritated from lack of sleep the past few nights, and his body was starting to feel the effects of it.

"How do you suppose we shall confront the old witch? I think we both know that it was most definitely the old hag, and why as well."

"I do not know, Richard. I am almost too tired to think right now, and I am also growing hungry from all of this exertion. Perhaps we can catch the post in Hunsford and ride into town." Suddenly he realized something as he reached into his pockets.

"That bastard! He stole my money as well!"

"Are you surprised? Look who we are talking about." Richard retorted.

"I know, but how are we going to get to town without any money, much less eat?"

"Well…" Richard thought for a moment, "I have always been sweet with that Betsy. You know Anne's maid?"

"I do not even want to ask how, but go on."

"I could sweet talk her into getting us some morsels of food from the kitchen. Tell her that I had to come on some secret mission near here, and she is not to speak a word of it to anyone. It is not like she would be stealing anyways. The wretched old wind bag owes us anyway for what she has done!"

Darcy was far from disagreeing with his cousin, in fact now more than ever he wanted to do her some serious physical injury even more than he had wanted to do to Mrs. Bennet last night.

"Do not let *me* stand in your way, but soon enough, we shall have to get word to town to let everyone know that we are fine. As to our *dear aunt*…" he gritted his teeth, "I am not at present in such a charitable mood as to overlook her treatment of me at the hands of one of my greatest enemy."

"That makes two of us. I just cannot wait until my father hears about this! I wonder what he will do about her now."

"He had *better* do something, or else he will not like what I will do… I may still do it anyway."

"Darcy… in all seriousness, I would let him deal with her. He seems to be the only one to bring herto heel, and after this… he *has* to do something. One does not abduct an officer in the army and bind them up then think that nothing will come of it."

At Darcy's questioning look he continued, "I was in uniform-still am in fact-though it looks like hell," He looked down at himself and shook his head, "but when they did this they did so while I was acting as an officer. One cannot commit such an offense and expect it to not go unanswered."

"But the material question would be how do you prove that it was her behind you being captured? Remember that it was me that they took. They shoved you and Bingley away, so really she could say that she had nothing to do with you being taken."

"True enough, but Wickham sure as the devil cannot use that defense, and after what he did last summer, I would just as happily settle for seeing him hang."

Darcy could not agree with him more, but he was not in much of a talkative mood, and he let Richard ramble on about what he wanted to see done with their aunt and their other captors until they reached the outskirts of Rosings Park proper. Both of them knew of several places where they could lay down and rest, and even nick some food before they got some rest. Soon enough they could send someone into Hunsford have an express taken to town to let their loved ones know that they were relatively safe, and where they were.

Richard was able to discreetly arrange for some food from the kitchen, a large pitcher of water, and some paper and ink with a quill since he was always a favorite with the staff wherever he went, and knew which servants were more trustworthy not to say anything to Lady Catherine or other staff members. They had found a loft that was not used much and laid down to rest before the sun had risen too much. It was not until one o'clock in the afternoon that they awakened, and by then the estate was crawling with workers going about their chores. They knew enough to figure that by then Lady Catherine would have heard about them having gone missing and would have some of her goons out looking for them.

"We shall have to wait until the workers go away for the evening before we can do anything. Blast! I wish that I could send a note to town to let Elizabeth know that I am well and as soon as I get back to town I intend to marry her no matter what objections anyone has!"

Richard chuckled at him, "This is amazing, Darcy. To see such a change in you... I have never seen you act in such a way since you have been around Miss Elizabeth."

"It is because she makes me feel alive, Richard. She has such lightness about her, and she is.... I do not know how to explain it. She has such a wonderful quick mind, and is so kind and thoughtful and loyal to those she loves and cares about. She is so vibrant."

Richard listened to him with brightness in his eyes as well. By six o'clock they had seen several odd things occur from their perch in the loft. From a distance, there appeared to be a carriage that conveyed them before, coming from the main road in Hunsford towards the general direction where they had been. They both expressed some hunger, and again Richard was the one designated to obtain food which he did with ease by telling the cook that he was there on secret military exercises and no one was supposed to know where he was.

Darcy wondered at how easily Richard always seemed to prevaricate, knowing that he would be seen right through if he himself ever tried to do such a thing. He knew that Elizabeth was already able to read him, and soon enough he would have to talk to her about how they came to be engaged and why they must marry sooner than later regardless of what has happened.

Elizabeth was never far from his mind and he wondered what she was doing at that moment, and wished more than ever that he could have seen her today as they had planned. He vowed that as soon as he could get to town-and clean up, he would go straight to the Gardiner's house and insist that she marry him immediately. He did not wish to take any more chances. His mind continued in its distracted thoughts until Richard returned.

"That was close! You will never guess who I saw going into the back servants entrance!" Richard exclaimed.

"Who?" Darcy demanded.

"Wickham himself! I *knew* that they were in this together, but what I need to know is what he is up to. I am going back there to watch for him. I only came back to bring you this."

"How can you be so sure that he has not gone already?"

"Because… I overheard that toady footman, Bill, say to him 'the old lady's in a right nasty mood. She'll be venting her spleen about the cock up with the gent's, so be prepared.'" Richard said in his best imitation of the servant.

"Well? What are we waiting for? Let us go and keep watch, and follow him, then we can ambush him and take the carriage that he came in. Maybe we should even tie him up and drag him along." Darcy growled.

"Do not think I have not thought about it, but perhaps I should go alone. I would not want anything to happen to you should I get ambushed myself."

"No, I think I should go with you to keep an eye out for anyone else, and if you get in a scrape I can help."

"All right then, shall we go?"

They walked down an obscure pathway towards the back of the house to watch for their prey, and when he reemerged from the house they followed him at a distance, so as not to be detected. When they arrived at the cottage-the same cottage that they had been held in earlier, they climbed back up the trellis to peer into the window. When Richard saw who was within he nearly lost his grip of the frame.

Chapter 8

A s Richard tried to regain his equilibrium, Darcy was fighting to tear past his cousin to observe what had shocked him so.

"What is it? What is going on, Richard?" Darcy whispered harshly.

"I do not think that you want to know, Darcy."

"*Why?*"

"Oh, Darcy that *scoundrel…*"

Richard's voice trailed off, and Darcy immediately climbed up next to Richard. He saw their nemesis, George Wickham lying on top of a form that looked hauntingly like their cousin, Anne. She was moaning loudly, and thrashing about beneath him as he took her. The outrage that they both felt could not be contained and they took action immediately, with Richard taking his elbow to break through the pane of glass and hurling himself through the window. Darcy quickly followed to help rescue his cousin, feeling the need to protect Anne from further harm from this beast.

George Wickham jumped back off of the bed with his trousers around his hips and his aroused parts still exposed. Anne was screaming as they entered the room. It was obvious that he had had his way with her, and Darcy felt the anger welling up within him as Wickham's face turned into a smirk.

"Well, well, well… look at what we have here… our two gallant heroes, but I am afraid that you are already too late to save dear Anne, here."

"Wickham, you bl__dy bastard!" spat out Richard.

"You shall hang for what you have done, you blackguard!" Darcy joined his other cousin.

Wickham laughed at them saying, "Oh? Shall I?"

He inched toward the side table where a gun sat inconspicuously half hidden by some newspapers, but fortunately Richard saw where his attention was directed and he moved quickly to reach the gun first.

" I am still too quick for you, George." Richard said.

"Not so fast!"

George moved just as quickly towards the bed grabbing Anne who had been frozen in shock during the whole scene. He held her in front of him as a sort of human shield.

"You would do well to watch where you point that thing Fitzwilliam. You would not want to have it go off accidentally and hurt your lovely cousin here *would you*?"

Just then the door to the room swung open to admit the man they knew as Denny. That man appeared very startled when his eyes met Darcy's, and Darcy wondered who else would show up. At the moment though, he did not care because he was so incensed at the violation that Wickham had perpetrated against his cousin that he was sure he could tear any man limb from limb. Through his furry he barely caught what George was saying to his accomplice.

"Denny... go get our *other captive*! I think it is time that we moved to safer quarters, and be quick about it!"

George was moving backwards from the room with Anne shielding him, and Darcy continued to inch forward until he spotted Denny holding onto his fiancée tightly. Elizabeth was struggling to break away from Denny's grasp, and when she spotted him she tried to run towards him. Unfortunately Denny was quicker than she was and grabbed her forcefully, pulling her back towards him and held knife to her throat.

"Darcy!" She cried out.

Darcy's mind was reeling, disbelieving what he saw. His heart broke to hear the desperation in her voice as he feared for her life. *How did they get hold of Elizabeth? What have they done to her?* His mind turned summersaults thinking of her being in these scoundrels grasp.

"*Denny if you hurt her so help me, I will kill you without any remorse whatever*!" Darcy growled.

"You must be wondering by now how I have come to acquire your..." He glanced over to Elizabeth and turned to him with a smirk, "lovely fiancée, Darcy. I must admit it was not as easy as I had anticipated. She is rather feisty, is she not?"

"Wickham you bl__dy son-of- b__ch! Let her go! Your issues are with me, not her... or Anne! Let them go!" He demanded heedless of his cursing in front of two ladies.

"Temper, temper, Darcy... No, no..." Wickham said rather matter-of-factly as he glanced at Elizabeth, "I think that I shall have to keep her... and your *other* intended for insurance purposes. I cannot have you or Fitzwilliam there trying to send me off to the stockade, and I am certain that these two may be worth *something* to somebody..."

"You shall be lucky if we leave you in enough pieces to send to the stockade after what you have done, Wickham!" Richard hissed.

"Now, now boys we must not play rough. You would not want anything to happen to your ladies would you?" George taunted.

"*What are you going to do?*" Darcy demanded.

"I am going to take these charming ladies with me to keep me company on a little trip. I may eventually let you have one or both of them back if and when I deem fit."

Richard growled, "If you know what is good for you then you will let them go-for if you take them your crimes will only be multiplied!"

"That is the material problem, is it not, Fitzwilliam?" He shook his head, "You will do everything in your power to ensure that I am locked up, and I have no intention of spending any time incarcerated, so I think I shall take my chances by taking these two ladies. They will be infinitely more entertaining than some fat old jailer."

The cur had the audacity to smirk at them again and moved towards the hall, while still holding onto Anne, and he directed Denny to take Elizabeth with them as well. Darcy and Richard were moving forward as fast as the other two men were moving back, and Darcy could see the utter terror in Elizabeth's eyes as tears ran freely down her face. Darcy was torn between furry, agony, and terror due to his own concern for her safety and also that of his cousin. As he thought of all of his options to free them, other thoughts intruded.

He knew George was capable of ravaging women even before tonight, but he had never thought that he would be so blatant... *and with Anne! What can I do? If I try anything to free them he may very well kill one or both of them, and if he takes them he may abuse them until he has had his fill of them and then dispose of them! I cannot even* imagine *what this Denny is capable of!*

George warned, "Do not try to do anything stupid. You would not want their blood on either of your hands would you?"

Wickham and Denny moved out of the door nearest the lane, each with a captive lady as they quickly darted towards the awaiting carriage that Darcy and Richard failed to notice earlier. As soon as the carriage door opened Wickham shoved Elizabeth and Anne in before joining them, and the carriage moved forward with a jolt. The driver's eyes widened when he saw Darcy and Richard and he urged the conveyance forward without waiting for Denny to embark.

As the carriage darted forward Darcy and Richard pursued it as fast as they could, but their legs were no match for two pair of horses-even with pulling a carriage.

"Darcy, this is ridiculous. We are no match for a team of horses." Richard huffed out breathlessly.

Darcy despaired as he watched his worst enemy taking off with his fiancée and cousin, though with more feeling for the former. He did not notice that Wickham's accomplice was left behind while trying to escape. Luckily Richard did and turned to chase after Denny. The two soldiers fought with fists, though Richard was much more experienced than the junior officer. The final result was a foregone conclusion, and the coward was actually begging not to be lock up in the goal. As far as Darcy was concerned he should be run through, but Richard would not let him do the man anymore harm.

"Darcy, we need horses and many more men to be able to pursue them, and we may be able to gain some intelligence from *him*," he nodded his head towards Denny, "that may help us to search for them."

"Richard..." Darcy gasp out, nearing tears, "what if he does them more harm? What if he... if he does to Elizabeth what he did to Anne?"

"I do not know what I can do about that. He is certainly capable and would do so if for no other reason than to throw it in your face, but I do not think that Elizabeth would stand for it. She is a fighter, Darcy. You must have faith in that... besides she is not alone. Anne is with her."

"Is that supposed to make me feel any better? Anne is no match for him, and he had another accomplice besides Denny here." He waved his hand toward the man.

They turned their attention to that man, "Where are they going, Denny?" Richard demanded as he shook him. "You had best tell us all that you know or else your punishment will be much worse than it already is!"

"I... I am not sure, Co-Colonel Fitzwilliam..."

"And *what* exactly is that supposed to mean?" Richard was losing his patience.

"I... I heard him talk about going to town after you and Mr. Darcy left. He said he was going to catch up with an old friend of his and they were going to lure you back here and..." Denny became quiet all of a sudden.

"And *what*? *What* was Wickham threatening to do?" Darcy demanded.

"He... he said that he was going to... to take her..."

Darcy turned, swung his right fist at the man, and dropped him to the ground with swift fist to his cheek. "You bl__dy b__tard! You were going to stand by and do nothing as I was forced to watch him rape my fiancée...?"

Denny remained silent, as he watched Darcy cower over him, flinching when Darcy came nose to nose with him.

"Darcy! We are not going to get very far if you beat the pulp out of him. We need him alive if we want any information he can give us." He turned to their captive and asked in his commanding officer's voice, "Where was he talking about going?"

"I... I... think he said something about a friend he had in town that would... enjoy seeing Mr. Darcy suffer."

Darcy met Richard's eyes as they registered the clue that could lead them to Anne and Elizabeth. Though there were a handful of people who may fit that bill, they both knew of one woman who would happily consort with Wickham and had an ax to grind with Darcy.

Mrs. Younge! That wretched woman! She will stop at nothing to get her revenge, and I have no doubt that she is the only person in town that will harbor him! Oh, my poor Elizabeth in the hands of such scoundrels! He thought despondently. He glanced at his cousin who was studying his face.

"We need to get to the stable at Rosings and arrange for transportation to town at once. I am not sure that I want to set eyes on Lady Catherine right now. The very thought of her malicious greed causing her own daughter's ruination and also causing Elizabeth to suffer the same fate! " He paused and considered what he already knew of Elizabeth's ruination... and at his hands. He felt his guilt rising within his conscience. *No, man you are the cause of her ruination*, he berated himself.

"You do not think that we should tell our aunt that her daughter has been taken?" Richard queried.

"*You* may tell her if you wish, but I am not going to waste anymore time while Wickham gets away with them! Besides... I can travel much faster on a single mount than they can with a team of horses."

After a moment's pause Richard said to him, "All right, I suppose that you are right. We can send word to her later-it really is better than she deserves." He glanced at the other man with them to say, "You come with us, Denny, just in case we need for you to put on a performance for us. Oh... and there is that little matter of a court martial too."

Denny looked at Richard as if he had lost his mind, "W-what do you want me to do? I-I mean I will do it no matter what, just... I beg you not to send me to the gallows."

"That all depends upon how well you perform. For if we find that you are lying to us, then I will not hesitate to send you to the gallows straight away, and if I find that you are still helping them, even though they left you to fend for yourself- then I will not only have lost *all* respect that might have remained for you, but I will personally run you through myself!"

"I-I am not telling lies, sir. That is all that I know... Wickham did not tell me anything else!" Denny protested.

Darcy was starting to recover more of his wits about him, and tried to think of where they could locate Mrs. Younge. *My documents at Darcy House should still be there where we sent our last correspondence, and we can obtain more assistance when we get to town.* He was still very worried about Elizabeth's safety and knew that Wickham would waste no time trying to ruin Elizabeth just to spite him. *If you harm her Wickham, so help me G_d I will not rest until I see you rot in hell!*

The three of them made their way to Rosings Park Stables, easily managed to obtain mounts, and sent word throughout the grounds to be on the lookout for a particular carriage and or a man by the name of George Wickham-just in case he did not manage to get very far. As fast as they could, they rode towards town taking half their normal time. There was little conversation between them due to the horses speed and Darcy being preoccupied with sorting out a strategy to rescue his beloved Elizabeth.

When they had come to the street where Richard resided, his cousin asked, "Darcy... do you think that we should consult my father? He may be able to bring more help quickly, and with Anne being abducted as well he will most certainly need to know what has happened."

Darcy thought it was a good idea as well, but he wanted to get the last known address of Mrs. Younge as soon as possible, feeling that it would help quicken their search.

"Yes, he certainly does need to be informed as well as the Bennet's and Gardiner's. I think that it might be best though, to go through my papers to find Mrs. Younge's address, and tell Elizabeth's family what has happened-in person. They do not need to learn about this from some impersonal note. I will go tell them right after I get what I need from my house, and then we can meet up at the Gardiner's house. In the mean time you go and let the earl know what has happened. I have a feeling that he will want to have a very serious talk with Lady Catherine." Darcy said darkly.

"Very well. Oh... we should notify the constable. He can get us more help to apprehend them, and he should have contacts throughout town." As soon as I get done briefing the earl on the entire situation, I need to get to the barracks and get this errant soldier to the stockade.

Denny shot the commanding officer a look of alarm, and Richard's response was to remind him, "Do not even try to worm your way out of this! The minute you chose to conspire with George Wickham, you as good as had yourself locked up or *hung* anyway."

The soldier's shoulders slumped even more as he rode the horse that had been tethered to Richards mount the whole journey to town. Darcy felt little sympathy for him. *Richard is right. Anyone who conspires with Wickham is signing up for nothing but trouble... but then not too many know his true character*. Guilt started to settle upon Darcy for having neglected to warn other's about his enemy's tendencies. He himself had not told his father of the many things he saw George do as they were growing up. *Pride is an awful object-especially when it leads to the harm of those you love*, he thought to himself. *I will make this right no matter what! No one else should have to suffer for my silence!*

They split up to fulfill their duties with Richard taking Denny to Matlock House, and Darcy headed to his town house. He not only wanted to obtain the address of his sister's former companion, but he also wanted to retrieve some weapons.

~*~*~*~

Elizabeth was terrified when Mr. Denny untied her and dragged her down the stairs at the cottage. She was even more terrified to see Darcy standing there, but wanted more than anything to run to him for comfort as much as safety. When her captor forcefully drew her back and thrust the knife to her throat, she began to feel the dread-not only of her present situation, but also that she would not ever see her betrothed ever again. She had not even registered Anne De Bourg's presence until they were both being dragged outside of the cottage to the awaiting carriage.

She held out hope that they would be rescued until the coach barreled down the road without Mr. Denny. The discomfort from being tethered for so long without being able to move much was pushed aside as her mind grasped that they were moving dangerously fast. Her concern shifted towards their safety within the carriage, fearing that they may soon capsize from riding so fast. After about fifteen minutes they slowed somewhat, and she noticed that Anne DeBourg did not seem to be nearly as frightened as she herself was. In fact Anne was far from it. Wickham had been smiling leeringly at them both, but Anne seemed not to mind… not one bit.

"Come, my darling…" He addressed Anne, "We are safe from Darcy now, and he will never find us."

"George… what was the meaning of using me as your shield? I could have been killed!" She demanded of him.

"Oh come now, Anne-you know good and well that neither Fitzwilliam nor Darcy would have done anything to harm you, but they would not hesitate to kill me. They do not even know about us…"

"Yes, but why did you have to drag *her* along with us?" she pointed towards Elizabeth, "You certainly did not need to bring along anymore baggage!"

Elizabeth's sense of fear and dread was soon overridden by her sense of outrage and offense at what she was witnessing. *Wickham and Anne are involved with each other? Were they conspiring to kidnap Darcy… and for what purpose?*

Wickham answered her silent question when he turned to her, "Oh… I am sorry Elizabeth. I suppose you would like an explanation? I mean a more thorough one than before. Anne and I have been *involved* for some time now and Darcy had to go and mess things up by engaging himself to you."

"Why would our engagement *'mess things up'* for the two you, if you are involved with each other? Why could you not just marry each other if that is what you want, and leave us out of it?" Elizabeth demanded.

"Because..." Anne broke in, "my mother is still in charge of Rosings until I marry, and she would *never* allow me to marry George. She has always set her sights on me marrying Darcy, and I was in a fair way of making that happen until you came along..."

"But, why would you want to marry someone that you did not love and did not love you?"

Anne snorted, "What has love to do with marriage? In *our* circles one does not marry for love, we marry for money... preferably *old* money, and as to why Darcy? Why not? He is handsome, wealthy, and would not likely put too many demands upon me."

Wickham snorted at her statement and she glanced at him and smirked, "I would have George here to help fulfill any other requirements that I should have."

"Do you not see how selfish and unfair that is? What if you should become with child?" Elizabeth demanded indignantly.

"All the better." Piped in Wickham.

"You people disgust me!" Elizabeth retorted.

"You know Elizabeth... now that I think about it; I now understand why my cousin engaged himself to you. You are both so uptight and pious, and you both enjoy arguing with each other. You really are perfect for one another."

Though it was getting dark, Elizabeth glared at the pair sitting across from her in the carriage. She hoped that she could find some way to escape and still wondered why Wickham even bothered to drag her along if he was involved with Anne. He continued to stare at her as they rode along, making her feel very uncomfortable. Finally when she had enough of it, she turned toward the opposite window from him, feeling that looking into the darkness was infinitely better than looking across to the duplicitous couple.

Elizabeth was tired and as she watched the passing darkness, she wondered if she would ever see Darcy again. Silently she prayed that he would find her before rumors started spreading about her captivity, for she knew that once ones reputation was lost-it was lost forever. She did not wish to be the source to Darcy's diminished reputation due to her under any circumstance, and she began to despair that what she had once never desired may never take place now. Tears ran down her cheeks, and she fought to gain some composure in front of the dissolute pair sitting opposite her.

No one said anything else and the rocking carriage, lack of nourishment, and fatigue finally caused Elizabeth to fall into a slumber. She thrashed around in her sleep. Her dreams reliving what had happened that day, and what may never happen between her and Darcy. Sometime later the carriage slowed down and she found herself in town again.

She became more hopeful that she would be returned until Wickham said to her, "Do not get your hopes up Elizabeth. We will be going to a very different part of town that even you are not accustomed to seeing."

"What are you talking about, George? What are you saying to Elizabeth? Why are we not going to some inn that is not in the... unfashionable parts of town?"

"Anne... we cannot risk being seen by anyone that knows you. If they see us then it will all be over and we could not continue with this... arrangement." At her petulant look, he quickly added, "I will not keep you there for very long, I promise. As soon as we can we shall go to some seaside resort and you can arrange for us to stay in a very elegant abode."

Again, Elizabeth wondered what they were planning to do with her, and why they would still need her if they thought that he had abducted Anne.

"Shall you not let me go? I am sure that I would be more in the way than anything, and then you can be off to wherever without my *baggage* to slow you down."

"Yes, but you know too much now for us to let you go-much as I would desire it you must remain with us. Oh... and do not even think about trying to escape. We do have other resources to keep you in check. For instance it could be leaked that whilst you were gone you were utterly compromised, and then not only you but your entire pathetic family would be ruined." Sneered Anne.

Elizabeth had had enough of Anne's derisive remarks, "I suppose that you would know all about pathetic family members, after all your mother would have been your best example of that and having spent your entire life with her must have groomed you very well for that position as well."

Anne raised her hand to strike Elizabeth, but she was too quick for the slighter woman, and George let out a loud chortle at their altercation. The two women glared at each other, and Anne sniffed at her without saying another word. They had been driving through a slightly dilapidated area of town and had come up on a Tudor style house that had seen better days, when the carriage finally stopped.

"Well ladies… we are home-or at least where we shall stay until we can go to wherever it is we are going to next."

Anne looked out of the carriage window with a deep frown. "You cannot be serious, George! You do not expect me to stay in a place such as this!"

"Yet you must, Anne. We cannot go to the finer areas of town. You must realize that you will be recognized and we cannot chance it."

She huffed, and followed him out of to the walk in front of the door then Wickham turned to Elizabeth to help her to disembark, but she refused any assistance from him.

He bowed lowly to her then came up right behind her to whisper into her ear, "Do not worry Elizabeth… I shall make certain that you are well *taken* care of. Anne does not have the fortitude that I am sure you have."

The indignity within Elizabeth came out as she turned to him, "That may be more to my advantage than yours, Mr. Wickham. I have always been known for my stubborn resistance when things did not suit me."

"Actually Elizabeth… that may work to my benefit- I do like a woman who shows more spirit and Anne does not have nearly as much as you do."

He grabbed her and shoved her forth to the old building. She saw a woman that looked to be in her mid to late thirties peering out of a window and then opened the front door. Their party entered and the woman quickly shut the door, but not before peering outside the door to both directions.

"George… what brings you here so late of an evening-and with guests?" She was glaring at Wickham.

"Hattie I came here as a stopover before I leave again for a while. A situation has arisen that necessitates my removal from the area for some time."

"You mean that you are hiding from the authorities after our old *friend* has gone missing." She countered.

He chuckled before he answered, "Well I must admit that I was not disappointed that he has gone missing, but I doubt that he will remain so for very long and I wish to absence myself from here-just for a bit…"

She was looking him up and down before she turned her attention towards Anne and her, Elizabeth noted. She narrowed her eyes at Elizabeth when she looked her over.

"I suppose that this is one of your little tarts, aye George?"

"Sadly no, Hattie. This is our old friend, Darcy's fiancée, Miss Elizabeth Bennet."

The woman, Hattie, looked at her with renewed interest, before turning her attention back to Wickham.

"Is she the one they have been looking for then?"

"Likely." Wickham answered.

Strangely, Elizabeth had mixed emotions about her disappearance being generally known. She wondered what had been said, and if anyone had seen Wickham and his accomplice take her from the park earlier.

"Where did you take her before you came here then? She was supposedly missing earlier today…"

"It is a long story and one I will not recount right now. Suffice to say that this is the second trip that I have made to town in the last twenty four hours, and it would not have been necessary except that Darcy had been so disobliging as to run off. I had to come back to get some insurance against his foiling our plans…"

"Ah… I see he was too quick for you again." The Hattie woman said dryly.

"Hattie, you wound me." Wickham replied.

"I seriously doubt it, George. You are as thick skinned as anybody I know; besides it is probably true."

"Well it will not happen again." He said with a scowl. "We have left him behind in Kent, and it will take him hours to catch up. That is if he can figure out where we are heading and I do not plan to stay here for very long, just enough o rest up before the next leg of our journey and we will soon be out of your hair."

The Hattie woman studied him for a moment before she asked, "And what is in it for me? If the authorities find out that you have been here what could make me keep quiet?"

Anne spoke up immediately, "I will pay you to stay silent, Mrs. Younge. At least until George has had a chance to execute our plans." She looked at Elizabeth for a moment before returning her attention to Hattie, "You can help to let people know that Miss Bennet and I are well, but that she has suffered a most *unfortunate situation*." Her eyes were gleaming as she looked back to Elizabeth.

Elizabeth had never met such a cold and calculating woman before and that included Caroline Bingley. The implications of Anne's insinuation made her shudder. Her impression of the haute ton was growing more and more dismal, but she did not allow that to cloud her judgment of the whole lot of them for she knew that there must still be some decent folks in that society to have begotten men such as Fitzwilliam Darcy and Colonel Fitzwilliam.

"Well then, I shall be happy to help in whatever way I can..."

They were shown to a parlor area before the woman called for a maid to show them to their rooms.

"Hattie, keep Miss Bennet nice and secure. We would not want anything untoward to happen to her now would we?"

"Do not worry. The room she will be in has a lock and no one but I will have the key."

"Mores' the pity." He muttered.

The maid led Anne to a room just to the right of the stairway and Hattie pointed to a room adjacent to it for Wickham, then she grabbed Elizabeth by the arm tightly and placed her into a small room that looked to have been a closet of some kind at one time. There were no windows, and the mattress was a thin feather kind with only a couple of meager blankets. It looked clean enough, and there was a short stand with a pitcher of water, and a small chamber pot. *At least I am not tethered to some bed, splayed out for anyone to take advantage of,* Elizabeth thought indignantly. For once, since this whole ordeal began, Elizabeth felt somewhat safe, but it did not keep her from sleeping lightly that night. Once during the night that she thought she heard someone trying the doorknob to her quarters and afterwards she could not sleep at all.

Early the next morning the door to the room opened and admitted Hattie and Wickham.

"It is time to rise and shine, Elizabeth. We must make haste in order to get to our destination in good time and we do not want any interruptions on our journey."

"Where are you taking me?"

"I thought I would let that be a surprise and how could it be a surprise if you were to know it before hand?"

Wickham approached her and helped her up roughly. Without letting go of her arm he dragged her downstairs where they ate at a small dining area where a surprisingly decent morning meal had been laid out. Though Elizabeth had not eaten for almost a day and a half she no longer had any appetite and even though Wickham tried to coax her to eat she refused, thinking would be a concession to him. Anne took no notice of them and happily went about devouring her meal.

As soon as their carriage was ready, they were taken out to embark to some other unknown destination. Elizabeth despaired of being discovered before something more untoward happened. She wanted to know where they were going and tried to watch for signs that would give her clues as to their direction. She caught a glimpse of a sign labeled 'Bath' after about an hour of traveling. *Bath... that must be the seaside resort where they are going.* The name struck up a memory... *Colonel Fitzwilliam was to go to Bath and retrieve Miss Darcy there. She was to meet with us for our wedding...* Tears began anew, as Elizabeth grieved over her present situation. How she wished to met Georgiana Darcy now, and get to know her as a sister.

Chapter 9

Richard arrived late in the night at Matlock House, and was surprised when he was informed that his father was still awake and in his study. He took Denny with him to ensure that he would not escape, dragging him to face the earl.

When he knocked on the door he heard a firm, "Enter."

Richard opened the door wide enough to admit himself and Denny and immediately noticed that his father looked haggard. His surprise matched that of his father who stood from his chair and rushed to greet his missing son.

"Richard," His father began, "we despaired of ever finding you and Darcy! What happened, and why are you here with... this gentleman?" He nodded towards Denny with an odd look.

"Ah... well, sir it is a complicated story, and if you do not mind I would love some port before I repeat it."

His father walked to the sideboard to pour Richard, and his companion a drink. Once he returned to them they sat down to enjoy the liquor. After a few minutes of enjoying a real drink since at least a day, Richard was not in too great a hurry to talk as he was still formulating what he was going to tell his father about his aunt.

"So... are you going to tell me what happened to you and your cousin or do I have to beat it out of you?" His father asked impatiently.

"I doubt what I have to say will be well received. It is rather unpleasant."

The earl regarded him apprehensively, then said, "Well, go on then and be done with it."

Richard took a deep breath and began his tale of how he and Bingley were shoved away from Darcy's carriage before George Wickham absconded with his cousin. He then told his father how he had almost managed to retrieve him until he was knocked unconscious and captured himself. The next part became more difficult because of who they found was behind the whole scheme. Though Richard wanted to spare his father some grief, it was not possible when he related to him how Lady Catherine conspired with George Wickham to kidnap Darcy in a last ditch effort to make him marry Anne.

"I tried to warn Catherine that Darcy never had any inclination to marry Anne, but she refused to hear it and would not brook listening to anyone who would nay say her."

"I do not doubt that, but this time she has gone too far and something must be done! There is more as, I am sure, you have already surmised." Richard studied his glass intently before he met his father's gaze.

"Are you going to tell me then? I cannot imagine how much worse it can get!" He huffed.

If you only knew how much worse it has gotten, you would likely throttle your own sister, Richard thought. He saw that the earl continued to watch him, and he knew that he had to tell his father what he and Darcy saw when they followed Wickham back to the cottage after he left Rosings. *Well... here it goes...*

"When Darcy and I followed the blackguard back to the dowager cottage, we were going to climb up a trellis and when we had just gotten to the first window... we saw.... we saw..." Richard kept swallowing.

"Yes? You saw *what*, Richard?" His father asked impatiently.

"We saw... George Wickham taking... taking... liberties with…with Anne."

"*What*?" The earl asked incredulously.

"It is true father. She was violated by George Wickham."

The earl stared at him disbelievingly before he blurted out a string of expletives. "I should have known that good for nothing, lying cur would have tried something else after Darcy sent him away from Pemberley forever! Especially after what he tried…" He abruptly stopped, when he realized that Denny was quietly listening to them.

Richard did not want anything leaked about their family, especially as it mostly involves *his* ward and there was a prisoner that would not scruple to use that information to his advantage. He looked at his father sharply to warn him to watch his words in front of others.

"Yes, I know… and it almost seemed as if she… could not or… would not fight him off."

"Well I am not surprised; Anne is such a slight mousey little thing. She probably knew that Wickham could easily snap her in half, and complied rather than risk further injury." The earl surmised. "I only hope that this does not cause her any more harm than it already has."

"True, and I doubt that Darcy will want anything to do with her at all-in the way of marriage anyway, but now she has been taken along with Miss Bennet. George took off with the two of them to keep himself safe from being run through by me and Darcy. In the process he left behind Denny here, to hold the bag so to speak. Wickham left in the direction of town so we came here. Darcy left to retrieve some crucial papers and then he was going to notify Miss Bennet's family of what has happened."

Richard's father stared at his son in disbelief, "Why is he *here* then, Richard? Why did you not have him *locked up* rather than bring him here to listen to our private dealings?"

"Sir, I may have use for him yet, and as far as what happened to Anne... he was there as well. If Wickham thinks that Denny here has gotten away then he may lead us to Anne and Miss Elizabeth. We think that he may have sought help from Mrs. Younge as well."

"Would it surprise you if he has? There are not likely too many people who would give him any assistance at all-other than to help him upon a scaffolding to await the noose. What I cannot understand is; if you know where he is, why do you need this scoundrel anyway? Why do you not just storm the worthless baggage's house and arrest him?"

"We need to know that he has not abandoned Anne or Miss Elizabeth, and the last time we tried to remove Anne from him, he abducted her while using her as his shield. We do not want that to happen again. If he thinks that no one is watching, then he may be lured away and that is when we will rescue Anne and Miss Elizabeth."

His father nodded his head comprehending the plan then asked, "If he has already taken Anne, what is to stop him from doing the same to this Miss Bennet?"

Richard could not help the chuckle from rising out of him, "You do not know Miss Bennet, sir. She is no mousey little thing and she has more spirit than some of the young green ears in the army. I suspect that should he be so unwise to do such a thing, she will set him straight and if he has any sense left about him then he will realize that Darcy would kill him if he were to try anyway."

"Indeed? She must be an amazing woman-though I should have guessed that any woman Darcy would align himself with would be anything but ordinary. Still... I wonder if it would be a good idea for him to continue his engagement if anything happened... I mean... what if..."

"Father, we cannot think that ... besides, Darcy will not let that cur stand in his way of happiness and frankly... neither will I. He has found a good match in her and it is the first time that I have seen him so besotted."

"She must be quite unique. I have met her family and they are..."

"Loud, noisy, unrefined?" Richard finished.

"That and much more! Did you know that she has an uncle in trade? I met her father last night and he is quite... unique as well."

"Yes, that he is and Miss Elizabeth takes after him more so than her mother in personality, but she takes after her eldest sister in looks. She may not be what you had envisioned for Darcy, but she is what he desires more than anything, and he is his own man. He does not require your permission, although I dare say he would appreciate your support."

Richard knew that his father would accede when he heard about Miss Elizabeth's *finer* attributes. He was always a softie when it came to a pretty face, regardless of their social standing in society and he managed to pass that onto his sons. He also knew that his father favored Darcy and wanted to see him happy in his adult life as his childhood was anything but.

"At least that is good to know. Her eldest sister is a very handsome woman, but still!"

"Father I have no objection to *those* relations and she makes him happy. They are fine upstanding people and they are much more pleasant than most in our society. As to the other issues, I think that they bear more serious consideration, and I think that someone needs to confront Lady Catherine and let her know that her scheming has resulted in her beloved Anne being *utterly compromised.* If the other lady has been harmed in any way though, I will personally see to it that Lady Catherine gets her just deserts as well. Miss Elizabeth was an innocent party in this whole thing, and she deserves none of it."

"True, it is awful having to imagine what those ladies are going through under the control of George Wickham. To think that my own sister was behind the whole thing! I wonder what she promised George in exchange for his cooperation?" The earl looked at Denny and addressed him. "What have you to contribute to this *Mr.* Denny?" he challenged.

Denny looked at him apprehensively before he replied, "I was offered one hundred and fifty pounds to help…" he swallowed hard, "take Miss Elizabeth."

Richard looked at the man sharply. *What the bl__dy h_ll is that supposed to mean? Was he also going to compromise Miss Elizabeth?* He became angrier the more he thought about it and made a mental note to confront Denny when they were alone. *He had better* not *have done anything to her, else I* really will *kill him!*

"I am assuming that you had absolutely *no intention* of doing so, *right*, Mr. Denny?"

"N-no, sir-it was all a big mistake to have even taken her away from the park…"

"You are d_mned right it was!" Both of the Fitzwilliam men bellowed out.

"Now you shall have your chance to make it *right*. As soon as my cousin returns with the address of Mrs. Younge, you will be in contact with her, telling her that George Wickham gave you her name and address and you have just escaped from us in Kent. You can even tell her that you can pay her to aide you… that should open her door faster than anything."

Richard turned to his father again, "Sir, it looks as though you have not slept for two days. Perhaps you should get some rest and then we can discuss what should be done about Lady Catherine after you have had some sleep. You cannot use the excuse that I have been abducted now, and Darcy is safe…"

"But what of poor Anne? What shall happen to her?"

"We cannot do anything about that right now. We are all exhausted and need to rest. I do not know about you, but I do better when I have a chance to think and I can only do that when I sleep-it is a soldier's thing."

The earl smiled, "I take it that I am being issued an order by a higher ranking officer?"

"No. Just a concerned son."

The three gentlemen retired for the rest of the night to catch up on some much needed rest, although Denny was not given a guest room. He was placed in a large windowless closet with a guard and a door that locked from the outside. Richard would take no chances of him escaping to warn his allies. He was so tired from the last two days that he did not even hear the carriage leave from Matlock House the next morning. When he did finally awaken to talk with the earl, he was told by the butler that the earl left at daybreak.

The debate raged within him as to whether he should follow his father to Kent or assist Darcy with his search for Mrs. Younge. After contemplating the risks of not going, he elected to stay close to town. *Father will not likely kill Lady Catherine and even if he tried she would still have her cane and she knows how to wield it. Darcy, on the other hand may very well kill both Mrs. Younge and George Wickham. That is if the cur would fight fair-which he usually does not!* Richard decided to stay in town and call upon his colleagues in the army to help them find the kidnapper and deserter.

When Darcy arrived at his town house, he was greeted by his very surprised but relieved housekeeper, Mrs. Jones.

"Mr. Darcy! Oh… my, what happened to you? Did you know that everyone has been out all over the countryside looking for you?"

Darcy could imagine that there was likely some excitement when he was rather publicly abducted in his own coach and in front of a whole crowd of people.

"I would imagine that there were a few people who may have been curious as to my whereabouts, Mrs. Jones. I do not suppose that you would happen to have some cold meats and some bread and tea would you?"

She looked at him oddly before she replied, "You know very well that I do and I shall bring it to you personally…" She hesitated for a moment before venturing to say, "Sir? Mr. Darcy… I do not know if anyone's told you this but… well the lady that they said you are to be married to has… has gone missing. They think that she may have been taken by the same people as took you."

"Yes…I know, Mrs. Jones. That is the reason I have come here actually. I may have some information that may help me to find her."

"Oh, that is wonderful news, Mr. Darcy. I hope those ruffians do not harm her…"

Darcy looked at her with a grimace, "I hope so too, and if they know what is good for them then they will guard her with their lives."

The housekeeper looked at him with a knowing look and left to prepare his repast, but before she could close the door Darcy called her back quickly.

"Mrs. Jones, I do not suppose that there would be any chance of me getting some hot water for a bath?"

The kindly older woman smiled at him and said, "I am sure we can arrange that as well, sir. I will bring you some dinner first, and when your bath is ready I will let you know."

"Very good, thank you."

Darcy went about looking for documents from almost a year ago, recalling what he had done when he found that Mrs. Younge was not as she represented, and had almost sent her sister into the clutches of George Wickham. The thought of both Elizabeth and Anne in his clutches now made him furious, and as soon as he found the woman's address he wanted to tear down there and break down her door to get to Elizabeth. Before he could do anything, however, his supper arrived and shortly thereafter his bath was ready for him.

Sitting in the warm tub helped to relieve some of the grime from sleeping in the loft at Rosings, but did little to relieve the strain on his muscles. He thought of every scenario he could to have prevented Elizabeth and Anne form being taken, but could come up with few good ideas and ceded that no other option was available at the time that would not have endangered his life or theirs. He slumped back in the tub and had nearly fallen asleep when his valet came to check upon him.

"Mr. Darcy …Is there anything that I can do for you, sir?"

"No…" Darcy was starting to wake more and reaclimated himself to his surroundings and asked, "What time is it, Altman?"

"It is almost two o'clock in the morning, sir."

"What are you doing awake at such an ungodly hour?"

"Many of the staff were having difficulty finding rest, sir."

The subtle reminder that he had such devoted staff who were obviously worried for him was touching. He wanted to reassure them that he was well, but did not want the word generally known that he was back in town least Wickham should find out.

"I thank you all for your kindness, but I am well-just a bit tired, and will need to be gone very early this morning again so if you could please see to it that as few people know about my return as is necessary, that would be much appreciated. I would rather keep things quiet for now."

"Of course, sir. I will see to it immediately. There are few who know, but they shall understand your need for their discretion."

"Thank you, you may retire Altman, I can see to my own needs."

Darcy stepped out of the now cold tub and donned his silk robe after he toweled off. He was actually very exhausted, and went straight to his bed and fell into it, falling asleep as soon as his head hit the pillow.

Early the next morning he was awakened by Altman's gentle noises as the gentleman went about preparing Darcy's attire, and polishing his boots. The house was starting to come alive again, and the smell of fresh bread was wafting throughout the house. The scent alone could easily draw him out of bed. His cooks were some of the best in all of England. Within a short period of time he joined Altman in his dressing room and was ready to eat a quick breakfast within twenty minutes.

Mr. Holder announced that Richard had arrived with Denny, and they joined him for his breakfast. The colonel seemed impatient to start the search, and was most irritating in his not so subtle hints to his companions as he watched them eat after he inhaled his food.

"I do not suppose that you would consider hurrying? We do have things to accomplish, and I told Colonel Hill that we would meet him at the Gardiner's residence within the hour."

Darcy was more than a little irritated at his impatience since Elizabeth was his fiancée and Anne was his cousin as well.

"What is *your* hurry, Richard? It is not as though we will need more than thirty minutes at the most to get to the Gardiner's residence, and we already have the address of Mrs. Younge's. I know that you sent word to have the place watched as soon as I told you, so calm yourself. You forget that I am also worried about Elizabeth and have more to lose should anything happen."

"Exactly-which is why I do not understand your hesitancy…?"

"Oh, do not mistake this as hesitancy. I know the area where Mrs. Younge lives. It is not the best area, but then Wickham has few options right now and even fewer funds. He cannot go far."

Richard harrumphed before he commented, "I wish that I had your confidence. You recall who we are talking about, correct? This is a man who can charm almost anyone and when he wants he can talk anyone into helping him out of anything."

"Point taken." Darcy allowed.

It did not take much longer before he was done eating and ready to travel to Gracechurch Street. . Darcy did not wish for anyone to know that he had been found yet or that he was in town for reasons of safety as well as privacy. He reasoned that he did not need the likes of Caroline Bingley and her gossiping to compromise Elizabeth's safety, so he drew the shades of the coach after he boarded it in the back of the house. Within twenty minutes they arrived in the back of the Gardiner's residence to a very surprised Charles Bingley.

"Darcy! What the devil happened to you? Where have you been and how did you manage to escape?"

"I will explain it all when we get inside. We do not need extra ears listening in on our private affairs."

"Of course. Let us go inside then." His friend replied.

They were all shown into the study where it looked like a major military campaign had been launched. There were maps of England's counties strewn about papers with all sorts of names, and in the middle of the melee was Mr. Bennet, Mr. Gardiner and Colonel Hill. They were obviously expecting them, and judging by the two former gentlemen, they had already been informed that Elizabeth was still missing.

"Mr. Darcy, what is this about Elizabeth being taken *again*?" Mr. Bennet asked with some agitation.

Darcy was still not ready to explain everything, but had some help in Richard who smoothly and concisely described most of what had happened at Rosings the evening before, which shocked Mr. Bennet and Mr. Gardiner. Once he finished, they began launching into more questions.

"How are we to find him now? They could have gotten as far as Yorkshire for all we know." Mr. Bennet asked.

"I doubt that they could have gotten that far, because George Wickham is not a man of many means and he has few true friends. We have managed to deduce who that may be and will be heading over there shortly to see if we are correct in our calculations." Richard answered.

"I do not suppose that you would divulge whom that *friend* might be would you, Colonel Fitzwilliam?" Mr. Bennet asked impatiently.

"I shall not say for now. We have good reason to think that Wickham would have turned to this person."

"Well then, can we at least join you when you when you go there? We have been quite anxious over Elizabeth's well being."

Darcy was slightly annoyed that his cousin had managed to jump into the lead role of rescuer even though their cousin, Anne, was also in some danger from Wickham as well. He chose to overlook *that* minor detail. If anyone were to be seen as Elizabeth's knight in shining armor, he was the one who wanted to fulfill the part of defender of her honor-not Richard. It was petty and unreasonable, but he could not help himself. He still felt insecure in her esteem, and felt even more so with Mr. Bennet.

His past behavior haunted his conscience and the fact that Richard was able to take command so flawlessly, thus gaining respect and admiration from Elizabeth's relatives grated on his nerves. That gentleman did not seem to notice, however, and continued to monopolize the other gentlemen's attention for three quarters of an hour with stratagems and contingency plans. When he had finally finished, Darcy scarcely paid him any attention for his focusing on the reactions of two particular gentlemen whom he dearly wanted respect from.

"I am going with you to wherever this Mrs. Younge's house is and retrieve my daughter…"

"But Mr. Bennet, that area is not a safe area to be-even for a soldier…" Richard replied.

"I do not care, colonel. This is my daughter we are talking about!"

"Sir," Darcy interrupted. "My cousin is correct. The neighborhood is very bad, and we could not possibly allow you to come… It is for your own safety, besides you can be assured that I will not allow anyone to harm Elizabeth or my own cousin, you have my word." He finished sincerely.

Mr. Bennet regarded him skeptically for a moment, and then looked between him, Richard, and Mr. Gardiner before he acceded to their plea. Darcy was relieved for the fact that he would feel even worse should Elizabeth's father be hurt or killed during their attempted rescue.

"I suppose you are right. I am too old to be gallivanting around town-especially the seedier areas, and Mrs. Bennet shall never forgive me if I got myself killed." He admitted ruefully.

Darcy understood his dilemma. If he were in the same situation, he would feel the same way, and Mr. Bennet's mention of being killed and leaving behind Mrs. Bennet and Elizabeth's younger sisters reinforced his stance. There was no way-if he could help it-that he was going to allow his soon-to-be father-in-law to come to any harm because he, along with Elizabeth would likely be burdened to take them on. *Unless they are all married off quickly that may still be the case, but at least Pemberley is very large and perhaps we can place them in the North wing... or the dowagers cottage even?* He pondered, but dismissed it just as quickly. He did not wish for Mr. Bennet to come to an untimely death.

"We shall ride in a hackney coach to the area. Wickham and Mrs. Younge know what the Darcy crest looks like, and riding in that area with... such a conveyance would only cause us to be discovered." Darcy said.

"Quite right." Offered Colonel Hill, "I have even instructed my men to dress in plain clothes. Should we be detected before we spot them, there is a chance that they he will get away, and from what I have heard of this man it is not safe for anyone if he is free to do more harm."

The gentlemen left shortly thereafter on their way to Edwards Street, where Mrs. Younge's boarding house was located, followed by soldiers in plain clothes. There were a few places that they passed in the hackney that made Darcy cringe. *How could George drag Elizabeth and Anne through such filth? He has no sense of decency at all! She had better be well when I get there, or else you will pay so very dearly, George!*

They traveled for about half an hour due to the crowded streets, and busy vendors plying their goods along the narrowed path it took them a little longer than even they had anticipated. When they came within two blocks of the establishment, they stopped suddenly. The driver refused to go any further, and the soldiers stood nearby to ensure that nothing untoward happened. As Darcy disembarked behind Richard, he took in their surroundings. There were many young children who looked filthy and unkempt, and the stench of the air was enough to make him nauseous. After taking in his environment, he hated George Wickham even more than before.

How dare he bring two gentlewomen to such a place, and then to place them under the same roof as that Mrs. Younge.... Despicable! There were many who held their hands out for money, seeing that he was dressed finer than anyone else there, he was their main focus. He did give a couple of people a coin or two when he saw that they had children in tow. Though their parents seemed negligent, he felt it unfair to let their children starve when he could do something to help them.

Richard leaned in to him to whisper, "Darcy, I would not encourage you to hand out money in a place like this..."

Darcy gave him a frown, and raised an eyebrow in question.

"They will put word out that some rich gentleman is passing out coins, and then we will be flanked by all sorts of beggars, besides-you are not likely to be helping their children... only feeding their drinking habit." He shook his head.

The intelligence shook Darcy to his core. He had always known that this area existed, and he had even seen some of it in other places, but it had never been so concentrated, nor had he seen so many destitute young people. These were the truly helpless of their society, and suddenly he felt guilt for the life he had been given. Richard seemed to sense his change in mood and reminded him why they were there in the first place.

"Darcy, recall why we are here. This is likely where Georgiana would have ended up if you had not condescended to take an early trip to Brighton and foiled Wickham's plot to seduce her." He shook his head and muttered, "I could never understand what it was your father ever saw in him. He was no good even when he was young!"

Darcy thought that he could not agree more, and maybe, perhaps they may be able to rid themselves of him once and for all-*and the sooner the better*. They came up to a Tudor style building that looked like it may have been a nice building at one time, but due to neglect or the area being overrun by the poorest of society it had gone into disrepair.

They followed the soldiers as they strategically surrounded the establishment. Then Richard directed Denny where to go. Standing near a general store of sorts, Darcy tried to imagine what Elizabeth must have endured while she was held by George. He watched as their group took their places and waited... and worried. Denny walked cautiously towards the establishment, and rang the bell. He waited for a minute before the door opened and a maid answered. After a few moments, she stepped aside to allow him entrance. They could not see him, but Darcy was assured that the whole house was being watched on all sides.

Everyone seemed to be getting impatient as they watched for nearly twenty minutes before Denny came out alone, and approached Colonel Hill, who joined him and Richard.

"Sirs, I am sorry to say that they are not here..." Colonel Hill began.

Darcy was as surprised as Richard as they both blurted out, "*What?*"

"Yes... you heard me correctly, but they *were* here earlier. Apparently Captain Wickham left early this morning with two ladies in tow. Denny was able to confirm that they were indeed Miss De Bourgh and Miss Elizabeth Bennet, but they traveled onward earlier this morning."

"*Well*? Where did they travel on to then? Surely she must know *something*?" Darcy exclaimed.

"She would not say, sir." Denny said, "She told me that she may be able to get hold of George, but that I had to await further word from him through her..."

"*So she does know where he is*! That bl__dy wretched woman!" Richard swore. "No doubt she is looking for someone to lay down some coin for information..."

"Or she does not know where he is and is trying to gain some profit..." Denny offered.

"Doubtful," Darcy said, "I think that she knows where he is going. She has been in contact with him for years and... that *'Bill'* fellow who was driving the carriage? If I am not mistaken, it is her son. She is sure to know where he is headed."

They all looked at him surprised and he explained, "I did actually interview her when she came to me for employment, and there were a few things that she actually told the truth about. The fact that she had a son was one of them."

"That is all *wonderful*, but how is that going to help us get Elizabeth and Anne back?" Richard snorted.

"For one, Denny can stay there and await word from Wickham while he is under her roof..." Darcy started.

"That is not possible... in case you have not forgotten, Denny is a prisoner now..." Richard interrupted.

"But you and Colonel Hill can arrange things, and perhaps you can have another soldier keep a watch over him."

"That might be possible. Ha!" Colonel Hill turned to his colleague, "This may even be worse that the stockade." He smiled.

"True Hill, but what other poor man would be so unfortunate as to have to live here with *him*?" Richard asked.

"That is easy...anyone who does not wish to be sent to the continent."

Colonel Hill was correct. There were few men who looked forward to going to meet Napoleon, and so volunteers were plentiful... even if they had to find other living arrangements. They managed to secure the area, and left Denny to stay with another man at Mrs. Younge's establishment. Apparently rooms were not the only things that she provided... with the right amount of persuasion they could have *other* sleeping arrangements as well.

Darcy was beginning to feel panic along with frustration. He desperately wanted to be reunited with Elizabeth, and had been looking forward to Georgiana having the sister she had always wanted. He then remembered that he had to write to his sister to inform her of what had happened. He did not want her to read about his abduction in any papers, nor of Elizabeth being taken as well. He contemplated going to confront his sister's former companion, and turned to do so when Richard caught his arm and swung him back towards him.

"What are you doing, Darcy? You may jeopardize this whole plan if you go rushing through there!" Richard hissed.

"I doubt that she will refuse to see me with the proper inducements."

"*What*? Are you planning on lining her pockets after what she has done?" He demanded.

"Richard, you and I both know that she is too greedy for her own good and judging by the looks of this place she will not hesitate to tell us where they have gone..."

"And what if she was telling Denny the truth, and she really does not know where they have gone?"

"She does and she will, after all it was her son that was driving the carriage- I am sure of it, although how he came to work at Rosings is a mystery. I am not sure what significance it holds, but I am sure that in time we shall find out."

"I hope that you are right, Darcy, because if you are not then you may be putting this whole plan in danger."

"All that I have to tell her is that I followed Denny to her house, and then I can keep this *plan* intact."

Richard hesitated, and then agreed, "Very well, but do be careful. You know what she is capable of."

"Do not worry, I can handle her."

Darcy walked away from them swiftly, and knocked firmly on the door. The same maid that had answered the door for Denny answered for him as well.

"May I 'elp ye, sir?" She was looking him up and down with interest.

"Is your mistress home? I wish to speak with her."

"Aye, she may be, can I give 'er yer name?"

He handed her one of his calling cards along with a coin, and watched her face as she glanced at it. She looked at the coin first and did not appear to recognize the name and Darcy on his card thought it possible she was illiterate. She curtsied to him, and went to a hall to her right. She heard some loud voice, before the woman came back to say that her mistress was busy at present and could not see him. He placed a guinea in her hand and told her that he would make it worth her while. The maid left again, and returned quickly to show him to a room.

Sitting behind a small desk, Mrs. Younge looked like a cat in search of prey.

"What a delightful surprise to see you here of all places, Mr. Darcy. Do not tell me that you are here looking for a room?"

"You can stop the small talk, Mrs. Younge. I am sure you know why I am here. I followed one Captain Denny here, and at once recognized the address." He lied. "I have good reason to believe that you know who I am looking for, and likely you also know where they are."

"I am sure I have no idea to what you are referring…"

"Cut the act, Mrs. Younge! You know where my cousin and Miss Bennet are, and I want to know!"

"Really Mr. Darcy… you presume too much!" She hissed.

"You may stop the dramatics now. I think I know of a way to jog your memory." He laid out a three more guineas and watched as her eyes widen a little.

She shrugged her shoulders, "I may be able to get in contact with him, but it may take me a little time…"

"I do not have a great deal of patience when it comes to people I care for."

"Yes, I can understand… George taking off with two of your ladies…"

"Mrs. Younge, you are trying my patience even more, *and for the record*, I have only had one fiancée"

She smirked, and said, "If you say so. It may take a few resources as well to get word to my old friend…"

Darcy knew exactly what she was hinting at and offered her what he thought of as whore's money. "Very well… if you can contact George Wickham and can provide me with his whereabouts, then I may be willing to offer you compensation for your troubles." He nearly spat out.

This was what it took to gain her full cooperation. "You can be assured that I will send word to you as soon as I may, sir. I suppose that you still reside in your old townhouse?"

Darcy nodded, and handed his card to the woman, "See to it that you do so as quickly as you can." He turned on his heel and showed himself out.

He made his way to where Richard was and he said to him, "She has not changed a bit. I am sure she knows where George is going, and we shall find out very soon, but…" He looked at the two colonels and said, "Just to be sure that she is not lying to us, and we should still leave Denny here."

They agreed to keep the house under surveillance, and Denny was to rent a room along with another soldier to keep an eye on the errant soldier while Darcy and the rest of the men returned to their posts. Darcy was starting to feel helpless and despaired that he would not be able to prevent George Wickham from harming her if he did not find her soon. *I will stand by you no matter what happens, Elizabeth, and I will make sure that Wickham pays for this!*

By Thursday afternoon, Elizabeth was growing restless from being kept indoors. Her hostile attitude was starting to annoy Anne De Bourgh. Those ladies took every chance they could to avoid each other, not that Elizabeth could go out of doors, Anne and Wickham planted two burly footmen outside her door, and there was no way that she would be able to overcome them to escape even if she tried.

Wickham had been in and out of the establishment, and offered to escort Anne to the park while taunting Elizabeth.

"If you promise me that you will behave and not try to escape, Elizabeth, I may take you out for a little walk. We all know how much you enjoy the exercise." He smirked.

Anne spoke up; protesting that it was too warm out and Elizabeth may very easily take the opportunity to run away."

"We can bring along some of those footmen, and then she will not be able to leave." Wickham protested.

"What? And then she can make a huge scene while they apprehend her? No I do not think so. We can go out a little later when the sun is not so high and there are fewer people around."

Elizabeth was disappointed, and was still trying to devise a way to run away and send word to town to her family on Gracechurch Street or to her betrothed, who she now dearly missed more than anything. She wondered if Georgiana was staying anywhere near the residence where she was kept, but did not figure that she would even have a chance to see her let alone meet her, since Anne was determined to keep her locked up inside.

I do not know why she even bothers with me. It is evident that she is happy enough keeping Wickham occupied, that he certainly does not need me for any reason. She recalled the last day while she was watching them and listening to them as they filled the house with loud moans whilst in his bedroom. She could not imagine allowing a man to do such things to her to cause her to moan out like that.

I wish that I could just get out and see the sun without a pane of glass to interfere. She saw all of the people walking through the lanes of the park, and the beautiful day outside, and was jealous of them and their freedom. Her mind began to work on a plan to get word to the outside, if she could gain someone's attention she could ask them to post it for her, and started to search for a quill, some paper, and ink.

When she found what she was looking for, she wrote a her letters. One to her father and another to Darcy. If she could find someone to pass it off to, she would offer to pay them for their trouble. When she was sure that no one within the house could see, she opened a small window to gain call out of and gain the attention of a passerby.

The middle aged woman of medium build looked kindly enough. When Elizabeth caught the woman's attention she addressed her quietly, "Excuse me? Ma'am?"

The woman looked up with surprise that someone was addressing her from nowhere, but did not realize until Elizabeth said, "Up here." Where the voice was coming from.

"I am sorry to bother you, but I need help most urgently. I have been taken from my family and loved ones and need to get word to them. Can you help me?"

Elizabeth was met by an alarmed and curious look from the woman, who glanced around before approaching the window, "What has happened my dear? Were you tricked into leaving?"

"No, ma'am." Elizabeth said quickly, "I was taken by force. I did not want to go, and have been held for the last few days. Please if you could find it in your heart to help me… by posting these letters, my family will know that I am all right, and they can come and get me."

The woman looked at her again with a skeptical look, but Elizabeth was desperate and wore that expression sincerely as tears started to well in her eyes. The lady seemed to sense this and agreed to take her letters and post them, and she would try to contact help.

"Miss, I am a companion to a young woman whose brother is quite wealthy, and has many connections. Though he is not with us now, her other guardian was to come and take us back to town soon. I am sure that once they hear of this they will not hesitate to help you… by bringing you with us to town if need be. In the meantime I shall post these letters for you, and I will come back to see that you are still safe."

Elizabeth felt instant relief at the kindness of this stranger and prayed that the post had not left Bath that day before the woman could send it.

"Bless you, madam. I shall make sure that you are compensated well for your trouble. Thank you so much!"

"Do not despair, miss. It is only what a good Christian must do. You need not compensate me for doing the right thing. Now I suggest that you take care. I would not wish for anything to happen to you." Then, as an afterthought, she asked, "By the way… may I know your name?"

"Elizabeth… Elizabeth Bennet."

"Well, Miss Bennet, I am Mrs. Ainesley, pleased to make your acquaintance."

"Thank you Mrs. Ainesley, Thank you *very* much"

Mrs. Ainesley nodded to her, and looked around again before smiling up to her. "I shall come 'round tomorrow about two o'clock. Try to meet me here, and let me know how you are doing, promise me?"

"I promise." Elizabeth agreed.

It was the first time in three days that Elizabeth started to feel hopeful. She prayed that the letters reach town in time to help her. Wickham was becoming more and more familiar with her at each passing day.

Chapter 10

By Friday Darcy was desperately awaiting word from Mrs. Younge as to the whereabouts of Wickham and thus Elizabeth and Anne. He enlisted the assistance of the runners from Bow Street as well as some private investigators to track down anyone who might know the direction their carriage was heading. He was fairly certain that they had at least stayed at Mrs. Younge's overnight then left very early in the morning. There was no one else in town that would harbor him, and town was most definitely where they were headed.

It was frustrating that the troops that Richard had sent were not able to arrive until after Wickham left with Elizabeth and Anne, and Darcy understood why the runners were unable to get there before then. They had enough on their hands with other crimes that went on—especially in *that* area of town. *Are the heavens conspiring against us now?* He wondered in despair.

For the tenth time he castigated himself for not going to the house on Edwards Street immediately after obtaining the address. He felt that it was safe to wait to go there due to George's usual lack of funds allowing further travel, but failed to take into account that his aunt, Lady Catherine, may have already paid him for his part in the abduction. *It would be unusual for her to have given him any money though. She would generally back out of paying for almost anything, claiming some unmentioned stipulation or other being unmet. He could have taken them anywhere by now!* Darcy searched his mind for answers.

Where could they go without drawing too much attention? Anne's name alone would be enough to cause recognition, and if someone saw their party they would think.... What would they think? George is so charming that he could conjure up any lie and make it sound plausible! Darcy was growing more frustrated as he thought of his dearest Elizabeth at the mercy of that man, especially after what he saw George do to Anne; he was starting to lose hope of Wickham not turning his carnal lust upon his much more attractive fiancée.

He felt he had to do something-anything, to distract himself. It was hard to stand by and wait. Richard was using all of his contacts within the army to gain more intelligence, but they were gaining no more information as to the whereabouts of Wickham or his hostages. Darcy decided to go to the Gardiner's home and find out if there was any new word there.

This is unbearable! How can I keep this up? I shall go mad! Darcy thought to himself as he donned his coat and gloves. He mounted his horse in the back of the house, for he did not wish to attract any more attention to himself. After his whole ordeal Monday night, it seemed as if all of London was eager to catch a glimpse of him and it grated on his nerves to be made into some sort of a spectacle.

Darcy was so lost to his own thoughts that he did not notice the express rider coming upon his house in an urgent manner. As one man approached the front of the house the other was leaving from the back. There were several people who had tried to engage him in conversation lately that he would just as soon avoid. Caroline Bingley being one of them. Both she and Mrs. Hurst tried to insinuate themselves into his home this past week wanting to discuss the '*debacle*' of Charles reuniting with Miss Jane Bennet.

It infuriated him how they seemed to be so insensitive to his most pressing concern of Elizabeth and Anne being taken. At one point he had even thought that they could just as likely be accused of supporting such a scheme to remove the two ladies he had either been rumored to or actually been engaged to marry in order for Caroline to try to pursue him. The very thought of being married to that woman caused him to shudder involuntarily. *I would just as soon join a monastery than marry that insufferable shrew!*

On Thursday, Darcy and Richard had come to Bingley's house and unfortunately arrived at the same time as Mrs. Hurst and Miss Bingley. Before he could avoid having to address them they quickly joined him.

"Mr. Darcy-what a pleasant surprise to see you here! Louisa and I were just saying before we arrived that we wondered what horrible things you had to endure during your captivity, were we not, Louisa?" Miss Bingley said.

Darcy was surprised at being addressed as such without an acknowledgement of Elizabeth or his cousins abductions-especially since Richard was standing right next to him.

"Oh yes, we thought that perhaps you might even wish to be away from town. You know there are rumors abound that you have announced your engagement to Miss Eliza Bennet! They even say that it came straight from you, but we knew that to be impossible." Mrs. Hurst looked at him appraisingly.

It would be impossible for me to consider marrying a woman like you, Caroline, Darcy thought to himself. *Elizabeth has much more class and grace than many of the women of our society.*

"That is quite right… we would know better than anyone else about that-especially after you helped us to remove Charles from Netherfield. Now Jane Bennet has managed to let Charles know she is in town. Can you believe the nerve! This could turn out to be quite the debacle! She must have written to him herself in order to worm her way back into his good opinion."

"Indeed!" Cried Mrs. Hurst.

At the mention of his part in separating Charles from Miss Bennet, Darcy cringed and noted that Richard was watching him closely.

"Actually, Mrs. Hurst, it was me that informed Charles of Miss Bennet's presence in town… after I managed to secure the hand of her sister, Miss Elizabeth." He managed to say with a neutral face.

The shocked look upon their faces made his irritation at having to see them worth the trouble. Mrs. Hurt's eyes grew wide and they both turned rather pale. They said nothing more, and soon Charles joined them in the foyer.

"Caroline… Louisa? What are you doing here, now? Did I not tell you that Darcy, Fitzwilliam, and I were going out this morning?" Bingley said to his sisters.

"You might have mentioned it…" Mrs. Hurst looked to Miss Bingley.

"Well then, is there something that you two needed, or were you on your way to Bond Street?" Bingley asked his sisters.

"Yes, we were actually on some errands." Miss Bingley looked at Mrs. Hurst, then scooted towards the door, "It was... nice to see you." She said to no one in particular before being handed her gloves and leaving.

"What was that all about?" A baffled Bingley asked.

"Nothing, I assure you." Richard said as he raised his eyebrow to Bingley.

Darcy was brought back to the present when he arrived at Gracechurch Street. He was greeted by the housekeeper, who announced him to Mr. Gardiner in his study. Colonel Hill was present again, and they were speaking with Denny. As soon as Darcy entered the room they stopped talking and looked at him.

"Has there been any word yet, of where Wickham may have gone off to?" Darcy asked Colonel Hill.

"No, not yet, we found someone who said a fine carriage similar to the one Captain Wickham used was headed towards the West, but I doubt that it was them." The colonel answered.

"Why?"

"They said that there was a couple that looked to be married, maybe traveling with a younger sister and the couple did not look as if there was any discord of any kind-they were sighted kissing. I hardly even thought it worth mentioning."

Darcy was disheartened by the news, and thought that he may just start canvassing the neighborhood around Mrs. Younge's himself if they did not get any breaks soon.

When Lord Matlock arrived at Rosings Park mid morning on Wednesday, he was in a very foul mood. After he had thought over what his sister had been saying all of these years, he half blamed himself for not insisting that she see sense and give up her ridiculous plan to unite Anne and Darcy. He for one always thought that his nephew could do so much better in terms of wealth and consequence.

He was very surprised when his nephew announced that he was marrying some country nobody from Hertfordshire, with no dowry or any connections to speak of, and who in fact had relatives in trade. The thought of all of that lost potential galled him, but he would not insist that Darcy break his ties with her. That would be even more disgraceful. Thinking about Miss Elizabeth's current circumstances though, brought him to the reasons for him being at Rosings, and not with his family in town where he belonged. His niece was abducted and ravaged by one of England's worst reprobates and the idea of anything coming of that made him furious.

To think that Catherine put my niece in the way of that cur! She will have to pay a pretty penny in order to bribe some young man to marry Anne now! Poor thing... she is nothing in the way of looks. It is no wonder that Darcy would want to look elsewhere. He thought to himself as he waited to be announced to his sister.

A loud voice could be heard berating the poor servant who went to announce him, and the man was flush when he returned.

"I am sorry your lordship, I should have led you straight in."

He nodded his head, and said to him, "I could imagine that Lady Catherine does not have absolutely everyone just brought in."

"No, sir." The man answered solemnly, as he showed him into the parlor.

"Andrew, what brings you here so early in the day? Has something happened to Richard, or Darcy? Or is it Beatrice?" Catherine asked.

He frowned at her bellowing and addressed her curtly, "*You know very well why I am here, Catherine!* I heard all about how you had Darcy abducted... and by that *cur* Wickham! Then to add insult to injury your ruffians took Richard when he followed!" He shook his head, "What were you thinking? Do you not even realize now that Anne is not here? That that same cur took off with her as well?"

"*What*? Anne is just upstairs resting! Of what are you talking about? Having my nephews abducted? *Preposterous*!"

"Oh? I know you cannot be absolutely *certain* that Anne is upstairs resting and as to my son and our nephew being abducted-*they told me themselves*! Apparently *you* were the one to sponsor Wickham in order to help with your scheme to force Darcy to marry Anne. Now tell me where he was taking Miss Bennet and Anne!"

Lady Catherine's eyes widened and she blanched at her brother's assertions. She shook her head and appeared flustered, for a moment. "I am sure that I do not know what you are talking about. You are lying! It was not my idea to involve Wickham in taking Darcy and making him see sense-it was Anne...."

"You *dare* to accuse me of lying? Admit it, Catherine! You have not seen her since last night! I know because Richard and Darcy came to town on two of your horses! Horses that they had to take in haste to gather help in finding Anne and Miss Elizabeth Bennet who were taken by George Wickham!" He growled.

"Then that no good hussy must be behind it, somehow!"

"Why? *What* could she possibly have to gain from having her fiancé abducted and brought here to have him married off to Anne? That makes no sense at all, and you know it! You were behind it, admit it! You were always going on about Anne and Darcy marrying to unite Rosings to Pemberley! Tell me was that your great scheme when you arranged to have our sister found in a compromising situation with George Darcy as well?"

"I had nothing to do with that! That was George Darcy's doing...you know how he was always after another lady with a title... and he could have had me..."

"Yet he did not want *you*, and now you plot to have his son kidnapped in order to try and force him to marry *your daughter*, whom I might add has been *utterly compromised*?" By now Andrew was furious and Catherine looked at him with astonishment.

"*Utterly compromised*?" She was becoming more excitable, which repulsed him, "Do you mean to tell me that Darcy and Anne...?"

"*No*! It was not Darcy who plucked her, but George Wickham..."

"*What*? That good for nothing blackguard ravaged my Anne?"

"*Precisely*! You were the one to arrange for him to come here in the first place, and though I feel terrible for what my niece has had to endure for your sins, I cannot find it in me to feel so terribly sorry for you! You are the one responsible for her ruination, but since she is my family I will do whatever is necessary to see to her reputation and well being."

"Andrew... she needs to be married now! If this is the case and we must see to it that Darcy marries her!"

"Absolutely not, Catherine! This is none of his doing or his responsibility and now he is publically engaged to Miss Elizabeth Bennet..."

"*That cannot be!*"

"Yet it is. It has been all over the papers for the last two days," to demonstrate his point he threw, Tuesday's *Times* on her lap, "Read it for yourself. He has publically declared himself and is now bound by honor to marry her. Oh... and do not think that I will try to persuade him to do otherwise. To dishonor his word now would be worse than marrying beneath him."

"You cannot be serious... she will make us a laughingstock!"

"No... *you* will make us the laughingstock for your ridiculous plot and the repercussions that we may yet suffer due to them. Maybe if you are *very lucky*, Darcy may allow Anne to stay at Pemberley with him and his new wife. I would not count on it though. If she has become with child he will not want to expose Georgiana to her in that condition."

"You sound so sure about yourself, Andrew, but how can you be so certain? What makes you think that he will still want that little trollop once George Wickham has had a go at her?"

Hearing his sister say such horrible, cruel things made the earl even more angry. It was the first time in his life that he had ever wanted to slap a woman. *Would I not know that it would be Catherine that should deserve to be assaulted? She is such a wretched human being, that I cannot stand to be around her...* He groused to himself. *I shall have to cut her off from any contact privately. She must be taught to heel once and for all!*

"That is enough, Catherine! To think that you would commission George Darcy's detested bastard to rape Fitzwilliam's fiancée in order to break them up is beyond unconscionable! Now he has gone off and ruined Anne in the mix- I hope that you are proud of yourself, for I am thoroughly ashamed of you! In fact you have caused so much disgrace to our family that I will not tolerated your presence in private. If I thought it would not cause a scandal, I would cut all public ties with you as well, but I will not ruin what has taken this family many generations to build! Consider yourself cut!" He stated as he looked at her directly and turned on his heel to leave. He could still hear her shouting her protests and epithets at him as he walked out to his carriage.

He had no further interest with what his sister's response was. Catherine had caused many arguments over the years within his household and throughout the family. It was also hard for him to forgive her for trying to seduce George Darcy before he married Anne. In fact it was due to her schemes that Anne had to marry that man.

~*~*~*~

It had been nearly thirty years since the earl had to confront a major family issue, and they always seemed to stem from the same person... *Catherine*. She never ceased meddling in other people's lives, and usually when she did, it was small things that would only irritate or inconvenience those who were her chosen victims ... *usually*. The last time she ruined their younger sister, Anne's, life, and all because she was on a quest to obtain George Darcy for herself.

Catherine had sent a note to Lord Westhouse requesting a private meeting outside on the balcony during a spring ball, and signed the letter with Anne's name. What Catherine did not anticipate was George Darcy hearing that man crow over receiving such a letter to some friends. He found out the details of the planned rendezvous and at the appointed time he arranged for a couple of his friends to distract Westhouse long enough to go to the aforementioned balcony. In the mean time Catherine had arranged for their sister to go out to the same balcony on false pretenses, knowing that the other gentleman planned to be there. Once she led Anne to the appointed place she quickly left to retrieve their father.

Her plan to marry the elder Darcy was quickly thrown over when their father came to where Catherine had left Anne, and found George Darcy with her in an embrace. It did not matter whatever protests Anne or Catherine put forth. Their father insisted that George and Anne marry, and Catherine was furious. Since then her jealousy of Anne living at Pembereley festered leading her to believe that if she could not have that grand estate, then her daughter would. *Such a waste! Had she been less selfish and underhanded, maybe she could have led a better life than she has. No... mother spoiled you too much for that, Catherine!* He had his carriage waiting to take him back to town, as he was not planning to stay for very long after he had spoken his peace with her.

The earl wished that he could help in more ways than threatening his sister, but she was either uninformed of her accomplice plans or too proud to own up to her part in this whole fiasco. *You did it to yourself Catherine, and now you can sit and stew in your own juices!*

~*~*~*~

When Mrs. Annesley arrived back at the rented house that she was staying with Miss Darcy, she had not thought to read the addresses on the letters that she was to post. Her first instinct was to call for the authorities, but then the young lady did not seem to wish for it. *There must be some good reason for her to stay mum about it, but why I cannot fathom! None-the-less I shall ensure that Colonel Fitzwilliam hears about this. He is sure to help once he hears about it, and he should be here very soon.* When she turned the first one over she noted it was addressed to one Thomas Bennet on Gracechurch Street, but when she looked at the other letter she paled.

It was addressed to her employer, Mr. Fitzwilliam Darcy. Her heart was racing at the thought of a young woman in danger that had any connections to the great man, and decided that she must use whatever resources she could to see that the letter got to him as soon as possible. It took great willpower for her not to tear the letter open and read it herself, but she knew that was wrong. Still she felt a need to see to it that everything that could be done was done to help Miss Bennet. She decided to enclose a note of her own to explain the circumstances, and where this building was located.

As soon as the missive was written she sent an express courier with letters in hand to Darcy House in town. She prayed that they would be able to return to Bath with the master and rescue poor Miss Bennet. She wondered how this could have happened in the first place until Friday morning brought most distressing news from town via the newspapers.

The times from Tuesday had read that a Mr. Fitzwilliam Darcy had been abducted with a crowd of reporters standing by, and he was carried away in his own carriage by three men who had commandeered his carriage. What was worse was that Colonel Fitzwilliam was also missing, and they had few leads as to his whereabouts. *Has the whole country gone mad? Are these kidnappings in any way related? How are we going to help Miss Bennet if the master and colonel are missing as well?* She knew that Miss Georgiana would be most distressed by such news, and felt that she need to find out more information before she broke the news to her.

It was with great delicacy that she instructed the staff to avoid mentioning what had been reported in the newspapers until they had heard from town. She knew that the express rider, Anthony, would return and could have more recent news from there, so she implored them to keep quiet until they knew more.

She still wanted to go back to the house where Miss Bennet was and she wanted to wait until their appointed time, but she was growing restless and anxious and felt that a walk in the park may help settle her. When Miss Georgiana finished her lessons for the morning they agreed to go out in order to enjoy the good weather and Mrs. Annesley also wanted to distract herself from all of the distressing news. They made their way around to the center of the park and decided to stop and sit for a rest.

Miss Darcy asked, "Is there something the matter, Mrs. Annesley?"

"Why do you ask, Miss Georgiana?"

"It is just that you seem… somewhat distracted, and I noticed that some of the other staff will not even look at me." Miss Georgiana sounded nervous.

"I am a bit distracted." She paused to contemplate telling her charge about her strange encounter with the master's fiancée. "I have met a young woman that has been taken away from her family and friends against her will, and I think that you may have heard of her… Miss Elizabeth Bennet?"

The young girls eyes widened as did her mouth to form an 'O' shape. "Y-yes, she is … she is engaged to Fitzwilliam! What has happened to her? Is she all right? What can we do to help her?"

"I thought you may have heard of her. I believe that she was abducted and brought here, but I do not know why. Her captors have her watched very closely from what I could tell. As to her well being… I think for the moment that she is doing as well as can be expected, but she is most anxious to be relieved of her circumstances, and I have promised her that I would send word to her family and… she had even written a letter to Mr. Darcy. I did not know who she was at first, but when I saw that she had addressed a letter to him. I knew that she must be the young woman that he was to marry. I have already sent an express messenger with a note and her letter to Darcy House in town." She did not want to reveal that it may not even be received by the intended addressee, but she hoped that someone would come or send word so that she would know how to deal.

"Oh, Mrs. Annesley, this is most awful! But… I am sure that once Fitzwilliam receives those letters he will come and help Miss Bennet and he will likely bring Richard as well. They will know how to deal with this, but we have to make sure that she is well… Do you think that we should contact the constable?"

"You can be assured that I will, but I must talk to her before I do. I got the feeling that she was trying to protect someone, and I have already made arrangements to meet her again today this afternoon to see how she is getting along. When she gained my notice from a window... she seemed as though she were pressed for time. Like she may have been discovered at any time."

"Do you think I could come as well? I would like to meet her, and do what I can to help."

"Miss Georgiana, that is very kind of you, however, if we were to be discovered then you may be put in danger as well and Mr. Darcy has entrusted your safety to me. I am afraid that you must wait to meet her when things are not quite so precarious."

She also did not want to add that she could be in great danger of being taken as well if she were to be seen near the establishment.

Miss Darcy looked somewhat disappointed, but seemed to understand the wisdom in what she said.

"I can understand that, but it is still so awful to think that there are people out there that would do such a thing. I wonder... did she say if she knew these people, or why they had taken her?"

"I cannot say, for I do not know, but you can be sure that once Mr. Darcy and the colonel find out they will be dealt with harshly, I am sure."

Her young companion nodded her head and looked away distractedly. She glanced in the same direction as Miss Georgiana. In the distance was a couple out for a stroll in the park. The young man seemed to resemble a small portrait that she had seen somewhere before, but she did recognize the woman. It was none other than Anne De Bourgh. *What is she doing here in Bath... and with a suitor?*

Judging by the way they were talking and how close they walked together there was no other explanation than the two being a couple. She had almost missed Miss Darcy's gasp, as the young woman turned away from the visual line of the couple.

"Is something wrong, Miss Georgiana? Are you all right, dear?"

"M-Mr. Wickham!" She looked at her with terror in her eyes.

"Mr. Wickham?"

"H-he is the man from Brighton." She said quietly.

That is where I have heard that name before. It was the reason why she held her current position, and immediately she understood the reason for her charges frightened look. Though she did not know all of the particulars, she knew enough to understand that the man tried to use his considerable charms to try to maneuver Miss Darcy into an impossible situation. She also knew that had Mr. Darcy not arrived to see his sister a few days earlier than planned she would have likely been bound to an opportunistic cur.

When she spotted the cousin to her charge and employer, she was very surprised that Lady Catherine De Bourgh would allow such a man anywhere near her '*dear Anne*'. From what she knew of that formidable woman, she thought that no one less than a titled man with great wealth, minor royalty or Mr. Darcy were good enough for her daughter. *I wonder if she even knows the man's reputation?* She pondered. That thought was quickly followed by another more alarming one.

I must remove Miss Georgiana, she seems to be getting more and more agitated and it would not do to have these two meet. Perhaps we should warn Miss De Bourgh about her gentleman? I doubt that she would bear his company if she knew what kind of a man he really is.

"Miss Georgiana? Shall we return to the house?"

"Y-yes." She looked at Mr. Wickham and Miss De Bourgh before looking back at Miss Darcy, "I should like to warn Anne about him, but I do not even know where she is staying. I had no idea that she was even coming to Bath."

"Would you like for me to walk you back to the house and then I can come back to the park and discretely follow them?"

"Oh-would you, please? I do not think that I could rest knowing that he could take advantage of my family again!"

"Then I would be delighted to do so." Mrs. Annesley assured her. "Let us return to the house and then I will come back here as quickly as I can."

They made their way to their residence and Mrs. Annesley returned to the park just in time to catch a glimpse of where they were heading. She became even more concerned when she noticed them walking towards the same house where Miss Elizabeth was being held. When they came to that very house she was downright alarmed.

What is this all about? Is Lady Catherine staying here, or did she rent it for Miss De Bourgh and her companion? Did they bring Miss Elizabeth here to keep her from marrying Mr. Darcy? Are they planning on forcing the master to marry Miss De Bourgh? No wonder she did not want me to contact the authorities! Mr. Darcy should know about this as soon as may be!

As she watched them go inside the house she wondered at the candor that the couple seemed to be exhibiting in public. They were obviously not chaperoned and that was enough to cause her concern, but then knowing who was inside made it all the worse. She knew from her many years of experience that a woman of Miss De Bourgh's station was expected to marry well and socializing with such a man as Mr. Wickham would jeopardize that.

We must get to the bottom of this! Lord I hope that Mr. Darcy is well and back home. I must write to town again and ensure that he is notified, and if nothing else, Lord Matlock needs to know. She turned back towards the house where Miss Georgiana awaited her and walked quickly, but not before observing the window where she had met Miss Bennet. She was not observed, and Mrs. Annesley hoped that she was still well. *I shall still return later to let Miss Bennet know what I have found out. I think that Mr. Wickham and Miss De Bourgh are up to no good!*

When Darcy returned home he was greeted by Holder who informed him that he had received two express letters and that they were on his desk. He immediately went to his study and found them, and was alarmed to see an express come from Mrs. Annesley but then he saw the letter with Elizabeth's handwriting. Quickly he tore it open and read:

Thursday 13 May 1809

?Bath?

My Dearest Fitzwilliam,

I have had this letter sent by an utter stranger and am in hopes that this has reached you in good time. As you can see by the address above I believe that I am being held in a house in Bath. It certainly looks as Bath has been described and I have seen the signs on the road, but I cannot be certain. I can see a park from a narrow window and there are passersby, and in giving this note to this as of yet nameless and kind person, I leave my destiny in their hands.

No doubt you are wondering how your cousin and me are, and I can easily say that Anne De Bourgh is doing quite well. In fact it seems that she and Mr. Wickham have had previous dealings with each other. They are on friendly terms and act quite familiar with each other. I have learned that your aunt, Lady Catherine, was not the mastermind of this whole scheme from Anne herself.

It appears that through her dealings with Mr. Wickham she has plotted to marry you and unite Rosings with Pemberley while still continuing her connections with him. I first learned of this when we were racing away from that cottage in Hunsford. Though it was dark, I know where we were, for I spent a great deal of time there before we left for town. I must say that I was alarmed at the friendliness between the two; however, nothing could have prepared me to witness their kissing.

When she told me of her plot to take you as her husband, and still keep Mr. Wickham I was furious for her duplicity against you. I would never wish to see you hurt in such a way, though I think I have known you well enough to know you would never be forced into any arrangement that you did not wish. That also brings me to my next thought. She had offered Mrs. Younge money to see to it that my reputation was in tatters. By what was said and insinuated, Mr. Wickham has promised to see to it that it is done by whatever means. He has not touched me in such a way and I think that Anne is drawing his attentions elsewhere-for that I can at least be grateful.

The thought of that man touching me makes me ill, and I would much rather die than bear it, though it seems that Anne feels rather differently. It may sound selfish under the circumstances to think only of my own happiness, but I have come to value you and realize what a good man you are. You are truly the best of men, and if it were possible, I would marry you today. I pray that you find this in good time, but if we shall never see one another again, please know that I have come to love and value you more than any other.

With all my love,

Elizabeth

As soon as Darcy read the letter he ordered his horse to be made ready immediately and sent a note to Matlock House to Richard and the earl and to Gracechurch Street. His carriage would also be sent there after him. Should Mr. Bennet or any of Elizabeth's family wish to join him they would be welcomed to stay at the house in Bath.

Before he left Darcy House, he made certain that he had his fa.... s pistols and a sword. He would take no chances with Wickham, and there was no way that he would allow anymore harm to come to Elizabeth. As to Anne... he still had no idea what to think, much less what he will do once everything was said and done.

Chapter 11

Darcy rode towards Bath as quickly as his mount, Zephyrus, could take him. Richard joined him as soon as he dispatched the intelligence to headquarters as well, but had a time keeping up with him on his somewhat slower mount. Mr. Bennet sent word that he would leave for Bath as soon as possible, but that Mr. Gardiner had some business matters that he needed to tend to and could not come with him immediately. As far as Darcy was concerned, that was just as well. The older gentleman would never be able to keep up with him or Richard anyway.

He was still astounded to learn of Anne's connivance in this whole scheme after re-reading Elizabeth's letter and could not believe that Lady Catherine would ever condone such a connection. As they traveled west towards Bath, Darcy tried to block the image of Wickham with Elizabeth and for a moment was actually relieved that Anne was keeping him occupied and distracted from his beloved. How much longer could she remain safe worried him more than anything.

The ride was long and hard, but he did not pay any heed to his surroundings or his fatigue and discomfort. He had a single purpose and that was to rescue his Elizabeth. At the speed that they traveled there was no conversation, but every once in a while the gentlemen would communicate by their expressions and most of the time Darcy was looking at his cousin with frustration due to his trailing behind him. Richard on the other hand expressed perturbation-mostly directed to his companion who easily had one of the finest horses in England and was quite possibly the fastest as well.

By the time they reached Reading, they were both extremely winded, and knew that they needed to rest their horses if they were to make it to Bath in the same day. They were also famished and needed rest, and though Darcy may have had the fastest mount, he was not used to being atop a horse for such long distances at a time. It normally took him at least a day to recover from the trip from Kent to town and now he was on another longer trek without much rest in the past few days.

Richard cautiously approached him with a suggestion after they had sat down for a warm meal at the nearest inn to the road.

"Darcy… I know that you want to get to Miss Elizabeth as soon as possible, and frankly I would like to get to Bath just to get to the bottom of this, but… do you not think that it would be wise to rest? Just for a little while?"

"No! Richard… you know as well as I do that George Wickham is capable of anything-especially after this! And do not forget that Georgiana is also in Bath. If George finds out that she is there, who knows what else he will do! We must get there as soon as may be!"

"*Listen to me.* We will not be able to rescue anyone in the shape we are in right now, and if we get ourselves killed along the way then there will be no one to stop Anne and George from doing whatever they please with Elizabeth. Would you prefer that?"

"Of course not!" Darcy said petulantly. "But, what is to stop him from doing what he will to her… maybe even killing her just to spite me?"

"He is not going to do anything to her until he can be assured that you are there to witness him doing it. That is what he ultimately wants anyway… to see you suffer and if you are not there to witness it then he will be less tempted. As for Georgiana, she is in the very capable hands of Mrs. Annesley and I do not think that *she* will allow anything to happen to Georgiana. Besides, was she not the one to write to you and tell you that she was intending to return to the house where Elizabeth is being kept and see to her well being herself?"

"Yes, she was and I trust the woman with my life right now- for if anything were to happen to Elizabeth then there would be no reason for me to keep going…"

"*Would you listen to yourself?*" Richard hissed, "You sound as if you are giving up already. Look… I am not saying that we should stop here and dawdle around. As soon as we are rested then we should go on to Bath, and rescue your damsel in distress. I know how these things go. Even in battle, I must allow my men to rest every now and then, otherwise they are no good to me and you are in the same situation. Do you think that we are just going to march up to the door where she is being kept and they will simply hand her over to you? Their whole purpose in taking her with them in the first place is to force you to see her suffer."

Darcy considered the wisdom of what his cousin said and though he was desperate to reunite with Elizabeth he also knew that they would likely have some challenges in retrieving her from her present situation. After a moment of contemplation he finally capitulated to Richards's request.

"Very well, but as soon as we and the horses are rested up, then we shall be on our way, agreed?"

"Agreed." Richard said with some relief.

When the maid had come with their meals, they requested that rooms be let for them to rest in quiet for a while. As soon as they were taken to their rooms they laid down to res, requesting that as soon as the horses were ready that they be awakened. Though thoughts of the past few days was enough to keep them awake before, as soon as they closed their eyes they went to sleep from sheer exhaustion.

It was early the next morning when they were aroused from their slumber. Both men were deep in thought as they ate their breakfast. Their horses were ready as soon as they were done eating, and almost as soon as Darcy mounted his horse he kicked Zephyrus into a fast gallop leading the way to Bath. Richard was soon catching up to him and they had a competition of sorts as to who could ride the fastest to certain destinations along the way.

By late morning they manage to make it all the way to the house in Bath where Georgiana stayed with Mrs. Annesley. Darcy was greeted enthusiastically by his sister as she leapt into his arms for a tight embrace. They led her to a quiet sitting room, where Mrs. Annesley was seated already.

"Oh brother...! I am so glad that you have come! Mrs. Annesley and I have been so worried about Miss Bennet, and I must tell you something..." She stopped suddenly and blushed.

Both Darcy and Richard looked at her in expectation and encouragement then looked at her companion for more explanations, though she only shrugged her shoulders and shook her head at what the girl was going to say and then joined them in awaiting her next words.

"Well? Are you going to make us wait here all day to hear it, Georgie?" Richard half teased.

"Of course not. It is just that... I have more news to tell you..."

"And?" Darcy demanded. "What news do you have to impart, dearest?" He asked with some strain, afraid of what she may have to reveal.

"Yesterday Mrs. Annesley and I went to the park and... we saw George Wickham... with Anne!" Her eyes were as wide as saucers as she looked between him and Richard.

He and Richard looked at each other with a frown. Darcy's mind started to race along with his heart, and he could feel himself breaking out in a cold sweat. *That blackguard was taking a stroll in the park with Anne in public while keeping Elizabeth locked up? What are they up to?* It galled him to think that his own cousin could betray him as much as it did when he finally realized what kind of a person George really was. *They deserve each other, and if they wish to keep the other's company then far be it from me to stop them. May they rot in hell for all I care!*

"Georgiana..." Darcy said quietly, "We already know about them. Apparently they have come here by design and with full knowledge of what they are doing. I do not know what you have learned from town, but Anne had George Wickham abduct me Monday night, but I managed to escape. When he discovered this, he came back to town and took Elizabeth in my place."

"But why would she do such a thing?"

He had no desire to go into the sordid details of what had occurred between George and Anne, but he would not scruple to reveal their duplicity in trying to trap him into marriage to Anne.

"She wanted to marry me to unite Pemberley to Rosings and if I were married to Elizabeth her plans would have been ruined-they still will be because, I will *never* marry her."

"I still do not understand why she would allow George to court her and want to marry *you*... or anyone else for that matter. And it still does not explain why they would take Miss Elizabeth with them. Unless they knew that you would find out where she was and come for her..."

That thought hung in the air causing Darcy to think that perhaps there was another reason that Anne and George allowed themselves to be seen in the park and in public. No one in their right mind would do such brazen things unless they wanted to be found, and for once, he was glad that Richard was there and made him wait to come to Bath.

"Darcy, she has a point you know. Neither Anne nor George is that stupid. They had this whole elaborate plan plotted out for some time by the looks of things. How else could they have managed to get a house in Bath in this neighborhood on such short notice? I think that they were planning on your coming here all along, though I doubt that they had planned on Miss Elizabeth getting word to anybody-let alone Mrs. Annesley. Perhaps we can use that to our advantage…"

"How so?" Darcy asked.

"They do not know that we are already in Bath and they cannot have been spotted that long ago, correct, Georgiana?"

"No, it was just yesterday that Mrs. Annesley and I saw them together in the park." She confirmed.

"That is to our greater advantage then. They would not expect that the news of their sighting would have reach town this soon. It would take the post about a day to reach town, and a letter would not be delivered on a Sunday, so they would have a couple of days to ready themselves for our eventual arrival."

"What makes you think that, Richard? Would Anne not want to conceal her association with such a man? And what of Aunt Catherine? She would be furious about that." Georgiana asked.

"For a beginning, Aunt Catherine was also involved in this *little plot*, though I doubt that she knows about Anne and Wickham's closer involvement. She *would* be, or should I say, *will be* furious once it is generally known that her daughter is associating with a fortune seeking cad and criminal-not to mention a deserter in His Majesty's Army. Father will no longer associate with her in private anymore even-though I must say I have no idea why he does not just cut all ties with the two of them!"

"They are still family, Richard, no matter how much we may wish to forget it. It will reflect upon us all regardless of how we do or *do not* wish acknowledge it. Society in general will judge us based upon our associations to them. What the earl is doing is acknowledging her as his sister because it is undeniable, but refusing to associate with her privately sends the message that he does not condone her behavior." Darcy speculated.

"I still think that we should tie them up together and ship them all off to the America's or Australia-perhaps in the eye of a hurricane." Richard chimed in.

Georgiana and Darcy both snorted at his idea, but Darcy would have to decide what he would do for retribution. Their behavior had to be answered for especially since word of Elizabeth's disappearance had been widely circulated and if she were missing for much longer her reputation would be irreparably ruined. Suddenly he had an idea that would possibly save face for at least some of them.

"I quite agree that they need to be punished, but I do not want you or Georgiana to suffer from their follies."

"After what has happened, I do not see how we can avoid it, Darcy."

"I have an idea of how we may be able to avoid it..." He looked at Richard and then Georgiana who were giving him their undivided attention. "People do not know about our aunt or cousin's involvement with this whole scheme, but they already know about some of the men who abducted me. The public also does not know where I am..."

"Yes?" Richard said impatiently.

"What if-when we rescue Elizabeth, we arrange for a quiet wedding here in Bath? I already have a special license and Mr. Bennet will be arriving here by late today or early tomorrow. Then we can tell people that we arranged to have her removed from town for her own safety and also in order for us get married quietly. It would spare her reputation, and if pressed we could say that we knew nothing of Wickham or Anne's involvement with each other. That would not be entirely false in any case."

"That sounds plausible, but what about that Darcy stance on always telling the absolute truth about everything?"

"Richard, I would not advertise such things openly. It is no one's business what occurred with us, but if pressed then that would be the official story and for the record I do not condone concealment, but this is protecting innocent people-namely Elizabeth and that is *paramount to anything*. You know enough people in the army that I am sure that you could convince them to go along with it, thinking it had something to do with our disappearance."

"It may work... for a few coins, I am sure." Richard said reluctantly.

"It would be worth it to spare Elizabeth."

Georgiana was looking at Darcy apprehensively and he felt at that moment that he had failed her, but he knew of no other way to resolve all of these difficulties without doing some subverting of the truth.

"I know that it is not what I would normally condone, but honestly I can think of no better plan without risking several innocent people's reputations and since it is being done to protect the innocent, I really feel it is the best way to approach this..."

"You are right, Fitzwilliam," Georgiana said quietly, "I know that you had also kept quiet about what happened last summer as well, and that was to protect me. I thought at the time that it was my own doing and that I deserved whatever reputation that I was given should I be exposed, but now I realize that it was not me that was at fault... at least not mostly at fault. George did what he did to hurt you... or us, and he was doing so by hurting innocent people. Nobody deserves to be treated thusly, and I understand why you need to do this. In fact... I am quite looking forward to having a sister within the household that I may be proud of."

Hearing Georgiana's support for his plan was a relief to Darcy. He was glad to hear that she was looking forward to getting to know Elizabeth, and understood why he needed to do or say those things. His next issue was the actual rescuing of his fiancée. In order for him to get her out safely he would need to communicate with her to let her know what his plans were to get her away from her prison.

"Mrs. Annesley?" He directed his attention to the lady, "When are you going to the house where Miss Bennet is being held?"

"I go around two o'clock in the afternoon." The lady answered. "But she was not there yesterday. I think the guards were a little too close for her to come to the window."

"Have you noticed anybody guarding the place on the outside?" Richard asked distractedly.

"Yes, there were at least two men at each exit on the front and back. I went there yesterday to check out the residence to assess the veracity of the young woman's words. Especially when I could not meet with her." When everyone looked at her with raised eyebrows, she explained further, "After I saw Miss De Bourgh with Mr. Wickham, I could not be too certain that everything was as it had been presented to me. I saw that in Miss Bennet's case, she was at least being truthful about being under guard."

"Well done!" Exclaimed Richard.

"Did you happen to notice if they were carrying any weapons?" Darcy asked with agitation.

"No sir, I could not tell if they were or not."

"Then we must assume that they are all carrying some sort of weapon." Richard said to Darcy. "Maybe we should request more help?"

"Richard, we are no match for at least four men who may or may not be heavily armed. There is no 'maybe' about it." Darcy answered shortly.

"I am not referring to just us, but Colonel Hill and his men. They will be joining us here."

"How do you know that?"

"Because I went by the barracks before going over to Darcy House. The man has an amazing collection of weapons. He even let me borrow a few-in case we might need them."

"Humph." Darcy replied, wishing that he had also stopped there before he left town. *If I had though, I may have taken more time to get here in Bath and my horse would not thank me for carrying such weight.*

"Seriously though, Darcy, we need to make certain what we are getting into before we rush in and get ourselves killed."

"I know, Richard." He with irritation. "It is just that I am worried about Elizabeth. I do not trust Wickham, and the docile Anne we have known is no more. What if they have done her any harm?"

"I doubt it. Like I have said, they do not know that you are already here and they will not be expecting you for another two days, at least. If you go and do something rash and stupid you may not only risk yourself but her as well. How would you deal with that?" Richard asked.

It was a sobering thought to Darcy. In no way did he want to do anything that would put her in jeopardy. If he had to risk his own life to save hers he would gladly do so, but he hoped that it would not come to that. His true desire was that by week's end they could be married and put this whole nightmare behind them.

"You have made your point." He said resignedly. "What do you propose that we do while we wait for them?"

"I propose that we send Mrs. Annesley out on her usual stroll, and make some observations for us while we wait. If there is anything unusual going on, she can come back and tell us. We should also let the militia's commanding officer know that we are here and that we suspect that a man who is wanted for desertion is at a certain residence... but that he has accomplices and they may be armed."

"Will they not want to go in immediately then, and arrest Wickham?"

"Not if they may have a small battle on their hands. No responsible commander would willingly put any civilians in harm's way."

"You had better be right." Darcy added.

They had no other choice but to wait for reinforcements, and more information. Richard took on the task of informing the local militia's commanding officer of the situation with Wickham, leaving out some of the more sordid details. Suffice to say they would be ready sooner than they had expected to enter the residence where Elizabeth was with many reinforcements. Apparently the local commanding officer had a particular dislike for those who would abandon their posts and was eager to make a point to those who might be tempted to do so.

Darcy would not openly admit it, but he thought he would not mind watching this particular punishment... *and Wickham is such a deserving man for it.*

Elizabeth was awaiting another visit from the kindly Mrs. Annesley in the narrow window in the pantry. If she could have wiggled herself through the panes she would have escaped by now, but she was a little too well endowed in places and it would have been impossible to wriggle through them without rousing too much attention not to mention the great possibility of getting herself stuck, giving the men guarding her quite a view.

Her dignity she could easily overlook, but the idea of a man seeing her exposed would have been mortifying, not to mention put her in some danger of being violated several different ways. *I hope that Mrs. Annesley comes with good news today. I cannot imagine having to live like a prisoner unable to go out as I please whenever I please, and at the mercy of these horrible people!*

She had been late meeting the woman yesterday and by the time she had gotten to the closet it was already twenty minutes past two. Elizabeth was greatly distressed that she had missed the woman and hoped and prayed that she would come again today. The relief that she felt when she saw that her guardian angel had come for her could not be expressed in words.

Mrs. Annesley waited across the park adjacent to the house under the shade of some trees until Elizabeth came to the window. When she saw the woman, she waved at her through the opened window with her handkerchief. The lady approached Elizabeth to address her as quietly as she could.

"Miss Bennet?"

"Yes, Mrs. Annesley? Are you well today?"

"Yes, Miss, I am fine, but I should be asking you the same question. I have been worried about you since I met you yesterday. I wanted to inform you of a great coincidence though."

"What is that?"

"I found out that my employer is your affianced, Mr. Fitzwilliam Darcy. I am the companion to Miss Georgiana Darcy…"

"Oh?" She asked with unconcealed excitement. "Is he well? Has he come with you?"

"He looks well enough for what he has been through and he sent me here to see how you are fairing. How long do you have before they become suspicious of your whereabouts, Miss Bennet? We should not risk you being found."

"We should have at least fifteen minutes, as the guards are… busy at the moment with a… chambermaid." She blushed at what she had said, but knew that she had a little time before she was missed. Elizabeth could hardly believe her luck when the woman related to her who she was and what she had done; Elizabeth's elation could be seen throughout her face and her eyes as tears formed in them. She thought that perhaps the heavens were taking mercy upon her and that is why she had found the one woman in Bath that could help her the most. The lady told her of how she sent an express to town along with her own letter describing the house and the address and now Darcy was in Bath arranging for her rescue as they spoke.

"I suspected that something was even more amiss yesterday when we saw a man Miss Darcy identified as Mr. Wickham escorting Miss De Bourgh for a walk in the park. They did not look as though they were having any difficulties, and she did not look as though she were distressed by his presence."

"No, she is not. She is apparently the one who orchestrated Mr. Darcy's abduction in order to force him to marry her and unite their two estates. They say that they have *other* agreements between each other and it shall not interfere with her being married to him. As to why they dragged me along…"

"I can easily imagine, miss. I have heard tales about the man. I do not even use the term gentleman because *that* he certainly is *not*. He has allegedly *interfered* with at least three men's daughters in Derbyshire alone and I am sure that that is not the beginning nor will it be the end of his transgressions. That is why we need to remove you from here as soon as may be. Are you in any immediate danger?"

"I do not think so. It seems that Anne has been keeping Mr. Wickham rather... occupied."

"Are you certain that you are all right for now, Miss Bennet?" Mrs. Annesley asked with concern.

"Other than being held as a prisoner by despicable people in a town that is foreign to me?" Her voice started to crack.

"Miss... do not despair. I am sure that once Mr. Darcy has all of his people in place that he will come right away. He would not turn his back on anyone that he has befriended much less intended to make his wife. I am sure that he will be here very soon."

"You make it sound as if he is a paragon of employers..." Elizabeth smiled through her tears.

"And why would I not? He is the very best of men."

"I have seen that in him as well. Apparently it is not just with me..." Elizabeth said as more of a thought than a statement. "Mrs. Annesley... would you please do me a favor?"

"Why of course, Miss Bennet."

"If anything should happen to me... I mean... if I should not be returned to my family... would you please let him know that... that I love him?"

"Of course I should let him know, but I think he should like it much more coming from you. He will come, you shall see, and you two will be married."

There was a noise coming from the hall, "Mrs. Annesley..." Elizabeth whispered, "I have to go now."

The noise from outside the pantry was getting louder and Elizabeth tried to hide under a cupboard but Anne found her before she could conceal herself completely.

"*What* are you *doing*, Elizabeth? Do not think that you can conceal yourself under there. You are not as small as a child, and contrary to any of your beliefs, we are not going to forget about your presence ... much as I might try. Oh... and cowering will get you nowhere either, *dear*."

Though Elizabeth was slightly humiliated at being found out she was not going to take the insults hurled at her lying down, or in this case crouched down. She stood up to her full height and approached Anne getting up within inches of her face.

"I would *never* cower to you, Anne. You are not so significant that I would ever even entertain that notion. In fact..." She looked her up and down, "you are of no significance at all. I really have no idea what Mr. Wickham or any man would ever see in you-aside from your dowry."

When Anne drew back her hand, Elizabeth quickly intercepted grabbing her at the wrist and leaned into her almost touching her nose to nose, "*Do not ever try to touch me again.* I will be the victor in any altercation with *you!*"

She continued to glare at the woman for a minute until she threw her hand down and turned on her heel to walk out of the closet. She did not notice Anne glaring into her back or her turning to see the open window as she went to the sitting room.

Wickham returned to the residence shortly, and Anne dragged him into the room they used as a study. Elizabeth could hear loud voices that seemed to only get louder until the door opened. She moved away quickly, but was unable to move fast enough to get away from Wickham's grip.

"Unhand me, this instant!" Elizabeth hissed. "Let go of me!"

"You are not going anywhere, Eliza, unless it is to your room upstairs." He leered at her.

She tried to loosen his grip to get away from him but he grasped her arm tighter and dragged her screaming upstairs to her bedroom as she swung her free hand at him and tried to pull away. He only seemed to grow more amused at her attempts at resistance as he dragged her along.

~*~*~*~

Mrs. Annesley had been standing stock still flush against the house for a moment listening to the commotion inside the house before dashing through the park to find Mr. Darcy and the colonel for help. She was out of breath when she reached the gentlemen who were with some other soldiers, and they could see that she was in great distress.

"Dear G-d! What has happened?" the colonel and Darcy asked in unison.

"Mr.... Darcy, sir... Miss Bennet... I think she may be in grave danger..."

"*What?*" Darcy's face paled. "We have to get her out of ..... immediately!" He grabbed his sword and started in a dead run towards the house.

A Colonel Brandon had called for his men to hold Darcy back for a moment. "Mr. Darcy, hold back for my men to get into position! You could be killed otherwise!"

"Like bl—dy h-ll I will!" Darcy struggled against the men trying to fight his way out of their grip.

Richard tried to reason with him, "Darcy, we have everything in place. Brandon is right! The men are at the ready. Do not go and storm the residence without our call. I would have no pleasure burying you as I would that cur, Wickham!"

"I will not be the dead man, Richard! Get out of my way!" Darcy demanded.

Richard looked to his fellow officer who nodded his head in silent response to him. Darcy and Richard along with a Colonel Brandon had arranged for the house to be flanked with a whole battalion of militiamen. They were already in their places with their weapons at the ready, and when Richard gave the command, and they invaded the residence with Darcy and Richard along side them.

Chapter 12

The thunderous noise from the front and back doors breaking down simultaneously brought both Darcy and Richard to a heightened state of awareness. They were both poised to go into the residence along with the militiamen, but Colonel Brandon insisted that Darcy stay back until the guards within the residence had at least been subdued.

Richard gave Darcy the signal that he could come forward as soon as the men were restrained, and Darcy rushed forth in order to retrieve Elizabeth. He made certain that he had his sword within easy access from its sheath just in case he had need to use it instead of the pistol he stashed within his waist band.

"Sir," Colonel Brandon said, "Miss Bennet must be upstairs, there is no one by the description given down here, but we are still searching."

Darcy raced upstairs as soon as he heard that Elizabeth could not be found on the main level. He prayed that he was not too late to rescue her, and began to search all of the rooms finding Anne within one. She wore a shocked expression, and started to address him.

"Cousin... I am so glad that you have come. I have prayed of being rescued..."

"*Save it Anne*! I know the truth of what you and George Wickham have planned; now the only thing that I am concerned about is finding my fiancée. *Where is she?*"

"Fitzwilliam... I am sure that I do not know to what you are referring..."

"I will say this only once; if anything has happened to Elizabeth, I will personally see to it that you and George are both transported-and not to some relatively mild place, Australia would not be far enough!"

"Fitzwilliam..."

"Not another word, Anne..."

Darcy would have said more, but he heard a faint squalling and left the room to follow the sound to a room at the far end of the second floor. After trying the latch on the door, he found that it was secured. A scream that he recognized as Elizabeth's emanated from behind the door and he took his foot and kicked the door in, nearly landing across the room.

When he looked to his left, he saw Wickham holding onto Elizabeth by the waist and the neck wearing a wild look about him. Darcy had his hand at the hilt of his sword ready to attack.

"I see that you have maintained your habit of arriving annoyingly early, Darcy. 'Tis too bad really, I was so looking forward to enjoying your fiancée's company too."

"*Get your filthy hands off of her, Wickham!*" Darcy hissed.

"Let me go you monster!" Elizabeth demanded to Wickham.

"Temper, temper... Eliza, you always have had quite a fiery temper have you not? I have always found it quite... attractive though do you not agree, Darcy?"

He noticed that Elizabeth's bodice was ripped and she had splotches across her neck matching his fingertips. Wickham grasped her tighter to himself infuriating Darcy even more. The sight was enough to enrage him as he assessed the best way to free her from her captor's grip without put her in harm's way.

Elizabeth suddenly stomped on his foot hard, forcing Wickham to loosen his grip of her and she managed to spring forward enough to move out of his reach. Darcy immediately maneuvered around her unsheathing his sword and lunged at his foe with deathly precision. Wickham hardly had time to counter-maneuver and looked at Darcy with widened eyes as if disbelieving that he had actually managed to strike him. His face turned a ghostly white as he looked down to the sword stuck through his right upper abdomen that had run thru his flank area. There was a copious amount of blood oozing around the puncture site and as he removed the sword from its intended target even more came pouring out.

George fell backwards towards the wall and slid to the floor leaving a line of bright red blood on the wall behind him. Darcy heard Elizabeth gasp and he turned to see her face turning a pale color. He immediately went to embrace her to himself to prevent her from falling to the floor when she fainted. His mind went from rage to worry within a second, thinking that she must have been traumatized to see such a gruesome scene unfold before her eyes.

Richard came in a moment later to witness the aftermath looking down upon them with his mouth agape.

"I see that the blackguard did not wish to go out without a fight, huh?" Richard said calmly, and then he looked at Elizabeth in his arms, "Is she all right, Darcy?"

Darcy looked down upon her pale face and said with great emotion, "She d_mned well better be or else I may just run our cousin through for good measure." Then he looked back up to Richard, "I think that she has been through so much and then seeing this." He nodded his head towards Wickham's now unconscious form.

"No doubt." Richard said as he studied Elizabeth's form, "Did he…?"

"No, I do not think so, but it was not for lack of trying. He said that he had been interrupted…. And I cannot help but think of what would have happened if we would have waited a moment longer…"

"But we did not, and she shall be well, Darcy. I think that we need to get her out of here and take her back to your house. We can send for the physician as well, just to make certain that she is fine."

"What about Anne? What is to be done with her?"

A voice from behind Richard answered, "Miss De Bourgh is being questioned and pending what the investigation reveals, she may be charged with aiding a deserter, but that is all that I can do with her. The charges of kidnapping will have to be dealt with by the magistrate here." Colonel Brandon came around Richard to see the resulting carnage from a few minutes ago.

When he saw Elizabeth's prone form and the state of her attire, his face turned even graver.

"I hope that we arrived just in time." He looked again to where Wickham lay and shook his head, "Such a waste of flesh."

Turning to Richard the other colonel said, "I presume we shall chalk this up to resisting arrest, and self defense for an assault?"

Richard nodded his head as he looked directly at Darcy, "It was long overdue, Colonel Brandon. George Wickham was anything but honorable and to don a uniform of the crown was an insult and a slap in the face to those who serve it respectfully."

Not much else was said as they left the house with Darcy still carrying Elizabeth. He covered her with his coat so that no one could see whom it was that he carried in his arms. They had already arranged to have a carriage waiting in the back alley in order to avoid the public curiosity of the neighborhood uproar.

When they ascended into the carriage Darcy had Richard pull the shades and he settled Elizabeth across his lap, ignoring propriety and daring his cousin to challenge his behavior. She was sleeping peacefully and some color had returned to her face. The fact that she was still unconscious though, worried him, and he wanted to ensure that a local physician had been sent for.

"Did you have one of the men send our request to Mr. Bales?"

"Yes, and to answer your next question, *yes*, I made sure that they gave him the *correct* address. Do not fret, Darcy, I can only imagine what she had been through these past few days, and seeing how sparse the kitchen was I can only imagine that she was not fed very well either."

Darcy looked up at his cousin sharply, "Do you mean to tell me that they did not even see to her basic needs? I shall throttle that little…"

"I would not worry about Anne. I am relatively certain that Colonel Brandon will see to her punishments if we would wish to pursue it, but the question is… Do you?"

"Why would you even need to ask such a question, Richard? I care nothing for Anne after what she has done, regardless of her being our relation. As far as I am concerned, I will not even acknowledge her if she should be allowed to stay here and that goes for Lady Catherine as well." Darcy nearly spit out.

"Perhaps we should wait until Elizabeth wakes up and ask her about everything that has happened while she was in captivity." At Darcy's glare, he quickly added, "I understand you are angry, but we must step back from this and consider all of the repercussions if Anne were to be publicly tried. The only reliable witness to this whole ordeal is Elizabeth. Do you really want her to be exposed in such a way?"

Darcy knew that it was an impossible situation, but did not want to think that Anne's treachery should go unpunished. He thought about the injustice of the situation for Elizabeth. If they insisted upon prosecution, then Elizabeth would face almost certain exposure and if they did nothing, then Anne would be almost getting away with murder.

"What solution is there? I cannot see that she should be allowed to get away with all of this and if we insist upon doing something then it would ruin Elizabeth-and she is the innocent in all of this!"

"I know and I agree with you whole heartedly. I shall talk with Colonel Brandon and see what he has to say about it. His reputation within the army is stellar-he used to be in the regulars until he came back from India and I would imagine that he saw a great deal of treachery over there-likely worse than here even."

"Personally, I cannot think of anything worse than what we have seen this past week..." Suddenly Darcy remembered that it was exactly a week ago today that he had proposed to Elizabeth and then they had consummated their bond-albeit unconsciously by one of them. He grew quiet thinking about that and Richard allowed him some peace and quiet to reflect on his own thoughts.

They were greeted at the house by not only Georgiana and Mrs. Annesley but also Mr. and Miss Bennet and Bingley as well. When Darcy descended the carriage with Elizabeth in his arms, everyone looked at them with alarm. He immediately explained:

"She is as well as can be. We think that she has been malnourished while she was captive and she has suffered a frightful shock when we retrieved her."

He looked at Bingley and Mr. Bennet when he said this, wishing that he could put their minds at ease, but not wanting to recount the gruesome truth of what scene occurred with George Wickham.

"I shall discuss this in greater detail with the two of you when Mr. Bales comes to examine her." He carried her up to the room adjacent to his own and lay her down on the bed.

Almost immediately Jane Bennet and Mrs. Annesley were at his side, and he was being shooed out of the room by the housekeeper, Mrs. Gordon. He tried to protest but the old woman admonished him.

"This is no place for a gentleman right now, Mr. Darcy. We shall see to Miss Bennet's care now and when Mr. Bales arrives you can see to it that he is informed of her circumstances." When he tried to speak she said abruptly, "We must get her changed into clean clothes and the poor thing must be exhausted and I am sure that she has not had a bath the whole time she was hidden away." He opened his mouth again, but she would not allow any protests, "There is nothing you can do for her right now but see to it that she gets some rest and she cannot very well be expected to do so with you hanging about. I promise you can see her when we get her settled, sir."

Darcy resentfully left the women to tend to Elizabeth. He knew that it was not his place-*yet*- to demand to be allowed into her rooms, and with that thought he went to the study where Mr. Bennet and Bingley were waiting for him with Richard.

I shall not endure being shut out of caring for her very much longer and as soon as she is well enough, we shall see to that remedy! He entered the study with a purpose and for the first time since Monday things were starting to look up.

Chapter 13

Elizabeth awoke from terrifying visions as she shot up in her bed. She did not recognize her surroundings and she looked around the spacious room that was lit up in the firelight. Her eyes settled upon the form in the bed staring back at her with darkened eyes.

"Fitzwilliam? W-what are you doing here? Where are we?"

He looked at her tenderly and brushed a lock from her face, "We are in your room at my house in Bath, dearest, and you are safe with me now. How do you feel?"

Elizabeth could sense the concern and deep emotion in his voice as he addressed her. "I… I feel as well as can be expected."

Her thoughts drifted back to the house near the park where she was held. "Did… did Mr. Wickham…?"

"He is dead… I… When I saw what he had already done to you… I felt my anger get the better of me and I knew I needed to end his treachery… before he…"

There was rawness to Darcy's voice that she thought she understood. He felt guilt at having taken a life-though that life was a miserable excuse for a man who had inflicted grievous injuries upon so many. His own character and sense of decency caused him to feel remorse for his own actions to end the life of another human being and she knew he had done it for her sake above anyone else's. Elizabeth felt an overwhelming need to comfort him.

"Shhhhhh, my darling… please, try not to think about it. I have… we will torture ourselves if we do and there is nothing that can be done about it now." The image of her beloved running her tormenter through was a vision she preferred to put out of her mind if she could help it. The nightmare she had relived threatened to intrude into her waking thoughts when she wanted nothing more than to forget the whole ordeal. Impulsively she kissed him tenderly upon his lips to which he responded eagerly.

Soon they were embracing each other; their mouths met and seemed to have joined as they tasted each other for the first time. Elizabeth felt a fluttering in her heart as he caressed her back thru the thin muslin of her nightgown and moved his hands upward to her breasts and began to massage her there. She brought her own hands to his neck and ran her fingers through his luxurious dark curls.

When she moved her hands down to his shoulders and began to match his movements she realized that he was not appropriately attired. His wool coat and vest were absent, and his neck cloth had already been removed exposing his masculine neck. She idly thought of how beautiful a man he was as she continued to explore his muscular body. *Why should I worry about his attire being appropriate when this whole situation with him feels... exquisite-so right?* He was kneading her breasts with one hand and moved his other down to her bottom. She stiffened immediately and he stopped his movement.

"Oh, Elizabeth! I am so, so sorry. You must think me an unpardonable beast! How could I have thought to do such a thing to you after what you have been through?" He berated himself.

She giggled in spite of herself causing him to look at her with a questioning glance and he frowned at her amusement.

"I am sorry, but am I missing something? What do you find so amusing, Elizabeth?"

"T'is your insinuation that I object to your caresses, my love... and... the fact that we are most assuredly in violation of propriety in such a situation as we find ourselves in right now. I truly had not thought about what happened there." She became more serious and frowned herself, "Nothing really occurred until just before you arrived and rescued me. He had *other interests* occupying him. I was only thinking of *our* situation at present. Were we to be discovered, my father would most assuredly insist that we marry immediately, but then he is not even here..." She punctuated this with a raised eyebrow at him.

"Ah... yes, that... well when I brought you here after you fainted, I was worried about you and wanted to make certain that nothing happened to you-especially after what you have already been through these past few days. As soon as I came to the door we were greeted by not only Mrs. Annesley and Georgiana, but Bingley and Mr. and Miss Bennet so you see... your father is here and though I think it would be a wonderful thing to be made to marry you immediately, I would not want to do so if that means putting you in a bad light."

To say that Elizabeth felt surprise that her father had come to Bath immediately after her letter was sent was an understatement. She could not fathom his traveling so quickly, and with her beloved Jane too. She knew that it must have been her betrothed that made the arrangements.

"I am guessing that my father's presence here now is thanks to you, and of course, Mrs. Annesley's quick thinking. I do not know how I will ever be able to thank you for saving me from those monsters and for bringing my most beloved family to me. As to your sister's companion-I do not know how to repay her for all of her kindness and attention…"

"Think no more about that-although I may give Mrs. Annesley a reward for finding you and sending your letters express. Had it not been for that-who knows what would have happened…" He shook his head, "and I still do not know what to do about Anne. To think that she could be capable of such treachery, I never would have believed it before, but after what Richard and I saw at the cottage and then what you wrote … I think that even my aunt would be shocked at her behavior-and *that* is saying something!"

Elizabeth recalled what had happened while she was in that house with George Wickham and Anne. They had engaged in some very physical acts between them and she was fairly certain that their sleeping arrangements were much as hers and Darcy's were at present.

"What is to become of her, Fitzwilliam? Has she been arrested as well as those others in that house?"

"She was held for questioning, but Richard and I are still unable to decide what should be done with her. I certainly will not acknowledge her or Lady Catherine *ever* again and it sounds as though the Earl Matlock will not abide her presence within the family, but may do so in public for nothing more than appearances sake. I thought that we should wait for you to awaken before we made any final decisions."

Elizabeth had suffered at Wickham and Anne's hands, and she was still rather angry at them for concocting this scheme in order for them to marry her beloved off to Anne. After she thought about it she voiced,"Fitzwilliam…? I do not know what your opinion of this whole mess is, but I think that the best punishment for her would be for us to marry and live happily ever after, for I think that to not be able to bask in knowing you or enjoying your society would be an excellent punishment in and of itself."

"You flatter me, love, but she has done so much harm. To think that she stood idly by while that monster was touching you in such a way…"

She touched his arm lightly to bring his attention to her, "But you came for me like a knight in shining armor, and made sure that I was safe. He was not able to complete anything, and as to the other nights… he spent them most happily occupied with her instead of me, so perhaps we should thank her for that as well?"

"Perhaps, but you must know that her actions shock me. They even shocked Richard and you can easily believe that he has seen a great deal of treachery while in the army. I wish I knew how long this was going on for between them. I mean after what he tried to do with Georgiana, it makes me wonder if she put him up to that as well in order to ruin our reputation so that no one of decent society would wish to marry into my family."

Elizabeth frowned, "If that is the case, then that is even more despicable than I had imagined. We had words earlier today-Anne and I, and they were not too pleasant. After I voiced my opinions of her to her face she tried to accost me, but I stopped her and turned on my heel. When Wickham returned she took him aside saying that I *'would be a much more difficult… chit than her cousin'* and demanded that he *'deal with me as they had planned before, with or without your presence'*. That is when he stormed out of the room and dragged me along with him…"

Elizabeth felt ashamed and embarrassed at what Wickham had done, tearing at her bodice and fondling her through her chemise. She knew that he intended to force himself upon her and she shuddered at the remembrance of his leering at her while he did so, telling her what he intended to do. She screamed and moments later Fitzwilliam Darcy had burst into the room. The horror she felt at his seeing her in such a state caused as much anxiety as seeing the man responsible for her tattered attire run through. Anne's threats to ruin her reputation intruded as well.

"I think that he had wanted to do something to me the night that we were in town. We had gone to that horrid Mrs. Younge's house and I was locked in a small closet. What little sleep I tried to get was broken by someone trying to enter the room, but they had no key. When they took me along the next morning she offered that woman money to spread rumors about town that he had… that I was…"

She broke down sobbing as she thought of what they had tried to do to her. Darcy held her tightly and rocked her in his arms, pulling her onto his lap, cradling her. Her head leaned against his heart and she could hear the steady rhythm beating more rapidly as he rocked her. His lips kissed the top of her head moving from her crown to her forehead then to her cheeks and finally resting on her mouth. It was not the hot passionate kind of kiss of earlier, but the kind compassionate ones that were the essence of who he was.

"I am so sorry that I did not rescue you away from them at the cottage. You have no idea how it tore at my heart to see him taking you away from me…"

Elizabeth's hands caressed his face, "I think that I do know what you were feeling because I felt it as well. I had no idea that they were involved with each other until our dash to town when they actually started kissing openly in front of me. At the time I had no idea why they would go to so much trouble to take me if they wanted to get away, but then I heard them today and it became clear. Their intention all along was to ruin me-my reputation by… by…" She started to sob again.

Darcy attempted to put her at ease, "Shhhh, shhhh, dearest. Do not fret, I am here now and I am not going anywhere. You and I are going to marry and we shall punish Anne by living *'happily ever after'* as you said. Though, after hearing what you had gone through, I am inclined to believe that a thrashing in the gallows would be too good for her."

After a moment of contemplation she asked, "Where is she now? Will she be able to come and go as she pleases?"

"To answer your first question, she was set up at the inn closest to where the militia is settled. Richard offered to guard her after I brought you here. Colonel Brandon is also being consulted. There is a chance that she may have to stand trial for conspiracy to aide a deserter for which the penalties are very harsh."

After hearing that his cousin may face some serious penalties, Elizabeth asked with concern, "Will she be hung, do you think?"

Darcy's hand stilled from rubbing her back as he sighed heavily, "I doubt it, but she may face deportation. The crown frowns upon anyone who would knowingly harbor a deserter and as much as I once took some concern for Anne, I am glad to know that she may finally face serious consequences for her actions. She has been spoilt her entire life and after hearing and seeing this side of her, I say *good riddance*."

They did not speak anymore about Anne. They were both tired and the last thing Elizabeth wanted was to mar her private time with Darcy by talking of unpleasantness. Darcy slowly lowered her upon the pillow and said, I shall leave you be dearest. I do not want you to feel uncomfortable."

Elizabeth felt his withdraw from her and suddenly felt panic at his pulling away from her.

"Please, Fitzwilliam... will you not stay a little while longer and hold me? I do not wish to be alone right now and..."

"Shhh, no need for explanations, my love. I would be happy to keep you company and warm you. I just did not wish to discomfort you in any way."

She smiled at the care he took of her. *How could I ever have thought him so proud and disagreeable?* "You would not be discomfiting me, love. I... I would feel so much safer with you."

"Well then, shall we get beneath the counterpane and rest? I promise to behave, if I can just hold you tight."

Elizabeth nodded her head and they made themselves comfortable spooned together. They lay for a few moments before Darcy asked, "Elizabeth? Do you suppose that we can discuss rescheduling our wedding date soon?" He was almost pleading.

She laughed, "I wish for the same closeness as well, Fitzwilliam, and I do not think that I want to forgo having you here to hold and comfort me. In fact I never wish to spend my nights alone again."

"Thank you." He replied.

"For what?"

"For putting me out of my misery once and for all."

They looked at each other with happiness that suffused their faces and kissed each other thoroughly before breaking apart and finding a comfortable position to lie together in. It was the first night that they were both able to sleep so peacefully... ever.

~*~*~*~

Richard came promptly at breakfast time just after everyone else had seated themselves. Bingley greeted him with his usual jovial manner.

"What news from the army today, Fitzwilliam?"

The grim look upon Richards face told Darcy that he had some not so pleasant news.

"Ahem...I... ah... have talked with Colonel Brandon today. It seems that some of the higher ups have gotten wind of what happened here, and...well, deuces! I have been informed that Anne is likely going to face trial for aiding a fugitive deserter."

Everyone at the table turned to him in astonishment except Georgiana. Darcy could only speculate as to her feelings about their cousin's fate.

Chapter 14

Georgiana Darcy had been preoccupied with her past behavior with George Wickham since last summer. She silently and continuously berated herself for having been so gullible to his charms and felt as if she had let her guardians down and besmirched the Darcy and Fitzwilliam names. In her despair, she resigned herself to never marrying due to her disgrace by consenting to an elopement with her father's godson.

When Fitzwilliam had come early to Ramsgate to surprise her, she knew that she could not bear to grieve her brother who had been like a father figure to her and confessed to their plans to elope. What he imparted to her afterward was that George was nothing honorable and had been courting her in order to obtain her dowry. At first she could not believe that her fiancé could have deceived her in such a way, conversely she could not fathom her brother would tell her any untruths either.

In the end, George ended up leaving Ramsgate without even so much as a backward glance. It hurt her more than she could express to have been duped in such a way and by someone she thought she could trust. After her experience she began to question her own judgment on everything. She began to turn inward and closed herself off from everyone close to her-even Fitzwilliam. The ache that she felt had been unbearable at times.

Mrs. Annesley came to her shortly after the whole debacle and she gradually learned to channel her frustrations in different directions. This is when she started to really focus on music. It became a balm to her when the darkness seemed to be swallowing her up. After a few months, the anger came, turning sharply towards the man who had brought this darkness upon her. Though she was usually a very forgiving soul, it was difficult for her to overcome such betrayal.

Georgiana knew that it was her *'Christian duty'* to overlook other people's trespasses. With George Wickham and Anne she knew that they had done this to hurt her deliberately and it was not likely that they had ever felt any sense of remorse for the hurt that they caused others. Part of her defense had been to withdraw from the outside world as much as possible, and with such a close relative betraying her she hardly knew who to trust… other than Fitzwilliam.

With the help of Mrs. Annesley, she was able to overcome the overwhelming emotions and begin to reconstruct her life. Her music and drawing helped to sooth her and as she gradually improved in performance, she also improved in her outlook towards life in general as well.

Seeing George Wickham again- *with Anne of all people*- made her furious. *Can he never leave our family alone?* At first, she thought that George had gone to Anne after he was found out by Fitzwilliam, but then she realized that Lady Catherine would never allow the association with a mere steward's son much less a courtship or marriage. *Has he managed to talk her into an elopement as well?* The idea was galling. *No… Mrs. Jenkins would never allow her to walk alone with a man, let alone with him! What is he up to?* She thought.

Her companion seemed to be concerned when she mentioned the name George Wickham. Georgiana's anxiety heightened when Mrs. Annesley offered to follow the couple to wherever they were headed. Upon arriving back at their house, a sudden urge struck her. *I shall follow Mrs. Annesley to see what it is that they are up to.* She was sure that her guardian would be very upset with her should she find out that she was being followed, but Georgiana could not dispel her unease.

Seeing the couple embrace and give each other a slight kiss shocked the young woman to no end. *How can they behave in such an outrageous manner? Aunt Catherine would have a fit if she saw what was going on and in public!* The Anne she knew would never venture to say boo to anyone let alone embrace and kiss a man in public. After seeing such a sight she knew that she must find out what was going on between the two of them.

The house where George and Anne walked to after they left the park was in a rather fashionable area of Bath-certainly nothing that George could afford. With her curiosity piqued, Georgiana went around to the side of the house to see her companion talking quietly to a woman in a narrow window. What she heard shocked her. *Anne and George have been involved with a plot to entrap Fitzwilliam into marriage? But why?* Her senses were reeling at such revelations. *Their relationship must have been going on for some time then…*

George and Anne have been involved with each other since before Ramsgate. She froze while grasping at the concept that her own cousin would have been involved with such a man as George Wickham, let alone force her brother to marry her. *Anne still planned to continue her duplicity with another man if she were to marry Fitzwilliam? What could they possibly hope to gain by taking Miss Bennet though? Jealousy? Anne has more than enough money, yet it is not enough for her?* She thought indignantly, no longer listening to their conversation.

They must have been together for....? It must have been for some time in order for them to do this! He was seeing her even during our stay at Ramsgate! Did she know? Would she have even cared? Thoughts were whirling in Georgiana's head, making her ill. She turned back before she could be detected by her companion and walked back home numb from shock.

When she arrived back at the house she made her way through the side entrance so as not to be seen coming in at a later time than she was supposed to have. Her behavior did not even register at first and when the housekeeper, Mrs. Gordon came upon her she was startled and subsequently frightened that the kindly woman would sense something was amiss.

"Are you well, Miss Darcy? You look rather pale." The woman asked.

She stared at her for a moment before she could form a response.

"Uh... yes, Mrs. Gordon, I am fine. I have just heard some alarming news..."

"Oh dear..." Mrs. Gordon looked worried, "We had hoped that you would be spared the knowledge, but apparently someone was lax in their duties."

Georgiana was puzzled over her comment and clarified, "What do you mean? What knowledge?"

"Why, about Mr. Darcy... and his betrothed going missing. We just heard today, that they have few leads as to who would have done such a thing! Lord bless me, I do not know what 'as gotten into people these days! Taking a man in his own coach-and with several witnesses! Even Colonel Fitzwilliam is missing!" The woman started fanning herself furiously.

The pieces to the larger puzzle were falling into place, but she felt the need to put the distressed housekeeper at ease about her newly acquired knowledge.

"Mrs. Gordon… Please allow me to put you at ease. I have learned that my brother managed to escape his captors," *likely due to Richard*, she thought with a little humor, "and I am sure that he will be able to help find Miss Bennet. He is a most loyal man and he will not allow anything to happen to her, I am sure of it." She said as much to herself as to the woman.

"Oh, bless me! That is wonderful news, Miss! We have all been quite worried about the master when we heard the news. It has been most distressing! I do hope that they find her soon, else you never know what those horrible ruffians will do to her…"

I can only imagine what they are capable of! Such horrid people! They should be stopped… her thoughts turned to a different direction. She knew that Mrs. Annesley had sent Miss Elizabeth's notes via express. *There is no other explanation for Anthony to leave in such haste yesterday other than with some express. Surely Fitzwilliam will come? Perhaps I should send a note to town to request more assistance in retrieving Miss Bennet?*

She thought about whom she could contact. *Miss Bingley? No… she could not be trusted to keep quiet about the circumstances. Colonel Hill? No… he would likely bring on more force and notice to the situation. Aunt Eleanor? Yes, she will let them know what is going on and she will know what to do about Anne as well! I am sure she will!* With her resolve, Georgiana, quickly penned a letter to her aunt in town, and when Anthony arrived back from his first errand, she requested that when he was rested enough he take her noted straight to town.

Friday 14th April 1809

Bath

Dearest Aunt Eleanor,

I have recently received some alarming news-which Fitzwilliam had been abducted and Richard, Anne, and Miss Elizabeth Bennet have gone missing. You can imagine the shock of hearing such news, but the way that I learned it was even more horrific. I had seen my cousin Anne here in Bath, and on the arm of George Wickham! My shock was great at having seen the man who had nearly been the cause of my public ruination and here he was with Anne who is supposedly missing! They were strolling in the park today near our house here and they seemed rather better acquainted with each other than one would suspect. In seeing their familiarity in light of what I have endured at that man's hands, I felt a need to follow them to their destination under the circumstances.

They were unescorted when they went to a rather nice townhouse here in Bath. Upon further investigation I learned then, that Anne was also supposedly abducted along with Miss Bennet, but now I know that this is obviously not the case. I had heard that Miss Bennet was within the house as well, but not quite so comfortably accommodated. Due to these overheard conversations I found out that she was still being held due to some nefarious plot to separate my brother from his betrothed!

It turns out that Anne was part of this plot to remove Miss Bennet from Fitzwilliam in order for her to marry him-though I have no idea why she thinks she is deserving of such an excellent man! It appears that she has been involved with George Wickham for some time as well, and had no intention of giving him up once she was married!

Now my greatest fear is that they will harm Miss Bennet to try and prevent her from marrying my brother. I hope that you can show my uncle this letter and he may be able to send help to rescue Miss Bennet before it is too late. I pray that you will also be able to send better news. With this I shall leave off by wishing you well and in good health.

Your Dutiful Niece,

Georgiana Darcy

As luck would have it, Anthony was rested enough to be able to take the letter to town that same afternoon. By night's end he had the missive delivered to Matlock House.

On Friday, Caroline Bingley received the distressing news that Fitzwilliam Darcy and his cousin Colonel Fitzwilliam had left town from Charles. She became desperate once she heard of his betrothal to that little country chit, Eliza Bennet, and was only slightly less peeved that Charles was planning on an association with her sister, Jane.

There is no way that I am going to allow that social climbing nobody to take the illustrious position of Mrs. Fitzwilliam Darcy!

After some thought as to how she could manage to end his engagement for certain, she decided to pay a visit to the countess Matlock. *Not only will she see the need to put a stop to this travesty, she can also help me to gain membership into Almack's.* On Saturday morning she went to Matlock House and presented herself as a concerned friend of Mr. and Miss Darcy's, to which the footman immediately showed her into the mistress parlor while he went to fetch the lady herself.

As she awaited the countess, Caroline walked around the spacious room noting the fine material for curtains, and the beautiful tapestries, not to mention the exquisite artwork and fine china. *This is how I shall be living once we are able to end Darcy's obsession with that impertinent little piece of baggage! I could even make Pemberley even more glorious with my decorating sense... much better than Eliza Bennet ever could! She has no taste, no style, in short nothing to recommend her,* she giggled to herself. While she awaited the countess she could not help but hear a servant's conversation at the back door to the room.

"I swear it Sam, another missive arrived from Bath just las ni'. Anthony said it was from Miss Darcy 'erself... said it was rather urgent!"

"Can you be sure it has anything to do with Mr. Darcy's lady?"

"No, but I did hear tha th mistress was quite distressed 'bout is contents. Somethin' 'bout entrapping er nephew... She was talkin' ta' is lordship... "

Caroline stilled at the mention of Mr. Darcy being entrapped into a marriage and wanted so much to find that letter. *I knew it! That harlot Eliza was trying to trap poor Darcy into marrying her! Ha! Eliza, two can play at that game! I must get to the study and find that letter before her ladyship comes down!*

She crept to the door that faced the main hall and cracked the door to peer out. When she saw the footman walk down the opposite hall towards the back of the house, Caroline quickly dashed towards the room she knew to be the countess' study. She knocked quietly and when she heard nothing, she crept into the room. It must be here somewhere, she thought as she looked around.

While she perused the room her eyes settled upon the fine ebony statue on the countess' desk set next to a matching one made of ivory.

She wanted to inspect the handcrafted work closer and in doing so, she knocked a letter off of the desk. As she bent to retrieve it off of the floor she noticed the signature at the bottom of the missive as well as the date at the top.

Unable to control herself, she greedily read the letter before she placed it upon the desk just as she thought it might have been. Once she was done she wanted to dance the jig herself, but controlled the impulse, and made her way out of the room as she had come.

Within moments of re-entering the parlor, the butler came in to announce that her ladyship was not able to receive her. By then her mood could not be affected by such a dismissal. With a wicked gleam in her eyes she sauntered back to her coach and headed back to the Hurst's residence.

Wait until Fitzwilliam learns about his dear cousin, Anne. I am sure that he will want nothing to do with the miserable little thing after this, and after Mr. Wickham ruins that Eliza Bennet, he will want nothing to do with her as well! Darcy will finally be free of the whole lot of them, and with a scandal hanging over him, few ladies would be encouraged to associate with the family-at least for this season! Then I can have him all to myself! Louisa will be so jealous of what a catch I made.

As soon as she arrived back at her sister's she immediately went to *share* her discovery with Louisa.

After breakfast on Sunday morning, Darcy and Mr. Bennet encouraged Elizabeth to rest. After being cooped up for several days, that was the last thing that she wanted to do. She did not think that she would be able to do so anyway and was certain that the only reason that she had last night was because she felt safe in Darcy's arms. Since it was highly unlikely that she would be able to commandeer him, she informed them of her wish to enjoy the park across the street from the house and she felt that it was a good way to get to know Miss Darcy as well.

"I have heard that the park across the way is lovely, and I would not mind having some company. Do you suppose that you could spare me some time, Miss Darcy, to escort me…?" She looked towards Jane who wore a slightly injured expression, "and of course my sister, Jane?"

Miss Darcy looked at her with wide eyes before she glanced towards Fitzwilliam who was silently nodding his head.

"That would be lovely, Miss Elizabeth."

"Please call me 'Elizabeth' or 'Lizzy', for we shall be sisters and that is what my sisters call me-usually." She and Jane laughed.

"Fitzwilliam," Georgiana turned to her brother, "May I go out before I start my lessons? I can easily start my music after we are finished."

"I think it sounds like a good idea, so long as you take at least one of the brawnier footmen with you as well. After having just gotten Elizabeth back, I am in no mood to go all over the countryside and fetch her again." Darcy addressed Elizabeth half jokingly.

"And I am in no mood to be dragged all over the countryside to be fetched again."

"Yet I would do it all over again if I had to." He responded seriously.

It was endearing to know that he cared enough to risk his life to rescue her, and was still looking out for her safety. Her sense of security last night stemmed from the tall dark and handsome gentleman she just so happened to be betrothed to. She was still shocked and surprised at their audacity to share a bed and was thankful that no one had come upon them last night. It was even more shocking to her when she discovered that he had managed to place her in the mistress chambers adjacent to his own rooms. If anyone noticed they had yet to comment and she was certain that her father would have protested had he known, but... then again *he* was not thinking about room assignments when she arrived either.

"'T'is a good thing too, for I do not think that I would have the strength or fortitude to go and rescue damsels in distress at my age," added her father lightly.

Elizabeth cringed at her his dismissive tone and dared to take a peek at Darcy who, thankfully, took it in stride.

He glanced at her before replying, "Then it is a good thing that she will soon be my wife, for I have no qualms about going to the ends of the earth for her. Speaking of which... sir, I wonder if we might discuss what I had began to plan yesterday? I find that I am most anxious to begin my duties to Elizabeth within more of an official capacity after this whole ordeal."

"I have no doubt you would, Mr. Darcy." Mr. Bennet said dryly.

Elizabeth blushed at his insinuations, but now she also secretly wished for Fitzwilliam Darcy to become more to her than her fiancé. She had grown to care for and love him and was anxious to marry him now. The irony that she had come to feel this way for him when just a few months ago she thought him rather rude and disagreeable struck her as amusing. *To think that I once thought him the last man in the world that I could ever marry now seems rather absurd!* She thought as she watched him discuss some mundane topic with her father.

Her thoughts were interrupted when Colonel Fitzwilliam came in and made an announcement of the fate of Anne De Bourgh. The look upon everyone's faces reflected shock astonishment, and even horror… everyone's except Georgiana's or so Elizabeth noticed. She briefly wondered at the lack of concern for her own cousin on Georgiana's part. Though there was no love loss between her and Anne, Elizabeth had no desire to see Anne transported or even hung. *Perhaps sending her to a convent or locking her in an attic for the rest of her life might serve her well, but this… I cannot imagine facing this.*

She could not help herself from asking, "Is it certain-absolutely certain that she will face a trial, colonel?"

He seemed surprised at her concern for the woman who had almost been responsible for her ruination.

"I would say that the chances are more likely than not that she will face a trial. Somehow the news that she was more of an accomplice than a victim has been circulated in town and the only people who know the truth of the matter are those present here, those that participated in the abductions, and my father. I think that I am reasonable enough to assume that no one here would say anything outside of these premises and I am certain that my father would never speak of it to anyone else-save my mother. There has to have been some sort of a leak, otherwise they would allow us to manage this within the magistrates and our discretion."

Darcy's face took on a grim look as he frowned deeply. "I cannot imagine that any servants would discuss this here. They know better than to talk-especially about things of this nature, besides that most of those present here now have been in service for our family for a long time."

"I do not know what to make of it either Darcy, but someone must have said something almost from the day that they arrived in Bath. There is no way that this could have made it to town overnight."

They looked at her father with more questions, "Mr. Bennet," Darcy asked, "When did you receive your letter from Elizabeth?"

"I received it Friday morning, by personal messenger, and before you ask, no I had not gone into specifics of that letter with Mrs. Bennet."

It was embarrassing to Elizabeth to think that her fiancé did not trust her father to refrain from sharing sensitive information with Mrs. Bennet.

"I was not insinuating that you would, sir. My thoughts tended toward who the messenger was. Do you recall who had the task of delivering it to you?" Darcy bristled.

"If memory serves it was a lad by the name of Anthony, but I doubt that he would have said a word to anyone. He seemed so quiet."

"He is, that is what has me so baffled. Anthony is one of our most reliable servants…"

"Fitzwilliam…?" The small voice of Georgiana could barely be heard.

Darcy looked at his sister, "Yes, my dear?"

"I think… that is to say… I know of someone else who also knows, or at least will know shortly about… Anne's involvement with yours and Elizabeth's abduction's…"

"Yes, Georgiana?" Darcy replied almost impatiently.

"The day that Mrs. Annesley and I saw George and Anne in the park holding hands…?" Darcy nodded for her to continue, "I… I… that is I had written to Aunt Eleanor to notify her of Anne's behavior as well…"

"Why…?" Darcy asked.

"That is no matter, Darcy! My mother would not say anything to anyone about our family if she thought that it might be harmful to be known, besides my father would tell her anyways." Richard retorted.

"I am only wondering what had made her send such a note to Lady Matlock, that is all, Richard." Darcy answered shortly.

Elizabeth sensed that there was a deeper reason for her writing such a letter when they were not even sure of the circumstances yet.

"Miss Darcy…" Elizabeth started softly, "Did something happen to make you write that letter? Was there anyone else that witnessed Mr. Wickham and Miss De Bourgh together?"

"I… I do not think so, but I cannot be for sure…"

Mrs. Annesley spoke up then, "I was there to witness the couple together as well and I did not see anyone else around, and I can also say that I have never spoken of this to anyone. It would also be difficult for me to believe that a servant from here would speak to anyone about such private matters. Every one of your servants seems so devoted to you, Mr. Darcy."

"I thank you, Mrs. Annesley." Darcy acknowledged her complement, "I think that I shall have to speak to Anthony to see if he saw or heard anything in town while he was there. In the mean time, we should be very careful with whom we speak to about this." He turned to her father, "Mr. Bennet, would you oblige me with some of your time? You may want to hear what I have to say as well, Richard, Bingley."

Those two gentlemen agreed to that they wanted to hear him out, and Elizabeth spoke up requesting to know what it was that Darcy was thinking about the news getting out. In her line of thought this also involved her and she felt she also had stake in this as well. Should this news get out, her reputation could be in taters as well.

"Would you mind if I joined you, sir?" She requested.

"Actually," He looked at his sister, "If you would not mind staying with Georgiana, it would be more helpful."Darcy answered.

Elizabeth was annoyed that he would bar her from such a discussion and was about to protest until she realized that the conversation seemed to be causing Georgiana some distress.

I suppose that I can do that, sir, but if you do not mind-would you be so kind as to keep me informed of any new developments?"

"I would not have it any other way, madam." Darcy stared into her eyes.

They parted from the breakfast parlor with the gentlemen joining Darcy in the study after the messenger named Anthony was sent for and the ladies prepared to go for a walk in the park. After Elizabeth, Jane, and Georgiana had donned their outerwear, they set off with the biggest footman as Darcy had requested to go with them.

Elizabeth joined her arms with Jane and Georgiana and set off for the center of the park. In truth she really wanted to enjoy the outdoors without the heavy burden of thinking about Anne's fate. She knew that it was likely that Georgiana felt some responsibility for this news having gotten out, but there really was no rational explanation even for that.

"Miss Darcy…?" Elizabeth tried to break the ice between herself and her future sister, "I do hope that you do not take this blame of what has happened to Miss De Bourgh upon yourself. From the sound of it, there is not likely reason to believe that your letter would have done anything of the sort."

"But that is not the only reason that I wrote to my aunt, Elizabeth. There are other reasons for me to write to my aunt of my cousin's behavior as it relates to George Wickham…"

Elizabeth instinctively knew that she was referring to Ramsgate.

"Does this involve another seaside resort town last summer?" She asked softly as she tried to catch the girl's eye.

Georgiana stopped suddenly and stared at her. "What do you mean? Has... has Fitzwilliam told you?"

"If you are referring to what happened at Ramsgate, then yes he has told me about that."

Tears formed in her eyes, and Jane and Elizabeth looked at Georgiana with great compassion and sympathy-one knowing the cause of her distress and the other only knowing that she did not like to see others in such distress.

"You must think me a terrible person..." She began to sob.

She took her hands and faced her, "No, of course not. I can easily understand how you could be taken in by his charms. In fact he had almost convinced me that your brother was such a horrible person that had treated him ill."

Georgiana looked at her with surprise in her eyes, "How could anyone believe such awful things of Fitzwilliam, let alone say them? He is the best man in the whole world."

Elizabeth smiled at her assessment thinking that she most defiantly agreed with that now.

"I tend to agree with you these days, but at one time, when he had first come to Hertfordshire, he did not make the best first impressions, and I am afraid that it was easier for me to believe Mr. Wickham's pretty words and charm than to see the depth of your brother's value."

"How could you believe that, Elizabeth?" She almost sounded wounded that she could think anything but wonderful things about Darcy.

Elizabeth laughed, which only seemed to puzzle Georgiana more, but she relented and related the first time that she and Darcy had met at the assembly in Meryton, and ended with his most insulting words along with her impression of them. The astonished girl was left wide eyed and speechless... for a moment.

"That was very wrong of him to say such a thing, and it is hard to credit, but it must be true, and you seem to have forgiven him for it."

"Yes, I have forgiven him for it, and I have learned that it is true that pride does truly cometh before the fall. If things had been different at Hunsford I may have even dismissed his proposal outright because of my wounded pride, and I may never have learned what a good man he really is."

"Would you have?" Again she seemed awed by such a confession.

"Very likely. I had a very poor opinion of him then, and some was due to that wounded pride, but that was also fueled by Mr. Wickham's lies as well. He was rather charming and flattered me with pretty words with fed my ego, and aligned with what I had thought of your brother, but since then I have learned that sometimes things are not always as they appear to be. Mr. Wickham was the wolf in sheep's clothing."

Georgiana was quiet for a moment before she said, "I think that that may also be the case with Anne as well. I have always thought of her as rather quiet and insignificant, but seeing her with him… and the way that she behaved! I was beyond shocked. She was not as she had ever been in my presence."

"No… I would imagine not. When I first saw her at Rosings, I thought the same thing, but then when I was… when I was taken away by Mr. Wickham and her, she was a completely different person. It was almost as if she were two different people."

"It must have been horrible for you." Both Jane and Georgiana said in unison.

"When I was taken it was, but my courage always rises with every attempt to intimidate me. I was not about to let them get the better of me."

"I wish that I were like that. To have such courage…" Georgiana said.

"I am sure that if you were to face such circumstances you may just surprise yourself."

The smile that lit up on the girl's face seemed to be one of relief, but then it was replaced again by worry.

"What do you think has happened, to leak this information out? I do not think that anyone here has said a word about it, and I am sure that Lord and Lady Matlock would not want such information out about our family."

"Whatever has happened, I think that your brother and the colonel will get to the bottom of it and in the mean time we shall continue on as if nothing bothers us. I, for one, wish to put this all behind me, and worrying about what will happen to your cousin will not help her in the least." *Although I do wonder if she really does have a demon possessing her.*

They agreed with Elizabeth assessment and moved on to discuss her upcoming nuptials until it was time to go back to the house. Elizabeth noted the wistful look upon Jane's face and hoped that very soon she too would have an announcement to make.

Back in town, Caroline Bingley sat in the Hurst's living room congratulating herself on initiating the first part of her plan to separate Fitzwilliam Darcy from Eliza Bennet and Anne De Bourgh. *Yes, you shall be mine, Mr. Darcy when one of your rumored fiancées is hung or transported and the other is exposed for the trollop that she is. Part two of my plot should be much easier to convince people of when they learn of the circumstances of her situation while she was gone.*

Chapter 15

The Darcy House in Bath was bustling with the ladies within busy planning the nuptials between Elizabeth and Darcy. Mr. Bennet sent an express to Gracechurch Street to notify his wife and their family that Elizabeth had been recovered and was in relatively good spirits. He further requested that they come to Bath if at all possible to witness the marriage of Elizabeth to Darcy. She was thankful that her mother was not there to interject in their plans for a very simple ceremony, and they were all enjoying the peace and quiet that would surely be interrupted when her mother and younger sisters arrived.

Both the bride and groom were anxious to be married soon, but each for different reasons. Elizabeth knew that her behavior Sunday night was beyond inappropriate, yet she could not bring herself to feel remorseful about lying with Darcy. She felt warmth and comfort within his arms both physically and emotionally. There was a sort of connection- a bond between them that she scarcely recognized which gave her an inner peace as well.

She suspected that she was now truly in love with him. People threw the word, love, around by saying that they loved someone or something and she had done the same, but this was different. Within herself she had a feeling of excitement as well as vulnerability. This sense of being at the mercy of someone else also made her feel... *nervous*.

Elizabeth's emotions were in an uproar, but she rationally explained them away as prenuptial nerves. Briefly and humorously it brought to her mind her mother's *nerves*; however she did not take to her room or flit about complaining of palpitations. Her energies were directed to constructive pursuits such as wedding arrangements and dress fittings. She even managed to embroider a special handkerchief with her new initials after tearing out a few stitches because she was not attending to her design.

Mr. Bennet *had* waited for a number of days for her to recover to write to her mother in order to make some arrangements for their wedding at the request of the happy couple. They knew that she would come via horseback if they had notified her sooner of her least favorite daughter's nuptials. Elizabeth suspected that her poor father had had more than his fair share of her mother's nerves these past few weeks and was now enjoying a holiday away from them. Jane had even seemed more at ease and was spending quite a bit of time with Mr. Bingley as well which in turn pleased Elizabeth.

Soon their paradise would be interrupted when Mrs. Bennet arrived with her entourage consisting of Lydia, Kitty, and Mary. They consoled themselves with the fact that the Gardiner's also agreed to join in their travel to Bath so at least there would be a few people of sense and education that would help to counter Mrs. Bennet's more senseless ramblings.

Darcy seemed to be getting more and more anxious as the days came and went. Elizabeth knew that he must not be looking forward to some of her relations presence and thought this was at least part of his source of disquiet even though he denied that it was. The subject was broached one night in her rooms after everyone else in the house was thought to be asleep. Her being in the mistress chambers went unmentioned by anyone either by ignorance or willful avoidance of the issue, thus he did not feel a need to make any changes to the set up or make any sort of issue out of it.

It had been over a week since her ordeal ended and every night he joined her in her bed, though they did nothing else. He was restless but quiet as he stared out the window, causing her to become uneasy.

"Fitzwilliam…?" She turned on her side to look at him, "Are you all right?"

"I am fine, dearest, why do you ask?"

"Because you are… restless. You seem unsettled. Are you anxious about my mother and sister's arriving on Monday?"

"No!" He answered immediately, "Why would you think that?"

"I know that you do not have the highest opinion about her-or my younger sisters for that matter and lately you just seem as if you are… preoccupied. Even now you seem tense."

She heard him chuckle a little bit before he responded, "I am tense because you are near, love, but it is not a bad sort of tense and as for your family, I shall be fine. If I have any issues that arise in that quarter, I know how to extricate myself from them rather artfully."

"Oh? And how would that be?" She moved to the edge of the bed to join him.

"It is simple, I shall tell everyone that I have an urgent business matter to attend to and I shall excuse myself."

"Very clever, but what if mama should ask you what possible urgent matter you could have late in the evening?"

He gave her a face that spoke of how distasteful that would be before answering, "I would tell her that it is a most private matter, and leave."

Her eyes widened as she challenged, "You mean to say that you would leave me to deal with her raptures on my own?"

"I never said that. After I leave the room then I would send Mrs. Gordon or an available footman in to summon you to help me deal with this matter." He grasped her by the waist as she sidled up to him and walked her backwards towards the bed.

She was amused by his subterfuge and would not object to his plans in the least if it spared her having to listen to her mother's incessant blathering or complaints about not being able to plan the wedding as would befit a man of Mr. Darcy's station.

"How would you have me '*help you deal with*' this '*most private matter*' then?"

"Well… I would much rather show you, than tell you…"

"What would you show me?" She asked in a husky voice as he lowered her on the bed.

He smiled slowly as he joined her, then brought his lips to hers, kissing her softly while moving his tongue over her mouth to gain entrance. She opened her mouth to allow his tongue into her mouth and her tongue dueled with his. Elizabeth could feel his hands snake around to her waist and then moved up her torso until they cupped her breasts. Her body instantly stiffened at this touch and he froze all of a sudden.

"I am so sorry, Elizabeth. I do not know what came over me. Please, please forgive me."

She looked at him with large eyes, as she breathed heavily. "I… that is… I am not offended, Fitzwilliam."

Darcy studied her face for a moment before asking, "You are not?"

"No. In fact it felt… rather tingly… and nice." She blushed, and then looked at him through her eyelashes. "You must think me a wanton woman."

"Absolutely not. I... you do not know how pleased I am to know that my touch makes you feel such a way."

She stared at him fully then moved her face towards him. His lips met hers with such a passion, it left her breathless. It took her a few minutes to realize that his hands had resumed their previous exploration as they loosened the ties to her gown then he cupped her breasts and his fingers began to knead the tips gently. A moan escaped involuntarily and she was not certain whom it came from. Her hands began to join his in exploration of her lover's body as she caressed his chest and wrapped her arms around her neck, running her fingers through his dark curls.

Soon his hand left one breast to venture down her side to her hips and the small of her back. His caresses became less gentle and more insistent as he grasp the hem of her gown and brought his hands to caress her inner thighs. In a swift motion he moved his hand to her most intimate place and began to massage her there. The surprise at his actions was soon supplanted by the sensations that his touch elicited. Her hands began to grasp at his hair almost pulling his head to her breasts. Darcy's touch caused her to open her thighs to him more as he continued to caress her core, and the sensation was...*exquisite*. Her breathing started to come in pants as she reached for something with him until an explosion of sorts came over her and she was riding a crest of sorts. Their mouths met in a crushing kiss as they moaned together.

When they were done, he turned away from her quickly and he apologized.

"I... Lizzy I am so, so sorry. I never meant to get carried away like that."

He got up from the bed quickly and made to leave, but she called to him as she touched his arm, "Fitzwilliam, please... I was as much responsible as you, and though I have no idea what happened, I do not object to it. At least as far as my comfort is concerned, but you seem to be... in distress again. Will you not allow me to help you? To relieve your source of distress?"

"Elizabeth... You have no idea how much I would love to make love to you again, but..."

He froze again as if he was unable to say anymore as he continued to stare at her.

It took her a moment to process what he had said and she wanted to clarify, "Fitzwilliam, to what are you referring? We certainly have not crossed *all* boundaries of propriety." She began to worry that her actions had caused him to think less of her. "What could we have possibly done before that would have caused this distress of yours?"

"Elizabeth... do you recall when we became engaged and you asked me to disclose our... *behavior* on the night I came to see you at the parsonage?"

She nodded her head in silent acknowledgement and continued to stare at him with great intensity.

He took a deep breath and began, "I had come to see you in order to propose and you were acting rather *off*, but at the time I did not think too much about it. Then you fell into my lap and you... you tried to get up and fell back upon me. You kept trying to get up again, but could not and when you were... moving in my lap, you caused a reaction within me. I knew that if you persisted that I... might be tempted to act in a very ungentlemanly way. Had a servant come by then we would most certainly have been forced to marry. Then you fainted and I ended up carrying you to your room where it was my intention to lay you down in your bed to rest. You woke up-or so I thought and you were so welcoming, and so friendly that you... embraced me. When you reacted to me in such a way, it was more than I had ever hoped that you would and I... we did some things and I... I took your virtue..."

Her eyes widened and she took a deep breath and began to hyperventilate. Darcy came around the bed to her side nd she pulled away as if she were burned.

He approached her cautiously, "Elizabeth, please understand-I had no idea that you were not, that you had been under the influence of some medicinal tea. If I would have known..."

"But it does not matter. You knew that I was not *'right'*... You had said that you heard that I had a headache..."

Suddenly Elizabeth frowned as her memory from that night was starting to come to her. The recollection of her falling into his lap, of their conversation, of his carrying her to her room... then finally she recalled the pain in those places he had caressed and how she had soreness there the morning after.

"So you do recall some of it? Elizabeth you must know that I had no intention of taking such advantage..."

"Yet you did..." She felt betrayed and violated.

"Yes, it was a weak moment, and I have never done that with any other woman. You are the only one that could incite me do such rash things and I truly believed that we would be married. That was the reason I wanted us to marry so soon. I could not bear it if something were to happen to you or to me before we were wed... especially if you were to... to become with child."

Elizabeth felt the hot tears forming in her eyes, causing her vision to blur as she started to sob silently. She turned to lie on her side away from him in order to prevent him from seeing her tears. *How could I have been so foolish to believe that he loved me? He is only marrying me because it is his duty to me. I have been so foolish thinking that he actually cared for me.*

The edge of the bed sank as he lowered himself on the mattress. She felt his hands caress her shoulders and then he pulled her into his arms for an embrace. Their bodies rocked back and forth and he picked her up and placed her upon his lap with little resistance from her.

"Please, my dearest love, you must believe me that I did not mean for it to happen. It was a weak moment, and I am afraid that my control is wanting whenever you are near. I am intoxicated by you and I shall spend the rest of my life devoted to showing you how much I love you. Please say that you will forgive me... please?" He begged as he kissed her temple and cheek.

Her body felt weak and tired, and she was exhausted after this whole unexpected development. The repercussions were just starting to occur to her. *What has he said to my father to allow us to marry so soon?*

"Fitzwilliam... Did you...have you told my father what happened that night?" She still avoided looking at him.

The look of contrition and worry upon his face told her the answer before he spoke it. "Yes."

Elizabeth felt the tears well up again, as she worried about what her father must think of their situation... of her.

"Why has he not said anything to me then? I would have expected him to be furious..."

"He was none too pleased with me, but he does not blame you, my love. We did not know about the tea until later, but he did not think any less of you..."

Her head bobbed up and down in a blank nod as she took in this information. Thomas Bennet had not been the strictest of fathers nor even the most affectionate, but Elizabeth did believe that he would have defended his daughter's honor-especially his favorite daughter.

Disappointment washed over her then for her father's lack of concern. She began to wonder why the men that she loved had betrayed her in such ways.

Many thoughts began to invade her mind. The repercussions of their behavior the last week could have easily caused others to think less of them should they be discovered. Up until then she did not think anything of it for they had not engaged in more explicit activities-until she allowed him to take certain liberties tonight, but they were very discrete in their sleeping arrangements. Her feelings of familiarity with him came to mind as well.

Is that why I have felt as though I know him so well? Did he feel that since he had known me in such a way that he had a right to make such arrangements as this?

"Elizabeth? Please speak to me. Tell me what is going through your mind, I beg you."

She looked at him again with tears in her eyes, as her last thought came to mind and was even more troubling to her than any of the others.

With her anxieties about their wedding she had not thought much about the subject, but now she began to wonder, *is this why my courses have yet to come?*

Chapter 16

Darcy worried about Elizabeth's silence as he watched the tears running down her cheeks. He knew that he had waited for an inordinately long time to tell her what had happened, but he had hoped that she would not react this way. The sadness in her eyes spoke volumes on her feelings of betrayal, but Darcy knew that he must explain and make her understand his undying devotion to her.

"Elizabeth, please allow me to explain to you why I had not informed you of this earlier…"

She looked at him with reddened cheeks and wiped away the tears from her face as she gave him her undivided attention. Her furious stares caused him to feel uneasy as he shifted from one foot to the other.

"I would not have you think that I was some sort of rake or cad for doing those things with you, and at the time that I came to you, you seemed perfectly lucid and in control of your faculties. You only seemed to be a bit off balance, and I had no way of knowing what was going on with you at the time. Then when you sat in my lap and certain… things happened to me, it was nearly impossible to ignore my overwhelming attraction to you…"

Elizabeth frowned at him and opened her mouth; however he stayed her by putting up his hand.

"Please, allow me to further explain, though it may be rather… embarrassing for both of us. When I think of you, I become aroused and when you are around me this feeling only intensifies. I cannot help it, but you must believe that I would never act upon it unless I received sufficient encouragement. That night when you fainted and I carried you to your rooms, you woke up and… Lord I do not know how to say this delicately… I received significant encouragement. So much so that I could not help myself."

Darcy began pacing back and forth, thinking how he should tell her of his complete capitulation to her.

"I have felt so strongly for you almost from the beginning of our acquaintance, and I will readily admit that I fought it for so long. Then you came to Rosings and were your wonderful self. When I saw you again it was difficult... nay... impossible for me to deny my love for you and I knew that I could not bear to spend the rest of my life bereft of you."

"That was when I decided to go to the parsonage and make you an offer of marriage. I could not ever imagine my future without you by my side and I can most assuredly promise you that I had absolutely no intention of engaging in... such behavior. All that I can do now is beg your forgiveness for my actions, and pray that you have it in your heart to accept me still."

Darcy felt exhausted after making such a confession, and he stopped pacing to stand before Elizabeth with such a remorseful countenance. They were both silent for a few moments before she took a deep sobbing breath, and looked at him with her widened eyes.

"I had thought that something serious had occurred that evening when you came after reading your letter that you wrote to me before leaving Rosings. After I awakened that morning I did not feel... as I usually do, and I had no idea what had happened-or at least had very little idea until I read your letter. I thought it rather odd at the time, but then later I had dreams-vivid dreams-about activities that occur between men and women. The odd thing to me was how I felt when it was you that was in those dreams. It felt... right and... I have no other words for it, but you were so kind and loving. You still are..."

He came to her and embraced her tightly, exclaiming, "Oh yes, my darling," Darcy kissed her head, and then palmed her face as he looked into her eyes, "I do love you... with all my heart. Will you say that you forgive me though? I could not bear to know that you despise me for my ungentlemanly behavior towards you."

She searched his eyes as he held her gaze, "Yes." She nodded, "I do forgive you, but I must ask you, why did you not tell me all this after you knew what had happened?"

"I was afraid that you would hate me for it. At the time you seemed almost ambivalent about our engagement, and I knew that I needed and very much wanted to persuade you to marry me. If I were to have confessed that then, would you have agreed to marry me, knowing how you felt about me at the time?"

The look in her face told him that he had hit his intended mark. She smiled timidly at him in acknowledgement of the truth.

"I am sorry to confess that you are correct about that, my love, but please know that I have come to feel the same passion for you as you have for me. At that time I based my feelings for you upon my wounded pride and the false words of others without taking into account the particulars of the situations surrounding those occurrences. Now, my feelings have changed for the better in regards to you. I have come to know the kind, gentle, shy, and loving man that you are. You are truly a beautiful person, and I thank the heavens for this opportunity to spend the rest of my life with you."

Darcy felt such relief at her exoneration of him that he kissed her soundly and she responded with equal enthusiasm. Her response was enough to cause his body to react with '*ungentlemanly*' reflexes.

"Dearest, as much as I would prefer to stay here all night and hold you thusly, I think it best that I leave…"

"But why ever should you go? No one is aware of our situation, and I would prefer you to stay with me. At least until I fall asleep?" Elizabeth begged.

Darcy could hardly resist her pleas for his presence in her bed. He knew that laying with her now would be sweet torture to him. He relented though, after recalling what they had both endured at the hands of Wickham and his cousin Anne.

Sleep was impossible for him to accomplish with her in such proximity since he had already known the delights of her warm body beneath him. Luckily for Elizabeth, she had no such issues. She fell asleep easily after they had found a comfortable position. Just before Darcy was about to withdraw from her bed, she began to cry in her sleep, but this time her tears were not due to his misdeeds. She was pleading for George to let her go.

My aunt and cousin shall pay for causing us such misery, my dearest Elizabeth, regardless of the scandal it may cause. No price is too high for the pain they have caused you, he vowed silently .

Early the next morning, Darcy removed himself from Elizabeth's bed and sent a footman to summons Richard before anyone else had arisen. His cousin wore his usual jovial smile when he met him in the study.

"What brings me to your study so early in the morning, Darcy? Do not tell me that you were so anxious to meet your future mother-in-law and some of your other future relations that you could not sleep?"

Though Darcy was in a foul mood, he snorted at Richards jibe towards the exuberant Mrs. Bennet and her younger daughters.

"Hardly, but then I am sure that with your personality and uniform I would very much enjoy spending many hours in such company…"

Richard looked at him with alarm, "Please do not tell me that you have summonsed me here in order to request that I play surrogate host to your future female relations?"

A soft rumbling chuckle escaped Darcy before he regained his serious expression again.

"That is a wonderful thought, but no. In fact I have called you here to request your assistance in the business of our rather less desirable female relations. "

"Ah, the issue of Anne and Lady Catherine… Yes, well I would much rather deal with the other ladies than have the rather onerous duty of investigating the treachery of our aunt and cousin."

"It is the price you pay for being a colonel in the army." Darcy retorted.

"Yes, and to think that had they not been stupid enough to conspire with a deserter, it would not even be an issue for me makes it even more disheartening. Really, Darcy, when you think about it, our relations are much more ridiculous than…"

Darcy looked at Richard sharply, and Richard tried to backtrack.

"Sorry, old man. I did not mean to offend you or your lovely bride-to-be. If it is any consolation, I do like the Gardiners, the elder Miss Bennet, and even Mr. Bennet… though he is a bit odd. It seems as though every family has its fair share of less than desirable characters."

"Touché, but right now my question is; how is the investigation going with relation to Anne and Lady Catherine's involvement in ours and Elizabeth's abductions?"

"You certainly know how to get to the point, do you not?" Richard smirked, "There will be a military trial, so it will not be made public, and before you ask, it was done at the request of my father. You know how he does not want this to besmirch our *vaunted* family name."

"I do not care about the publicity at this point after having witnessed Elizabeth thrashing about in her…" Darcy caught himself, but the hint of realization registered upon Richard's face. "Never mind. Anne may be our cousin, but after what she has done she deserves the public censure that she will surely receive."

"Oh, I do not think that you need worry about that Darcy. Anne would have suffered public censure regardless." Richard offered.

"Why?" Darcy asked suspiciously.

Richard looked to his side and then to the floor before he met Darcy's gaze hesitantly, "Because, Darcy, she is with George Wickham's child."

Darcy's eyes widened and he gasped at the stunning news. "H-how… how do you know this?"

His cousin shook his head sadly and walked to the window to look out to the street below.

"She had been ill and the commander here wanted to have her seen before deciding if they could remove her to town to stand trial. She confided this to the army physician they sent. I just happened to be outside the cell when he came to examine her. Apparently she has known about it for at least a month. So you see… either way you look at it, she would have been ostracized… unless…"

"Unless she managed to force me to marry her, you mean." Darcy finished grimly.

"Yes." Richard agreed.

"Why did you not mention this before? What will happen to her now?"

After taking a deep breath, Richard replied, "Truthfully? They rarely hang women-especially pregnant gentlewomen-for charges less than treason. For this? She may be transported, but then again they may send her to goal, or if someone is bribed with enough money, then they may work out something where she is… committed to an institution."

Darcy's mind was reeling in the revelations about Anne's fate. He wanted for her to pay for her part in Elizabeth's abduction, and near rape, but this seemed a higher price than even he would demand. *To bear the child of such a man, but I cannot feel too sorry for her. She did try to separate Elizabeth and me and then tried to foist that monster's child upon me.* He shuddered at the thought of being bound to such a woman, and was now more thankful than ever that he had gained the hand of a most loving and passionate woman that Elizabeth is.

"What… what of Lady Catherine? What shall they do with her?"

"They have no evidence-at least direct evidence- that links her to this, so we can do nothing with her-unfortunately. I have heard that father will not even acknowledge her-even in public now, though. Before he told her that he would only do so in public while banishing her from our private affairs. After this whole business with Wickham and Anne… well suffice to say that he wants to *cut off* that branch of the family."

"Do you mean to say that he knows about her…?"

"Present situation? Yes, and is all right to say it. Pregnancy is not a disease… well maybe in this case it is. "

"I have no doubt that that may be a very real threat to her. It is difficult to know what George has been exposed to since his tendencies were to lie with questionable women."

"No doubt. I hope that the image of father going to tell Lady Catherine about Anne will give you some comfort." Richard smiled at him mischievously, "Apparently when he informed her of her daughter's *condition*, she was almost apoplectic. She vowed that she would disown Anne after this. That was after she tried to deny that her *perfect daughter* could not possibly have been responsible for this whole fiasco, and that it was most assuredly the fault of George Wickham and…"

He took a deep breath before looking at Darcy, "She even tried to insinuate that… well… that Elizabeth was responsible for this. Father informed her that we had witnessed Anne's perfidy wilts engaged in intimate acts with said man. When she tried again to deny that her delicate child could do such a thing, he threw it at her that Anne was far enough along with child to know it. It is kind of hard to deny the facts when faced with such blatant evidence."

"Indeed." Darcy could offer no more words to such a sad conclusion to a young woman's life. Had she just been with child, then it could have easily been disguised, though he found that thought distasteful enough. She could have been sent away and the child cared for quietly away from society. Her mother would have seen to it that it was kept quiet, but now her crimes were compounded and it was nearly impossible to keep from the public.

The two gentlemen sat quietly reflecting upon the fate of their cousin until they heard the bell for breakfast. Darcy was now anxious to adjourn to the parlor, for he knew that Elizabeth would be there likely approaching her father with trepidation after his revelations last night.

When they made their way to the room, he noticed that Elizabeth had not come down yet.

"Is Elizabeth to join us this morning, Mrs. Gordon?" He addressed the housekeeper.

"No, sir. Her abigail said that she was feelin' under the weather an had requested some tea be brought up. When th' girl brought them to her, Miss Bennet was asleep again. She figured she was needin' her rest 'afore the rest of her family arrived today.

The news that Elizabeth was ill concerned Darcy enough to contemplate sending for the physician. He did not want her ill just as they were about to take their vows.

Chapter 17

Darcy stopped his pacing when Mr. Bales finally emerged from Elizabeth's room. He insisted she be examined regardless of her protests to the contrary. Bingley, Jane, Georgiana and Mrs. Annesley sat quietly talking amongst each other while occasionally looking at him. Elizabeth tried to assure him that she was well and that her illness would pass soon enough. His determination came after he had entered her room only to hear her retching in the dressing room.

Afraid that she was coming down with something, he sent for the physician and was now anxious to learn what was to be done for her. As soon as the door opened he was ready to pounce upon the poor man.

"Well? What news, Mr. Bales? Is Elizabeth all right? What is the matter with her?"

The elderly man smiled at him and shook his head. "Sir, your fiancée is well now, but I have advised her to rest as much as possible. She seems rather fatigued-no doubt the nightmares of what she has gone through are causing her troubles resting at night. As to her other ailments… it could be many things, and I have told her to eat small bland meals."

"So this is simply due to… sleeplessness? Then why…?"

"I do not know for certain. It could be many things and may resolve itself; however, I have told Miss Bennet that should her complaints continue, to have someone summon me."

Darcy noticed that the man seemed to be avoiding eye contact with him and he wondered at it. *Is he withholding something from me? Is there something he does not wish to tell me?*

"May we see her, Mr. Bales?" Mr. Bennet asked calmly.

"Of course, sir. I would request that you allow her some time to rest though. Oh… I would like to examine her in another week or so if she is still here, as well."

"If she needs to be then we will make sure not to travel until you think it would be wise." Darcy answered.

"Very well. I shall see myself out then."

Darcy did not glance back as he wanted nothing more than to see Elizabeth at that moment. Mr. Bennet shook hands with the physician before the man left them and followed Darcy, Bingley, Jane, Georgiana and Mrs. Annesley into Elizabeth's room. When Darcy saw her, he immediately noticed her flushed face and in another second saw the dark circles under her eyes. He approached her with some trepidation.

"Dearest, you look fatigued. Have I been keeping you up too late?" He whispered to her, to which she blushed and shook her head.

A little louder he asked, "How are you feeling? Did Mr. Bales say what could have caused you to take ill?"

"No… he only thought that it may have been stress, or…"

"Or?" Darcy questioned.

"Nothing," She said softly to him avoiding his gaze, "but I feel well now, Fitzwilliam. In fact I thought that I might like to take a walk to the park a little later."

"Nonsense, the physician said that you needed to rest and I intend on seeing to it that you follow his orders." Darcy answered.

"Yes, Lizzy, Mr. Darcy is right. Once you are completely better, we can take a walk." Jane insisted.

"Well Lizzy, I knew that you were not looking forward to seeing your mother and younger sisters, but this is a bit much to try and get out of visiting with them." Her father teased. "You do realize that once your mother catches wind of your illness that she will not rest until she has seen to every aspect of your recovery? She would not allow it to prevent your wedding after all."

Though Darcy refrained from cringing at the mention of Mrs. Bennet's impending arrival, in his mind he was devising ways to keep the matron occupied and out of everyone's way. He was certainly not looking forward to her or the younger Bennet ladies arrivals. Their consolation was that the Gardiners would be traveling with them and he did find that he enjoyed their company very much and Elizabeth seemed to be quite attached to them.

"I would not hear of any illness disrupting our wedding, sir. That is why I sent for Mr. Bales immediately upon learning of Elizabeth's condition. He is the best physician in Bath and is very well known throughout southern England for his excellence as a physician."

"Ah, that is good to know. If Mrs. Bennet should start having an attack of nerves, we may need to call upon the gentleman again. I, however, shall return to your fine library and await the invasion." Mr. Bennet said lightly.

Darcy wondered at his jesting at the expense of his family and could not fathom his dismissive manners towards all of his family. He could never see treating Elizabeth in such a flippant way. His ideal for a marriage was one of mutual respect and caring-*and a bit of passion never hurt either*. Turning his attentions back to her, he wished for some privacy to talk to her and looked at the room's occupants trying to convey his desire. Georgiana was the first to take the hint.

"Miss Bennet... do you suppose that you might be able to help me plan for tonight's dinner? I am afraid that I know so little about your family's preferences for desert or even entertainment." Georgiana directed her attention to Elizabeth's sister.

Darcy silently blessed his sister. *I should increase her pin money just for that.*

Jane Bennet looked at her hostess with surprise then back to Elizabeth. She hesitantly acceded to the request made of her. Once she made her good-byes, Bingley followed along with Mrs. Annesley, whom he noted looked back to him with the hint of a frown. He understood her unspoken censure not to trespass on propriety by staying overlong in the room alone with a single woman, even though they were betrothed, and she left the door cracked.

Once they were all gone, he approached the edge of the bed to sit next to Elizabeth.

"Elizabeth... please tell me if there is anything else that is wrong with you. I will make certain that you receive the best of care-you know I would do anything for you, do you not?"

She sighed heavily before she took his hand and replied, "Fitzwilliam... I am well right now. There is nothing the matter with me. Mr. Bales is simply being a little over cautious that is all."

He raised their joined hands and kissed her fingers. "When it comes to you, there is no such thing as being *overcautious*. Will you not tell me if there is something else? I cannot but help to think that something else is wrong."

Elizabeth raised their hands and kissed the back of his fngers. "Dearest... do not worry yourself. Even if I should suffer from some minor ailment, Mr. Bales assures me that I shall be fine."

"But... how can you be so sure?"

"No one can be sure about anything. These past few weeks have taught me that, but I have also learned that there are just some things that I cannot control and that I should not fret over those things that I can do absolutely nothing about."

"What makes you think that I cannot try to prevent something from happening to you?"

"Fitzwilliam…" She sighed again, "Sometimes, *things* are not always as bad as you imagine them to be. For right now, we know nothing, and it would be best if we do not dwell upon it… Please?"

She said no more as he studied her face in non-comprehension.

"If you wish." He hesitated for a moment before saying, "I should apologize for keeping you awake at night. It was abominable of me and I promise that I shall leave you be from here on out-at least until our wedding."

"I was not complaining was I? I would much prefer you to stay with me. After all, Mr. Bales also thought that my lack of peace was due to those nightmares and you go a far way to helping ease my mind."

He felt some relief that he would not be banished from her room from now on, but he would keep their interactions as chaste as possible-*at least until our wedding, anyway.*

"Then, if it is all right with you, I shall join you. It would not do to risk your health." He chuckled.

She smiled at him, but said little more. It was obvious to him that she would not discuss more of what the physician had said and he decided that she was correct. *Worrying about it would not help matters if there was nothing that could be done*; or so he kept saying to himself as he embraced her.

As expected, Mrs. Bennet and the youngest girls arrived with a flourish. Upon her arrival she demanded to be shown to Elizabeth's room immediately. Though Darcy was tempted to say that she was indisposed and could not be disturbed at present, he thought that in doing so she might cause an even louder uproar and agreed to show her to her daughter's rooms. He wished that Mrs. Gardiner would join them, but she had to tend her children at the moment so he decided to take the ladies to Elizabeth himself. Her mother seemed to be in a lather about something that he could not quite make out until the lady blurted out something that she heard from town.

"Oh... is such a great thing that you would keep our Lizzy after what has happened to her, Mr. Darcy. We were so afraid that you would give her up after this whole ordeal."

He was perplexed as to why she would think such a thing and asked, "Why would her being abducted cause me to give her up? It is not as if she had gone and eloped. She was, after all, taken by force and without her consent."

"Aye, but that is the whole crux of the issue. I, for one, would not wish to chance taking on another's child as my own if I were you, but then I should not be the one to complain." She said in a kind of stage whisper.

Darcy was taken aback at her insinuations about what happened while Elizabeth was captive and it took a great deal of self will not to lose his temper with his beloved's mother.

"Mrs. Bennet... I assure you that your daughter *was not touched* in any such way by that fiend so there is no possibility of her being *ruined* by him. Furthermore, I should request that you not speak of such things-especially where your younger daughters might hear it. It is most assuredly false and could not only ruin her reputation, but yours as well!"

She seemed undaunted. "Well I am only repeating what has already been said. Many are thinking you to be too kind to our Lizzy under the circumstances."

"Under *what* circumstances, Mrs. Bennet? I have just stated that Elizabeth was not touched by George Wickham...or anybody else while she was captive and I should know because she has said as much to me."

The woman looked at him with a condescending smile and said nothing else, which further irritated him. Her smug look seemed to indicate that she thought that Elizabeth would only say that to trick him into marrying her. *You have a very poor understanding of your daughter if you think that she would do such a thing and an even worse one if you think that her being raped by that monster would stop me from marrying her.*

"Mrs. Bennet, what would give you such ideas in the first place? Who told you these things about Elizabeth's ordeal?"

"Why it is all over the society pages, Mr. Darcy. Have you not heard?" She seemed genuinely surprised that he had not read about it.

He was aghast that it would have even been mentioned, but then to hear that it was in the society pages? *This is not to be borne!*

"No! *Who would have said such things?*" He demanded.

"I do not know who would indeed, but then it had to be true if they were saying such things in print." The woman tried to reason.

Darcy would have said several things to such ridiculous reasoning, but then he figured that it would only fall upon deaf ears anyway.

"Mrs. Bennet…" He pinched the bridge of his nose, "I beg of you not to mention this to Elizabeth. I would not want for her to become even more ill from the stress and worry of hearing her name bandied around in the gutter press in such a way."

That woman's eyes widened as she nodded her head in silent ascension.

"Oh… absolutely not. I would not wish to jeopardize that! In fact if there is anything that I may do to speed up her recovery, then I shall see to it immediately."

Suddenly an idea struck Darcy. *Perhaps I can spare Elizabeth this for a while longer.*

"Actually, Mrs. Bennet, the physician did say that she need as much rest as possible and she must avoid anything stressful. Perhaps you might want to freshen up before seeing her… and even rest up yourselves. I am sure that your journey must have been quite long. My staff can see to Elizabeth's needs easily as they are very efficient and I am sure that you could direct them to do whatever else you deem necessary for her care. In fact, maybe you might want to consider restricting your visits. It would not do to travel such a distance for the wedding only to become ill as well."

I hope that Mrs. Gordon will not resign after this, he thought to himself.

"Oh, yes! How thoughtful of you, sir. We will do that straight away. I am sure that you have many servants seeing to my Lizzy's comfort anyway and I am actually a bit tired myself. Maybe I should call for a bath too…"

As she continued to ramble on, Darcy vowed to get to the bottom of such malicious talk about Elizabeth. This time he knew that it could not have been due to Anne or even Denny. Mrs. Younge, he would not put it past, *but then with such bribes as she has received, she would not wish to chance risking my further wrath should I find that it was her saying such things-besides no one would believe such a woman anyway.*

Mrs. Bennet was still blathering on about how many servants he had, and what fine possessions he owned when he was brought back to the present. *I now understand why Mr. Bennet would want to hide in his library. It is the last place on earth this woman would ever deign to go. I would tear my own ears off if I had to listen to such nonsense!* It amazed him further that Elizabeth could have come from such a woman and he was thankful all the more. *Maybe she was a foundling...?* He immediately changed courses in the hallway and discretely requested the footmen to request Mr. Gardiner and Mr. Bennet in the study.

Within a half hour of depositing Mrs. Bennet and the other girls in their rooms, Darcy was on his way to the study. *I will get to the bottom of these vicious rumors and make the perpetrator pay dearly!*

Chapter 18

Caroline Bingley was anything but happy. Her brother, Charles, left her with her sister Louisa and her husband Malcolm Hurst. To make matters worse Charles had gone off with Jane Bennet and Jane's father to assist Mr. Darcy in his quest to *rescue* Eliza Bennet. When she first heard of the *little country chit's* having gone missing she prayed that some town drunkard had carried her off and had his way with her before drowning her in the Thames.

Unfortunately it was that Mr. Wickham and Mr. Darcy's mouse of a cousin Anne De Bourgh that was behind it all, and they were able to easily locate Eliza. She had heard that George Wickham was killed during the rescue and that Miss De Bourgh was taken in for questioning. She managed to fill in some of the gaps in information and embellished a little bit, then compounded her transgressions by repeating those embellishments to a few select others.

What followed from her actions turned out to be quite a sensational story in the gossip press and she could not have been more pleased with the end results. *With everything that is being said there would be no way that Eliza could remain unscathed from the scandal and Mr. Darcy will have to give her up in order to maintain his reputation.*

The challenge Caroline faced now was finding a way to get to Bath in order to prevent him from making the biggest mistake of his life by not marrying her. She was desperate enough to consider taking the post chase, but decided to cajole Louisa and Malcolm into taking her there, by persuading them that it would be good for his gout to visit the resort town.

It took Caroline almost six days to convince the Hurst's to take her to Bath, and they only agreed then after a friend's generous offer to allow them to stay at their house in the town. *Things could not be better. I shall make sure that I have plenty of fine gowns, and I shall take those articles with me to present to Mr. Darcy. Surely he will see the error of his ways when he sees them and realizes the impact it will have upon his reputation,* she thought to herself as she gazed out of the window. *He should thank me for saving him from such a fate, and I know exactly how he should show his gratitude.*

When Darcy summoned his future father-in-law and Mr. Gardiner into the study the gentlemen stopped speaking to each other to look at him. From the expressions on their faces it appeared that they already knew what he was there to discuss.

"I assume that you have both heard the vicious rumors about Elizabeth by now?"

It was more of a statement, and they both nodded their heads in acknowledgement of it.

"Can you tell me what exactly has been said, and when you first heard about this, Mr. Gardiner?"

"I am afraid that this came about a few days ago and though I have tried to track down the source. I found that once it was traced to some of the society with which I do not associate, no one was willing to divulge that information-at least not to me."

Darcy knew that several members of his set would know better than to divulge their sources of information to anyone from the outside, but then those members whom he associated with would have nothing to do with idle gossip.

"Can you at least tell me how far you were able to trace this, sir?"

"I was able to trace it to a servant in the Thrasher household. According to the girl, her mistress was talking about a scandal involving Miss De Bourgh and Elizabeth being involved with George Wickham. The story that she heard…" He paused and blushed, not wanting to repeat what had been said, "They were saying that Elizabeth and your cousin were involved in a romantic triangle and there was some rivalry between her and Miss De Bourgh. Apparently there is word going around that Elizabeth is carrying his child."

Darcy could feel the rage building within him. He knew that he had heard that name *Thrasher* before, but he could not place it at the moment through his furry. He would request that his aunt, Lady Eleanor, see if she could trace the rumors any further when she arrived later that afternoon.

"I thank you for going to all of the trouble of locating the source of the rumors, and I will take it from there. My immediate concern now must be Elizabeth's reputation. It has been severely unfair to her to have such things said about her and the only way that we may be able to protect her would be for us to marry immediately. In fact if she were well enough, I would marry her today."

"Do you really suppose that your marrying will help things, Mr. Darcy? Will not the whole of your society judge her more severely if you were to marry in such haste?" Mr. Bennet asked.

"Those who know me, would know better than to assume that I would associate with anyone who was in collusion with George Wickham, let alone marry them. When we are married and the official announcement is made, my friends will stand by me and should anyone say something disparaging about my wife, they will defend me unwaveringly."

"You have great faith in your friends, sir." Mr. Bennet commented.

Darcy looked directly at him and said, "I am very particular about whom I associate with, and everyone who knows me, understands that. If my friends say something as fact then it is regarded as such."

It sounded arrogant even to Darcy's ears, but he spoke the truth. His friends were not known to gossip and did not partake in such a senseless pastime. If they said something they were listened to with interest, because like him, they did not just speak to be speaking. They said something worth hearing.

"We shall have to rely upon that." Mr. Bennet said grimly, "When do you propose that you marry then, Mr. Darcy-if not today that is?"

"I had hoped that perhaps if everyone from both sides of our family arrived as expected then, tomorrow."

Darcy could tell by the look upon the gentleman's face that he was none too pleased with his answer, but he honestly believed that it was in both of their best interests to do so as soon as possible... *before anything else happened.*

"Then I hope that you are planning on delivering the news to Lizzy and her mother. I would not envy you for all of the riches in King Solomon's mine for having to *tell* one lady... the other I simply would not envy you your hearing." Mr. Bennet said dryly.

Mr. Gardiner chuckled at the truth of it and Darcy knew that Mrs. Bennet would likely try to argue otherwise. As to Elizabeth... she would be another story. He knew enough about her to know that she did not take too well to being*told* to do anying. *Maybe I could convince her to dress well and tell her that we are going for a ride, and then take her to the church?* He immediately discarded that notion. *She would be more furious about that than telling her the truth. Any way that I choose to inform her about everything that has happened will not be pleasant. As much as I prefer to spare her the tawdry details, she has to be informed. I will not start our marriage with disguises of any sort. Especially by keeping this from her.*

Darcy went straight to Elizabeth's room from the study. He knew that he was going to impart some information that would upset her and requested that Mr. Gardiner ask Mrs. Gardiner to be available should she need some reassurance. *Mrs. Bennet would only make it worse and I will not have Elizabeth distressed anymore.* He knocked upon her door and heard faint footsteps coming across the floor to the door. When Georgiana answered he was surprised, although pleasantly so.

"Uhhh, Georgiana… is… is Elizabeth well?"

"Yes, she and I were just discussing music. Did you come to join us?"

He hesitated before he would answer, "I, uh… actually wanted a moment alone with her," He looked to Elizabeth, "if you are agreeable to that?"

"Of course. Georgiana and I can catch up in a little while and I thought that since I have spent so much time in this room cooped up, I might re-emerge into the gardens at least and enjoy them before the rest of your guests arrive."

"I would not mind accompanying you." He turned to his sister, "Would you care to join us?"

She nodded silently in agreement and left them for a moment to retrieve her pelisse and gloves. Darcy decided to take this opportunity to discuss his plans for tomorrow in privacy when his sister left them. He came over to her side of the chase where she was laying with her legs hanging over the edge and sat in the chair next to her.

"What is on your mind, Fitzwilliam?"

"What makes you think something is wrong?"

"Because I can see your muscles tense in your jaw and that usually happens when something is bothering you."

He smiled despite his news and quickly regained his resolve to discuss his plans with her.

"You know me too well, dearest. I... um... wanted to talk to you about our wedding plans..."She sat up at the mention of their nuptials and stared straight at him. "We... that is your father and uncle and I have been discussing our plans, and due to new circumstances, we have decided that we should marry as soon as possible. Tomorrow even." He blurted out.

Her eyes opened wide and she stared at him, "Why such a rush?"

"Today, I have received some most distressing news. It involves you-well what happened with you while you were gone." She raised an eyebrow to indicate for him to go on. "Apparently there have been some rumors that... well that you were not so reluctant to go with them..."

He was immediately at her side when he saw the indignant tears forming in her eyes.

"They said that they would ruin me. In fact they swore that they would!" She bit out. "I began to think that it might all have worked out finally, but now it seems impossible!"

"Elizabeth, please, sweetheart, listen to me. We are not going to let anyone destroy our chance at happiness. That is why I am planning for us to wed tomorrow. Once we are safely married then these rumors will be dispelled, and it will soon be forgotten in place of other gossip."

"Fitzwilliam, do you honestly think that once we are married that it will change anything? People will say what they wish to believe and since I am not of your social circle, they will... they will find it easier to fathom... the worst!"

"Shh, no, no, darling. Once we are married then I shall publish the announcements and then those of my true friends will know the truth of the matter. They know me well enough to know that I would never associate with you if I believed that you had plotted against me with my worst enemy... but in order to do this we must first marry. Would you consider this?"

She thought for a moment. "Are you sure that you would still want me after all of the trouble I have caused you?"

Darcy was taken aback at her reluctant response. "Why would you ask such a question? Of course I still want to marry you. There is no one else that I would rather marry and recall that I know the truth about the whole situation. It does not matter to me what others say because I know the truth."

"But, your family… Georgiana…"

"They will be unaffected. My love, our family has enough clout and rank that we do not need to worry about what others think or say and as I have said… my true friends will know the truth about the matter anyway. They will support me, so you see… there is no need to worry on my account."

Georgiana had been standing behind the door and came in quietly.

"Elizabeth… my brother is right. You need not worry about us. Our real friends know about our relationship with George Wickham… even without knowing what happened with me, they know that he was a man not to be trusted and they also know that Fitzwilliam would not marry any woman who would associate with that man. You need not worry over that and as for me…. I would be delighted to call you sister as soon as may be."

Elizabeth smiled at the pair through her tears and then looked back at him. "Well then Fitzwilliam… I suppose that I shall marry you tomorrow-if that is your desire."

"It is. Very much so." He replied hastily as he grabbed her hand to kiss the back of it. "Nothing would make me happier."

Actually there were a few things that would make Darcy happier at the moment, but he would not entertain those thoughts until tomorrow night, when he could claim Elizabeth as his own. He decided that a walk outside would help to calm them, and allowed for his sister and his fiancée to do most of the talking, as he was content in listening to them getting along as she did with her sister's, and more specifically as she did with Jane.

By the time that they had come inside from the gardens, the Matlock's coach had just arrived with the rest of his family. When the earl stepped out to hand down his Aunt Eleanor, Darcy noticed the tense look upon both of their faces. He braced himself for what he knew was coming, but was ready with his defenses.

Richard also arrived while they were outside walking and Darcy was thankful that he would not have to face that inquisition all by himself.

Richard, Darcy, Georgiana," The earl greeted them; "Will you be so kind as to introduce us to your companion?"

Darcy quickly recalled his manners, "Pray, forgive me, Lord and Lady Matlock... May I introduce you to my fiancée, Miss Elizabeth Bennet? Elizabeth, this is my Aunt and Uncle Fitzwilliam's, the Earl and Countess Matlock."

They paid their respects to each other and gave their civilities amongst stilted conversation, before Darcy asked them to join them in the parlor after they were settled.

Once they were out of earshot, Richard leaned over to whisper to Darcy, "That went much better than I expected. I am surprised that they did not insist that your engagement be broken."

Darcy glared at his cousin, "After what I have had to endure these past few weeks, they have nothing on my glares of incivility, my stubbornness, or my furry. Might I also remind you, Richard, that it was your father who said that he would not hear of me ending my engagement? It would be far worse for me to abandon my responsibilities now, and besides all that, I have no wish to do so. Elizabeth and I will marry tomorrow morning and that is final."

Richard held up his hands, "Do not look at me. Were I to be my own master, I would have chosen her for myself..."

Darcy's face was flushed with a look of further furry and indignation, and Richard's words died upon his lips. He wisely decided not to tempt fate for the moment.

When the earl and countess had refreshed themselves, they came down to join the rest of the party before dinner that evening. As luck, would have it, Elizabeth decided to take mercy upon Darcy and informed her mother of their plans to marry tomorrow while the new arrivals were indisposed. Though he could not be sure, he was relatively certain that he could hear her protests from across the house and he had to acknowledge the truth of Mr. Bennet's sage words- he did not envy Elizabeth her good hearing at that moment either. Once Mrs. Bennet calmed to a more tolerable decibel or five lower, he heard Elizabeth's footsteps in her rooms and went over to join her.

"How did it go with your mother?"

"I am surprised that you did not hear. She was unsurprisingly unhappy, but then we knew that she would be."

Elizabeth seemed out of sorts still, almost to the same level as she was when he informed her about their need to marry immediately.

"What is it, Elizabeth? Did your mother say something else to upset you so?"

"N-no, but she did tell me how much of a mess I have made of things..."

She took a deep breath and let out a small sob, which broke his heart. He embraced her to him tightly, trying to transfer his warmth to her as he rubbed her back in small circles. Darcy became furious at his mother-in –law-to-be for distressing Elizabeth, wishing that he had been the one to break the news to her and regretting not having done so.

"What did she say to upset you?"

"S-she s-said that I have disgraced myself and you as well, and that I should be thanking you for taking me on and then she let into me for us having to marry so soon. That was when she started shrieking."

He grabbed her shoulders and held her away from him in order to look her in the eyes.

"Elizabeth, your mother is no different than she has always been with you. I am surprised that you are so upset about this, and besides she is talking nonsense about your need to thank me for wishing to marry you. It is I who should be thanking you-after my abominable behavior. Had it not been for me and my family, you would not have been in this situation in the first place."

She said nothing more, but allowed him to continue holding her until she calmed. He summoned her maid when she felt up to dressing before dinner so that she could meet his aunt and uncle more formally, and secretly prayed that Mrs. Bennet would have an attack of apoplexy to the extent that she would be rendered mute-for eternity. He left her in capable hands and went to change his own attire. When he was ready he knocked upon Elizabeth's door so that he could escort her to the parlor before rejoining his guests. As they were coming out of her sitting room door to the hall, they were greeted by his aunt, Lady Eleanor.

Upon seeing the couple emerge from the door of the master suite, she wore a frown that was mostly aimed at him, but said nothing as he stiffly offered her his opposite arm. No one spoke of anything and Darcy wondered about her disquietude, knowing that once they were out of earshot of servants or any audience, that the great lady would not withhold her opinions. Luckily they arrived in the appointed parlor before the rest of his guests, and his aunt took the opportunity to talk to them both.

"Darcy, I am shocked at your behavior, taking such liberties of placing your fiancée in the mistress chambers before you are married. I should hope that you will tell me that it was in preparation of your nuptials tomorrow, but somehow, I do not think that to be the case."

Darcy was properly chastised for his blatant misbehavior, and had completely forgotten about his relative's placement within the family's rooms. He knew that his aunt was not pleased, but since they were to marry tomorrow, he did not think she would object to Elizabeth staying this last night in the mistress chambers- if he removed himself to a different room. He was also surprised that she was already aware of their plans to marry the next day.

"How did you know that we had planned to marry tomorrow?"

"Richard. You know he cannot keep a secret-especially when it comes to family gossip. It is a wonder that the military has him in intelligence." She looked Elizabeth over as she said this, "Miss Bennet, I understand that you·have four sisters?"

"Yes ma'am." She was still blushing from the countess mention of their room's proximity.

"I also understand that you did not have a governess growing up?"

Elizabeth looked at her with curiosity.

"Again, Richard took the liberty of informing us all about your circumstances." At Darcy's look of alarm she clarified, "Do not worry, he was singing only praises for Miss Elizabeth and Miss Bennet... Oh... and your father, Mr. Bennet. I understand that you like to read, is that correct?"

"I do, ma'am."

The countess waved her hand, "We do not have to be so formal, Miss Bennet, you will be a part of the family by this time tomorrow, so you may call me 'Aunt Eleanor'."

Darcy was shocked at her easy acceptance of Elizabeth and could only assume that Richard had his hand in it. Before they were joined by the resident big mouth he wanted to ask his aunt a favor.

"Aunt Eleanor... I have no doubt that you have heard..."

"The rumors surrounding your Miss Bennet's supposed compromising situation with George Wickham? Yes, I have, and I have my suspicions as to who started them, but I have not heard anything from *my* sources...*yet*."

She looked at Elizabeth before she expounded upon her efforts while she was in town to find the culprit responsible for besmirching her favorite nephew's name by slandering his fiancée.

"I do not take lightly to anyone who spreads about rumors-whether true or false-especially as it regards my family. Your fiancé, Miss Bennet, is well known for his *upstanding moral principle*, steadfast dedication, and loyalty to his friends and close family members."

The countess made eye contact with him then, and said directly to him, "Which is why I find your room assignments rather... surprising."

Darcy's back straightened and he was about to respond to her unspoken reprimand, but they were joined by Georgiana and the earl who greeted them with polite formalities. Georgiana took a seat between their aunt and Elizabeth and placed her folded hands in her lap, but said nothing. Their uncle was more quiet than usual and his wife teased him to goad him out of his blackened mood.

"Andrew, you really must not frown so much least your face should become permanently frozen in that expression."

He scowled at his wife at first before the corners of his lips upturned into a small smile.

"I will endeavor to remember that from here on out, dear, least I be accused of turning to stone." He turned his attentions towards Darcy. "How are you both this evening?"

"We are fine, sir. I trust that you are rested after your journey?"

The earl snorted before answering, "I started to fall asleep on the last leg of the journey until some boob tried to run us off the roadway by overtaking our coach, then the idiot had the gumption to slow down considerably after passing. Needless to say our journey here was a great deal longer and more tedious than necessary."

"Did you see who it was that almost ran you off the road?" Darcy asked with concern.

"No, but be assured that if I ever find out from our driver or footmen who they are, I shall *read them the riot act*!"

As he and his uncle continued on in their banter the elder gentleman finally spoke about his preoccupying thoughts.

"I suppose that Richard has already apprised you of the situation with our errant family members?"

"Yes."

"That is good, for I have no desire to dwell upon such unpleasant matters. I have done all that I shall for them, and now that they have made their beds, they can sleep in them. I have washed my hands of the pair!" He turned to Elizabeth and said, "Forgive me my manners, Miss Bennet. Normally I would not discuss such things in front of others; however, seeing that you will soon be a part of this family, and have unfortunately been a victim of Catherine and Anne's schemes I feel no compunction about discussing it now. In fact, Eleanor and I prefer to discuss things out in the open as such, for we have found that within marriage it is nearly impossible to keep secrets for very long without the other party finding out about it... *eventually*. Let that be one of your first lessons in matrimony, it will help you to get along better than many of our set."

Darcy was surprised and heartened that his uncle was making an effort to accept Elizabeth into their fold. He was also proud of Elizabeth as she proved that she could engage in intelligent and lively conversation with the earl.

"I would think that is good advice for anyone who is marrying, sir." She said with her usual easy manner.

His aunt and uncle chuckled to listen to her respond so sensibly. She would not cater to them and she was not afraid to express her own opinions as either. They continued their conversation about what they felt constituted a good marriage and then started discussing their personal hobbies. Darcy was somewhat surprised when he learned that Elizabeth, like him, enjoyed playing chess.

He was about to ask her about setting up a match later on in the evening, but the Gardiner's and the Bennet's made their way into the parlor. Darcy's attention was instantly focused upon Mrs. Bennet and what she might say or do, and he also noticed that Elizabeth became quieter when her mother entered the room. After he made all of their introductions, he went to stand behind Elizabeth in support of her as well as assurance to himself.

For the most part, *her mother* conducted herself rather well under the circumstances. She did not speak unless it was to offer her deference to the earl or countess and seemed to be generally in awe of his family's station, dress, and most especially the countess' jewels. Darcy found Mrs. Bennet's behavior diverting and thought to himself that he was glad that she did not know that his own wealth well surpassed that of his other family members-including Lady Catherine.

In his own opinion there were too many women within his own social circle that were like Mrs. Bennet and Caroline Bingley that could only see him for his wealth and position and too few like Elizabeth who valued the man behind it all.

Thinking of Caroline Bingley gave him the cold chills. He had a feeling that she at least knew something about the rumors concerning Elizabeth, if she was not behind them, but he had no proof. He would wait to see what the countess' sources turned up, but he thought that he may hire an investigator himself to ferret out information as necessary also. No stone would be left unturned, and when he found the bottom feeder that did this to his Elizabeth he would make certain that they knew what it was to have their name dragged through the gutter press. After they finished their meal, they enjoyed the usual separation of the sexes. The earl took a moment to speak with Darcy in relative privacy while Mr. Gardiner and Mr. Bennet wandered over to the book shelves to find a few new volumes on horticulture to peruse. Richard and Bingley began a loud game of billiards and even had to be reminded to keep their boisterousness down a bit.

"I see that your fiancée's father and uncle also have a passion for books, Darcy. They seem to be well read and well bread for a tradesman and a small country gentleman."

The reference to Mr. Gardiner made Darcy bristle, and he felt a protective urge to defend him to his uncle and also his friend who, it seemed, might also become his brother soon enough.

"Though Mr. Gardiner and Bingley are tradesman, they are also very intelligent and loyal to their families," *To a fault at times in Bingley's case*, he thought to himself, "and they likely do better than some gentlemen of our association as far as their fortune."

"Those are good traits, my boy, but what should the *ton* say if they found out your wife has an uncle in trade? Or even more that your new sister married a man with roots in trade?"

"What could they say? I am not ashamed of them... most of them, anyway. They are good people-better than many of our acquaintance..."

"Easy, Darcy. I was not criticizing your choices or the men themselves, I just want you to realize what it is you are getting yourself into."

"It is not as if I have not thought about it before, but I am willing to take relatives a thousand times worse for her."

"That is good to know, because she will be getting relatives a thousand times worse with her association with you...er...us."

The earl sobered quickly, "It really is too bad that we cannot prove that Catherine was in collusion with her daughter, because I know that she was aware of what was going on with you and Richard. What I cannot fathom is how she did not know about Anne and George Wickham... to be carrying on in such a way. If there ever was a soul to really feel for, it would have to be that child Anne is carrying! I have been racking my brain to find a way to help the poor mite, but the only thing that I can come up with is to send Anne to some friends in the north..."

Darcy frowned, thinking about all of the innocent people that had been affected by their selfishness and duplicity, and that it would be carried over to the next generation. He may be able to help them find placement for the child in a good home, and he would see to it that Lady Catherine made her contributions to the child's upbringing. It was, after all, partly due to her overlooking her daughter's behavior that the entire situation was created in the first place.

I shall deal with that another time. For now I have much to anticipate and refuse to waste my time or my happiness on them. Tomorrow, Elizabeth shall be my wife and I can protect her from the likes of the Lady Catherine's and the Caroline Bingley's of this world.

Soon after, the gentlemen joined the ladies and were treated to an assortment of Mozart, Bach, and Handel by Georgiana, Elizabeth, Mary, and Lady Eleanor. When Elizabeth accompanied Georgiana at the piano forte, Darcy's heart stood still listening to her beautiful soprano. She sang with such feeling and spirit... and passion. Darcy's mind began to wander to other areas of her passion, losing himself in the memory of their evening at the parsonage.

His body started to respond physically to his imaginings and he had to shift in his chair and cross his legs to hide the evidence of his desire. When Elizabeth finished with her piece she came over to sit next to him which exacerbated his desire for her. Never was he so thankful that a night of entertaining was done when Lady Eleanor played Mozart's piano concerto number twenty one. It was such a fitting piece at the end of the evening, he took his time arising and stayed behind until his body had calmed enough to walk the halls to his room. He felt fortunate that Mr. Bennet allowed him a few minutes alone with Elizabeth as well. Her father seemed to recognize their need for some privacy before the morning. It would be a very long night for both he and Elizabeth, for this night was one of anticipation. Tomorrow night would be one of satisfaction.

When everyone but Darcy and Elizabeth were gone from the music room, Darcy wrapped his arms around Elizabeth's waist and held her tight against him.

"Are you as excited about tomorrow as I am, dearest?" Darcy asked her.

She looked up at him and smiled, "Yes, I think so. At first I was a bit nervous about this happening so suddenly, but now I am actually looking forward to it. Since I have gotten to know you and have seen the kind of man that you are, and heard the stellar testimonials of your character I cannot believe my luck in winning your affection. I cannot wait to start our new life together."

Her beautiful expressive eyes were smiling up to him along with her beautiful lips that were begging to be kissed, and he took this opportunity to do so. He began lightly, brushing his lips with hers. Gradually she began to respond likewise causing a cascade of emotions to run through him. His passion for her grew in his kisses as he demanded of her and she gave willingly to him. They were lost in each other's embrace and barely registered the throat clearing coming from Lady Eleanor who was standing in the doorway to the great hall.

They quickly disengaged from each other, but not without regret. His aunt offered to escort Elizabeth to her rooms, and gave Darcy a meaningful look.

"Tomorrow, you may both loose yourselves to the moment, but tonight you must find a way to control your... passions." She threw another meaningful look to Darcy, "I have taken the liberty of having your valet set up some of your things for tomorrow in my suite. I shall be staying in the one adjacent to Miss Elizabeth's for tonight."

They both blushed with embarrassment, and Lady Eleanor laughed, "Do not look so forlorn, Fitzwilliam. After all it is only for one night."

With her final words she whisked Elizabeth to her chambers, and made certain that the doors were secured. Darcy was not looking forward to this last night without Elizabeth in his arms and he barely slept all night. At the break of dawn he woke and was the first person ready in the household. He was getting married today and absolutely *nothing* was going to stop him.

Chapter 19

Elizabeth was awakened by the early light streaming through the curtains. *I am getting married today*, she thought happily. She sat up in bed quickly and threw off the covers, but before she leapt out of the bed she was very nearly ill. The thought of anything interfering with their plans to wed was banished from her mind in the next instant. *I refuse to allow it! No, nothing will stop us from attaining our happiness! I will not be ill, especially not today of all days!*

She tried to turn the handle to the hall which was still locked, and then she tried the one to the sitting room. As luck would have it, it opened where she was greeted by the Countess Matlock. *I should have known*, she thought anticlimactically.

"Good morning to you, Miss Bennet. Did you sleep well?"

"Yes…no… well perhaps not. It was difficult for me to sleep, due to…nerves, ma'am. And you? Were you able to sleep well?" She said with more politeness than real concern.

The older woman chuckled a little before replying, "You do not strike me as a woman who is *'struck by nerves'* easily. Perhaps you felt a need for a comforting presence?"

Elizabeth blushed scarlet from her ladyship's inference to her and Darcy's sleeping arrangements which were surprisingly precise. The elder woman smiled at her with a hint of sympathy mixed with amusement.

"There is no need to be embarrassed, Miss Bennet. I was young once too."

It took Elizabeth another moment to gather her wits before she could speak.

"I… we have not… that is we did not do anything, we…"

"It is none of my business what you and my nephew have or have not done. What matters now, is that you do not appear to be thwarting propriety in the face of such a scandal as you are now embroiled in. That is why I made the sleeping arrangements that I did last night.

Though Darcy proclaims that his staff is most loyal to him, there is no telling who might let some little bit of information slip and that will not aid in restoring your reputation, Miss Bennet."

The frankness in which Lady Eleanor spoke was eye opening to Elizabeth. She knew that those false rumors would significantly damage her credibility and reputation among the *ton*, but then her behavior while at Bath would do nothing to exonerate her either.

"I know that Lady Matlock and I do appreciate what you are saying, though we have done nothing more than…"

Her last words died on her lips as she recalled what had happened in Hunsford. What she was saying did not impress the lady either.

"My dear, you may not have done anything besides hold one another, but had anyone witnessed the two of you, it would be difficult to persuade them that you were innocent of other things as well. Oh… and I sincerely meant for you to call me *'Aunt Eleanor'*, for at ten o'clock we shall be family."

Elizabeth was duly reprimanded and avoided eye contact with Lady Eleanor when she asked, "How did you know…?"

"About your sleeping arrangements with my nephew? It was not that difficult to figure out when I knew where his chambers were and saw where you were situated. I am rather surprised that your father has not insisted that you marry immediately after such a blatant breach of propriety."

Elizabeth bristled at her veiled, if unmeant, criticism of her father then recalled that the countess could not have had a chance to really know him over one nights polite conversation.

"I think that at the time of my room being assigned, my father was simply happy to have me safely returned to him. Mr. Darcy brought me straight here from… the other place."

Lady Eleanor's face suddenly changed from amused curiosity to motherly concern.

"So Darcy placed you here in the room next to his to keep you safe?" She nodded her head and said more to herself than to Elizabeth, "It makes sense now. He probably did it as much for his peace of mind as for yours."

Elizabeth heard the empathy and understanding in the countess' voice, and then realization dawned upon her. *He needed to know that I was safe and that he could protect me.* At that moment she comprehended what her companion was saying. *It makes sense. He protects Georgiana with the same devotion that he does me. Because he loves me unconditionally he wants to protect me above all else.* She felt special-truly loved-by such a gift as he had given her...*his heart.* Even her own father-of whom she was favored above all others by, had not even exhibited this much love and devotion to her... *ever.* In that moment she knew that she would do anything to protect that gift with all *her* heart and soul and endeavor to be worthy of it.

The amount of power that that feeling gave her was uplifting, exhilarating, and quite scary to her. Never before in her life had she realized that she could feel such a way towards another human being, not towards Jane or her father had she felt this way. *I really do love him!* It was surreal for Elizabeth, but it elicited a sense of contentment within her. *There will be no regrets for me when we are married because I only ever wanted to marry for the deepest love.*

They were silent for a moment before the quiet was broken by a servant's knock on Elizabeth's dressing room door.

"I suppose that you should be made ready for this special day. Once you have bathed, I will have your breakfast set up in here. You can be made ready afterwards and then we shall go to the church." At Elizabeth's look of protest, she finished by saying, "It would not do to have your groom see you before the ceremony."

Elizabeth was slightly amused at her adherence to those rather superstitious practices and also disappointed at not being allowed to see Darcy before they met at the altar, but decided to obey her directives. *Not too much longer and we shall see each other and then no one will be able to separate us.*

While she enjoyed her bath the maid came in to announce that her mother wished to speak to her. The tranquil peace was short lived.

Darcy had thought about going out for a ride on Zephyrus, but thought better of it. He would not risk being thrown from the horse. *If anything happened to me then Elizabeth could face dire consequences since we are not yet married.* He still worried that she may have become with child since their encounter at the parsonage, but pushed those thoughts aside. *Nothing is going to happen to me today. I will not take any unnecessary risks. There is too much to lose. Within a few hours we will be husband and wife and then I can protect her for the rest of her life.*

Before breakfast he decided to go out for a walk in the park instead. He kept hoping that Elizabeth would have the same idea and meet him there, but as he made his way through the sun dappled trees, he scarcely came across another person, let alone the one person he most wished to see. When he made it to the opposite side of the park he noticed that a familiar carriage was being brought from the side of a house. *What is the Hurst's carriage doing here in Bath?* He asked himself.

Quickly he darted across the street, to the courtyard behind the house to see if he could see who had taken up residence in the building. There was another carriage behind the Hurst's which still had an inordinate number of valises left to be unpacked. *Judging by the initials Caroline Bingley and Louisa Hurst must be among the occupants of the house.* Darcy froze for a moment, wondering why they would arrive unannounced to the town where their brother had recently come with Miss Bennet. A feeling of dread overcame him, and he decided to go back to his house. *I need to make some arrangements before things get out of hand*, he thought as he briskly walked home.

Upon his arrival, he summonsed two of his most trusted footmen to the study. When they arrived he went on to explain his plan to ensure that this day was not disrupted in anyway by any unexpected visitors.

"Mills, Wilson, I have made a startling discovery that may disrupt our celebration today and I need for you to do some things for me...."

Darcy went on to explain his plan to the two men, then sent them on their way to do his bidding. He felt more at ease with those tasks taken care of. Now he needed to discuss what he saw across the park with Bingley and Richard. Once they had awakened they were sent down to join him in the study where he informed them of his observations this morning, but not until after he received some lighthearted ribbing.

"We heard that you were up early enough to rouse the roosters Darce. Were you thinking about tonight?" Richard asked. "Or do you need some advice as to what your husbandly duties entail?"

He winked at him while Bingley guffawed, to Darcy's disgust.

"No!" Darcy snorted, "I hardly think that three minutes of carnal activity constitutes being an expert on such subjects, Richard... especially when that includes disrobing one's self as well."

"Well we all know that *you* would take at least twenty minutes, Darce... and most of it would be spent laying out your clothing and hanging them up!"

Bingley was still laughing at the cousin's antics, when Darcy's mood sobered somewhat as he glared at his cousin.

"The reason that I have asked you both in here so early on my wedding day is because when I was out rousting the roosters and contemplating my future felicity," He raised his brow in a challenge to Richard, "I stumbled upon a most alarming discovery."

"And what discovery was that?" Richard asked.

"Apparently Malcolm Hurst along with his wife and," He turned to Bingley, "your youngest sister have come to Bath and they are staying across the park from us."

Bingley shot up with alarm, "*What*? They are here, *now*?"

Bingley's choice of words caught Darcy's attention.

"What do you mean by, '*now*', Bingley? Were you *aware* that they were coming?" Darcy asked.

"Ah... well... not exactly that they were coming-just that they might... come." Bingley offered meekly.

"And you did not think it important enough to *forewarn us* that they might be coming?" Darcy asked indignantly.

"Well, it is not as though I knew for certain that they were going to come-especially the week of your wedding. I thought that Hurst would have more sense."

You underestimate his power of hearing... or at least his ability to avoid a nagging wife, thought Darcy. It was yet another instance where he was coming to value Elizabeth as his wife-to-be. She would never try to interfere with his plans and she was most certainly not a nag... or a bundle of nerves-normally.

"There is nothing to be done about it now, Bingley. They are here and obviously since they have not come demanding shelter in Darcy's house, we shall not have to acknowledge their arrival until they come over to present themselves." Richard suddenly froze.

I see you are thinking along the same lines as myself, Richard, thought Darcy.

"Yes, and it is only a matter of time before they are come to tear up our peace." Piped in Bingley absentmindedly.

When the cousins stared at him he said, "What? You think that I am stupid when it comes to those two? I know that they have tried to separate Jane... Miss Bennet from myself..." He looked at Darcy who wore a chastened expression. "And it is very likely that they have heard what has been said in town and now want to tear me apart from her again… but it will not work! I will not allow them to dictate my future happiness! Jane and I will be married despite what they may wish… even if I need to use…"

Bingley froze again when Darcy and Richard stared at him as if he were a man possessed.

"It is true. We are engaged as well, and we have even obtained Mr. Bennet's permission. The only reason that we waited to make the announcement was because of you and Miss Elizabeth's situation. Our intention was to make the announcement at your wedding brunch." He looked sheepishly at Darcy. "I hope you do not mind?"

Darcy's head was spinning, but he quickly regained his wits. A new plan came to mind quickly… or rather an addendum to his original plan came to him. *If Mr. Bennet is amenable to this new arrangement it may save us all some trouble… and it may save me from offending either Richard or Bingley.*

A note was penned quickly and sent via footman to the house across the park. *If anyone thinks that they can come to tear up our peace, they have another thing coming to them!* Darcy thought with a gleam in his eyes.

At nine o'clock Elizabeth was on her way to the church along with her father, the Matlock's, Gardiner's, and Jane in the Matlock's spacious carriage. Elizabeth was both relieved and dismayed that her father had insisted that her mother go to the church with her younger sisters *and* Georgiana. She felt guilty at how he had finally convinced her to accede. He told her that Colonel Fitzwilliam would be accompanying them to the church and of course she was never averse to throwing any of her daughters in the way of a single gentleman-especially one in a redcoat.

That poor unfortunate man was convinced to agree to that part of Darcy's plan by a promise-more like bribe-of a whole case of his best whiskey, and there was also the fact that he was also a co-guardian to Georgiana. Mr. Bennet confided to her that he thought it was a bargain on her fiancé's part and that her future sister-in-law would forgive them… eventually.

Darcy and Mr. Bingley had already ridden ahead of their party earlier to finish up some last minute arrangements. According to his aunt, she and her husband would be riding back to the house with Mr. Bingley and Jane and then their family party would move to a different house in order to give the newlyweds some privacy.

Contemplating how she felt, Elizabeth did not feel as she had always thought she would as a new bride, but then she attributed that to what she and Darcy had already shared between then. If she had to assign any emotion at that time she would have described it as anticipation and excitement. She knew that she wanted more than anything to be his wife now.

When Elizabeth's carriage pulled up to the church they were the last to arrive and as she entered on the arm of her father she was surprised to see that she was not the only one to share that honor. Her father offered his other arm to a very surprised Jane and he escorted them both up the aisle. It did not dawn on her until they reached the alter that not only was Darcy awaiting her, but Mr. Bingley also awaited Jane. *A double wedding? How wonderful to be able to share this day with a most beloved sister!*

She smiled widely at her intended and he gave her one of his rare dimpled smiles and winked at her. His handsome features and the glowing look in his eyes as he gazed upon her took her breath away. It was a few moments before Elizabeth noticed that Jane was looking at her father questioning his actions until he leaned to whisper something to her. After the surprise nuptials were announced -to the gasps of her mother and the three youngest Bennet daughters- the reverend began the ceremony.

Elizabeth's head was swimming with all of these new developments as she slowly began to concentrate on the words to her vows that would forever bond herself to Mr. Fitzwilliam Darcy of Pemberley and Derbyshire.

Most of her attention was focused on the man himself whom she had gotten to know and now thought of as the best man of her acquaintance. In November she would never have guessed that her life would have taken so many turns as to bring her to this point, but she was now indebted most thankfully to whatever forces of fate delivered her to this point in their lives.

He likewise did not seem capable of removing his eyes from her all throughout the ceremony and she could barely recall when the reverend turned his attentions towards Jane and Mr. Bingley. Their focused attention remained on each other until they were pronounced man and wife. At first she was uncertain as to how they would acknowledge their new status, but that answer was quickly resolved when Darcy' eyes met hers and he took her face in his hands to bring his lips down to hers in a soft and not so chaste kiss as his tongue surreptitiously grazed over hers.

Their families broke out into loud applause and a little whistle from Colonel Fitzwilliam. When she and Darcy signed their names upon the registrar it was surreal to her that this would be the last time that she would write the name Bennet beside her name. Charles and Jane followed them to sign and when they came out to greet the well wishers they were all surprised to hear a commotion towards the back of the church.

"*What is going on here Charles? What have you done*" Demanded Caroline Bingley.

Her new brother-in-law was momentarily speechless, but her husband straightened to his full height and took on his impervious look.

"Why, Miss Bingley... I think it would be quite obvious. These fine lovely ladies have just made us the happiest of men... by becoming our wives."

Elizabeth noted a gleam in her husband's eyes as he announced their marriages and she decided to join him in his merriment.

"Yes, *Miss* Bingley... *Mrs.* Bingley and I look forward to catching up on the latest news from town... I am sure you would be more than knowledgeable about everything that we have missed since we have come to Bath."

With great pleasure did the newlyweds march past the uninvited intruder towards their carriage without as much as a backwards glance. Had they bothered to notice, Caroline Bingley would have been seen to be sporting a paler than normal complexion and a mouth in danger of falling to the floor.

Chapter 20

After the Darcy's and the Bingley's entered their carriage, everyone was silent. Elizabeth was elated that her new husband had arranged for her beloved Jane and Mr. Bingley to marry along with them. *It is just like him to arrange something like this without so much as a hint as to what he was planning... though I shall not complain about that.* She looked at the newlyweds across from her and Darcy who were still enraptured with each other. *Jane appears to be so happy and Mr. Bingley looks... almost like Fitzwilliam looks at me. I know that Jane did not know about this. She would have surely said something... or at least hinted at it. I shall have to ask Fitzwilliam how this all came about.*

She turned to the man himself to find his eyes darkened, simmering, and focused solely on her. *I wonder what is going through his mind?* Elizabeth smiled at her new husband and felt a blush come over her as he gazed at her with such dark intensity that she had not seen in him before. Her thoughts were interrupted by Mr. Bingley's clearing his throat.

"I say, Darcy... you were absolutely correct about Caroline showing up for the wedding. How did you know that she would be there so early?" Mr. Bingley asked.

"I had Wilson and Mills go out into the park to discuss our plans for the wedding today and gave them leave to speak as loudly as they wished when they were just in front of the house where the Hurst's are staying. I let them know that we would be at the church by eleven o'clock." Darcy explained.

"But... the ceremony was moved from ten o'clock to at least nine thirty. Why did you tell them to say that we would be there by eleven o'clock?" Mr. Bingley asked with confusion.

"Because I knew that we would in all likelihood still be there by that time..." Darcy looked at his watch to check the time, "I was only a few minutes off, but then she was a few minutes early too."

Elizabeth did not know what her husband was up to, but was not disappointed that Caroline Bingley had missed their weddings. *She would have likely not only objected to her brother marrying Jane, but* strenuously *objected to Fitzwilliam marrying me. Miss Bingley will no doubt be falsely polite to Jane, but if she does come for our brunch then she will have few qualms about unleashing her sharp tongue against me. No matter... I can handle her.* Her thoughts were interrupted by the carriage slowing down as they approached the Darcy's house. The gentleman stepped down first, and then handed out their brides before escorting them inside.

Mrs. Gordon was the first of the staff to greet them, "Welcome home Mr. and Mrs. Darcy and welcome back Mr. and Mrs. Bingley. We have everything ready for you and your guests..."

"Mrs. Gordon... How did you know about Mr. Bingley and Miss Bennet's marriage?" Darcy asked with a hint of piqued interest.

The housekeeper blushed and looked down to the floor before she sheepishly said, "Ah... the lads, sir. When I went callin' fer 'em they weren't available... I went to find out wot they's up ta an well... I found out."

Elizabeth laughed gaily. It amused her to no end that no matter where she was or what the circumstances, servants would always gossip amongst themselves. That thought then took a turn in her mind to what Lady Eleanor said earlier that morning about even the most trusted servants talking within the household.

She still felt as though she and Darcy were very discreet with their behavior while they were above stairs, but realization dawned upon her that any one of the maids would have known about their proximity to one another. *It would not take any stretch of the imagination for them to go from sleeping in the same suite to sleeping in the same bed.* Her face must have changed expressions along with her thoughts because Darcy looked at her with concern.

"Are you all right, Elizabeth?"

She saw his anxiety and quickly tried to reassure him, "I am fine, Fitzwilliam, I was only thinking about something that was said..." She stopped suddenly, not wanting to tell him about her conversation with his aunt... especially not immediately following their wedding.

"Dearest..." He looked around them, and saw that Mr. Bingley and her sister were staring at them. He motioned towards the study as he urged her to come with him. "May I have a private word with my wife before we join the festivities?"

Elizabeth obediently followed him to the quiet study where he took her into his arms and brought her up against his hard body while burying his face in her hair. She returned his embrace with one of her own, wrapping her arms around his waist and burying her face into the crook of his neck. His woodsy scent was calming to her.

"Elizabeth... I can sense your distress. Will you not share with me what was said and by whom, so that I may know who to credit with souring your mood?" He finished by kissing her temple and pushing her away slightly so that he could gaze into her eyes.

"It is nothing really, Fitzwilliam. I was just thinking about a conversation I had earlier this morning with... your aunt..."

"*Aunt Eleanor*? I cannot imagine what she could have said this morning that would have caused you such distress all of a sudden... and right after taking our vows..."

"It is not that... well, not really. I was only thinking about... what she said about how even the most trusted staff will talk amongst themselves..."

Darcy seemed to understand then, what she was distressed about.

"Dearest, you do not need to worry over what has been said here. It will not go outside of this house and even if it did, no one would pay it any heed to it because we are married now."

"But does it not disturb you that the upstairs maids know that we have slept in the same rooms?"

"No, because they also know that we slept in two separate beds and were already engaged to be married when we did so. It would not be unreasonable to have such accommodations, especially with a sitting room between us as there is... Elizabeth... what is *really* bothering you? You have not seemed yourself lately."

She looked at him sharply before she withdrew from his embrace.

"Why am I not myself lately? I do not feel '*myself*' lately." She was almost petulant. "I have had a great deal to take in-in a very short amount of time- and then to have to endure what I have and to be under such suspicion as I have..."

Tears were beginning to burn her eyes as her vision became blurry. Though she knew herself to be happy about marrying him, she could not understand why she felt so out of sorts at times. She did not wish for her husband to see her cry- *and on this of all days*-she turned away from him to avoid his gaze. Elizabeth could feel the heat from Darcy's body as he came up behind her and pulled her back into his embrace as he turned her around to face him.

"Elizabeth…" He said gently, "No one who matters to me will look at you with anything other than respect. Not my friends or my family. They all know what history I have had with George Wickham and they know the truth of the matter when it comes to whom I would associate with as well. I would *never* have married you if I had even an inkling of a hint that you were in collusion with that man. As to our servants saying anything outside of this household that may disparage the Darcy name-they all know that should they say anything of such a nature and I find out who said those things, they would be dismissed without references. Besides all of that, hardly a soul would believe them if they did say such things." He smiled at her.

Elizabeth was finding consolation in his words and was slightly amused at his last statement.

"Does that mean, Mr. Darcy, that your friends and family think you a candidate for sainthood?"

"Not likely. I have been known to have a few vices… such as pride…" He laughed.

She laughed at his jest about one of their conversations that they had while she stayed at Netherfield when Jane was recovering.

"Shall we go and join our guests in celebration of our wedding, Mrs. Darcy?"

The new appellation made Elizabeth's heart skip a beat and her toes tingle. She could scarcely believe that she was now married to the man she had at one time thought of as the last man in the world she would ever consider marrying. She thought it was a great honor to have gained his admiration and affection.

"That would probably be a good idea. Do you suppose that Miss Bingley will join us?"

"I doubt that we could be lucky enough for her to stay away." He said almost grimly as he offered her his arm and escorted her out to the dining room where some of their family had already begun gathering while they were in the study. As they made for the door they could hear some loud shouting across the main floor, and they quickly left the study to see what the source of the noise was, but arrived only to see Wilson and Mills emerge from the front door.

"Is everything all right?" Elizabeth asked them.

"It is now, ma'am." Wilson said.

~*~*~*~

Since Lord Matlock wished to converse with Mr. Bennet, he rode with him in the Bennet's carriage and Lady Matlock had the misfortune of riding back to the Darcy's house with Miss Bingley after the ceremony. She was not looking forward to visiting with that woman for any length of time at all. The only reason she allowed for the unusual arrangement was to gain some intelligence on her suspicions as to who had been spreading those lies about Elizabeth in town.

Her conscience niggled at her for all but forcing Richard to sit next to the woman, but that was better than forcing poor Georgiana to sit near her. She had always viewed Caroline as a snide, harpy, social climber and had little good opinion of her after she found out that she said some unkind things about the daughter of a friend. *The lady's perfume was always so... pungent too.* It was another thing that Eleanor Fitzwilliam did not like about some women... *she lacks good sense about scent.*

She had always said that if they were wearing something that strong, then they must have something even stronger that they had to mask. In Miss Bingley's case she always suspected her of having very excessive feminine scents, and thus tried to avoid her whenever possible, but something about her odors this day triggered something within her mind. It was a familiar scent that she had smelt not so long ago.

"Miss Bingley... what is that you are wearing?" She addressed the orange clad woman.

"This?" Miss Bingley said in an excited voice, "Why... this is one of the latest fashions from London, ma'am-but then I am sure that you already know..."

Lady Matlock wanted her to cease her nonsense before she truly became ill, thus she interrupted her companion's rambling, "I was *referring* to your perfume, Miss Bingley." She said flatly.

"Oh," The woman smiled smugly at herself and her niece, "This is a new scent from town as well. There is only one shop that sells it and you can believe that it is not in the... less desirable areas of town..." she leaned forward towards Eleanor as if speaking conspiratorially.

It was difficult for the lady to refrain from rolling her eyes at the ridiculousness of Miss Bingley's assertions as she tried to block out her voice until she heard her companion utter something that sounded suspect.

"... and even Miss Thrasher thinks it a good scent on me, though I do not think she takes her own advice half of the time..." Miss Bingley chatted on. "I am sure that that Miss Eliza Bennet would disagree. She seems to enjoy running around smelling as though she had rolled around in the gardens, or the dirt... why *you* would have been *shocked* at the time she came three miles to Netherfield through mud, just to see her sister who had caught a cold!"

There was something about Miss Bingley's speech that caught Lady Matlock's attention-aside from her disparaging remarks about the new Mrs. Darcy. She also did not appreciate such a woman railing against Elizabeth in front of Georgiana who seemed more and more uncomfortable with Miss Bingley's choice of conversation.

"Miss Bingley, did you say that you know of a Miss Thrasher?"

Her companions eyes lit up, "Why yes, your ladyship. She and I have known each other very well, for some time... since our first season together."

As if that would impress me, Miss Bingley, thought Lady Matlock. "Have you seen her lately?"

"Oh yes, ma'am, only just this past week."

Lady Eleanor suspected that it was Miss Bingley that had come to her house to visit, when her footman said that '*a rather unfashionable lady, with odd tastes, and wearing orange*', had come to visit her. She could not get the scent that was overpowering from her rooms for the longest time and this scent was oddly the same as the very one threatening to undo her stomach at present. Her suspicions came to the forefront of her thoughts as to how Elizabeth's name had come to be linked with Anne and George Wickham in the first place, and how anyone could have come across such intelligence... unless they had read her letter from Georgiana.

The funny thing to her was that that letter was in her study and *that* woman was only shown to the parlor, however... *that scent was overpowering in both rooms...*

The idea of anyone going through her personal correspondence was enough to set her off, but she needed to gather further evidence before she launched an attack upon Caroline Bingley. She was one of the few women whom the countess would put nothing past in order to sabotage Darcy's plan to marry another woman.

"Miss Bingley...I had just this past week received some visitors who commented upon a particular fragrance in my study and it is very like the one that you are wearing now." *Never mind that they were my housekeeper and her assistant, and they were trying to figure out how to dissipate the stench.* Baiting the lady even further, she said, "My guests had said that it was rather an unforgettable aroma."

Miss Bingley's eyes opened wide and she straightened up then smiled brilliantly, "Really? Well, I was not going to mention this, but I had come to your house to..." she paused for a moment before going on, "discuss my concerns about your nephew, Mr. Darcy's... ah... association with certain people. It concerns me that he may be risking his reputation with such an imprudent match as he has made... I could also not discount what it could do to poor Miss Darcy here..."

The more venom Caroline Bingley spewed about Elizabeth Darcy, nee Bennet, the more Lady Eleanor was seeing red. She knew in an instant that Caroline Bingley must have been the source of the gossip in town that was circulating about Elizabeth. It took all of her self control to keep from throttling the nasty woman sitting across from her in her coach. Had it not been for her family in the carriage, she would have likely killed the woman on the spot. Georgiana turned pale and looked at her with worry written in her countenance.

Luckily the carriage arrived at the Darcy's house and Richard stepped out and handed the ladies out. Richard offered one arm to Georgiana and the other to his mother. Lady Matlock did regret that her favorite son and niece had to endure such displeasure, but felt it could not be helped. When they were ushered inside, Lady Eleanor requested a private word with Miss Bingley before they joined the others for brunch.

"Will you join me in the small sitting room before the rest of the guests arrive, Miss Bingley?" She turned to her son, "Richard, would you please escort Georgiana to the parlor?"

Miss Bingley had no other choice but to acquiesce to her ladyship's request. They removed to the small sitting room where Lady Eleanor turned a sharp eye on the sycophant social climber.

"Miss Bingley, I shall not mince words now that we are in private. It is peculiar that you should mention that you were at my home last week, because it has occurred to me that just after you visited me, some rather alarming rumors began to circulate about the former Miss Elizabeth Bennet being taken to Bath by a George Wickham. They had also included mention of some animosity between Anne and Elizabeth because of an alleged affair that was said to have gone on. This all came about after I had my servants send whomever the visitor was away from Matlock House '*last week*'. That was also the day I had to start fumigating my study to be rid of the peculiar stench that was apparently left there by you, Miss Bingley, *and* that was also the day that I found my desk in my study had been rummaged through."

She had turned to see Caroline Bingley with widened eyes and her complexion was even paler than usual, but Lady Eleanor would offer no mercy. Her companion offered no protests of her innocence, but only looked half put out, half defiant... for a little while longer.

"I have since discovered that a certain 'Miss Thrasher' was also a source of those rumors, *but she* has also claimed that she was not the original source. I know for a fact that the rumor was spread after the fourteenth as well, Miss Bingley, because that was the date on the letter from my niece, Georgiana, who happened to mention in her letter some rather private details. I need not tell you what was in that missive as I'm sure you already know."

"But..." Caroline Bingley was half pleading with her in desperation.

"No, Miss Bingley, there are no '*buts*'! I keep my things in order for a purpose besides being particular. If someone were to rummage through my things, then I know that they were tampered with. I knew that day that someone had tampered with my letters, but I did not know who... until now. You were the one that said all of those terrible things about an innocent woman..."

Caroline opened her mouth and shut it repeatedly, and looked as if she were a fish out of water. She tried to protest again.

"But, she does not deserve him..."

"*That* is where you are wrong. *You* are the one who does not deserve my nephew. He loves her and she loves him just as much. He never even cared for you with your pining after him and your sycophantic clinging behavior. Could you not tell that he would gag when you came near him? *We all did.* You are certainly not the epitome of fashion or sense either, and I think that as far as those things go, Mrs. Darcy has more than ample amounts of that to get through the hurdles of the *ton*."

By this time the lady was in full lather, and wanted to go in for the kill.

"Furthermore, when I get back to town, I plan on throwing the new Mrs. Darcy a ball, and I will ensure that all of those at Almacks know about your duplicity. If I were you, *Miss Bingley*, I would not even dare to show my face in town or even here in Bath for a very long time. I would think you lucky if my nephew did not have you thrashed for what you have done to his wife! Now... *Get out!*" She demanded of the pathetic woman in front of her.

Caroline Bingley was still standing with her mouth agape for the second time that morning when Lady Matlock called for the footmen to remove her from the house before she did any bodily harm to her. When her source of ire was finally removed, the whole household could hear Caroline cursing the footmen like a sailor as she demanded to be '*put down this instant*'. *It is too late for that Miss Bingley, I have already* 'put you down' *once today already today.*

The countess was still too furious to rejoin her family and began pacing until she had regained a semblance of calm. She then went to rejoin her family and Mr. and Mrs. Bingley who looked at her fearfully.

Within a few minutes, Darcy and Elizabeth joined her, and he asked, "So, what is going on now?"

"Not now, Fitzwilliam. We shall talk later." She shook her head.

This is going to be a long story, she thought to herself.

Chapter 21

The wedding brunch commenced once the countess and guests of honor were settled down. Darcy saw that his other guests were all very quiet when they joined them. He and Elizabeth heard the argument, but had no idea what it was all about because of their own tete-a-tete. It was clear to him also that both Mr. and Mrs. Bingley were more than a little uncomfortable, and Georgiana looked a bit...*nervous. Obviously there was an unpleasant scene prior and judging from everyone's expressions it probably pertained to Caroline Bingley. No matter, she is not here now and that is just as well. She would not have added to anyone else's enjoyment anyway*

Elizabeth must have noticed Georgiana's turmoil as well, because she was very solicitous of her. "Georgiana... would you care to sit with us here?" Elizabeth pointed to a chair between them.

It touched Darcy to see how well the two most beloved women in his life got on and it was just one more reason that he was thankful he chose Elizabeth for his wife. Had he married a woman like Caroline Bingley he knew he would not have been as happy as he was now, and none of those women would have taken the pains to get to know his sister.

Georgiana looked to Elizabeth and said shyly, "Thank you, that is very kind of you, but I could not separate you and Mrs. Bingley..."

"Nonsense, you are family now too, and you must bear sitting between us to keep us from quarrelling as to who will be happier in their new role as a wife..." Elizabeth laughed, as she looked at her new husband with her bright eyes.

His sister gratefully accepted the invitation, but Darcy saw how nervous she still was and worried that she may still be upset after having witnessed whatever happened between their aunt and Caroline Bingley. He made a mental note to talk to her later as he was curious as to what occurred with them in the carriage ride back from the church. Not that he minded Caroline's absence in the least-in fact he thought he might thank his aunt for saying or doing whatever it was that she did to cause that orange nightmare to leave. His thoughts were interrupted when he heard Mrs. Bennet's proclamations.

"I shall be the envy of all of Hertfordshire to have my two eldest daughters situated so nicely. 'Tis a good thing as well for our other girls-especially after those horrible rumors in town. Who would have thought after such a scandal that anyone would have had my Lizzy?"

Darcy wished that he could gag Mrs. Bennet or banish her to another part of the country… preferably on the continent. He watched his new wife as she cringed at her mother's harsh and embarrassing words and then he was grateful when his Aunt Eleanor spoke up.

"Mrs. Bennet… It is fortunate for our nephew to have found Mrs. Darcy. He seems much happier now than he ever was, and as to those rumors in town-that is just what they are-rumors. No one really pays heed to them, especially if they can be proven false and I am sure that they will not continue to haunt *our* family much longer. After the ball we will have in honor of the Darcy's marriage everyone will see what a gem she really is and this whole thing will be summarily forgotten."

Lady Eleanor always knew what to say to redirect those with less sense, thought Darcy.

"A ball? Did you say that you were having a ball, ma'am?" Mrs. Bennet asked with enthusiasm as her eyes lit up.

"Yes, I did, Mrs. Bennet. It is what we do for all our newly married family members." His aunt said matter-of-factly. "When Darcy and Elizabeth come to town we will arrange a time and send out invitations." She paused in a manner that Darcy could only describe as dramatic for Lady Eleanor, and she said, "Oh… and of course you and your family must come. I am sure that Georgiana would enjoy the company of other girls her own age."

Darcy wanted to cringe at that last statement as he wondered if she intended for his sister to attend the ball…or if she intended her to stay home and '*attend*' to their new sisters. *The later would be almost more preferable, then the younger Bennet girls would not expose them all to censure. Mrs. Bennet can manage that quite well adequately on her own- no sense in compounding the problem, though… poor Georgiana*, he bemoaned inwardly.

"Oh! How wonderful! That would be most fortunate for my other daughters…."

Mr. Bennet interrupted his wife at that moment, "Mrs. Bennet, please may we enjoy one day without discussing another event? Today we are supposed to be celebrating our two eldest daughter's marriages and we have yet to celebrate."

Mrs. Bennet's mouth went agape and she looked as though she were going to say something else. Lucky for everyone she was stopped by Richard.

"Here, here... You are absolutely correct, sir. I must first have a taste of the fine feast before I can consider such an occasion celebrated." He piped in.

Darcy refrained from rolling his eyes, and thought to himself, *'I would consider a feast of a different sort to celebrate my marriage and I would not invite anyone but Elizabeth'*. He loved his family dearly, but at the moment he wanted nothing more than to enjoy his newly married status-*alone with Elizabeth.*

"Then by all means let us get on with the celebrations." Darcy said flatly, while thinking, *'Then you may all leave us be to enjoy ourselves...'*

His eyes met his aunt's. She was staring at him and Elizabeth as they sat side by side. Elizabeth was flushed and her color looked bright and... she was glowing. Her gown complemented her complexion which Darcy could not help but notice emphasized her lovely bosom. When he looked down upon her from his vantage point due to his height, he noticed her décolletage displayed to her best advantage and he wanted nothing more at that moment than to take her upstairs and feast upon her.

Lady Eleanor looked at him with a raised eyebrow and a small smile upon her lips. Darcy knew enough to realize that she likely understood his line of thought at that moment and he looked away from her in embarrassment as the rest of the party talked amongst themselves, ignorant of his discomfiture. He idly wondered how long they had to continue their hospitality until they could be left alone, when Elizabeth addressed him.

"Fitzwilliam...?"

His thoughts were disrupted by the sweet voice of his new wife, who had found amusement with something.

He looked at her inquisitively and asked, "What do you find so amusing, Elizabeth?"

She giggled again, "It is only that your cousin and I have been trying to engage you in our conversations for the last five minutes. What is so enrapturing as to hold your undivided attention, sir?"

Darcy wanted to show her what it was that held his attention so, but knew that his family would never forgive such a breach in propriety were he to act upon his desires at that moment to remove her abruptly from the room and carry her to their bedroom. He smiled back at her then leaned in to whisper to her.

"I have been contemplating the very great pleasures of finding out what delights await me as your husband, my dear Mrs. Darcy."

Her flush overspread her face and across her bosom which inflamed his desire for her. She looked up at him through her eyelashes and said, "I am sure that we shall enjoy many a night in the library... discussing books... or would you prefer we do that in the ballroom?"

"I was not thinking about entertaining ourselves in either of those rooms in such a way as I had envisioned, but now that you mention it... perhaps we should consider trying other activities in there as well..."

He laughed in a low rumble, which caught the attention of the others in their party. They realized then that they were being observed by everyone within the dining room. Darcy blushed at their family's scrutiny of them, and dawned his *'Master of Pemberley'* mask immediately. Elizabeth looked down at her plate and began to pick at her food, but he could tell that she was as amused as was he.

"Why such a dour look Darcy? Do you not wish to let everyone know that you are actually capable of smiling now and then... or looking like the rest of us mortals?" Richard teased.

Darcy wanted to say, '*Why do you continue to act like an idiot, Richard? Do you not wish to show everyone what excellent strategists you are... or do you prefer everyone to think you a buffoon?*'

Out loud he said, "I believe that they all know that I have that capacity, Richard..."

"Yet you do not demonstrate it nearly enough for us, Darcy. You have such a brilliant smile... when you chose to show it." Lady Eleanor stated.

The whole room erupted in laughter -including Elizabeth and though Darcy did not enjoy being the butt of jokes he could not help but take his aunt's words any other way than how they were meant... as compliments. His lips turned up at the corners and he demonstrated to his new family that he did, indeed, have that capability.

Elizabeth leaned in to whisper to him, "You know dear, that Lady Eleanor is correct? You are truly a beautiful man, and when you smile your beauty is even more emphasized."

"And you, my lovely wife, are a magnificently striking woman anytime."

She looked at him under her eyelashes, for a moment before their privacy was once again interrupted. Lord Matlock stood up to give a toast to the newlyweds.

"Ladies and gentlemen, I wish to give a toast to Fitzwilliam and his bride, Elizabeth, as well as to Mr. and Mrs. Bingley on their marriages." He nodded towards the other newlywed couple, "May you have a long and happy life together and know what it is to have a family that will stand by and with you through thick and thin-and of course... many you be blessed with many, many children."

Everyone raised their glasses to toast the couples and they continued to enjoy each other's company for about another hour before Darcy caught Bingley's eye while he was engaged in a conversation-or more accurately he was listening patiently to- Mrs. Bennet's ceaseless chattering. He was relatively certain that his friend was just as anxious to have his new wife to himself as Darcy was to be alone with Elizabeth. *Bingley you have much more patience than I ever would with that woman and I certainly do not envy you your close proximity to Longbourn either.*

It was just one more thing that Darcy could be grateful for. Though he loved Elizabeth with all of his heart, he did not know how he could bear to be so near to her mother. *Mr. Bennet would not be so bad... for the most part. It is no wonder that Elizabeth is so favored by* him *and not so much by her mother-she has too much good sense.*

Bingley smiled reluctantly at him and leaned in to say something to Jane then said to Mrs. Bennet, "I am sorry, Mrs. Bennet, but there was something that I wished to show Jane... u-upstairs. Would you mind excusing us?"

"I am sure that you can send a servant to get whatever it is that you would like to show our dear Jane, sir." Their mother-in-law said, oblivious to their desire to be alone.

"Uh... well...it is not... something that I can send a servant after..." Bingley answered with a hint of nervousness.

Apparently their new mother-in-law was not too adept at taking hints and said, "Oh, of course! You are probably wishing to give her some wedding presents... perhaps another family jewel or something?"

"My dear, Mrs. Bennet... you are likely correct. I have no doubt that Mr. Bingley would like to spend a little time *alone* with his new bride in order to show her the *'family jewels'*, but he would probably enjoy doing so without an audience."

Bingley blushed at his father-in-laws tongue in cheek remarks, but those with more sense knew that he was right. The gentlemen wanted nothing more than to begin their married lives together in a more intimate setting, and their family wanted to have some fun at the newlyweds' expense.

Bingley eagerly nodded his head at the proffered excuse and bade them all a good afternoon before he slipped out of the room with his wife.

Traitor! Darcy thought with frustration, as he watched his friend assist Jane out of her chair. Darcy cursed the fact that as the host and hostess, he and Elizabeth had to stay to entertain their guests until they left. He was becoming frustrated at the situation and thought he might go mad before their family finally left.

It was difficult for some of the gentlemen present to keep a straight face and it seemed to him that they were continuing to stay just to drive him to distraction. Darcy thought of the *'family jewels'* he himself would like to give Elizabeth upstairs-well anywhere really-*but upstairs would be most preferable.*

Edward Gardiner, who had been quiet throughout much of the meal said, "Margaret and I should be going. Our nanny is likely to go mad with four children who have been cooped up for so long." He looked at his nieces and asked, "Would any of you girls care to join us in our carriage? I am sure that your cousins will be happy to see you this afternoon."

"I shall be happy to join you and Aunt Gardiner, uncle. 'T'is our Christian duty to spend time with our younger family members, and I am sure that they will appreciate some readings from the scriptures as well..." Mary spoke up.

"How droll, Mary. Can you imagine being kept inside all day and then have someone come and entertain you by reading some scriptures the whole afternoon?" Lydia replied.

"I will come with you, Uncle Gardiner." Catherine spoke up, "I am sure that I can find some better way to amuse my cousins for the rest of the afternoon."

Darcy was thankful that he was already married, because if his new family had acted this way before he had taken his vows, he was sure that the Earl and Countess would have tried to talk him out of marrying Elizabeth. *No, they would still value her for who she is...*

Lady Eleanor spoke up, "Andrew... I think that it is time to go as well. It was a rather long night sleeping in a foreign room and then getting up so early. I would imagine that Georgiana is a little tired also."

"Then I shall call for the carriage, dear." Lord Matlock turned to address Richard, "Will you be staying with us, son, or do you have other accommodations?"

Richard looked as though he were contemplating his options while looking pleadingly at Darcy, who frowned at him, thinking, *'There is no way I am going to keep you here on my wedding night, cousin. I do not need you in the way while I enjoy my new wife.'*

"I believe that your father is awaiting your answer, Richard. I would imagine that Georgiana would enjoy visiting with you while you are still here." Darcy happily offered to an un-amused Richard.

"That is so... thoughtful of you Darcy, but I doubt that Georgiana would see it that way. I am sure she thinks of me as her old boring guardian-cousin."

"That is not true, Richard." Georgiana protested, "Fitzwilliam is correct-I would not mind it at all if we could visit while I stay with Uncle Andrew and Aunt Eleanor."

Darcy smiled at his cousin triumphantly, as he made for the door to call for Richard's things. *Soon Elizabeth and I can finally be alone, without worrying over the servants talking about our arrangements.*

"Well...then, I suppose that I shall be going with you and my parents, Georgie." Richard said with a hint of defeat.

Darcy understood his reluctance to join his parents, who had already been reminding them both for the last three years that it was high time that they got married and started a family. Now that Darcy was married, Richard's mother would have only him to focus on. *Better him than me.*

Mr. and Mrs. Gardiner's coach was ready before anyone else's, and they left with all three of the Bennet sisters. Before they left Darcy and Elizabeth saw them out.

"I cannot thank you enough for your hospitality while I stayed with you, aunt and uncle." Elizabeth said to them.

Her Aunt Gardiner smiled and said, "You are always welcome to our house, Lizzy-and you as well, Mr. Darcy. It is too bad that *you* will not get to travel to the Lake District with us, but you shall enjoy Derbyshire just as much…perhaps even more now." She grinned at the couple.

"That, I will ensure, Mrs. Gardiner, but maybe I can show her the Lakes as it is not so far from Derbyshire as London or Hertfordshire." Darcy added.

Mrs. Gardiner was still smiling jovially, "I hope that you do, sir, but I doubt that you will do much traveling once you get to Derbyshire."

She looked again to Elizabeth and hugged her before saying softly, "Congratulations, Lizzy. Your uncle and I wish you all the happiness in the world that can be spared from ourselves. Take care of yourself, dear, and endeavor to be patient with him. Men cannot change overnight, and sometimes it may be *us* that must change-remember that."

When she released her niece, she embraced Darcy lightly, "Take care of our girl, sir."

"You know that I will. I will not allow anything else to happen to her if I can help it." Darcy assured them.

They saw the rest of her family out without too many words, other than promises to reunite in town before the Matlock's ball… until they said their goodbyes to Mr. Bennet.

"Take care of my treasure, Darcy. She has been as dear to me as I am sure she will be to you."

Darcy could see the sadness in her father's eyes and the unshed tears in Elizabeth's eyes as they said their adieus.

"I shall miss you, Lizzy. You know that I shall not have a bit of sense spoken at the table from here on."

"Do not say that, papa. We will come to see you, and of course, you must come and visit us as well. I hear that the library at Pemberley is one of the most extensive in the whole country and I could not imagine you passing up an opportunity to avail yourself of it."

"In that case, I may come whenever I may. Maybe even when you least expect me." He teased.

"You will be most welcome at anytime, sir." Darcy added good naturedly.

They watched as he left the house and entered the carriage with Mrs. Bennet. Elizabeth continued to watch until it moved out of their sight, before she turned her attention to the Fitzwilliam's and Georgiana.

"Lady Matlock... I thank you for your kindness towards myself... and my family." Elizabeth blushed.

Lady Eleanor smiled, "It is nothing really, my dear. You are family now, and what I said was true about the ball. We gave one in celebration of James' wedding. It is just too bad that we cannot also celebrate Richard's as well, but we shall keep looking until he finds the right woman. Then the last one for our set will be Georgiana."

Darcy noticed the slight hollowness when his aunt mentioned the last of their generation being Georgiana. There was no mention of Anne, but he could tell that it saddened her how things turned out. He was reminded then of the earlier hoopla with Caroline Bingley.

"I hope that we can see you and Georgiana before you go back to town. I am rather curious about a few *things*." Darcy hinted to his curiosity about what was said to their missing guest.

"Again, Darcy... that is a very long story and since it is your honeymoon, I do not wish to ruin your day. We shall talk later. Today you need to devote to your new wife." She said with motherly affection.

Darcy accepted her words of wisdom and tried to block out any unpleasant thoughts associated with his imaginings. He said his goodbyes to his sister affectionately, kissing her on the cheek and accepting one likewise from her before he helped her into the carriage.

"We shall see you later, Georgie. When we get back to town, we will bring you back home." He looked back at Mrs. Annesley, Richard and his uncle and said, "Take good care of her in my absence, would you?"

It was more a statement than a request, but he knew that they would take good care of Georgiana while he spent some time with Elizabeth- besides Mrs. Annesley would be with her as well.

"You know we will, Darcy." Richard said.

Before he handed his sister's companion in, he and Elizabeth thanked her again for all that she had done to assist in recuing Elizabeth.

"Madam, we cannot express how grateful we are that you were where you were when you met with Mrs. Darcy. Had you not found her, there is no telling what would have happened..."

Darcy could not go on, as it was too horrible to think of what George Wickham would have done to her, had they not know where to look for her. Elizabeth expressed her gratitude once again to her guardian angel.

"I cannot tell you what it meant to me to know that there was someone out there that was looking out for me when no one else knew where I was. It must have been fate that brought you to that street when you happened along. I thank you from the bottom of my heart for everything that you have done for me, Mrs. Annesley."

"You are most welcome, ma'am. I would have done it regardless, but now that I know who it was... I cannot but agree with you. It *must* be fate that brought me there."

They closed the carriage and watched as the last of their guests rode away. Darcy turned towards the house with Elizabeth on his arm. He knew enough of Bingley to guess that he was making more headway in getting to know the new Mrs. Bingley, and he wanted to make the same kind of in roads with Elizabeth-least Bingley out do him.

With that in mind, he turned to her and asked, "Would you think me a presumptuous rake if I were to ask you to join me upstairs in our chambers, Mrs. Darcy?"

She looked at him and responded saucily, "Only so much as you would think of me as a wanton hussy for saying that I think it sounds like a fine idea, Mr. Darcy."

He offered her his arm and escorted her to their chambers above stairs, and stopped at her door.

"May I come to you in half an hour?" His voice was low, and he looked at her with unbridled desire.

"Yes... you may."

Darcy leaned down to brush his lips with hers. He had only intended for it to be a light and quick kiss, but he could not resist her allure. His tongue darted out to brush against her lips and insisted on being admitted entrance into her mouth. She responded to him and allowed him his desired goal. Their mouths dueled with one another until they needed to come up for air.

She leaned into him and ran her hands through his hair. Darcy grasped her waist pulling her tightly to him and he ran his hands up and down her back to her shoulders, arms, and finally cupped her breasts. It was a good thing that there were no footmen around to witness them, but he would not have cared right then. His desire for her at that moment was becoming almost unbearable. He wanted to take her right there, but settled for picking her up and opening the door to carry her into the room then placed her upon the bed in quick measure.

Elizabeth lay back, pulling him with her. He covered her with his body, his hands never leaving her body… caressing her breasts, down her sides to her hips and they finally landed at her apex. She thrust her hips towards him as he paid special attention to that area which he most desired at that moment. Her moans were intoxicating to him, almost drug like in their draw to her.

He felt her hands entering his coat and then unbuttoning his vest, until they invaded his fine lawn shirt. She was trying to untie his cravat and he decided that he must make some inroads to joining her in her quest to undress one another. This game was exciting… mesmerizing even, in its effect upon him. She managed to remove his outer layers of clothing down to his shirt and trousers, when he decided that what he wanted most was to see her naked with her beautiful mahogany hair down around her.

"Lizzy…?" He asked, and then had to repeat her name again to draw her attention from her task at hand.

"Lizzy… may I remove your hair pins? I have wanted to see your hair down since… our… since Hunsford."

She withdrew a little and he regretted mentioning their first time together. They lay in the bed breathless, looking at each other, studying each other's face.

Elizabeth frowned for a moment, and then said, "I wondered about that. I had not recalled taking my hair down." Her chest was still heaving and though he wanted nothing more than to enjoy her bounty, he knew that he needed to gain her trust in order to proceed.

"I had done that. I did not think that you minded, but I guess…"

"Shhh," She put her finger against his lips, "We shall not discuss that incident, my love. Had you not… done what you had, we would not be here now. Let us not think of the past except as it gives us pleasure… Now, about that pleasure…"

"Where were we?"

He smiled at her, happy to resume his attentions on his activity prior to mentioning the incident at the parsonage. She sat up and allowed him to remove the pins to her hair and he was entranced as he watched her hair fall over her lovely shoulders. Shoving the neckline of her gown over her shoulders as he unbuttoned it, he was starting to enjoy her lovely flesh. Soon he had the bodice removed and wondered how much more he would have to remove before he got to the final layer as he shoved the rest of it down past her hips, thighs, knees, calves, until he had her dress and petticoats removed.

In the meantime he felt her hands upon him as she pulled the tail of his shirt out of his trousers and ran her hands down his naked back. Shivers ran up and down his spine, driving his desire further. He helped her remove his shirt and threw it over to the side of the bed, and then returned his attentions to her corset, unlacing it hastily until it fell from her torso. She remained only in her chemise and he in his trousers and boots. Before he made any further moves, he decided it might be prudent to remove his boots as they may prove to be an impediment to his plans.

She sat up in bed with a look of desire in her eyes as she studied his physique, matching his interest in her...person. He returned to her arms lowering her to the mattress as he kissed her jaw and neck, moving slowly down to her breasts, where he found the immediate object of his desire. Shoving the straps of her chemise down over her shoulders, he was able to gaze upon the most perfect breasts he had ever seen in his entire life. His lips automatically moved to the pink buds at the tips of her mounds, suckling her there.

Elizabeth ran her hands through his hair, massaging his scalp as he worshiped her body. He was reveling in her touch, and thankful that she was the extraordinary woman that she was. Her hands were upon his back pulling him to her as she moaned her pleasure out loud.

Darcy could stand the tension in his body no more, and he abruptly pulled away from her, stripping away his trousers. As he approached her, she looked slightly alarmed, but did not resist him as he kissed her lips... tasting her tongue and caressing her mouth with his. His hand grasped the last bit of barrier in the form of her chemise between them and pulled it down past her hips, her legs, until she was finally free of the last impediment. Finally he was able to see her... all of her.

He could control his desire for her no longer, and moved over her-as he caressed her most intimate areas with his manhood. Soon she opened her thighs to accommodate him. When he felt her warm moist entrance he wanted to enter her slowly in order to avoid any discomfort to her, but when he finally thrust into her he could not quite slow himself. She was tight, but the barrier that he had felt before was no longer there. Darcy gritted his teeth trying to maintain some control over his body's excitement.

Elizabeth was panting; her sweet warm breath was blowing against his neck as she moved her hips up to meet him. When he felt her moving to his rhythm, he started to quicken his pace moving against her harder. She was moaning her pleasure, calling out his name, meeting him thrust for thrust when he felt her body contracting around his manhood. It was too much for him to bear and he finally felt his release. He felt the tension removed from his body as his seed flowed from him to her.

He felt as if he had run for miles chasing after some object and finally found it. His breathing was still rapid as he looked down into her eyes to see the love and adoration that he had always craved. *I am finally home, and home is not a place… it is this contentment that one feels when they are finally fulfilled within the arms of the one that they love and who loves them back in equal measure.*

Pushing up from her, he could not help but smile and kiss her deeply, once, twice, three times.

"Elizabeth Darcy, I love you with all of my heart and I will always cherish the gift you have given me this day."

She smiled at him and said, "Fitzwilliam Darcy, I love you with all of my heart and entrust you with it for the rest of my days. You have made me the happiest of women on this day, and I will cherish you forever."

It was some time before they recalled that they had requested bath water to be brought up, so enthralled were they with this newfound and deeper intimacy. They decided that they did not wish to part with each other's company and therefore bathed together.

Chapter 22

Almost four weeks later Darcy awoke to an empty bed, and immediately looked around their room for Elizabeth. He thought he heard some noises coming from her dressing room, and lay back thinking she was just refreshing herself after another night of passion. When she did not return to him shortly, he sat up to the side of the bed, and listened for the noise again. He walked towards the door to where the it came from and noted the clock on the mantle read just a little past five o'clock in the morning. As he opened the door to her dressing room, he came upon Elizabeth retching into the commode. He was instantly alarmed and quickly went to her side and pulled her hair back from her face.

When she had finished expelling the contents of her stomach, she sat back on the cool marble floor of her dressing room to rest against his chest and between his legs.

"Elizabeth… darling… what is the matter? You are pale and sweaty. You look…"

"I look wretched and frightful, Fitzwilliam, I know… and I feel just as awful." She brushed the back of her hand across her mouth.

"I shall call our family physician, Mr. Tyler, right away, but first I must get you back to bed…" He made to pick her up off of the floor, but she stayed him with her hand.

"No, please dear… can I just sit here on the cool floor for a few minutes and then I will have my strength back… at least enough to get to our bed."

"Do not be ridiculous, Elizabeth. Allow me to carry you."

"Oh, but the cool tiles feel so good, please just allow me to sit for a few moments?"

How can I deny her anything when she feels so wretched? He hesitated for a moment then relented.

"All right, but then you must permit me to carry you even if you feel strong enough to walk. It appears as though you have expelled all of your meal from the whole of yesterday and I do not want you to faint from lack of nutrients." Darcy implored. "When I get you settled back into our bed, I will summons Mr. Tyler."

His tone was one that would brook no opposition, and under the circumstances she was in no shape or mind to object to anything he proposed.

"I will, but do you suppose that I can get cleaned up a bit before he arrives? I know that I must look terrible…"

"Darling I am sure that he has seen people in worse shape…"

"But, Fitzwilliam, I think I would feel a little better if I were to wash off this sweat and stench."

He knew it was a reasonable request and could think of no reason to deny her if it would help her feel better. Darcy called for a footman to send word to Mr. Tyler, and had another fetch some warm water for a bath. Once the servants were dispatched to do their jobs, he picked her up and took her to a chair on the other side of the door, but sat her in his lap. Her illness frightened him greatly. Not only had she seemed rather not herself lately, she was also more tired than ever before. Even her father commented upon it, but she dismissed everyone's concerns saying that she had been moving from place to place in the last month and had also just gotten married. It made sense to them, but he wondered what could have caused *this*.

Retching is not typically a sign of fatigue. Darcy reasoned. He was truly worried that something serious had come over Elizabeth, but did not wish to alarm her. All sorts of scenarios ran through his mind as he recalled his mother going through her illness before she died. As he sat in the chair cradling his Elizabeth, he began to rock her and held her a little tighter as two servants filled up her tub. She was almost asleep when they finished their chore, and he had a maid arrange for some fresh linen to be brought in for them. His intention was to clean her up himself.

Once the room full of people was excused, he threw off his robe and nightshift and attended to her gown as well. She complied with his gentle tugging as he undressed her as well.

"Are we to bathe together again, husband?" Elizabeth teased tiredly.

Darcy was a little relieved to hear her teasing and responded likewise, "Certainly, my dear wife. It is easier than leaning over a bathing tub, and I would have called for one sooner or later anyway.

This will save the servants from having to do some extra work, and I do not mind it in the least."

"Well in that case who am I to disagree with such logic?"

He lowered them both into the water with her back leaning against his chest and felt her soft form molding to him. Though he would have liked nothing more than to enjoy her in other ways in such a position, he was-for the very first time- not aroused. That did not concern him as his mind was on her health. Darcy knew that Elizabeth was by far the healthiest woman of his acquaintance, which was another reason he was so concerned.

The issue of her health pervaded his mind as he cleansed her from top to bottom. As he was finishing his ministrations, a knock came at the door, and he called out, "Yes?" in his deep baritone voice.

There was a short pause before Elizabeth's maid answered hesitantly, "U-uh, Mr. Darcy... uh... th' physician is here t-to see Mrs. Darcy, sir."

"All right, please have him wait in our private sitting room. We shall be out in a moment."

"Very good, sir."

Darcy removed them both from the tub and gently pated Elizabeth dry.

"You take exceptional care of me, my love," Elizabeth said to him affectionately, "and I think that your ministrations helped me much more than any physician could. I feel so much better now."

"Yet, I still insist upon Mr. Tyler seeing you, love."

Darcy helped her into a fresh gown and placed her robe around her before he dressed in his own clothes. There was no sense in his donning a new nightshift. He was not going to be able to go back to sleep even if he wished it due to his concern for Elizabeth.

He turned to pick her up and she exclaimed, "Fitzwilliam, you shall hurt yourself and I think that I should be able to walk now. As I said before, I feel much recovered."

Ignoring her protests, he carried her to their bedroom and laid her upon the bed. The maid had already changed the sheets and opened the windows to let in some fresh air as the room had smelt of the discarded contents of her stomach. As soon as he had her settled, he left her in the bed to talk to the physician.

A white haired slim man was patiently waiting for him when Darcy entered their sitting room and the gentleman stood to greet him.

"Mr. Darcy, sir, I came as quickly as possible… but you appear to be in good shape…"

"I am, Mr. Tyler. It is not me who is in need of your services, but my wife."

"Your wife, sir?" He paused for a moment, before saying, "Oh! Yes, yes, I do recall reading that in the papers about a month ago. Well then, what can I do for Mrs. Darcy, sir?"

"She has taken very ill this morning… to the point of retching several times. I know that people do this at times with no ill effects, however, she has been unusually tired lately and has not been herself."

Darcy noticed the man looking at him with a blank expression, seemingly unimpressed by what he had heard thus far.

"I see… May I take a look at her then, and see what I may be able to make of her symptoms?"

"Yes, of course," Darcy motioned for the door to the bedroom and opened it to admit them, "Please…"

They approached the bed where Elizabeth lay watching them as they came to her.

"Elizabeth, this is Mr. Tyler, our family physician. Mr. Tyler, my wife Mrs. Elizabeth Darcy."

"It is an honor to meet you, ma'am. Now… can you tell me in your own words, what is it that has been going on with you?"

Elizabeth elaborated upon what Darcy had already told the man, and Mr. Tyler asked some questions that Darcy did not understand before the elder gentleman requested, "May I have a few moments alone to examine Mrs. Darcy?"

Darcy was hesitant to leave her, until she reassured him, "My dear… Sarah is here. I shall be fine."

As he left he looked at her wistfully, and proceeded through the door. Searching for something to distract him, he grabbed the first thing that he saw which happened to be a book of sonnets. It was difficult to read when he was in no mood to think of light thoughts. He rose abruptly from his chair and began to pace anxiously until the door between the two rooms opened.

"What news, Mr. Tyler? What is wrong with my wife?"

The smile on the man's face was puzzling to Darcy until he explained, "Sir… your wife is fine. This is perfectly normal for a woman in her condition."

"*Fine*? How can you say that she is *fine*? She was in her dressing room early this morning retching up everything that she has eaten in the last twenty four hours!"

It was infuriating to Darcy that the man continued to look at him so calmly. *Does it amuse him that Elizabeth may be dying while he stands here telling me that this is all fine and perfectly normal?*

"Mr. Darcy, what she is experiencing is normal for a woman who is with child. Though it is disturbing for most men to watch, it will soon pass and just to be on the safe side, I have instructed her to take things easy for now. No heavy meals… light foods like toast, plane biscuits, should help settle her stomach-especially in the mornings, and she must get plenty of rest. She says that you have only married about a month ago, but her symptoms suggest that she is further along… either that or she may be carrying more than one child."

The rest of what the physician said barely registered as Darcy struggled to grasp what he heard. *I am going to be a father? Elizabeth is pregnant?*

"Mr. Darcy…? M-Mr. Darcy?" Mr. Tyler said.

Darcy focused his attention back on the man. "You were saying?"

"I said that I have also requested that your wife rest more often, and before she rises in the morning she should have some dry toast and tea. As to some of her other symptoms… I am afraid that there is not much else that I can do. Her irritability likely stems from the pregnancy as well, so until she is delivered, she may continue to experience that."

Suddenly Darcy imagined his witty, vivacious wife turning into Mrs. Bennet. It was enough to make him shudder.

"Do you think that it will only be temporary?"

"Mr. Darcy, I have delivered many women, and Mrs. Darcy is no different from them. What is happening with her now is only the result of the pregnancy, and as I have said… It will pass. She will be fine as long as she takes things easy and I will check up on her again in another week or so unless you need me sooner."

"Do you think that it is a good idea for her to refrain from… certain activities?" Darcy wondered what specific limitations she had in relation to… their marital relations.

The elder gentleman chuckled a little, "The only restrictions upon her activities are that she should not over exert herself, and that she should have frequent rest periods. She should also refrain from horseback riding as well-if she has been so inclined."

Darcy was still stunned at the new turn of events, and absently thanked the doctor for coming, before offering to see him out-which the gentleman declined saying that Elizabeth wished to see him now. He went into their bedroom and slowly approached Elizabeth. She was looking at him with her beautiful wide eyes, smiling at him tenderly and reached for his hand. He grasped her hands in his and kissed the back, and then her palms, and finally her wrists.

"Thank you." He said as he gazed into her eyes.

"For what?" She asked with surprise.

"For loving me, for becoming my wife, and for this." He reached his hand down to caress her abdomen.

He leaned into her and kissed her passionately and she returned it in equal measure.

Darcy arranged for Georgiana to come back to Darcy House the day of the ball since she would not be attending. His sister agreed to entertain Elizabeth's younger sisters while they attended Lord and Lady Matlock's ball- much to the consternation of Mrs. Bennet. Both Elizabeth and Jane were relieved that Lydia and Catherine would not be running around a ball room making a spectacle of themselves, and Mary seemed to be genuinely looking forward to spending a quiet night with Georgiana. They had found a mutual interest in music and in some reading, and Darcy was becoming more impressed with *that* Bennet girl's improvement since the two young women made acquaintances with each other.

Things were looking better and better as he prepared to take tea with the countess before leaving Matlock House with Georgiana. They were shown into her sitting room and invited to sit on either side of her.

"Darcy, how is Elizabeth faring this afternoon? Is she resting before the ball?" His aunt asked.

"Yes she is. She was not feeling well this morning and was told by Mr. Tyler that she needed to take things easy for now."

"Is she going to be up to attending the ball?" The countess asked with concern.

"Yes, she is feeling much better this afternoon and I have seen to it that she is able to rest without any disruptions." *At least until her sisters converge upon us.*

"Darcy... I have been meaning to talk to you about the day of your wedding. You recall that we had some issue that needed to be addressed later?"

"I do not know how anyone could forget. Caroline Bingley left in such a huff, and did not even join us for the wedding brunch-not that I am complaining, why do you ask?"

"Because the reason that she left was me. I told her to leave and never come back. It was Caroline, Darcy, who had those rumors spread around about Elizabeth." Subtlety was never one of the Countess's strong suits.

Darcy was only partially stunned. He had suspected Caroline Bingley all along, but did not have any proof.

"H-how do you know this?"

"Because she reeks, Darcy." The Countess nearly chuckled at Darcy's look of confusion. Tapping his knee as she had when he was a child, she continued. "Apparently she had come to '*visit*' me, and I did not receive her, however, she managed to get the servants to allow her to wait inside my parlor, feigning a closeness that does not exist. She apparently thought that she needed to examine the desk in my study as well because she snuck into that room after she was shown to the parlor, and read a personal letter from Georgiana to me."

Lady Matlock went on to describe what happened next as she confronted Caroline Bingley with all of her evidence against that woman. When she finished, she watched as Darcy went from angry to furious, and finally to an indescribably rage at that woman. "I shall have to have a talk with Bingley, and then I shall have another with Miss Bingley." Darcy bit out.

I will throttle that little bitch for everything she has put Elizabeth through! He was about to storm out until he heard Georgiana's voice.

"Brother... please wait. This has all been due to my carelessness. I should have never sent that note in the first place. I feel that this all my fault"

Lady Eleanor spoke up again staying Georgiana's apology, "Nonsense dear, you should never fear writing to your own family for advice. *She* was in the wrong for having done what she did. It might interest you to know that I have already taken the necessary precautions relating to her. I would imagine that she is finding it more and more difficult to gain admittance *anywhere*."

Darcy knew more than anybody that it was like a social death sentence to lose the support of the countess, but to him it still would not be enough to punish Miss Bingley in such a way. *Elizabeth has suffered needlessly, and all due to that conniving wretch, Caroline Bingley! Running her through would be too good for her!*

He thought that he would pay a visit to his friend, and now-brother, and discuss what he had learned from Lady Matlock. *If she is sent to Scotland and never comes back it will be too soon.* Once he had mastered his roiling emotions, he politely bowed to his aunt, and made for the door with a worried Georgiana in tow.

"Come now, dearest, I need to talk to Bingley", *and if he has any sense left he will remove Caroline to Scotland, never to return again.* He assisted his sister into the carriage, and absently leapt inside. To the Bingley's they would go.

Chapter 23

Darcy arrived in a silent rage at his brother-in-law's home with Georgiana in tow. He was so infuriated at Caroline Bingley that he barley paused at the front foyer before he insisted on being announced to his longtime friend. Georgiana was shown into Jane Bingley's sitting room and he was hastily shown into Charles's study where his bewildered friend looked at him as though he had gone mad.

"What is wrong, Darcy? You look as if the French are about to invade England."

"That might be a great deal more pleasant Charles!"

"What has gotten into you to come storming over here... not that I mind seeing you or your family, but you seem to be overly agitated. I have never seen you like this before."

Darcy pinched the bridge of his nose to try to stem his tirade and began to pace, stopping in front of Bingley who was sitting at his desk. He leaned forward and braced himself-grasping at the ledge tightly.

"You are aware, of course, about the rumors circulating here in town about Elizabeth being *intimately involved* with George Wickham."

Charles gulped hard and nodded his head in confirmation.

"Were you also aware that it was your sister, Caroline, who started them in the first place?" His voice was deceivingly calm.

Darcy was eyeing his friend, trying to gain some insight as to how much Charles Bingley knew of the situation. He watched as Charles frowned and then blush before he nodded his head again slowly.

"*How could you...?* How could you allow her to do such a thing to an *innocent woman*... and not just *any* innocent woman, but *my fiancée-now wife? Your wife's sister?* Did you not think to ever *check* her?" Darcy hissed.

Charles was still frowning, and looked at him, with his face still very flushed, and then he looked down and rubbed his face with his hands.

"I did not know about Caroline's involvement with those rumors until about a month ago, Darcy, you *must* believe me. I did not even find out until... until... until our wedding day. That was when Caroline left your house in Bath right after your aunt... had a talk with her."

"Why did no one say something *then*?" Darcy demanded.

"That was our *wedding day*, Darcy! You did not expect us to tell you something like that, did you? You would have been as furious as you are now... maybe even worse, considering that Caroline was in Bath at the time..."

Darcy knew that Bingley was speaking the truth. If he had heard about Caroline's viciousness then, he would have likely strangled her when he got his hands on her. *Who am I kidding? I would happily still strangle her now, if she were in front of me.*

"Where is she *now*, Bingley?"

Charles looked away from him, and then stood up from the desk before he turned away from him entirely.

"When you and Elizabeth were sequestered wherever you were after we arrived at your house the day of our weddings... the Countess Matlock took Caroline aside. That was when you heard all of those loud voices- well mainly the countess' voice, but that was when we heard about Caroline's role in the rumors about Elizabeth. She apparently found a letter addressed to your aunt... and... she read it. Whatever was in that letter gave Caroline enough of an idea that she started that speaking with her... friends... though I must admit knowing how rumors go, I am not entirely convinced it was all Caroline's doing..."

"*Get your head out of the ground, Bingley!*" Darcy exclaimed with frustration. "You know how she is! She has been jealous of Elizabeth almost since we went to Hertfordshire! Caroline was always making such cutting remarks to and about Elizabeth while we were there-all because she felt Elizabeth was a threat to her! I wish that we had been blunter about my wishes never to have anything to do with her a long time ago. Now she has cast a shadow over my wife's character, and you know good and well how difficult that is to overcome in this town!"

Darcy started pacing again in front of his friend. There was no hiding the fact that he was becoming more agitated the more he thought about it.

"*Where is she now*? I would have some words with her, so that she would know that she will never again be welcomed to any of my homes, nor any homes of my other family members here in town…"

Bingley held his hand up to stay any further words from him.

"Darcy… I should have told you before, but after that day-our wedding-I wrote to Louisa and Hurst, and informed them what I heard from the Countess and Caroline's conversation and why I could not have her in my household anymore. I could not allow such an insult to my Jane… Oh, and to Elizabeth, of course. I am still in charge of administering Caroline's inheritance until she marries or attains the age of twenty five, whichever one comes first. She will soon be of age, but I have written to my solicitor, and have arranged for her to obtain her inheritance early. My sister can no longer rely upon me to supplement her financial shortfalls due to her imprudence."

"That still does not answer my question, Bingley. *Where is she now*? If she is not under *your* protection, am I to assume that she is staying with the Hurst's?"

Bingley shook his head, and looked at him warily. "Hurst would have nothing to do with her after he heard what she had done, and he was even more disgusted when he heard that the countess would publicly cut her and anyone associated with her. He gave Louisa little choice. She was sent to some of our relations in Scotland shortly after we were married."

"Well that is a relief. At least now she cannot go around spreading anymore rumors here in town. It still infuriates me that she dared to do such a thing to my Elizabeth, and she will not even be really punished for it."

"Oh, I would not say that, Darcy. The Filken's only reason for accepting Caroline into their household was to help with the children. Apparently my cousin's wife had taken ill after giving birth and it will take some time before she is well enough to take on the responsibility of six children, and seeing how much Caroline despises children… well let us just say that this is going to be as close to hell as she will get for a little while." Bingley chuckled.

The thought of Caroline Bingley taking care of small children was frightening, but knowing what he did about the Filkens, Darcy knew that they would not allow Caroline to shirk her duties or treat their children poorly. *She has basically been put upon the shelf and turned into a governess... and in Scotland to boot! I must admit that short of killing her, this would be a good second option for a punishment for her*, Darcy thought with some satisfaction.

Darcy smiled a little at his friend, "I suppose that you are correct, but it still galls me that she did this and it is Elizabeth who shall have to suffer the consequences for some time…"

"Do not worry, my good friend. If anyone asks, I will set them straight… as embarrassing as it is to me and my family. I think that most people already know the truth about who started the rumor and why. Caroline has been pursuing you for years and she had been bragging to the other ladies of the *ton* about how she would one day become the next *Mrs. Darcy*. They all laughed at her behind her back when they read about your engagement… and public declaration. She was humiliated beyond belief… at least to her sensibilities anyway. Her reputation is already shred to pieces for what she did to you and Elizabeth."

Darcy could sympathize with Bingley's plight. They were essentially in the same boat with rumors circulating about their families and neither deserving of the censure. Besides, Jane was also going to be affected and she was his sister now too. He offered the olive branch to Bingley in a gesture of… *understanding*.

"I feel for you my friend." He paused and thought for a moment, "You are still planning on coming to the ball tonight are you not?"

Bingley smiled one of his genuine smiles, "We would not miss it for anything, Darcy. Of course Jane and I will be there."

They shook hands and Darcy made to excuse himself to ready for the ball. He was shown to Jane's sitting room where his sister and the new Mrs. Bingley were happily chatting away as if nothing in the world bothered them. *This is yet another reason that I am grateful that I married Elizabeth… she does have some relations for whom she need not blush.* He greeted his sister's hostess and talked briefly with Jane before he made to leave.

"Mr. Darcy," Jane said, "I understand that Elizabeth was seen by a physician this morning. Is she all right?"

"Ah," He looked at Georgiana, slightly perturbed that she mentioned Elizabeth's illness this morning, but then checked himself. She was not told the reason Elizabeth was seen, or what her condition was...*yet*. At present, he wanted to keep that a secret between him and Elizabeth. "She is fine now. She has been rather fatigued and had some difficulties earlier this morning, but we have been reassured that she will be fine."

"Is she still able to attend the ball? It would not do for her to wear herself out dancing." Jane said.

"I have made sure that she is well rested today. That is why she is not with us now, so that she may be rested enough to attend the ball tonight." And it would not be any imposition what-so-ever for me to sit out many dances with her. *That would also be an excellent excuse for her to decline dancing with any other man*, Darcy thought with satisfaction.

Jane looked at him with a hint of concern. "Are you sure that that would be in her best interests, sir?"

"I am not entirely convinced, but Elizabeth has assured me that she will be fine and she wishes to go. I will not deny her, but you can rest assured that I will make certain that she is not overtaxed and she will rest if she seems to be overtired."

"I shall trust your judgment then, and if you need any assistance in convincing her, I will be happy to help."

It was touching how the two sisters were still very protective of each other and Darcy could only hope that this sisterly affection grew to the same proportions between the Bennet's and Georgiana-though more so with Elizabeth and Jane. Noting the time, Darcy made his excuses as he needed to ready for the ball and the three younger Bennet girls would be arriving at Darcy House soon. The last thing that he wanted was for Elizabeth to have to deal with the influx alone.

As expected his house was in an uproar when Elizabeth's sisters arrived. Luckily Georgiana had become more accustomed to their mannerisms and had actually befriended Mary and Catherine. She was still a little intimidated by Lydia who seemed a bit loud and untamed... or so she confided to him.

Both he and Elizabeth ate a light meal in their private sitting room before readying for the ball. Mrs. Jones made certain that they were well supplied with bland and dry foods as well as plenty of tea to help keep Elizabeth's stomach from revolting. As they sat across from each other at their small table in their sitting room, Darcy enquired about her health.

"Are you certain that you feel up to attending tonight, Elizabeth? You do know that no one would blame you for not going under the circumstances…"

"Fitzwilliam, I think that under the circumstances, it is imperative that I do go. If anyone learns of the reason for my being absent, then you know that the rumors will only be given more credence. I think that I shall just have to grin and bear it, besides… I feel much better now and Mrs. Jones has taken such good care of me today."

Darcy knew that she spoke the truth. *No, it would not do for anyone to learn that she has already become with child.*

"All right then, dearest, but you must promise me that should you become fatigued or start to feel ill at any time that you will let me know and we shall leave immediately."

"I shall promise to let you know, but I think that the best thing to do would be to ensure that it does not happen and then we can enjoy this night together."

"Darling, you know that my idea of an enjoyable evening does not include guests… or clothes, although a different sort of dancing might be entertaining." Darcy teased.

"Perhaps later we can have our own*private* ball?" Elizabeth laughed.

"I look forward to it."

He leaned forward to capture her lips and what started as a light gesture, soon turned into something else entirely. Darcy had a glint in his eyes as he felt the stirrings of passion overcome him. He moved to her side and grasp her hands to help her stand then smiled seductively at her.

"Do you suppose that we might be able to start a dance now? Then perhaps we can finish here tonight, as well? I may need some practice you know, and I *was* denied that this morning…."

"I think that I might be able to arrange that, sir, but I seem to recall a time when you thought that dancing was for savages…"

"Yes, and right now I am feeling rather primitive, madam." Darcy picked her up, carried her laughing to their chambers and laid her on the bed.

"I think that I might be able to give some attention to your… needs…" Elizabeth said as she pulled him down to her in a deep searing kiss.

Her hands began to work on the buttons to his waist coat and then moved deftly to his cravat, removing it easily. Darcy's hand were busy freeing the tiny buttons to her bodice while he fondled her breasts through the material, but he grew frustrated when his body demanded that he move quickly and he grasped each side of the offending garment and tore it open, to Elizabeth's shock.

"Sir, I will have you know that this is one of the few gowns I have left that still fit me in... certain places."

"My dear, we can easily afford new gowns that will 'fit you in places', but please, for my sanity, make sure that they are easily removed." Darcy pleaded as he moved to release her from her corset and chemise all the while placing small kisses along the exposed skin of her back and shoulders.

"Husband... can I not assist you in removing your rather inconvenient garments as well? You are being selfish..."

Darcy moved to face her once again and kissed her soundly before pulling away, "By all means, dearest. I would not have you think me selfish." He gave her a rakish smile.

Elizabeth quickly assisted him in removing his shirt and trousers when she met with his boots. Darcy had been helping her to shed her last few bits of clothing and was working on her garters while massaging her core, when he realized that his boots were in the way. By this time he was too tense with a burgeoning erection to wait for their removal and said to her, "Forgive me, love. I fear that I cannot wait any longer to have you."

She did not have any time to respond before he grabbed her hips and thrust into her deeply then began to move in a frantic rhythm. Her hips came up to meet his, matching his tempo and he could feel her body responding to him as she moaned out his name in pleasure over and over. In no time at all he could feel his manhood being squeezed by her core as she found her release and he could hold himself off no longer and joined her in an extremely satisfactory orgasm. They lay joined in a breathless post coital bliss, regaining their senses again, but not separating from each other.

It was some time before they called for their bath and as a matter of expediency... and enjoyment, they bathed together.

After they had bathed and dressed, Darcy came to Elizabeth's dressing room to escort her to their coach. When he saw her in her pale yellow silken dress that complemented her figure and complexion so well, he could not find the words to express how truly handsome she was-even more so than usual. He could not help but think that their afternoon love-making session may have added to her glow, but had to push those thoughts away else he might embarrass himself in front of her maid.

Sarah had just finished putting her hair up in an intricate up do with some jeweled pins which only added to her lovely mahogany hair. She wore his mother's pearl and diamond choker and earrings and a broach with diamonds and yellow topaz.

"Mrs. Darcy, please allow me to say how well you look, and to say that you look every bit the society lady... not that that is any surprise." Darcy complimented her.

"I would venture that you are probably one of the few people who will be there tonight that think that."

"Nonsense love, Aunt Eleanor would not invite anybody there tonight who would disparage you and if anyone dared, they will have not only my wrath but that of the whole Fitzwilliam and Darcy clans as well as our friends. You must know that I will never tolerate anyone saying terrible, untrue, and unkind things about you."

"You are truly the best of men, Mr. Darcy."

"I am truly the luckiest of men, Mrs. Darcy, with you by my side." He offered her his arm, "Shall we?"

He escorted her to their coach where her parents and the Gardiners were already awaiting them.

"Is this not the most exciting thing to be going to such a prestigious ball, Lizzy? 'T'is too bad that your younger sisters could not come. I really do not understand why they should have to stay behind. This would be an excellent opportunity for them to meet other rich men..."

"Fanny..." Mr. Gardiner said in exasperation, "They are too young to attend a ball of this sort. Why... even Miss Darcy is not attending tonight..."

"Yes, but Mr. Darcy could have had a word with the countess to allow her to come and them my girls could have gone as well." She retorted.

Darcy was gripping Elizabeth's hand tightly and though no one could see his face he took on a scowl towards his mother-in-law.

"Mrs. Bennet," He said in clipped tones, "Georgiana is not yet out, and I do not think that she needs to be exposed to so many impertinent questions and conversations tonight-especially after the ordeal Elizabeth and I endured only a little over a month ago." *Not that she will not have to endure that at home, but at least the exposure within my own home will be minimized. I only hope that after tonight she will forgive me.*

"Oh, that! I do not think that people will be still talking about that now. There have been other things that have occurred in town since then…"

"Mrs. Bennet… Mr. Darcy and his family are quite prominent families here in town and if there has been any talk about them at all it is not likely to die a quiet death -for people love to have a nice bit of gossip regardless of whether or not it is true." Mr. Bennet stated.

"Well… it is nice to be able to say that you have such connections, is it not, Lizzy?" She turned to Darcy and asked, "Do you suppose that there will be any member of the royal family there, Mr. Darcy?"

"I doubt it. Though the earl and countess have traveled in that set, they are rarely graced with such notable personages at their functions… unless it has to do with matters of state." Darcy answered.

Mrs. Bennet did not seem to be deterred and continued to prattle on until they arrived at Matlock House. Never had he been so relieved to attend a ball. His only consolation was that he would no longer be the object of interest by the match making mamas of the ton. He stepped out of the coach and handed Elizabeth down and they entered the House. Since they were the guests of honor, they were the first to arrive, but soon they were greeting the onslaught of guests that his family had invited.

Elizabeth leaned over towards him as they greeted what he thought was the three hundredth guest and said, "I thought that Lady Eleanor said that this was to be a small sort of affair?"

He leaned over to answer, "This *is* a small sort of affair for her, dearest."

"Please do not tell me that I must dance with all the gentleman here?"

"You do not have to dance with any gentleman here… except me, of course and I think that Richard and my uncle would wish to dance at least one dance with you, however."

"I think that is only fair, since your cousin did help to rescue me, and your aunt and uncle are throwing this ball in our honor."

"Then by all means, please do so, but do not expect that I shall be dancing with a great deal of other women. You know how much I despise the activity… unless it is with you of course." He raked his eyes over her and stared at her with his burning gaze.

"Dearest, I think that I am a little over dressed for your sort of dance right now, and we have only just greeted our guests."

"Yes, and now that they have met us we have fulfilled our obligations." He was half teasing, half serious.

"I think that we would not be forgiven, should we do that, besides, Fitzwilliam, my other invitation is open at anytime."

"Well then, I may just have to sprain my ankle in the first set, and claim a need to go home with my wife to comfort me…"

She giggled softly, "You are encourageable."

"Only with the proper motivation." He whispered to her as he reached behind her and caressed her bottom. He delighted in the affect it had upon her complexion as a blush overspread her chest and face.

Once the line of guests had dwindled and the musicians were warmed up sufficiently, the first strings of the first set sounded. Darcy escorted her to the dance floor and stood up at the front of the line followed by the earl and countess and then his cousin the viscount and another guest, Richard and a Lady Regina, Bingley and Jane and several other couples.

Darcy kept an eye on Elizabeth, watching for any signs of fatigue and he was relieved when she seemed to be in relatively good shape after the first set. The next was to be a quicker paced dance and though he was leery of her dancing again he allowed her to accept the next with the Viscount Matlock, and finally a third with the earl. By the time she had finished the third set, she was starting to look a little fatigued and he encouraged her to sit and rest with Mr. and Mrs. Gardiner and Mr. Bennet while he went to get her some refreshments.

While he made his way across the room towards the punch table, he was arrested by some idle discussion that he overheard between two society matrons.

"I do not see how the new Mrs. Darcy could be seen as anything special, Harriet, I mean look at her- she really has nothing to recommend her… other than her charms, or so I have heard."

"Well I have heard that she has charms aplenty, Martha. You know she was said to have been having an affair with his steward's son before she married him? I mean really, if she were to be tripping in the pasture, why do so with a lowly servant's son… but then I guess that is the way that those of the lower ranks do things…"

The conversation was enough to infuriate Darcy all over again after the afternoon at the Bingley's. He decided to make his presence know, and came up behind them.

"Lady Sefton, Mrs. Granville... can you not find anything else to amuse yourselves with than false tales?"

Both ladies turned around towards him and their complexions turned a very bright red color when they recognized their intended victim's husband had overheard their very unkind remarks. When they said nothing to him, he continued, "If you are not finding anything more entertaining here, then I am sure that the Countess would not be offended if you excused yourselves early. Not everyone has the same opinions as to what constitutes entertainment."

He finished by nodding curtly to them and turning on his heel back towards the refreshment table. With drinks in hand, he gingerly made his way back to where Elizabeth and her family as well as some new acquaintances were talking. Darcy handed her a glass of punch, and stood brooding over what he had just overheard and reacted to. With self recriminations he revisited what had happened. Mrs. Granville and Lady Sefton were notorious gossips and both of them had tried to entrap him into marriage with their daughters at one time or another.

He knew that they were likely bitter over his choosing a wife that was not from town, but still he would not tolerated anyone disparaging Elizabeth... even if it was just bitter grapes.

Elizabeth was watching him and asked, "Are you already disgruntled that I made you come here, Fitzwilliam? You seem to be distracted."

He was brought out of his thoughts, and frowned momentarily before he tried to paste a smile on his face, "I am not disgruntled, dearest. I..." *How can I tell her why my mood has soured?* "You know how I feel about these sorts of events, and it is a bit crowded in here."

"Would you care to go out on the balcony then? I could use some fresh air right about now."

Instantly his concern for her health was at the forefront of his mind.

"Are you all right, Elizabeth? Should I call for the carriage?" He said with great concern.

"No you do not need to call for our carriage. I am fine. I was only thinking that it has gotten warmer in here with so many people."

He felt some relief, and offered her his arm, "In that case I will walk out with you."

Once they had attained the balcony behind the settee where she was sitting, they found that they were alone for the moment. She reached out to take his hands when she turned to face him.

"Fitzwilliam, what is the matter... really? I can tell that something is upsetting you."

He looked at her for a moment before he kissed her hands, and looked away again. "I cannot speak of it, my love. It is somewhat distressing."

She reached up and turned his head to face her with her tiny hands, "Fitzwilliam, please tell me. I think that I can handle almost anything after what I have heard for the last month."

"I have heard a couple of the *'society matrons'* discussing those rumors that have been going around."

"Just now?" Elizabeth asked, and when he nodded his head, she asked, "I cannot say that I am surprised, after all there are quite a few single women here, and I am sure that their mother's are not likely to be fond of me." She said lightly.

Darcy looked at her with something akin to astonishment. "How can you talk of something like that so lightly?"

"Darling, I did not come here tonight thinking that all the rumors surrounding me would suddenly have disappeared. I know that it will take time for people to learn that those things said about me were false." She took his face gently in her palm. "It will not happen quickly."

"I worry about what people might say when they learn of your condition as well..." He started, but she pulled away from him, and looked away.

"Are you ashamed of ... of my... condition?"

He saw her eyes watering and it tore at his heart to see her distancing herself from him, and he wanted her to know that he still loved her regardless of what others said.

"My love, please do not misunderstand me, I have never been as happy as I was this morning. Well at least after I learned why you were so ill, but no, I am not ashamed that you carry my child. Quite the contrary. What I meant to say a little less inelegantly, is that others will be unkind still when they learn of your condition so soon..."

She looked at him with a blank expression and then frowned, "I have no intention of announcing anything right now, at least not until I feel the babe quicken. That is what I understand is usually done, or so Mrs. Jones assures me. We will not know anything until my confinement begins anyway and I had thought that… maybe we could stay in Derbyshire after the babe is born. It is not as though we have to announce to the whole world what my condition is. It is none of their business. This does not change how we will act or feel does it?"

What she said made perfect sense, and Darcy realized that he was borrowing trouble. They really did not know when their child would be born, but it would not change how they felt about each other or their child. He sighed deeply and answered her.

"You are perfectly right, dearest. It really is no one else's business, but our own."

They stared into each other's eyes and smiled before they both leaned into and claimed the other's lips. Elizabeth reached up to grab the back of his neck, running her hands through his hair while he embraced her tightly and moved his hands from her waist to her round bottom. Their kiss grew from comforting to something more until the doors behind them opened to admit a witness to their intimate moment.

"I say… there seems to be a better show out here than inside." The distinct voice of Richard Fitzwilliam said.

"What are you doing out here, Richard?" Darcy growled.

"I just came out to fetch our guests of honor. The earl and countess wish to have you present before we entered the dining room, but it looks as if another feast has already begun out here."

"Richard… bugger off. Can a man not enjoy a private moment with his wife during a ball?"

"Of course, but you have had enough *private moments* by now to have enjoyed the lovely Mrs. Darcy quite thoroughly."

Darcy glared at his cousin who was smirking remorselessly at him, and then he noticed that Elizabeth also seemed to find some amusement in their situation.

"You have to admit that we will incite more rather than less talk if we stay out here for too much longer, darling." Elizabeth said.

"At present, Mrs. Darcy, I care not what others will say. The only thing that I wish to incite…"

"Uh… Darcy, unless you want to incite the ire of my mother, then I suggest you come back inside before she comes out here to join you."

True to form, the countess came out to the balcony as well.

"Darcy, Elizabeth, it is time to start the supper dance, then once we are finished there you may enjoy the outdoors again." She spoke in a tone that commanded their presence, and turned away from them but before she left she stopped, turned again briefly and said, "Oh, and I almost forgot to tell you… the supper dance happens to be a waltz." She smiled at them and left them to follow her.

"Well… I suppose that we should continue inside then, Mrs. Darcy."

"Indeed we shall, Mr. Darcy."

After they danced the scandalous waltz, the rest of the evening went off without a hitch. Later Darcy learned that the two matrons he heard talking earlier were also overheard by a close friend of the earl and countess. They had heard his biting words to them as well, and were invited to leave again, but took no heed of the invitation. They were soon cut by most of the room, and left before the dinner set with a great deal of mortification. As to Darcy and Elizabeth, they were noted to be the best dancers on the floor that evening. They did not stay for the entire evening, however, leaving at one o'clock in the morning, to the protests of Mrs. Bennet and the relief of the rest of their party.

Though Darcy's mind was willing to dance again with Elizabeth, that night neither of their bodies was willing. As soon as their heads landed in the pillows they were fast asleep.

As the carriage made its way through the woods of Pemberley Park, Elizabeth noticed that they were slowly climbing up a hill and when they reached the top of the hill, Darcy struck the roof with his walking stick.

"Look out to the west. There is Pemberley, dearest. Welcome to your new home."

He pointed towards the large three story stone mansion with great pillars, and in front of the manor was a lake with a stream feeding into it. The whole house looked as if it had been there forever and belonged in this location. She could see the clear reflection of the house in the lake. There were no artificial plants and the shrubbery, though well maintained, were not perfectly coifed as they were at Rosings. Elizabeth was breathless at the beauty of her new home. Never before had she seen such a place so perfectly situated.

Her usual calm left her to be replaced by trepidation. *Of this I am to be mistress of? What if I am no good at it? What if it proves to be so daunting that I fail miserably?* Her thoughts were interrupted by her new sister's voice.

"Well? What do you think, Elizabeth?" Georgiana asked excitedly.

"I think... I think that... that I have never seen anything situated quite so well in my life..."

Her response seemed to please the other two occupants of the carriage as they were both smiling at her with matching dimples going ear to ear.

"Shall you like it here, do you think?" Darcy asked with a hint of eagerness.

Elizabeth looked at him with a hint amusement, and a wide smile of her own, "Yes... yes, I think I shall like it here very much." Her nerves started to wane as she repeated to herself, *So long as I have William's love and faith, I shall be the best mistress of his household.*

Darcy leaned to her and kissed her upon the lips, unembarrassed in front of his sister. "Good, because I hope to spend many long years here with you... and our family." He took his walking stick and tapped on the roof of the coach again, and they began moving a little more quickly towards the house.

When the coach pulled to a stop in front of the house, Elizabeth saw a great many servants standing on the steps waiting to greet them. Darcy emerged first and helped Georgiana and then Elizabeth out to be introduced to an elderly, but spry looking woman.

Darcy introduced the woman as 'Mrs. Reynolds', and informed her that the housekeeper had been with the family for nearly four and twenty years.

"It is a pleasure to finally meet you Mrs. Darcy. We have all been looking forward to meeting you ever since we heard that the master was to marry and bring his wife home to Pemberley."

"I hope that I do not disappoint you then, Mrs. Reynolds." Elizabeth answered.

"I doubt that you will ma'am. If what the master says in his letters is true then we shall get along just fine." The kindly woman informed her.

Elizabeth looked at Darcy with a blush and Darcy responded to Mrs. Reynolds, "It is true, in fact I am afraid that I have not done the new mistress justice by extolling her many fine qualities."

"Then, sir, I have no doubt that the new mistress will do quite well here."

Hearing her husband's confidence in her abilities helped to dispel Elizabeth's uneasiness, and she gradually began to relax as he continued to introduce her to the rest of the household staff. She was amazed that he knew them all and it struck her that such a great man was able to name all of his staff without assistance. She was not even too certain that her father could do so, and the staff at Longbourn was nowhere near the size of Pemberley. It struck her then that she still had a great deal to learn about her new husband, but she did at least feel secure in two things.

He is the very best man I have ever known, and he loves me with more devotion and faithfulness than anyone else. I think that I shall quite enjoy getting to know more of him as we grow together in our love.

Chapter 24

Elizabeth sat down upon a chair on the balcony at Pemberley to join Georgiana as they watched Darcy ride in from inspecting the crops. This late in September the tenants were readying for the coming harvest and she knew that soon he would be out in the fields till almost dark. The time that they had now was precious to them and she was always eager to see him return home-especially if it meant seeing him ride atop his horses.

She secretly enjoyed watching him as he mounted and dismounted upon the animals as it showed his physic to the best advantage with his strong lean frame taking command over his mount. This evening was no different as he came to the back of the house where she was situated. He was in his shirtsleeves and it was unbuttoned to the middle of his chest. *Such a nice view*, thought Elizabeth.

"How are you all this evening?"Darcy asked both of them.

"We are well, sir, and how are you after such a long hot day atop that horse?"

"We are both well too." He laughed as he came over to kiss his sister and then her lightly on the cheek and brushed his hand over Elizabeth's swollen belly. His work clothes were dusty from the day of riding, and she knew that he would wish to bathe before they ate supper. It was a prospect she was looking forward to because they had made it a habit to bathe together whenever practical.

"How is the planning for the Harvest Ball coming along?"

"Oh, we are all done with that now, brother, but then it is not too difficult with the help of Elizabeth and Mrs. Reynolds. It will be the best one yet!" Georgiana proclaimed.

"I am sure that it will be, Georgie. Is there anything that you two cannot do in quick order?"

"Well… there are a few things that take time. We still have not gotten the things out of the attic for the nursery, nor picked the colors for the walls. Perhaps if we are very lucky we can persuade someone to help us." Elizabeth coaxed.

Darcy laughed, then said tenderly, "If it were up to me I would have them painted blue and be done with it. As to the things in the attic, we have plenty of servants to retrieve anything that you wish, dearest and if we do not then it would be simple enough to have our family bring whatever we need from town with them next time they come. You should not overexert yourself."

Elizabeth's eyes lit up, "You have no need to worry on that subject, husband. Mrs. Reynolds would not allow it. She would be offended if we did not request her help anyway. That reminds me... Jane and Mr....uh... Charles will be coming for the ball. I still need to have some rooms readied for them, but I do not know which ones he used when he was here before."

"Oh..." Darcy said with a pause, "I suppose that his old rooms will not do anymore, now that he and Jane are married and now that they are family. We should probably use the rooms that my aunt and cousin used to use-you remember, Georgie... the blue rooms down the hall from the master suite?"

"Yes, those rooms would be perfect." She said softly.

Both Elizabeth and Darcy looked at her when she suddenly withdrew.

"Is there something the matter Georgiana?" Elizabeth asked.

The young woman looked at them and frowned before looked towards the ground. "N-no, well y-yes." Then she shook her head and looked at both her and Darcy, "It is just that I think that it is so sad what happened with Aunt Catherine and Anne. To have lost everything...her estate and her child as well..."

Both Darcy and Elizabeth made to sit on either side of her, and embraced her.

"Georgie, dear," Darcy said, "Fate has a way of dispensing justice as it should be. The consequence of their actions was far reaching, and many people were hurt- not the least of all, Elizabeth. You must not grieve for those who have gotten what they so rightly deserved."

It had been two months since Anne died giving birth to her son who was born breach. Her pelvis was not wide enough to deliver him and the midwife could not turn the child around to move him into position. Lady Catherine was with them when her daughter succumbed and started ranting about how this was all the fault of *that little harlot from Hertfordshire'*. After the funeral she had come at Elizabeth accusing her of killing Anne. When the Earl, Richard, and Darcy subdued her before she could get to Elizabeth, she was taken to her rooms and sedated by the physician.

When the family saw that her mental state was only deteriorating more, they felt the only thing that they could do was to have her quietly removed to a facility for the mentally incompetent. Upon her removal from Rosings and further investigation into the estate business, a newer will of the late Sir Louis De Bourgh was found. At the reading of the newer will, it was discovered that should Anne not marry, the estate would automatically go to Richard Fitzwilliam.

Being thrust into the new roll of being a major estate owner, Richard decided to resign his commission and with the help of his father and Darcy, he was on his way to learning how to manage his properties and assets. Consequent to his inheritance, he found his desirability within the *ton* had increased tenfold-which caused him to stay away from town for the time being. Darcy seemed to find his cousin's new predicament rather amusing, and found great enjoyment in teasing him about it as well.

Neither Elizabeth nor her husband talked much about the whole kidnapping incident, as it brought them no pleasure at all. The last time it was even mentioned was when Darcy had to serve as a witness to the trials of the other assailants. When the magistrate suggested that their crimes could bring a death sentence, he and Elizabeth advocated for another suitable punishment. The Darcy's felt that since the main instigators were already dead, or confined to an institution-the others could be shown enough mercy to be transported to Australia for the rest of their lives.

The Harvest Ball would be the first major event that Elizabeth would oversee. Her guest list included all of the prominent landowners in Derbyshire and even some in the surrounding counties. Some of those guests even included a duke and duchess and more than a few earls and countesses which helped to add to the prestige of the event. Though she had a great deal of input in the planning, she also had the help of very competent staff and Georgiana who had helped plan them in the years prior. She was now doing exceedingly well in learning her new role as the Mistress of Pemberley.

On the night of the ball Elizabeth took a great deal more care in dressing than she had at the Matlock's ball celebrating their marriage. They had forgone her formal presentation until the next season, which would be postponed now that Elizabeth was expecting. This later event was one of the causes for her taking more time to get ready this evening, as she did not wish to demonstrate how much she had really grown into her roll. The current fashions of the dresses did help to somewhat conceal her girth, but it seemed that she was doomed to carry the babe in her front.

While she studied her figure in the looking glass, she did not see Darcy come into her dressing room and observe her.

"Do not worry, Elizabeth, you look as stunning as ever."

Elizabeth looked at him in the mirror and smiled, "You are just saying that because you are my husband and also the reason why I look like I am a chubby drunken sailor instead of the elegant Mistress of Pemberley."

Darcy made a low chuckling sound, as he embraced her around her middle to caress the swell there, and began to place small kisses from her ear to her shoulder.

"You are not chubby, you are with my child... besides, do you have any idea how utterly gorgeous you are right now?"

Elizabeth placed her hands over his as they caressed her abdomen and she turned to face him, wrapping her arms around his neck. She could not get as close as she once could, but they managed to reach each other's lips and kiss with as much passion as they ever had before.

"Elizabeth...? Must we attend this ball?" Darcy growled.

"It would not reflect very well upon us, and me in particular if we were to stay above stairs for my very first ball now would it?"

"Darling... everyone around here already thinks you are a paragon of virtue and hospitality. You do not need to impress anyone..."

He began to place more small kisses from her ear and along her jaw until he reached the swell of her now even fuller breasts. The sensation of his warm lips upon her caused her to moan out in pleasure until he felt his hands reach for the hem of her gown.

"Dearest… Sarah would not appreciate it if she had to iron this gown again after our frolicking about just before we were to open the ball."

"Darling, that is what she is paid to do."

Darcy slowly moved her against her dressing table until he could lift her bottom to perch upon the edge of it. He continued his ministrations to her until she relented and allowed him to caress her in the center of her core until she needed to feel him within her. His movements were ecstasy to her and she moved her hips to intensify the feeling he was eliciting with his hands. She was taken by surprise when he removed his hands from her and moved swiftly to remove the barrier of his trousers. He joined her in coital union. His actions were bringing her some relief as he increased his thrusts to aid her to her completion and then she felt another crest wash over her. It was not long before she felt the warmth of his release within her, and his movements gradually slowed. His moans of relief had matched hers, and soon they were both breathless and perspiring. *I shall have to clean up again before I am presentable.*

Darcy smiled at her lazily and said, "Of all of the dances I have ever had, Mrs. Darcy that was by far the very best of my life." He quickly withdrew from her, re-buttoned his trousers, bent to kissed her, and continued, "I think I will refresh myself and I will meet you in about fifteen minutes?"

She could do nothing more than nod her head and when he had left her to tend to himself, she regained her senses and called for Sarah. *Hopefully she will not be too upset with me for this*, she thought as she took in her appearance and wrinkled dress. Her maid came promptly and had her dress back to its pristine condition and Elizabeth's hair back in a presentable fashion within the allotted time- with some assistance.

As promised, Darcy returned to her within fifteen minutes and seemed to take great delight in watching Sarah tend to her hair and appearance.

"You look even more remarkable than before, Elizabeth."

"And I wonder why? But you look as handsome as ever too, Fitzwilliam." Her eyes raked over his form, "Shall we prepare to go dancing again?"

His eyes lit up and she could see the darkness that still reflected the passion he felt for only her, "I suppose, but I rather prefer the other dance we had earlier."

She could feel the heat rise from her chest to her face and finally the roots of her hair. Shaking her head she rose from her seat and accepted his proffered arm. They walked down the family wing and met with Georgiana as she left her rooms.

"Georgiana, you look…" Darcy seemed almost stunned as he took in his sister's appearance. "Lovely."

Elizabeth was very pleased with the way that her newest sister's dress turned out. The pale rose set off her complexion to her greatest advantage and the empire waist complemented her womanly figure as well.

"Thank you, Fitzwilliam. You look quite handsome tonight as well, and you too Elizabeth. Why… both you and my brother seem to have the same rosy complexion tonight."

Neither of them said anything and if anyone were to look at them at that moment they may have been said to easily resemble a ripe tomato.

Darcy offered her his other arm and escorted them both to the ball room where they could hear the musicians warming up. Soon they were in the midst of welcoming the first guests which happened to be the Earl and Countess Matlock. There would be a little time before the rest of their guests arrived, so the family had some opportunity to visit before everyone else descended upon Pemberley.

Lady Eleanor approached Elizabeth and leaned in to whisper to her, "You are looking rather well, Elizabeth. How are you feeling?"

"Very well, thank you, Lady Eleanor. You are looking as beautiful as ever."

The countess laughed, "I thank you, but I truly meant what I said, my dear. Your condition certainly seems to agree with you… Much more than Lady Anne's ever had." At Elizabeth's look of interest, she continued, "Your predecessor was a small woman, much like that of her namesake, and she was not nearly as hearty as you are and she could not even dream of giving a ball in your condition. Her constitution would not have allowed the activity. I think the high coloring that you have now speaks to that." She smiled a knowing smile at her.

Elizabeth blushed and looked away, where she spotted her husband talking in earnest with his uncle. Soon those gentlemen joined the ladies and Lord Matlock repeated the complement paid by his wife. Elizabeth had barely said her thank yous, before the rest of the guests started arriving in droves.

The ball officially began with Darcy and Elizabeth opening with a traditional weaving of the hey, and shortly after that Elizabeth was approached for many more dances. She could tell that Darcy was not too keen upon her spending the whole night dancing-especially if it were not with him, but she was able to beg off some of the dances claiming fatigue. Many of her society equals saw her talking easily to their husbands and sons, and they were able to see how she and Darcy interacted with each other and their closest family. It was apparent to them that their society accepted her without reservation, and many of the society ladies were eager to become acquainted with her afterwards.

Lady Matlock played a material part in her acceptance, Elizabeth knew, due to her considerable influence among the *ton* and at Almack's, and then there were the stories that had been circulating about the source of those vicious rumors surrounding the new Mrs. Darcy. It had become more widely known that one Caroline Bingley started those false rumors because of jealousy, and she had been sent away-nearly disowned by her family for her abominable behavior. The last rumors even had her dismissed from working as a governess for some middle class merchants in Scotland. Apparently she could not handle her duties, and she was sent to live in a small village on whatever inheritance she had left after paying some familial debts-at least that was the last rumor that Elizabeth had heard of Miss Bingley. Charles and Jane never spoke of her.

It seemed that the *ton* had not only all but forgotten about the gossip following Elizabeth, but they had moved on to another scandal. *Such is life*, thought Elizabeth, but poor Jane and Charles... to have such unfortunate relations. It made her thankful that her father had finally heeded William's advice to have the three youngest of her sisters sent to a finishing school in order to learn some restraint and they were starting to show some improvement... at least Mary and Kitty were. Lydia still had a long way to go to be considered finished and Elizabeth wondered if that was even possible in her case.

Before the ball came to a close, everyone was declaring it a success. To finish the night though, Darcy made a special request. He wanted the waltz to be the very last dance of the evening.

At the musicians cue, Elizabeth excused herself from a conversation about perennials that had lasted nearly three quarters of an hour to find her husband who had been watching her from across the room.

"I thought that I should never have been able to escape that conversation with Lady Thurston." Elizabeth proclaimed.

Darcy chuckled, "I enjoyed watching you from across the room, but I knew better than to interrupt."

She looked at him almost indignantly, "Could you not have rescued me though, Fitzwilliam?"

"Why? Then you would have been approached for a dance by some other gentleman."

"Darling... the only gentleman I want to dance with is you... besides you shall always have my last dance." She smiled at him lovingly as they started their waltz.

Soon after their intimate embraces on the dance floor, Darcy and Elizabeth found an even more enjoyable dance... in their private suite.

Chapter 25

C hristmas at Pemberely had not been so scenic since Lady Anne had been Mistress of the manor and all of the credit went to Elizabeth and Georgiana. They both planned the decorating, and gotten a little carried away in Darcy's opinion, but the results were magnificent. He worried that his wife was doing too much preparing the house for the holidays and decorating the nursery, but she insisted she was perfectly capable of doing both-in spite of her *delicate condition*. When he tried to object, his sister offered her services to help Elizabeth with the arrangements. The result was magnificent. They had managed to transform the house into a winter wonderland.

When Pemberely was opened to visitors, they were awed but none so much as Mrs. Bennet. With many reservations did Darcy and Elizabeth invite their families to their home for the holidays. The matron showed up a full week prior to Christmas, to the master and mistress' horror, and upon seeing the great house could not stop exclaiming upon all of the fine things within each room. One morning, while Darcy and the rest of the manor tried to avoid the woman, he came upon his wife and mother-in-law arguing. *She has finally succeeded in exhausting her daughter*, he huffed to himself as he listened with disgust.

"Lizzy, you know that you should be resting as much as possible. I can manage the household. My goodness, I have been doing it at Longbourn for nearly four and twenty years."

"Yes, but mama, I am entirely capable of running my own household…"

"Oh, do not be so silly child! You are so great with child and besides… look at your figure!" She pointed at her daughter, "Mr. Darcy will not want to have anything else to do with you if you continue to gain weight as you have. You are not even due for at least…what? Another two months! You really must take care, or hope that you bear him a son, else he will not want anything else to do with you."

Elizabeth rolled her eyes as her mother continued ranting. When she was done, Elizabeth cheekily responded, "Mama, if I am to stay slim, then I must *move* and the most efficient way to get things done is to continue to *do* what needs done. As you have noted I am not due for a little while anyway, and you are a guest-not a servant."

Darcy thought for sure the last statement would stop her mother, but the lady was very determined.

"Nonsense! They still need to be supervised, and you are not in any condition to do so! In fact you could do with some more help until you enter your confinement. I am sure if I speak to your father that he would consent to stay... or at least allow me to stay on until you have delivered."

I am sure that Mr. Bennet would not want to be away from home, but if you offered to stay here while he left, then I have no doubt that he would happily agree to that as well, thought Darcy with great frustration. He finally decided to enter the fray.

"Mrs. Bennet... I am sure that Elizabeth and I can manage. We have a very competent staff and a more than ample supply of midwives *and* a physician to see to her health and well being." *And you can be certain that I will not let anything happen to her if I can help it at all.*

"But they are no replacement for her own mother, sir! Just look at her. She has gotten so large-I am sure she will have a grown babe rather than a normal sized infant." She looked him over, ignoring Lizzy's paling face, before she pronounced, "It is likely due to your size."

They were both shocked into silence as she continued until the lunch bell was sounded. Fear of Mrs. Bennet's determination to stay on after everyone else went home, compounded by an uncertain due date for Elizabeth was causing the couple much grief. Her mother was determined to be there for the birth of her first grandchild and Darcy was doubly determined that she would not.

It was a great relief to them when the Earl and Countess of Matlock arrived to help assuage the frustration they had with Mrs. Bennet. Lady Matlock was able to help diffuse the lady, engaging her in conversations regarding the fashions of town, and what she was going to do with the younger girls to *formally* bring them out.

"Oh, but your ladyship... they are all now out! It has been so for nearly a year." Mrs. Bennet proudly proclaimed. "In fact... my own Lydia could very well find a husband before the other two!"

Darcy could tell by the look upon Lady Eleanor's face that she was quite surprised as well, which Mrs. Bennet mistook as being impressed.

"It is true. She is a child after my own heart-so very amiable and energetic…"

As she expounded upon Lydia's many attributes *he* could not help but to think, *she is certainly as silly as you and as to being amiable and energetic-that is not necessarily a good thing. Poor Aunt Eleanor, having to endure Fanny Bennet's ranting on about her silliest daughter as if Lydia's behavior was a good thing.* When Mrs. Bennet mentioned Richard being a good match for either Lydia or Kitty, he was sure that he saw his aunt staring daggers at her though.

"Mrs. Bennet… Richard must have a wife who understands the many responsibilities of running a large estate, as well as have some experience with being a hostess to many distinguished guests. She must also be able to handle the complexities of a household budget. I understand that your daughters have been at home their entire lives?" Lady Eleanor asked.

Mrs. Bennet hesitated a moment before responding, "Well… yes, except my Jane and Lizzy… they spent a great deal of time in town with my Brother and Sister Gardiner. The other girls never had the wish to go, but… I am sure that they can learn as quickly as the eldest two…"

Not likely, thought Darcy, *but that does explain how Elizabeth and Jane turned out as well as they did. 'T'is too bad that the others did not spend as much time away from their mother and father as well.*

"Perhaps, but then they would have to spend some time in town, would they not?" Lady Eleanor easily replied.

"I suppose… I shall talk to Mr. Bennet and my brother and sister when they get here about the girls spending some time in town. I think it would be good for them, and then perhaps they can all meet some gentlemen." Mrs. Bennet simpered.

How does she do that? All Aunt Eleanor has to do is say something so easily and unaffectedly and immediately Fanny is all sense. Darcy was in awe of his aunt's talents. He would have to find some way to repay her for distracting his mother-in-law as she had.

~*~*~*~

The whole family was able to come together in Derbyshire to enjoy the holidays even finding time to go out and enjoy the weather on a couple of sunny days. When Georgiana suggested that they go out to the pond to skate, several of the younger people enthusiastically and happily agreed to join her. Since Elizabeth had never done such a thing in her life, she wanted to come along to at least watch if she could not participate, but Darcy had his reservations when she mentioned going out.

"Elizabeth the snow is very deep in some place along the pond, and though it is bright and sunny outside, it is still very cold."

"Fitzwilliam, I have navigated along snow drifts before, and as for the cold the others are going out in it and you are not protesting their excursion outdoors... besides... with all of my bulk, I am much warmer than I usually am anyway." She protested.

"My dear, I have no doubt of your snow drift maneuvering abilities, but then you were not great with child," He instantly regretted his words as soon as they rolled off his tongue when she glared at him, "I am not saying that there is anything *wrong* with you, but it is just that your sense of balance has been a bit off lately and I would not want to see you or the babe injured."

"Mr. Darcy, I am perfectly capable of walking out of doors without falling over and if you are so concerned then you can join us and I will show you just how well I can do so." She lifted her chin up.

Though Darcy had no desire to go outside to watch the others skate and likely fall upon their backsides, he did not want Elizabeth to go out and risk injury, so he thought it best to go with her to insure her safety. When he and the rest of the party gathered after changing into outdoor attire, he reluctantly assisted Elizabeth out to the pond to watch the others as they skated on the ice.

He reflected as he helped Georgiana to don her blades to skate that he still worried as much about her risking injury, though for different reasons. Last year she did not venture out much, but he figured that it was more due to her moods after the Wickham debacle over the summer. Back then she was the only one that he had left of his immediate family... *How things can change in such a short period of time.* The whole ordeal of the past year tried them all, but now they were here at Pemberley... together, and having such a joyful time. His Elizabeth was now great with his child and they were happily married.

"Husband...?" Elizabeth addressed him.

He looked at her startled, then raised an eyebrow to indicate that she had his attention.

"A penny for your thoughts?"

He smiled at her and said, "I was just thinking about how my life has changed this past year. There have been so many of them... most for the better, and I am not even sure how it happened."

"I certainly know that to be true in my life," She smiled up at him as she caressed her mid section and said, "I blame it on the tea."

Darcy looked at her incredulously, "And what, Mrs. Darcy, does tea have to do with anything?"

"That is simple, Mr. Darcy. When you came to Hunsford, my life was going on as it normally had, and then I drank that tea of Mrs. Hanson's because of a headache that I got when Col-Richard told me about what you had done with regards to Charles. Then you arrived at the parsonage and ..."

He chuckled at her reference to his indiscretion and realized that things could have turned out so much worse. *Had she been in her right mind what would have happened?*

"Elizabeth," He said suddenly serious, "Do you suppose that you would have accepted me if you had not drunk that tea, and... then we did what we did?"

She looked away thoughtfully, taking a few moments to consider his question.

"That is hard to say. I did not know you as I do now. There were so many things about you that I did not understand then, and at the time I did not understand your character, but... since then I have come to consider you as one of the best men that I have ever known." She looked at him with such tenderness and sincerity.

He did not want to imagine the alternatives to what else could have happened then. Just the thought of it was too painful to him, and so he leaned down to give her a quick peck on the lips.

"Then I believe I shall send dear Mrs. Hanson a big thank you for giving you that tea. Perhaps I shall ask her for a sample when next I wish to persuade you into something?"

They both laughed and scooted closer to each other as they watched Richard and Georgiana skating alongside each other on the ice. They were laughing and holding on to each other's arms to keep from falling down while Lydia, Catherine, and Jenna and John Gardiner skated, or more like slid on their bottoms while moving across the pond. Darcy could not recall when he had had so much fun.

He could not believe his amazing fortune, now that he had almost everything that he could ever want. Soon... very soon he would have everything he had ever dreamed of.

~*~*~*~

The Fitzwilliam's, Bennet's sans Catherine, and Gardiner's left Pemberely two days after twelfth night to the great relief of Darcy and Elizabeth. Charles and Jane Bingley stayed behind to help Elizabeth and Darcy with the impending birth and unbeknownst to the Bennet's, to look for an estate closer to the Darcy's. Charles apparently figured out what Darcy already knew... one can never be too far from Mrs. Bennet.

Catherine stayed to keep Georgiana company as the two had begun to form a true friendship towards the end of the Bennet's stay, and he thought that he could see some improvement in both of them as they spent more time with each other and away from Lydia. For her part Catherine was less flighty, and boisterous, and more thoughtful and reserved. In turn Georgiana seemed to be growing more outgoing and talkative-though she would *never* be close to what the two youngest Bennet daughters were at their best. His sister also seemed to enjoy the company of another young woman of her age to associate with, and who was nearer to the same situation in life. Catherine even seemed relieved to be free of her mother's ranting.

After what Fanny Bennet had put them all through during her stay, he was glad that she was finally convinced to leave. It took many promises by Lady Eleanor that she would help to find some good masters for Lydia and Mary and if they did well enough, she might even allow them to come to a ball towards the end of the season. Darcy did not worry much over his aunt having to include them though as he was convinced that it would take more than one season before his aunt would consider them *'ready'* to be out.

~*~*~*~

Things were starting to settle down as it neared the end of January when he had a frantic summons in the wee hours of the morning to a fire at a tenant's home at the other end of the estate. Elizabeth hardly stirred when he got out of bed. He did not want to

awaken her as she rarely slept well at night, and he knew that sleep
was important as she neared her confinement. *I shall be back as soon
as I can, dearest and in the meantime the staff will be here to take care
of you.* He leaned over to kiss her cheek tenderly and left their rooms,
but not before looking back at her wistfully.

Soon he was riding off towards the fire along with several of his
men, Charles, and a few other tenants. An uneasy feeling came over
him as he rode the ten miles to fire. *I pray that all goes well, and that
nothing happens to any of us.* As soon as he set his eyes upon the
blaze, he leapt off of his horse and began yelling directions to put out
the flames and save the family and livestock.

When Elizabeth woke up in their bed alone she wondered where
Darcy was. She rang for Sarah, and when her maid came in to her
room, she asked her if she knew where Mr. Darcy was.

"Aye, ma'am. They said he an several other men went to a fire on
the other end a th' estate."

Elizabeth was worried and slightly upset that Darcy had not
informed her of the fire, but soon forgot everything else when a pain
tore through her midsection. It lasted a few seconds, but returned
again, and then again. The pain was starting to grow enough to make
her moan out and Sarah became alarmed when she returned to the
master's chambers with her breakfast tray.

"Shall I call for Mrs. Reynolds, Mrs. Darcy?"

Elizabeth did not think that the pains were serious enough to
alarm the housekeeper until another pain shot through her again that
not only pierced her midsection but went through her back, and lasted
longer than the previous ones.

"Ooooooooooooh." Elizabeth grasped her abdomen and grimaced.
"Sarah… I may have spoken too hastily… perhaps we should call for
Mrs. Reynolds… now."

Sarah ran to summons the housekeeper immediately, and came
back to check on Elizabeth. It seemed to the latter that time was
moving very slowly while she waited for assistance. When the elderly
woman arrived in the room she took one look at Elizabeth and knew
that it was time for her to deliver.

"How long have these pains been comin', Mrs. Darcy?"

"About twenty minutes ago they began ... and..." Elizabeth stopped as another pain hit her.

"Ooooooooh... "She had to take a deep breath, "and they have been lasting up to a minute or two."

"And how long are they apart, ma'am?"

Elizabeth had to think for a moment, but before she could say anything, another pain tore through her.

"Never you mind... Sarah," She said without even looking at the girl, "Go have Mills call for the midwife and if they can spare it, the physician." When the girl stood unmoving, staring at the scene, she turned and said, "Go! Now!"

When the pains had grown to almost unbearable proportions, Mrs. Reynolds began to bark out orders as efficiently as any army sergeant, taking control of the situation. She had the kitchen warming up hot water and the footmen filling the tub full of warm water. Elizabeth wondered at her insistence in preparing a bath when she was going into labor and inquired about it.

"The warm water will help to relax your muscles and ease your body as the babe moves down in your pelvis. It makes it easier on both you and the child." She explained succinctly as she readied the room for the birth.

It soon seemed as if the room was in a flurry with several maids hanging blankets in front of the fire to warm as the footmen that had not gone out in the fire brigade were carrying the water. Elizabeth suddenly recalled that her husband was not there to support her and began to panic.

"Has my husband been notified, Mrs. Reynolds? Does anyone know if they..." She gasped as another pain came, stopping her from speaking. "Does anyone know what has been going on at the Gibson's?"

"No, ma'am, we hadn't got word of what is happening yet, but I did have one of the men send word to Mr. Darcy."

Jane arrived in the room along with Kitty and Georgiana. They all wore the same terrified look upon their faces when they saw Elizabeth grimace with another pain. Elizabeth was immediately flanked with the three young women who sat beside her helplessly.

Jane reached over to hold her hand, "Oh, Lizzy... We came up here as soon as they told us. You look..."

Elizabeth managed to laugh a little before another pain tore through her and she moaned out, "Oh, Jane," She began breathlessly,

"You need not find kind words to describe my appearance. I know I must look awful right now."

Her sister smiled, and said, "You still look as lovely as ever. You are having a child and this is... to be expected."

"Where is... uuuuuummm, where is Charles?" She moaned out.

"Oh... well... I thought that you would be told, but... no matter, he went with Mr. Darcy to the tenant's home. I would think that with so many men that they would have the fire under control if not out by now though."

"Ah, I see." Elizabeth groaned again with another pain and started to double up as the contractions became stronger. Mrs. Reynolds placed her hands over her stomach and felt the tightening with a frown. She began to move her hands all over Elizabeth's stomach.

"Mrs. Darcy... I think we need to get you moved to the tub. Th' men 'ave got it filled up enough and it'll just have to do. If we need more we can 'ave the cook send more up, now..." she reached for Elizabeth's arm. "We need to get you up."

Elizabeth took another deep breath as the contractions kept coming in quick succession and stopped. They managed to help her to stand and started walking towards the bathing room. She was starting to wonder if anyone had really told Darcy about the impending arrival of their child, when the doors to their bedroom burst open and in walked a soot covered Darcy. His eyes were sweeping the room wildly and he immediately went to her.

"Elizabeth," He looked down at her as he embraced her to him. "How are you, darling? I came as fast as I could, and I am sure that Zephyrus will not soon forgive my rough riding of him here, but you are more important to me right ." He leaned down and almost kissed her but suddenly they recalled the audience until she grasped her middle again.

"Ooooooooh."

Had she not been in so much pain, she might have laughed at his utterly terrified look, but soon she was wearing the same when she noticed a gush of bright red blood running down her leg. Mrs. Reynolds saw it as well because she started barking out all sorts of orders, but Elizabeth hardly heard what she was saying. Darcy picked her up immediately and ran with her to the tub room placing her in the water according to the housekeeper's instructions.

She could barely hear their voices, but could tell that they were all practically yelling, and she could hear them order Kitty and Georgiana to leave. She thought she could hear the voices of the two midwives, Mrs. Walton and Stacy as they talked calmly to whom she could not figure out. Her pain was easing a little when she was immersed in the warm water, and then she felt hands pushing down on her abdomen. They felt like huge hands, but she knew that touch... they were Darcy's hands.

There was a great deal of pressure on her bottom, and then a tearing, almost ripping sensation there until... finally the pain was gone. She heard some faint cries before she could not hear anything else.

Chapter 26

Darcy was frantic. When Elizabeth lost consciousness he went into a panic. He heard his child cry, and even knew that he must be all right from the volume he exerted, but his wife laid in the tub unable to be aroused. The midwife was shouting orders for Mrs. Reynolds and Sarah to help push down on her belly which was still rather swollen for having given birth, but then he knew little about what to expect. The two servants were surrounding them and pushing with all their strength on her abdomen again. He snapped out of his fog and assisted them in their task until he saw another head emerge from Elizabeth.

Mr. Tyler had been correct about her carrying twins, and though they were a little early they seemed healthy, but Elizabeth was still not waking up and what was worse is that she was now in a tub full of bloody water. The midwife ordered him to get her out of the warm water, and for the other women to open the windows to let the cold air in. He immediately complied and lay Elizabeth on the bed which had been prepared for her. They dried her off and began to massage her midsection watching for clots to come out, and finally he saw the sacks which had linked his children to her for the past few months.

When Mrs. Walton inspected them she saw the source of the premature labor. One of the bags of water had a large clot on one edge which had begun to detach from her womb. Though Darcy knew very little about childbirth, he knew that it was dangerous for both mother and child and even worse when carrying twins. He did not understand why they kept massaging her abdomen and when he looked at the women Mrs. Stacy answered his unasked question.

"We have to make the uterus contract… to make it shrink else she may bleed to death."

Darcy could feel his tears well up. He prayed fervently that they would be able to make her uterus contract and that she would stop bleeding. It seemed as though he was lost in his thoughts for a long time when they finally declared that the bleeding had slowed down considerably. They cleaned her up again, and placed her under the clean linens. When he finally dared to look at Elizabeth she was as pale as his shirt... maybe even worse, but she was still breathing and she seemed to be resting peacefully. There were cries heard from the tub room as Sarah and Mrs. Reynolds came round to where he sat beside Elizabeth and that was when it registered to him that they had two children- two people who were a part of both of them.

"Mr. Darcy... would you care to hold your son and daughter, sir?" Mrs. Reynolds indicated the tiny bundles in their arms.

He looked up at them numbly and nodded his head. Darcy wanted nothing more than to have all of his family healthy and with him at present. He climbed up beside Elizabeth and held out his arms to take them. When they were each placed in his arms, he noticed how much they resembled both he and his wife. They had dark hair and wide eyes, but he could not decide whose noses they favored or what color their eyes would be as they had the typical slate blue of all newborns. They were also quite tiny, but the midwives assured him that this was normal for twins.

Elizabeth lay so quietly that he did not want to wake her, yet he also wished for reassurance that she would be all right. *I shall not leave your side again until you are well, my love. I am so sorry that I was not here earlier...* His guilt nearly overwhelmed him. Georgiana, Jane, Bingley, and Kitty stepped into the room almost tiptoeing towards where he and Elizabeth lay side-by-side.

"Is she going to be all right, Fitzwilliam?" Georgiana asked.

He studied her for a moment before he answered. "I do not know, Georgie. I pray that she will, but the midwives will not say one way or another..."

Darcy felt himself chocking with grief, feeling so guilty about what he had done to her to have brought all this on her. He knew that it was quite possible that she had conceived that night at the parsonage, and now... in his selfishness, she was paying so dearly for what *he* had done. His sisters moved up to him. Georgiana embraced Darcy as he felt the tears coming from his own eyes. They stayed in that position for a few more moments before separating - with him still clinging to his children.

"They are beautiful brother, may we hold them?"

He was reluctant to relinquish them, but he knew that his other family wanted a chance to see them as well. He handed over his daughter to Georgiana, and Jane eagerly took his son.

"Have you any names for them, yet, Fitzwilliam?" Jane asked quietly, as she and Bingley marveled over the miracle in her arms.

The question made him start. They had not really considered naming them yet, but he knew that they would eventually have to be given names. At present, he did not want to consider it without Lizzy's input. He would wait until she was awake and able to help pick out their names. Suddenly he realized that he had not yet answered Jane's question.

"No... we had not agreed to anything definitely. We had thought that we had some more time before they would come." He smiled a crooked smile, but it soon faded as he turned to look at his wife. *Please G-d, do not take her away from me too*, he begged silently.

"Fitzwilliam," Georgiana hesitated, and then looked at the others in the room, "Would you care to refresh yourself while we stay here with Lizzy? I promise that we shall not leave her side." Her eyes were pleading with him to take care of himself as well.

Darcy had forgotten that he was covered in soot after he left the scene of the fire when he had come to Elizabeth as she gave birth to their children. He saw the sense in what she suggested, but did not want to leave her side just in case she should take a turn for the worse while he was away.

"If anything happens then we shall come and get you, Darcy." Bingley reassured him.

After some more coaxing, he was finally convinced to go and clean himself up, and went to his room where the footmen had just finished removing the bloodied water and the maids were busy cleaning up. Mrs. Reynolds had already ordered more water brought up for his bath and more footmen had been sent down to fetch the heated water while he waited. He sat in his dressing room as Hobbs went to work removing his dirty boots and assisting him with his clothing, getting him down to his small clothes in order to bathe.

The hot water felt good on his skin washing away all of the soot, sweat, and ...blood. He washed himself mechanically watching the water grow more dirty as he went to his task. It was a relief to finally be clean, and it was something he had been looking forward to since he left Elizabeth to go tend to the tenant's fire. His plan for the morning was to help her bathe while he joined her in the tub... but that was not to be.

Hobbs stoked the fire in the room, yet he still felt cold and their bedroom was already blazing to keep Elizabeth warm. He finally dismissed his valet to have some privacy, and laid back with his eyes closed to rest. This whole day had been so awful… his tenant, Gibson, had lost one of his daughters in the fire when she succumbed to the smoke. As his eyes closed he could still see her tiny lifeless body as they carried her out of the house covered in soot. She was still in her sleeping gown, and it looked as though she were only sleeping.

He felt great sadness for what that family had suffered. He could not imagine losing either of his children now, and especially not Elizabeth. It was too much to fathom. He broke down and sobbed in overwhelming sorrow for the loss of life, and fear of what he may still lose. The grief seemed so overpowering. *Lord, please not Elizabeth too, please do not take her from me, I beg you,* he prayed. *I cannot go on without her…* Memories of his mother's death flooded his mind as he remembered what happened before she slipped away from him just after Georgiana was born. He had suffered so many loses in his life thus far and did not think he could bear much more. The heaviness in his heart weighed him down, aging him, making him feel ancient.

A knock on the door alerted him that the outside world was still going on despite the heaviness in his heart.

"Enter." He commanded in his 'Master of Pemberley' voice.

Hobbs was standing in the entrance looking a little uncomfortable. "Sir, Miss Darcy and Mrs. Reynolds asked if you would like to have your supper brought up here to your rooms, and also if… you would wish for some Bourbon from the cellar."

"That would be fine, Hobbs, thank you. Oh… and would you fetch my things? I think that I shall get out now. I imagine that I have been gone long enough… Miss Darcy and Mrs. Bingley probably want to eat their supper as well."

The servant cleared his throat and said, "Actually, sir, I believe that Miss Darcy has requested that dinner be served in the sitting room … if that is all right with you, that is?" Darcy smiled a little at the care that his young sister was taking of him now. It was ironic that he, who had taken care of her for so long, was now in a position to have that favor returned.

"That is fine, Hobbs, let her know that I will relieve her shortly. I can dress myself." At his man's look of surprise, he replied, "I can manage to look presentable, besides it is only my sister and perhaps Mr. and Mrs. Bingley and Miss Catherine."

"Shall you like a shave, sir?"

"Not tonight. I do not want to be away from my-Mrs. Darcy's bedside just in case… anything happens."

"Very good, sir."

His man left him to his devices as he dressed himself and made to look more presentable without looking too much like a small child dressing himself for the first time. When he was done he went to Elizabeth who remained unconscious. *'She is still breathing'*, he said to himself in relief as he watched over her. There was still no color in her pale face and the midwives both tried to reassure him that nothing had changed since he left them.

"The biggest obstacle has been overcome, and that was the heavy bleeding right after the babes were born. Her bleeding has almost stopped and it is near normal."

"How can a person lose so much blood and… and…?" Darcy asked of Mrs. Walton.

The elder woman said with compassion, "Women have a great deal more fluid in their body when they carry a child and then when they deliver all of that fluid can come out with the babe, so it really is not that unusual… not in most cases."

"I noticed that you looked at the afterbirth… why?" Darcy was curious as to what she had searched for.

"I wanted to find out why she was havin' so much pain and things were comin' so quick. Then there was the blood… some is normal like I said, but this… it was dark red mixed with bright blood. Sometimes when there is a problem with the bag of waters it can tear away from the womb early and causes some problems."

"Is that what happened then, with my wife?"

"Likely… but what I doon' understand is how it got that way. Last time I saw somethin' like it was Mrs. Smith on another part of Lambton, but 'er 'usband took ta beatin' 'er an' thas how it likely happened with her." She scratched her chin before looking at him, which made him self conscious least the woman think that he ever laid a violent hand on his wife.

"I can't imagine what happened ta Mrs. Darcy though. She did not by chance have a spill at some time or another did she?"

Darcy could not think of any mishaps that Elizabeth suffered, but then he noticed Georgiana frowning and biting her lower lip.

"Georgie… do you know of anything that could have happened to Elizabeth?"

His sister's eyes widened and she looked down to the floor, then to the wall above him.

"Once… when we were decorating she had taken a small tumble while decorating over by the mantle in the great room. It was quite frightening to see, but she seemed fine… at least she said she was fine. I was a bit concerned and thought she should maybe see the physician or at the very least one of the midwives, but she insisted that she was fine, and that she had only injured her dignity."

Darcy was alarmed at this new report and was more than a little upset that not only Elizabeth, but Georgiana had failed to tell him about the incident.

"Why was I not told of this before?" he demanded.

Georgiana's eyes teared up and she shook her head, "She… she… Elizabeth made me promise not to tell you. I wanted to tell you but then she said that you would only worry, and so I promised not to say anything, but do you think that it happened then?" She looked genuinely worried about her new sister's state of health.

"It could have." Mrs. Walton said, "But even then there would be no way of knowin' about it until she gave birth. There really is no way of knowin' what goes on in there until they deliver… well sometimes we can guess, but when you canno see inside the womb, you canno' tell what the problem is. We may never know what really happened."

Darcy was thankful that the woman was compassionate enough to try to assuage his sister's feelings of guilt, and he understood her sense of remorse for not telling him about Elizabeth's mishap earlier. He would have worried a great deal, and like the midwife said… they may never really know how they had come to this. The most important thing now was getting Elizabeth back and restored to good health.

The whole family ended up taking their meal in the sitting room while Mrs. Reynolds and Sarah stayed with Elizabeth. As soon as they were done eating Darcy, Georgiana, and Catherine stayed with her. The Bingleys were both exhausted from the events of the day, and Jane seemed unwell, and the last thing Darcy wanted was for Elizabeth to become ill with something else besides recovering from childbirth.

He also wanted to notify the Bennets of the births as well as what had happened to Elizabeth, so he requested for Jane to write an express to them. He did not know how he could write such a letter to Mr. Bennet with his own sense of overwhelming guilt over this as well bearing such devastating news to Elizabeth'.

"Jane... would you mind terribly if I asked you to send word to Longbourn... to Mr. and Mrs. Bennet? I would request it of Bingley, but I am afraid that they might never get the message. Sorry, Bingley."

Everyone who had ever seen Bingley's handwriting laughed, including Mrs. Reynolds. *At least we can still make light of some subjects.*

"That is quite all right, Darcy. I am sure that my angel can write quite well, and she can probably add more to the letter than I ever could." Bingley replied good-naturedly.

"I will be happy to do that, Fitzwilliam. Perhaps since it is so late, I shall start it tonight and if there is any change by morning then I can add to it?" Jane offered.

"Very well. I thank you, for everything. You have been such a great support to us, Jane..."

She smiled at him sympathetically and leaned in to kiss his cheek. "It is no more than she would do for me, dear brother."

Darcy watched them leave the room before rejoining Elizabeth on the opposite side of the bed as Georgiana and Catherine as they sat in chairs beside her. It was endearing to see how much care their family took of each member. He briefly considered that could not fathom a woman of the *ton* or their families taking so much care of one another. They usually delegated such tasks to the servants, but with this family... he felt as though he were enclosed within a loving cocoon, and it warmed him and lightened his burden. He requested that his babes be brought in and asked for Mrs. Reynolds to be sent up again.

When the longtime housekeeper arrived he made a few inquiries as to finding a wet nurse, to which the ever efficient servant replied sheepishly, "I have already made some arrangements, sir... pending your approval. Mrs. Dillon from Lambton was able to come on such short notice when she was told of Mrs. Darcy's condition this afternoon. It was only right after all Mrs. Darcy did for her after her brother passed."

Darcy's lips upturned. *I should have known that she would have already thought of this and it is heartening to know that the townspeople are already valuing Elizabeth for what she is-kind, compassionate, and caring.* "That is fine, Mrs. Reynolds. I thank you for everything you have done for Mrs. Darcy since... well since she has come to Pemberley."

"It is my job to help the new mistress learn her position. This place is too great to do by herself as a young wife and then with a babe-or two on the way, there was no way I would let her do it on her own. Besides… when she wakes up, she will likely be too weak to nurse one infant by herself, let alone two."

"Quite right, Reynolds. Quite right."

He looked down at his daughter in his arms and cradled her to his chest. The brother and his sisters had some conversation, but then regressed to their own thoughts, then tried reading to occupy their time. By the middle of the night he woke up and saw that Georgiana had also fallen asleep with his son cradled in her arms. The babies had not awakened since nearly midnight, and they were still relatively dry so he laid down his precious cargo before he took his son and laid him next to his sister, before waking Georgiana and Catherine.

"It is late you two and I am sure that you would sleep better in your own beds." They both looked at Elizabeth who was lying still in the bed. "I will stay here with her. You need to get your sleep anyway and these chairs are no place for that."

They both arose to leave, but Catherine turned just before reaching the threshold, "You will call for us if…?"

"Yes." He said uneasily.

They closed the door softly and he removed his coat and vest, then finally his cravat and boots to join Elizabeth on their bed along with their babies. He kissed each one before trying to settle himself, then made certain that they would not be smothered by anything before he lay back on the pillows with her hand in his. Darcy needed to be touching her… to stay close, as if he were holding her to this world.

He was able to close his eyes, but his dreams were so frightening filled with fire, and blood and death. He kept waking to check on his family, to reassure himself that they were fine. He would drift back to sleep only to be awakened again. Close to dawn he finally succumbed to sleep. The next time he woke he felt cold hands squeezing his. When he opened his eyes, they were met by a pair of large brown ones staring back at him… studying him.

"Fitzwilliam? Why are you in your day clothes?"

Elizabeth had come back to him.

Chapter 27

W hen Elizabeth woke up, she felt exhaustion overcome her, as if it was a tremendous effort to open her eyes or talk. Her body was very sore and her head was spinning. She could not recall how she managed to get in her bed, and then she felt warm hands upon hers and immediately scanned the room. From the slight light coming through the windows, she knew that it must be either dusk or dawn, and she tried to focus her eyes on the clock sitting upon the mantle. She could barely make it out, but saw that it was almost six o'clock in the morning. As she looked beside her she saw her husband looking extremely disheveled while his eyes never left her.

Why is he wearing his regular clothes instead of his nightshift? In her befuddled mind she had almost forgotten about the horrendous day before and she asked, "Fitzwilliam? Why are you in your day clothes?"

He stared at her for almost a full minute with tears in his eyes before he said, "I was waiting for you to come back to me…"

In the next moment he was coming to kiss her. It was not a kiss filled with passion-not the one of lovers, but one of a person who had been away from their beloved after a long journey. She instinctively knew that something had been troubling him and cradled his head in her hands, concerned that he seemed to be clinging to something.

"Fitzwilliam…" She said softly, "What grieves you so?"

He pulled away in surprise then embraced her tightly to himself, kissing her numerous times upon the cheeks as his tears fell upon her.

"You have come back to me, my love. I was so worried that you might die, but now you are back…" Darcy kissed her hard upon the lips then.

"But I am here. I have not gone anywhere…" Suddenly she placed her hand over her abdomen and the events of yesterday came flooding back to her. Panic rushed through her wondering what had happened to their baby. "Fitzwilliam… what happened…" Elizabeth could feel the tears begin in her own eyes and her breathing accelerated as she worried about the child she had heard crying before she lost consciousness. "Where is our baby? Is it...? Did it...?" She took a deep sobbing breath and he pulled away from her again and stared at her.

His smile gave her some comfort, but she would not be satisfied until she knew.

"Fitzwilliam-what happened to our baby?" She demanded.

"Shhhh-shh, it is all right Elizabeth. They are fine... now you are all fine."

He nodded his head to her right, and there she saw the most precious sight of her life. There next to her lay two babies looking so innocent and peaceful. He had them swathed in some light blankets, and she tried to push herself up to view them better, but was too weak to manage. Darcy stood up and helped her to sit up, adjusting the pillows for her to sit against. She realized then that that position would be uncomfortable for some time, but would not complain as to the cause.

He came around their bed again to sit by her, handing her their son while he held their daughter. She removed the blankets from around them and could make out their dark hair, and touched their downy soft skin. Her tears were now coming freely as she gazed upon them.

"They are so beautiful..."

Darcy smiled at her and said, "They are a part of both of us... our love... our union, and... they do favor you a bit."

"And you as well, but what are they?"

He looked at her for a moment forgetting that she did not know the gender of either of them.

"We have a son-in your arms, and here is our daughter." He looked down at his tiny cargo, and smiled again. "Soon we shall have to choose names for them... I did not want to even think about it until you were... until you woke up." He frowned again, and she caught the trepidation in his expression.

Suddenly it struck her that she had not recalled the birth of at least one of their children, but she recalled the pain she endured, the blood loss beforehand, and his disheveled appearance, coupled with his behavior towards her when she woke up- Something must have happened, but I do not remember what. It must have been enough to frighten him thoroughly though.

Being the curious creature that she was, she asked, "Dearest... what happened yesterday when... after... you placed me in the tub?" She had thought it was at least morning judging by his thick beard and his haggard appearance. "It is morning is it not?" "It is..." He hesitated for a moment before he replied to her question, "You had fainted while you were in the tub... after he was born... there was so much blood, but your womb wound not contract as it was supposed to and that is when we discovered her presence." He nodded at the babe in his arms. "We managed to deliver her, but it took some time before the bleeding stopped. We-I feared for your life. I have never seen so much blood come from one person without them... without..." He took a deep breath, "It is too difficult to even say in relation to you. I cannot think about it even now. Part of me would have died with you if you had left me."

She had not thought about her own demise though she always knew that it was a possibility with childbirth. The idea that she might have never been able to see her children grow up, to see their milestones met, or grow old with her husband was a sobering moment for her. In that instant she understood what he had endured while she was unconscious. He still wore worry on his handsome face, and she wished more than anything to set his mind at ease.

"My love, I am here now. Nothing is going to take me away from you... or them. I am too willful a creature to allow anything to come between us again."

They smiled tenderly at each other and joined their hands with one another while holding their babes in their other arms. Darcy put her hand to his lips and kissed the back of it.

"Thank you."

"For what?" Elizabeth asked.

"For loving me enough to marry me, and for them."

She put his hand to her lips and said, "You are very welcome, but then I shall have to thank you as well, for loving me enough to marry me and for helping me to bring them to us. It takes two, does it not? To make a child- and now we have two- and are one family." She yawned and her eyes started drooping due to fatigue.

"You are quite right, my darling." He paused for a moment then asked, "I would ask if you have any names picked out, but I think we have a little time, and you need to rest. Shall I take him and help you to lie back down?"

She smiled sheepishly, "I wish that I could stay awake to enjoy them, but I am very tired. Shall we lay them down again between us?"

"For now I will lay them down here, but then I want to keep watch over you all. I will not risk anything happening to any of you again."

Darcy placed the babes down on the large bed between them and came around to help Elizabeth find a comfortable position before he joined her on the bed and watched over them all until he succumbed to sleep as well. That was how Mrs. Reynolds and the midwives found them hours later when they came to check up on their patients.

When Darcy woke and saw Elizabeth's beautiful eyes looking back at him, he felt relief that the huge weight that had been hanging over him was lifting. He had noticed the massive amount of blood that she lost with the delivery of the twins and was amazed that she was still with him. It was a testament to her excellent overall health that she had not succumbed like many others before her to the complications of childbirth. He had even vowed that if she survived, he would never put her at such risk again. *Now she has come back to me.*

The beginning rays of the morning's sunshine filtered through to the room and he blinked his eyes once, twice, then a third time to be sure that he was not dreaming, and when she asked him why he was dressed in his day clothes he could not be happier. He leaned forward to claim those lips that he feared would never smile or speak to him again just last night.

Her first words upon awakening were ones of concern for him and all he could do was grasp her and shower her with kisses of relief, and gratitude for being the wonderful woman that she was. *How could I be so fortunate to have such a woman? I must truly be blessed to be so favored.*

Elizabeth's frantic voice registered to him and he wanted to immediately relieve her distress when she began to ask about their children. It dawned upon him that she may not be aware that they were two babes and not a lone child.

"Fitzwilliam-what happened to our baby?" She demanded.

"Shhhh-shh, it is all right Elizabeth. They are fine... now you are all fine."

He nodded his head and waved his hand to where their son and daughter slept, and she tried to sit up to get a better view, but was too weak to move much on her own. Darcy moved to help her sit up and brought their son to her while he cradled their daughter as he sat beside her. In that moment he knew that this was one of the proudest moments of his life. *Yes... this is pride under* very *good regulation, my love.*

Now that his Elizabeth was improved and their children were well, his life seemed more content than ever. He understood the true feeling of completeness with the woman he loved most in the whole world while holding their children safely in their arms together for the very first time.

The family had been left in privacy to the relief of Darcy and Elizabeth, as they all felt their need for rest and privacy. Elizabeth was still very weak after the double birth with its subsequent loss of blood and then the babies themselves were starting to prove to be a bit demanding.

Their feeding schedules were not synchronous and the couple was even more grateful to Mrs. Dillon and Mrs. Reynolds for coming to their aid. For the first few days their families had even volunteered to step in and help with the newest additions to the family-including Charles Bingley.

The proud aunts would sooth the babes, taking turns walking with them in the room and even Catherine seemed to find enjoyment in reading to them from nursery books. It soon became apparent that they would have to look for two nursery maids, which was not a difficult task considering the reputation of Pemberley's master and mistress. By the tenth day they managed to move two chambermaids into the position, and Mrs. Reynolds had hired on two young women from Kympton to fill their vacated rolls.

A more difficult task was the naming of the precious babes. While Darcy preferred *'Elizabeth'* or *'Victoria'* for their daughter and *'Thomas'* or *'William'* for their son, Elizabeth preferred *'Emma'* or *'Adelaide'* for her and *'Andrew'* or-well really just *'Andrew'*. Since the local parson wanted to ensure that the baptism occurred *before* they celebrated their first birthday, a compromise was reached.

On the first day of March 1810, William Thomas Andrew and Emma Elizabeth Adelaide Darcy were christened in the church at Kympton with their entire family present and though they may have been a bit on the scrawny side at birth, they were now quite robust for twins. Most of the household attributed this to the fact that they fed eagerly, especially when at their mother's breast.

Their godparents, the Bingley's, Aunt Georgiana, and Richard Fitzwilliam stood as proud as ever when the children were presented. With the ceremony was over the countess began *strongly hinting* to her youngest son to start working on his additions to the family.

"Richard, you know that your cousin is *two years younger* than you and yet now he has a wife and two children. I should think that it about time for you to start thinking about following his example."

Apparently there is a little bit of Mrs. Bennet in every woman thought Darcy with amusement as his cousin stood looking at his mother in horror.

"Mother... I am sure that there are several women among the *ton* that would *absolutely love* to become your daughter, but as I should have to reside with them thereafter, I would prefer one that I can actually *live with*."

Lady Matlock smiled at him, "You are right of course, because if they were some silly little thing- or worse, much like some I have had the misfortune to come across as of late, I would much prefer you a bachelor. *Not confirmed* of course, as I would still like to see you well settled... with a *deserving* woman.

Richard gave her a cheeky smile, but was prevented from saying anything when Mrs. Bennet spoke up.

"You know, sir that I still have two daughters at home and I am sure that you would find them quite amiable..."

"I thank you for that generous offer, Mrs. Bennet. However as I am starting to learn how to manage a new estate right now, it would be quite difficult for me to also learn how to be an adequate husband as well."

Besides that, those two are still quite silly, Richard. Darcy was amused at how his mother-in-law could make even him wish for the frontlines of the continent. It also amused him to no end to see his cousin, who had always ribbed him of being the focus of match-making mammas, getting a little taste of his own medicine. He thought about his cousin's future though, and thought that eventually he may need a good wife who suited his outgoing cousin as well. *I shall have to ponder that another time.*

Miss Catherine, it seemed had become smitten by the parson at Kympton, who though widowed, was still quite young and had no children. They had become acquainted while the Darcy's were discussing the christening. It seemed as though she may have found in him a man that could appreciate her following rather than leading, [i]and he is a great deal more sensible than Collins when it comes to parsons.

It was no surprise that when Lady Catherine was placed in a *'special residence'* her parson switched his loyalties to the new owner of Rosings Park as well. Richard had confided to Darcy that he was considering finding a new position for the pesky parson.

"I do not suppose that you would have any openings in any of the parishes around here, would you Darce? I cannot tell you how grateful I would be to be rid of the odious man."

"And yet *'that odious man'* would then become my problem? I think not, Richard. You inherited Rosings with everything that came with it and that includes the Hunsford Parsonage along with the parson."

"Oh, come on now, Darcy. Your estate is large enough to separate you from the man. He would be far enough away that you would not see him nearly every day."

"That is still not enough of a separation for me. Though I do feel for your plight, I do not wish to make it my own. I think that Elizabeth and I have made enough concessions in agreeing to come and visit you early in the summer. Perhaps you could make your mother the offer that if she agrees to take on Collins, that you would agree to take on a wife?"

The nasty look that graced Richard's face was enough to cause Darcy to laugh.

"I think not." Richard said petulantly, "With my luck, she might very well take me up on the offer, and then lord only knows what kind of woman I would end up with as payback for inflicting him upon her."

"Well you know that Elizabeth's two sisters are still available..."

Another dour look appeared upon his cousin's face.

"If they were all like *Mrs.* Bingley... or especially like *Elizabeth*, that would be another story."

It was Darcy's turn to don the stern look. Though he knew his cousin was jesting, there was a time when he thought that Richard may have actually considered making her an offer, and at the time, Elizabeth likewise seemed to favor his cousin. Now he at least knew that she loved him every bit as much as he loved her.

Richard laughed, "You have nothing to fear from me, Darce. It is quite obvious that Mrs. Darcy loves you above all others... well maybe not above Emma and William, but then they *are* a more adorable than you."

"Well, at least we agree on that." Darcy said wryly. "I am sure that one day you will find the same happiness, just remember never to settle."

Bingley joined them in the conversation then, "I cannot agree more. There are several ladies among the *ton* that would *love* to latch onto a man with an estate of Rosings size..." His face grew dark. "It would be best to find someone who will make you happy."

They said little more as they allowed their minds to contemplate the fate of Miss Bingley. She was exactly the kind of woman that they all wanted to avoid in marriage. Bingley's cousin dismissed Caroline for dereliction of duty when her charges were found one too many times hiding from the wicked governess, who would apparently throw temper tantrums more often than the children themselves. She was set up with her remaining funds away from that family in a town where no one knew their connections to her.

It seemed that even in the far north, she was still too vile a woman to be associated with. Her dreams of becoming mistress of a great estate went only so far as becoming the mistress of some gentleman of questionable character and already in possession of a wife and heir... with an entailed estate. There were rumors circulating too, in town that she had borne a child from such an affair. The Bingley's distanced themselves from her by declining any association with her, going so far as to refuse to receive her in their homes. Jane would occasionally take pity and send some small sum to aide in expenses for a youngster living within her household however.

For their parts, Darcy and Bingley were every bit as satisfied in marriage as they had ever hoped to be-even more so. Now they were close brothers as well as friends.

Soon after the Christening of the Darcy children there was news that the family would be expanding even more. Jane and Charles revealed that they were expecting a child in August, but what made

Mrs. Bennet nearly apoplectic was their other intelligence- that they would be leaving Netherfied for an estate near to Pemberley. One would have thought that someone had died rather than the happy announcement that was made. At last the two sisters would be as close as a day from each other, likely less, and they all hoped that someday Catherine might join them in the north as well.

Epilogue

When the Darcy's introduced Kitty to the Kympton parson, Jacob Jennings, they had little notion that it would lead to a budding relationship. Catherine 'Kitty' Bennet and the parson got on quite well. In fact they got on so well that he proposed and she accepted his hand. He had wanted to obtain Mr. Bennet's consent, but it had to wait until that man made one of his predictably unpredictable visits to Pemberley. It was not long before Elizabeth's time became consumed with her household responsibilities and the planning her sister's wedding.

During this time, Elizabeth decided to take some time out from running the household, and the rearing of her children to commemorate their wedding and so she proposed for her and Darcy to go out to the dowagers house at Pemberley to spend a couple of nights alone. *It is hard to believe that a year has already passed and now we have not one but two children. I would never have imagined such a scenario one year ago*, she mused as she made plans for a private celebration.

Since her husband was more than willing and eager to have her all to himself- especially after such a long and difficult planting season, he gladly agreed to the scheme. They managed to find some time before they would leave for Rosings to go to the cottage, leaving William and Emma with Mrs. Dillon and their two nursery maids as well as their aunts Kitty and Georgiana. They set of in a phaeton one late afternoon, arriving at the cottage just before dusk where their cook had prepared a meal, and only Sarah and Hobbs remained behind to assist with their needs.

As soon as they arrived they were quickly assisted to refresh themselves before they were whisked to a lovely dinner of creamed broccoli soup, chicken with berry sauce, fresh parsley potatoes and a chocolate torte.

"I see that you managed to have all of my favorite foods here, Mrs. Darcy. Pray… what is the occasion?"

Elizabeth was slightly hurt that he had not recalled the first anniversary of their nuptials, but she feigned indifference.

"Does a wife need to have an occasion to seduce her husband, sir?"

She could tell that her words were having some effect by the way that he looked at her with his dark eyes burning into her.

"So you went to all of this trouble to *seduce me*, madam?"

"That thought had occurred to me, husband."

"Then I must confess that I wonder now at having gone to so much trouble to obtain this,"

He pulled out a velvet box from his coat pocket and presented it to her with one of his rare dimpled smiles. When she received it from him, she eagerly opened it and found a beautiful silver necklace lined with diamonds and Garnets to symbolize their children's birthstones. Tears formed in her eyes as she thought to herself that she should have known that he would not forget their anniversary.

"They are beautiful…" She looked at him with her large dark eyes filled with gratitude and leaned forward to kiss him.

Darcy accepted her thanks and eagerly returned her kisses finally leaving them both breathless when they came up for air.

"Was this a part of your seduction, Lizzy, or was that just a prelude to what is to come?"

She could do naught but laugh and kiss him again for asking such a thing, abandoning their desert for something more delectable. When they came up for air again they decided to take themselves to the master bedroom and Darcy picked Elizabeth up in his arms and carried her to their bed. They moved to each other's embrace quickly, neither one of them wanted to part from their other half. Soon lips were joined with hands and his hands came to her luxurious silky mahogany locks, while hers ran through his wavy ones. They began to move their appendages to other parts of their bodies caressing each other from chest to waist until they finally reached the area's begging to be touched most- at one another's center of desire.

It did not take long for them to undress and instead of calling for their personal servants; they did the honors for each other. Elizabeth was still a bit self conscious about her figure after having had twins because her figure had not returned to its normal shape, but Darcy assured her that he appreciated her ample bosom and loved her shapely figure that she now sported.

"Do you know what a beautiful woman that you are, my Lizzy?" Darcy murmured in her ear, as she was helping him off with his shirt.

"Do you have any idea what a handsome man that you are, my darling Will?" She managed to pull his shirt over his head as he was working on her stays. He kissed her passionately and continued to peel off layer after layer of her clothing while he massaged her breasts, teasing her nipples by rubbing them between his thumb and forefinger.

When they had finally managed to remove the last obstacles between each other, they began a new and fervent exploration of the others body. He began again with her breasts, which he seemed to have a new appreciation for since she had given birth. As he suckled her, she could feel her arousal building in her core, and began to caress and grope at his bottom feeling his firm muscles there. It was an added aphrodisiac to her to feel all of his potent and powerful muscles rubbing against her as he paid her such attentions.

Darcy moved from suckling her breasts to kissing a pathway down her abdomen to her hips and then to her inner thighs. The warmth of his breath exciting her as much as the feel of his lips in a place only he had ventured to go. When she felt his lips upon her womanhood she shuddered with pleasure as he began to suckle her there. The pleasurable sensations he elicited were enough to drive her mad with passion until she felt her crest coming upon her. She grasped the sheets beneath her, and prepared to enjoy the sensations he elicited in her.

He stopped suddenly and moved over her thrusting his manhood into her moist folds. They began moving in a rhythm as old as time and soon were moving in perfect harmony. Her crest was building greater and greater, and Darcy could feel that he was teetering on the edge as well. It did not take much time after they had found that harmony to come to completion together. They lay there in silence gazing into each other's eyes, breathless but still full of unspent desire.

They laid there for a few more minutes to catch their breaths until they heard the tub being filled with water. The cook had been keeping water heated for them to bathe in, but since they had not arrived until late there was not enough for the both of them to do so alone.

"Would you mind terribly if we were to bathe together? We could help each other rinse off." Darcy offered suggestively.

"Do you even need to ask?" She asked with a hint of amusement, "Was that not one of the first things that we did together on our honeymoon? I think it would be a fitting end to our night together."

"My dearest… whoever said that that would be the end of our night?" He asked teasingly.

They rose from their bed and joined each other in the bath, dismissing their servants for the rest of the evening so that they might enjoy some more time alone with each other. As it turned out, they were able to enjoy each other countless times before exhaustion finally claimed them. The next day was spent in each other's arms as much as possible between meals, and the night ended much the same as the first. It was with great regret that they left the dowagers cottage after the second day, but they were happy and anxious to see William, Emma, Georgiana, and Kitty.

Shortly after they returned home, they were packing for a trip to Rosings. It was decided that Kitty would stay behind with Mrs. Annesley in order for her to continue with her contact with Jacob. Elizabeth also sympathized with her reluctance to return to Longbourn before their wedding as well, and agreed to give her sister this reprieve. The trip was uneventful, and Richard greeted them enthusiastically upon their arrival, but he wanted to pull Darcy aside to ask him many questions about the running of an estate, and about recommendations concerning various topics that had come up.

The gentlemen ended up spending the first two weeks touring the estate surveying the ground and visiting with the tenants who seemed generally glad to have Richard as the new landowner. They also seemed rather taken with Elizabeth and Georgiana since neither Lady Catherine nor Anne had ever come to pay them any visits when they resided there.

It was during these tours that Georgiana and Richard began acting towards each other as more than cousins or as a guardian to charge, but was not generally noticed by Elizabeth or Darcy. Elizabeth had been ill for a couple of days and Darcy stayed behind to see to her needs while the other two went out to visit the tenants. Later Darcy confided to his cousin that he was still worried over Elizabeth's health, but dared not voice his concerns to her then-he just wanted to stay near and protect her as best he could.

Richard started to look at Georgiana as Darcy looked at Elizabeth and because of the new couples urging and Elizabeth's continuing to feel under the weather, they stayed for some time longer than they anticipated. By the middle of the summer Georgiana was insistent that she would never wish to part from Richard...ever. The Darcy's and Richard spent more and more time together and it became more and more obvious how right the new couple were for each other. Their eyes lit up whenever the other entered the room, and it came as no surprise when late into their visit Richard approached Darcy to request Georgiana's hand in marriage. At first he was a little reluctant to agree, but with Elizabeth's encouragement and her various ways of persuasion, he finally agreed to the match after grudgingly admitting how happy they were together.

By the first part of July the Darcy's along with Richard and Georgiana went on to Hertfordshire from Kent to attend Kitty's wedding to Mr. Jennings. The parson had come with his fiancée and her chaperone in one of Darcy's carriages for the wedding. In mid July of 1810 Kitty and Jacob were married in the church near to Longborn with her mother gloating over the neighborhood ladies that she had managed to marry off three daughters in a little over a year and very likely would be able to accomplish marrying them all off within the next. They were both relieved that they would not be spending much time there after they had said their vows. After the ceremony they planned to go on to the Lakes for their honeymoon, and again use the Darcy carriage… *as part of the wedding gift of course.*

When they returned they would reside in the parsonage at Kympton, thus bringing the sisters even closer. It was just after their wedding that Elizabeth began to suspect the cause of her ongoing *'illness'* but she dared not mention anything to her husband until she was certain of the diagnosis. She waited until she had better information and felt the quickening of the babe before divulging that information to him.

Naturally Darcy was very concerned about Elizabeth becoming with child so soon after giving birth to William and Emma and especially after he had nearly lost her with their births. He tried to hide his fear, but Elizabeth could sense his uneasiness and tried to reassure him that this time would be different. She could tell that she only carried one baby this time due to her smaller size, but she knew that he would continue to worry until this child was born. The only thing that could distract him was the ongoing nuptials of their sisters and so she tried to keep him focused on this as much as possible.

Georgiana married Richard in the fall of 1810 to the very mixed emotions of Darcy and Elizabeth. They both wanted their cousin and sister happy, but knew that they would miss her terribly since she was much farther from her brother and new sisters at Rosings. At first it was difficult for all of them to adjust, but as her letters became fewer, yet more cheerful Darcy learned to gradually let go. He finally realized that life would go on regardless of how much he worried or tried to control it. The only thing that he could do was provide the best care and guidance to those he loved... *Fate will take care of the rest.*

Jane and Charles Bingley moved to nearby Blackridge Park, in the summer of 1810 when their lease expired at Netherfield. It was convenient to have sisters so close by when Jane gave birth-without any complications whatever- to a charmingly beautiful little girl named *'Margaret Rose Bingley'* who went by the name of *'Rose'*, for she was that sweet. Not long after little Rose's appearance Jane Bingley began to show signs of being with child again, such was the passion in their marriage. A short time after *'Geoffrey Jennings'* was born to Kitty and Jacob; he was joined by another cousin, *'Charles Edward Bingley'*. There were more children to follow but none were as close as these first few cousins, though *William Darcy* was always the one to look out for them all... with the help of his slightly younger sister Emma-who was usually the lookout.

There was one incident that would be long talked about, when the cousins were visiting Pemebrley. The two Bingley children, the Darcy twins, and Geoffrey decided to have an adventure in the woods. They went to one of the tallest, sturdiest trees near the southern pasture and built a fort high in the branches, but when it got too dark for them to make it home safely, they decided to stay where they were least they get lost. While the others were scrounging for some berries and nuts to eat, little Emma was looking out over the woods in the waning sunset, and called the cousins when she spotted the search party that was sent out to find them. They were overjoyed when Darcy and Bingley finally found them and led them back to the house, but they were suitably punished when they were made to muck out the horse stalls for a week for causing such an uproar.

~*~*~*~

On March 15, 1811 Elizabeth went into labor again, but unlike the first time, Darcy was at her side the entire time. He insisted on having not only a physician but both Mrs. Walton and Mrs. Stacy present... *'just in case anything happened'*. Elizabeth labored for eight hours and at the end she was again in the warm tub with her husband at her side-much to the consternation and urging of the physician, but neither midwife would send him away.

Only when she was able to deliver their second son, *'Bennet Charles George Darcy'*, without any complication what-so-ever, was Darcy relieved to welcome another child. Both mother and son recovered easily, he was one of the greatest joys of their life. Not only was he well mannered and even tempered, he had the same mischievous sense of humor as his mother-which only endeared him more to his father. Elizabeth and Darcy would eventually go on to have two more children without any complications, and the families would live to become very close to most of their cousins.

By the spring of 1811, the Fitzwilliam's had an announcement of their own. Lady Eleanor would gain her first grandchild and she was over the moon. Richard's brother, Andrew and his wife had yet to produce an heir, but Georgiana and Richard apparently had no such issues.

The Darcy, Fitzwilliam, Bennet, and Bingley families had expanded in every direction and one loss that few mourned. Lady Catherine had been in a private sanctuary for the mentally infirm when she suffered from apoplexy. It was said that after her nephew Richard Fitzwilliam refused to allow her back into the Rosings Estate she went into a fit of rage from which she never recovered. He felt that she would be a poor influence upon the new staff, and did not wish to risk losing such good help... *especially with a child on the way.*

The once forceful woman was left to suffer the fate of being fed porridge and soups or broths for the remainder of her short life by some lowly staffers at the facility. It was rumored that her last words before she succumbed were, 'That little harlot should have never gotten to be Pemberley's mistress. It was my Anne's rightful position, and now she is dead and it is all that woman's fault!' She was buried in a far corner of the Hunsford Village's cemetery-next to her *'dear Anne'*. Mr. Collin's was able to officiate without too many tears during the service-much to his 'dear Charlotte's' consternation.

With Georgiana married and well settled, Elizabeth and Darcy decided that they would not mind another sister staying with them and so invited Mary to come and live with them, much to the relief of Mrs. Bennet. She was beginning to despair of that child ever marrying... especially since the retired Colonel Richard Fitzwilliam had recently married. The town of Meryton had few prospects or so she thought, but by the time the sermonizing Mary had returned for a trip to Hertfordshire, she met an old family friend.

John Lucas, brother to Charlotte and son to Sir William and Lady Lucas, had grown into a fine specimen of a man and had just finished his abbreviated grand tour. Since he had not seen the usually retiring Mary since before she left for Derbyshire he was very... impressed with her many improvements so much so that he asked for and received permission to court Mary. When she came back from Pemberley to Hertfordshire and began her courtship with John Lucas it was obvious that she would leave them as well. By late spring of 1811 he had proposed and been accepted by Mary.

They consoled themselves that at least Georgiana would have a sister close by, and so it was with great joy that they received the news of Mary Bennets betrothal to that gentleman. The wedding was set for mid July since neither of them had any desire to wait any longer than absolutely necessary to get married and begin their lives together.

~*~*~*~

The last and youngest of the Bennet sisters, Lydia, was much harder to reign in. Her wild ways and silliness could not be curbed by

Jane's patience or Elizabeth's uncommon good sense. They both took turns hosting the girl, and finally gave up and given her back over to their mother and father. During a ball with the regiment that had come to stay-again at Meryton- the young woman rekindled her friendship with one Mrs. Forster who proceeded to invite her to come and stay with her and her husband in Brighton. She developed an attachment to one soldier there by the name of James Saunderson.

One night while staying with the Forster's, she absconded with the soldier under the premise of eloping. He took her as far as town and no further, where he claimed many liberties with her, and had almost left her there alone, without friends, or funds. It was at a Mrs. Younge's house that he planned to abandon her. When word reached Darcy House where the errant Lydia was, Darcy and his 'brothers' took great pains to locate the errant Saunderson working on him until he agreed to marry the silly girl. It must be noted that by the time this took place, Lydia was getting on far enough with child that it could scarcely be concealed. Due to Richards's connections in the army, he was able to have the couple shipped far north... after James was commissioned in the regulars.

Due to the distance from the Saunderson's and the rest of their families, those cousins were never that close to the rest of the families. In fact, they did not have any more correspondence with that family after they were sent to North America... to a post in Canada.

The Pemberley, Rosings, and Blackridge estates thrived under the management of the Darcy's, Fitzwilliam's, and Bingley's. Eventually, it would be known that Richard's elder brother's wife was unable to bear children, and so the title of Lord Matlock went to him by default. Richard and Georgiana then became one of the wealthiest landowners in the country... besides the Darcy's. The families continued to remain close throughout the rest of their lives... and lived happily ever after... for the most part.